CATCH HER
IF YOU CAN

By Tessa Bailey

BIG SHOTS
Fangirl Down • The Au Pair Affair • Dream Girl Drama
Pitcher Perfect • Catch Her If You Can

VINE MESS
Secretly Yours • Unfortunately Yours

BELLINGER SISTERS
It Happened One Summer • Hook, Line, and Sinker

HOT & HAMMERED
Fix Her Up • Love Her or Lose Her • Tools of Engagement

THE ACADEMY
Disorderly Conduct • Indecent Exposure • Disturbing His Peace

BROKE AND BEAUTIFUL
Chase Me • Need Me • Make Me

ROMANCING THE CLARKSONS
Too Hot to Handle • Too Wild to Tame
Too Hard to Forget • Too Beautiful to Break

MADE IN JERSEY
Crashed Out • Rough Rhythm • Thrown Down
Worked Up • Wound Tight

CROSSING THE LINE
Risking It All • Up in Smoke • Boiling Point • Raw Redemption

THE GIRL SERIES
Getaway Girl • Runaway Girl

LINE OF DUTY
Protecting What's His • Protecting What's Theirs (novella)
His Risk to Take • Officer Off Limits
Asking for Trouble • Staking His Claim

SERVE
Owned by Fate • Exposed by Fate • Driven by Fate

BEACH KINGDOM
Mouth to Mouth • Heat Stroke • Sink or Swim

STANDALONE BOOKS
Unfixable • Baiting the Maid of Honor • Off Base • Captivated
My Killer Vacation • Happenstance • Wreck the Halls

CATCH HER
IF YOU CAN

a
novel

TESSA BAILEY

A V O N

An Imprint of HarperCollins*Publishers*

hc.com

FIRST EDITION

Interior text design by Diahann Sturge-Campbell

Feathers illustration © Yuliia Borovyk/Stock.Adobe.com

Library of Congress Cataloging-in-Publication Data has been applied for.

ISBN 978-0-06-338088-2

ISBN 978-0-06-338087-5 (simultaneous hardcover edition)

Printed in the United States of America

25 26 27 28 29 LBC 5 4 3 2 1

CATCH HER
IF YOU CAN

CHAPTER ONE

Eight Years Earlier

Boys smelled like goat cheese.

Thus, fourteen-year-old Eve Keller had put them into one category: NOPE.

No, thanks. They were *all* the same. Not for her.

That opinion changed on a brisk autumn day in late November.

Eve held the snack-size bag of Fritos between her teeth. She needed her hands free to unload her school iPad and science notes, but before she managed to unzip her backpack, the two guys throwing a baseball in her friend Skylar's backyard caught her eye. One of them she recognized. One of them she didn't. In their smallish Rhode Island town of Cumberland, coming across an unfamiliar face wasn't typical.

If she'd seen this newcomer before, she would have remembered.

He had a different way of standing. Braced for a blow. Chin up, hands half curled at his sides. Eyes narrowed as if suspicious of his surroundings, his demeanor very still and observant, while conversely, his black hair moved every which way with the wind. Something else that marked him as an outsider? He wore a jacket, instead of a hoodie, as was the custom with the local boys, even when temperatures dipped to the twenties.

As if sensing her curious gaze, the young man's head turned and caught her staring from the kitchen window. Apart from a slight widening of his eyes—what *color* were they?—his expression didn't change. But those hands completed their curl at his sides.

Quickly, Eve looked away, surprised to feel goose bumps lifting on her arms inside her sweater sleeves, no idea she'd spend the next eight years holding back four words from being said aloud. Four words that would keep her awake at night, choking her at times.

I saw him first.

"Who is that?" Eve asked her best friend, Skylar, who was the only freshman at Cumberland High with an At-a-Glance business planner—and she had her nose buried in it now.

"Who is who?" Skylar asked, distracted by her color-coded to-do list.

"That big dude with your brother."

Skylar's brunette head popped up. "Huh?" She turned in her chair to follow Eve's line of sight out the window. "I have no idea. Wait. Why is he kind of hot?"

Eve snorted and sat, ripping open her chip bag. "The hot ones are always the biggest assholes."

The other girl snorted too. "If he's hanging out with my stepbrother, that definitely tracks."

Eve woke up the home screen of her iPad.

"Maybe he's on Elton's travel team," she murmured, once more glancing out the window.

"Uh, yeah. No. Look at his form. Is this, like, the first time he's ever thrown a baseball?"

"Maybe he's a cousin on your stepdad's side," Eve suggested, refusing to be caught staring again. Although keeping her attention glued to her iPad screen was annoyingly difficult. "Imagine you just called your new cousin hot."

"Stop."

"Stop being a pervert."

They ducked their heads to muffle the sound of their laughter, though Eve put an end to her mirth a lot sooner than Skylar, not wanting to make it weird. Or make it seem like she was too invested. Their friendship was still new, right? Skylar might welcome Eve at her kitchen table to do homework today, but girls their age were fickle. They switched up friend groups as often as they changed their nail polish color. Skylar was already getting teased for hanging out with Eve and it was only a matter of time before that got old.

Ignoring the dread that sank low in her stomach, Eve fished out another Frito curl and popped the chip into her mouth. "What do you think is going to be on the quiz tomo—"

"Oh my god, they're coming in here."

"What? Oh." Eve clapped her hands together to get rid of the Frito salt, then ran what she hoped were five nonchalant fingers through her chin-length blond hair, surprised to find her pulse being weird. "Whatever."

"Yeah," Skylar breathed, her casual shrug looking more like a flinch. "Whatever."

Both girls kept their heads down when the two boys came in through the back door into the kitchen, though Eve would admit to sliding a quick sideways glance at the new guy's footwear. Lace-up boots, not sneakers. Definitely not from here.

Elton greeted Skylar the same way he had since their parents got married two years earlier. "Oh god, you're *still* here?"

Skylar's middle finger was already up. "Die, Elton."

He stomped into the kitchen and yanked open the first cabinet. "Did you eat all the good snacks?" Foil packaging rustled. "What the hell. All that's left is your mom's health food shit."

"You're not looking hard enough." Skylar spoke to her stepbrother like she was communicating with a toddler. "Move the granola bars to one side. See beyond the front row, genius." His cry of good fortune had Skylar sending Eve a smirk. "Pathetic."

Eve rolled her lips inward to stifle a laugh. It would probably sound too breathless if she let it out, because her entire right side was on fire under the new boy's scrutiny. He stood without moving at the entrance to the kitchen, hands in the pockets of his worn jeans, eyes quietly amused. Until they rested on Eve and that sparkle turned . . . serious?

"This is Madden," Elton said around a mouthful of whatever he'd taken from the snack cabinet. "Ms. Donahue next door? That's his aunt. He's visiting."

"Oh." Skylar's face was the color of pizza sauce as she fidgeted to face the tall, silent new guy. "Are you here early for Thanksgiving break, or something?"

Madden cleared his throat. "We don't celebrate Thanksgiving in Ireland."

Eve's fingertips started to tingle. It wasn't *just* that he had an accent. A gorgeous one with inflections in unexpected places and lilts in others. No, it was deep. Deep as the black sky she stared into at night, focusing on the vast, bottomless well of ink until the stars disappeared in her periphery. There was some hesitance in his tone, as well, that she understood. Most of Elton's friends would already be digging in the refrigerator, entitled to whatever they got their hands on, but this guy would barely enter the kitchen.

Please don't be an asshole, Eve found herself wishing.

A ridiculous wish that wouldn't come true. And who cared, anyway?

She refocused on her work.

"Are you going to tell me their names, or should I guess?" Madden asked, with the barest touch of humor.

He's still looking at me.

Eve could feel it. And a quick peek confirmed she was right. Maybe . . .

Maybe Elton had already told him about her father.

That would explain why he continued to stare at Eve.

"Fine." Elton sighed. "This clown is my stepsister, Skylar. She's a decent pitcher or I would have thrown her annoying ass out by now."

"Decent?" sputtered Skylar. "I could strike you out in my sleep—"

"And that's her friend Eve," Elton said loudly, throwing an empty Fritos bag at Skylar.

Eve gave a tight smile without looking up from her work.

"Hi, Skylar." Then, in a rumble, he added, "Hello, Eve."

A ripple moved upward from Eve's toes, culminating in a feathery sensation in her belly. Suddenly, she needed to get *out* of there. She'd learned very early not to expect too much good from people, but if this guy was giving her extra attention for the reason she suspected, she didn't want it. So ridiculous to be disappointed in someone with whom she could barely make eye contact, right?

Right.

Eve started to gather her things. "Oh, um. I just remembered . . ." Might as well beat him to the punch. "My dad needs me to line up the music for tonight."

Skylar nodded, her expression giving nothing away. "Okay."

"Eve's dad owns Cat Fight. That strip club just off Pendleton Street at the edge of town," Elton said absently, his head buried in the fridge, rooting around for a soda. "She very rudely refuses to sneak me in."

"Elton . . ." Skylar sighed, witheringly. "Can you not?"

"Can I not, what? I'm sixteen. Her dad owns a place where women get naked. I'm not supposed to think about it twenty-four hours a day?" He took a swig of his all-natural soda and winced, looking at the label. "Back me up on this, Madden."

Eve tucked her hair behind one ear and continued to gather up her things. "Go ahead," she murmured. "Ask me if I'm going to work the pole one day. I'm sure you're dying to know." The ensuing silence caused her to add, "Everyone asks. It's fine, really."

Liar. It wasn't fine. It's why she dreaded going to school every morning.

Madden's brow knit together, but he said nothing.

Blue.

His eyes were a deep, sapphire blue.

"Eve?" Elton steepled his fingers in prayer. "I'm also willing to do part-time work, if your dad needs a busboy."

"He doesn't," she breezed.

"Boobs."

Skylar threw a stylus at her stepbrother's head, hitting her target. "Dude. Shut *up*." She pushed back her chair. Then to Eve, "I'll walk you to the end of the driveway."

"You really don't have to."

Her friend was already moving in her purposeful bounce toward the archway that separated the kitchen from the front of the house. "Nice to meet you, Madden," Skylar said. "Don't let him and his douchey friends rub off on you."

Instead of responding to Skylar, Madden looked Eve in the eye as she passed. "I won't."

The weirdest thing happened. Eve believed him.

Walking by Madden on her way out was like journeying past an open doorway that led to a babbling brook and fallen, moss-covered logs. A nighttime sky overhead. The chirping of crickets. Peace and mystery embodied in a human being. Eve couldn't tell if her steps slowed as she brushed by his sturdy frame or if she imagined time turning lethargic, her skin growing hot and feverish when those blue eyes studied her. Studied her throat and cheeks and the fist around her backpack strap.

A moment later, when Eve emerged from the house in front of Skylar, she had to stop herself from gasping for air out loud.

"Holy shit. Holy shit," said Skylar, speed walking up beside her. "I can't believe there is a fine-ass *Irish* guy in my house. What planet is this? Did I act okay? Did I say anything dumb?" She fanned herself furiously, even though the outside temperature was in the forties. "Do you think he would go for me, even though I'm a freshman?"

I saw him first.

I saw him first.

Those four selfish words clogged Eve's windpipe momentarily, memories of Madden's blue eyes and safe, babbling brook presence distracting her from more important thoughts. Such as, Skylar was her only friend. A *true* friend. The only person who'd ever stood up for her at school against the boys who hounded her constantly about the club, asking uncomfortable questions that made Elton's jokes sound like a lullaby. If Skylar had a crush on the new guy, she wouldn't get in the way of that.

Anyway, he'd probably be gone in a week.

Their friendship, she really, really hoped, would last a lot longer than that.

"Um, yeah," Eve forced out, feeling winded. "Who wouldn't go for you?"

"Really?" Skylar looked back at the house. "I can't go back in there. Wait. Yes, I can. What should I say? Maybe I should just practice pitching. That'll impress him."

Eve smiled with as much warmth as she could muster. "Show him your breaking ball, babe. He'll be putty in your hand."

Put him out of your head.

He'll be gone soon enough.

But time was determined to prove her wrong.

CHAPTER TWO

Present Day

As long as she lived, Eve would never judge a mother. Not ever again.

Raising kids was a physical and mental assault. A war waged in the trenches, but instead of grenades, the weapons were half-drunk cups of apple juice and unflushed toilets. Being cute didn't excuse the noise they emitted, either. The screeches that erupted mere moments after peace had been achieved. The *Encanto* soundtrack slapped, but it didn't slap this much. She wanted to slap herself at this point to make sure she could still feel something. And she'd only been parenting for three weeks. *Three.*

By the time she hit six weeks of this warfare, she'd look exactly like the Barbie she stepped over now on the way to the bedroom shared by Lark and Landon.

Fried, wearing a shirt as pants, staring into the void.

Yet somehow, she could still love her niece and nephew with her entire being, despite them trying to land her in an early grave. Exactly why Eve hadn't even hesitated when Ruth, her sister, had come to Eve and asked her to take temporary legal custody of the children while she put herself through rehab, plus a comprehensive recovery program. Her friends had organized an intervention and pooled resources to send Ruth where she needed to go.

I don't know how long I'll be gone. Or if I'll even succeed.

I've tried before and failed. I could very well fail again.

Please be sure you want the kids, because they could be with you for a long time.

Another one of those demonic screeches rent the air.

"No," Eve said in a strangled whisper, stepping over the threshold into what used to be her yoga space that doubled as an office. "No more screaming."

"He keeps pretending to bite me," Lark exclaimed, pointing at her twin brother.

Landon folded his hands together in his lap and giggled.

"Okay, but what that scream communicates to me is that he has not only bitten you, but completely severed a limb from your body." Holding on to her patient, even tone, Eve continued. "Before you scream, please ask yourself, is it worth it? You know? Do I *need* to pierce the sound barrier over fake biting?"

"Yes," Lark responded with a solemn nod.

That's the other tragic thing about kids. They didn't pick up on sarcasm.

What a waste.

"You guys promised me you would start getting ready for school." Eve cataloged the room through a twitching eye. "But it looks like you've just been breaking crayons. How did we get here?"

"Landon wants to wear a chef's hat to school."

"Can I?"

"Yes. As long as it isn't the *only* thing you wear. I don't see why not."

"He wears it all the time," Lark said, throwing up her hands.

Landon chomped on some air. "So?"

Lark screeched.

"Ah!" Eve wagged a finger at her, like an old schoolmarm instead of a twenty-two-year-old woman who owned a burlesque club. "Not warranted, that screech. Not even a little."

"If he wears his chef's hat, I'm wearing lipstick."

"Fine. Let's go. Clothes on. Breakfast is almost—" Ah shit. Eve backed into the hallway, sniffing the air, already knowing the scent of charred sourdough was going to greet her. And it did. "Breakfast is definitely burned. I'm going to put down two more pieces of toast. You two better be dressed by the time they pop up. Go."

Okay, fine, they were cute when doing what they're told. Lark turned and opened one of her designated drawers, which was built into the bottom of the IKEA bunk bed Eve had put together over the weekend. Landon snagged yesterday's jeans off the floor, even though Eve specifically remembered him sitting in a puddle of syrup in them. Know what? She'd just pretend she didn't see that.

The smoke alarm went off.

"Cool. Our neighbors are going to love this," Eve called over her shoulder, jogging into the kitchen to find one of her old copies of *Entrepreneur* magazine, left over from a time when she could afford the subscription. She stood on one of the dining room chairs and fanned the smoke detector with one hand, whipping her phone out of her back pocket with the other to determine the time. They were running late. Of course they were.

"Please stop beeping," Eve muttered, fanning harder. "There's already more than enough screeching in this apartment."

And now her neighbor was banging on the wall.

That was new.

Eve's vocal cords must have gotten to him.

"Who's knocking?" shouted Landon over the noise, streaking past Eve in jeans and a chef's hat, skidding to a halt in front of the door.

"No one. It's just our neighbor . . . saying hello. Hi, Mrs. Rudolph!"

Landon wasn't listening. While Eve continued to fan the bleating device furiously, Landon unlocked the door and yanked it open.

Madden Donahue stared back at Eve from the hallway.

She dropped the magazine, her knees dipping out of pure shock to find Madden filling up her doorway with his serious eyes and wide shoulders, the impact of both upsetting her balance. Oh man, he looked pensive and restless, distracting her further.

Story of my life.

Since the afternoon they'd met during her freshman year of high school, Madden Donahue had taken up rambling acres of space in Eve's mind. She'd seen him first and she'd simply . . . never stopped seeing him. Not even in her dreams. Rules didn't apply there. In her dreams, she didn't have to avoid Madden out of loyalty to her best friend, Skylar, who'd always carried a torch for Madden. Didn't have to make vague excuses or run for cover, the way she'd been doing since Madden had started showing romantic interest in Eve, the year she turned eighteen.

In dreams, she didn't have to think about the difference in their social status.

She could let her wealth of feelings for Madden overflow.

Perhaps those feelings had piled up enough to upset her balance, because her chair wobbled and she began to topple. It was suddenly happening, and she really didn't have time for a broken leg. *Please, no.* Not when her sister had just left town with no timeline to return, leaving Eve with her two children and her burlesque club sinking further and further into debt.

Please, not one more thing—

Madden caught Eve's waist between two strong hands, steadying her.

"Easy, love." Even with Eve standing on a chair, at six foot three, Madden barely had to lift his chin to make eye contact with her. "Don't scare me like that."

Eve had two reactions to Madden's touch. His sudden presence.

There was Fantasy Eve who allowed herself to continue toppling straight into his baseball-catcher arms and be spun around the kitchen while she laughed, youthful and carefree. Once their amusement cooled, she would perch her inner thighs on his hips and work herself close enough to make him groan, before thanking him for being her hero.

Asking him coyly what she could do to repay him.

Reality Eve ignored the tingles shooting upward from Madden's palms and fingertips to her nipples. She ignored the surging pound in her chest. The sexual awareness. The pure rush of pleasure over simply seeing him. Being graced with a reminder that Madden Donahue existed in this world.

All she could do was bite her lip and avoid eye contact while he lifted her down off the chair, reached up, and pressed a button to make the smoke detector quit its blaring. With the situation under control, Madden stared down at the two children craning their necks to look up at him, giving them a curt nod, as if they were tiny little adults.

"You're the man who had a fight with Eve," accused Landon, adjusting his chef's hat. "Huh?"

Yes. Yes, he was.

Two weeks prior, Eve had taken the stage at the Gilded Garden for the very first time. A last resort. Maybe if she performed and fulfilled the prophecy of everyone she'd grown up with, she'd get enough locals talking to spur some business. Alas, she never removed so much as a silk glove, because Madden had stormed the stage and carried her off over his big, baseball catcher shoulder. While they argued backstage over her choice to become the night's entertainment, he'd discovered the five-year-old twins passing the time with coloring books in her office. The cat was out of the bag. Eve was raising her sister's kids for the foreseeable.

However, Madden's stoic expression didn't budge at the question. "You must be thinking of somebody else. I'd never fight with our Eve."

"Yup, it was you," Lark confirmed.

"You have to get out of bed a lot earlier in the morning to gaslight these kids," Eve said, attempting a smirk, despite her racing heart.

"I get to wear lipstick to school today," Lark added.

Madden's eyebrows went up. "Well now. What color?"

"Pink!"

"And here I thought you'd say blue."

Lark trapped a giggle behind her hand.

"Kids, um . . ." Realizing she was still wearing her dove gray silk, lace-edged shorts, and a matching tank top she'd worn to bed, Eve crossed her arms over her breasts. "Go finish getting dressed, please. Don't forget socks and shoes."

"Don't forget the toast!" Landon shouted, running full speed to the bedroom, his sister hot on his heels. "And don't burn it again!"

Eve took a comically deep breath, attempting to distract herself from Madden's presence. An impossible feat—and she knew that by now, didn't she? If he was in the room, he absorbed 100 percent of her focus. Just sucked all of it in like a big, muscular Irish sponge. "Let's not talk about the fight."

"I specifically came here to talk about it," he countered, no hesitation. "Or what caused it, anyway."

Eve squinted an eye. "I'd rather not."

"I'll make the toast." He glanced sideways toward the door, a muscle flickering in his jaw. "Would you mind putting on a sweater or a robe, so I can think straight, love?"

It took her approximately five seconds to complete a swallow, the blooming sensation between her thighs was so intense. And so tied to this man, the only one who got this reaction out of her. God, it was so useless. "No need. You were just leaving."

"You're not running away from me this time, Eve." Madden gave her a firm nod. "Now. It's a proper conversation we'll be having this morning."

Her nerves fluttered. "Why?"

"We've things to sort out, you and me. And . . ." A line appeared between his brows as he dropped his head forward. "I don't have a lot of time."

"Why?" she asked hollowly, knowing she sounded like an echo.

"I'm leaving for New York this afternoon. I've been picked up by the Yankees."

CHAPTER THREE

Four Years Earlier

Madden sat on the back steps of the Page house, hovering on the periphery of the noise, like he always did. A giant white tent had been erected in the backyard, the interior lit by strings of lights and large brass lanterns. Local friends overflowed onto the lawn, reminiscing, making plans for the summer.

A celebration in honor of Skylar's high school graduation.

In the fall, Madden would be starting his third year at Brown, along with Elton. Although Brown wasn't a far journey from where he currently sat, he hadn't been back to Cumberland in over a year. Not since his aunt Fiona passed away and he'd come back to make her final arrangements.

A memory came meandering in, as this particular one was wont to do.

On a daily basis.

Eve standing beside him at the wake, being pointedly ignored by his aunt's friends from church. A seventeen-year-old girl judged for her father's chosen livelihood. Madden had been in such a state of shock to have his aunt gone without any warning and overwhelmed by the social pressure of a funeral that the rebuff of his friend hadn't quite processed right away. Not until she'd slowly slipped out the back door and disappeared.

To this day, that haunted him.

Still in his suit and fresh from the burial, he'd looked for Eve everywhere. He'd called her with no luck. Knocked on the back door of Cat Fight, visited her house, enlisted Elton to help him. But . . . nothing. Obviously, she hadn't wanted to be found.

He hadn't seen her since. In over a year.

She'd helped him plan the funeral, along with the Pages. Made the uncomfortable phone calls to his parents to inform them of his aunt's death, so he wouldn't have to resurrect those old ghosts. He could still remember the way Eve had tried to remain stoic while the phone was pressed to her ear, as though he couldn't overhear their toneless response to the passing of the family black sheep. Instead of asking him why he didn't want to speak to his parents or why they didn't even consider making the trip to Rhode Island for the funeral, she'd kept her no-nonsense demeanor and helped him track down a suit and tie, giving him exactly what he'd needed at the time.

Then she'd cut him off.

It still confused Madden somewhat why he'd allowed that to happen.

Eve was his friend. Eve meant *a lot* to him.

There were times during high school when he'd worried she meant too much to him. As they both got older and his heart started to beat faster every time Eve came around, he'd wondered if some distance between them wasn't wise. He'd aged into adulthood before her and had no right to look for her around every corner, conjure her in every dream. As wrong as it felt, he'd allowed that distance to yawn when he left. He'd gone to school, done his best to put sixteen-year-old Eve out of his head, and lived the lifestyle of a college athlete. Parties and women and blurred recollections.

Here he was now, though, searching for her among the party-goers in the tent.

Heart in his fucking throat.

Madden yanked at the starched collar of his dress shirt. Ironic that he'd be wearing the same damn suit as the last time he'd seen Eve. Almost like no time had passed at all.

But when he saw her arrive a moment later in a white strapless dress and gold sandals, her hair in a long tumble down to the middle of her back, it became obvious that time *had* passed. Eve looked older. Like an adult. A young woman who might walk into one of the parties thrown by his teammates over the years. Every head in the room would turn.

That image made his eye tick.

Aye. He'd been right to stay away.

Madden watched Eve hesitate at the entrance to the tent. She turned like she might leave, giving herself what looked to be a silent pep talk. Shifted in her sandals, turning the small purse over in her hands.

He was up and striding in her direction before a conscious decision was made.

"Eve," he said, as soon as he was close enough to be heard. He wanted that indecision gone from her face. However, nothing could have prepared him for the knockout blow to his chest when that wide, amber gaze landed on him, her soft mouth parting on a gasp. Elation. It slipped along her features like a golden ray of sunshine, before she locked that reaction down tight, leaving her guarded. Like the Eve he remembered.

Only, her beauty was amplified now, perhaps because he was allowing himself to fully notice it for the first time. He couldn't *stop* himself from noticing. It ate him alive, her beauty. The supple glow of her skin, that fluid slope of neck into shoulder, the maturity of her posture, her unique style of clothing, that lifted chin he remembered so well.

Found you.

Finally.

"Madden." Eve took an audible breath, braced in an almost indetectable way, then went up on her toes to kiss his cheek. Back down onto the flats of her feet, just as quickly. "Hi. You're in Cumberland. I didn't know."

The urge to pull her into a hug dominated him, as it always had, but there were other layers to the impulse now. He'd only caught a hint of her scent. He wanted *more*. And damn, Madden wanted to hold her tight and apologize for the day of the funeral. He would if he didn't think it might hurt her pride. Or cause her to disappear again.

Complicated was this girl's middle name.

They had that in common.

"Congratulations," he said, sliding his hands into his pockets, before she could see they were unsteady. "You graduated this week, as well."

"I did." She looked up at the tent, then down to the ground. "End of an era. I can't say I'm sad to see it go."

Madden swallowed the twinge in his throat. "The worst of the eejits graduated with me, didn't they?"

"Yeah." She cleared her throat. "Most of them did."

But not all her bullies left the same year as Madden, it seemed. The guarded shadows in her gaze made that obvious. "Eve, I . . ."

Eve looked up. "Yes?"

I checked in with the younger lads on the baseball team after I graduated to make sure you weren't being hassled. I tasked them with shutting down any bullshit.

I didn't forget about you.

"Never mind," he said, tipping his head toward the entrance. "Do you want to walk in together?"

"In a minute." Eve exhaled, her gaze straying to Madden's lower abdomen. "How are you feeling? Is your new kidney still up and running?"

"Last time I checked," he returned dryly. "It's been over two years since the surgery. If my body was going to reject it, I'd be toast by now." He winked at her. "Must have gotten a good one." His flippancy about his kidney replacement was meant to keep the mood light, but she didn't laugh. Not Eve. She'd taken his kidney disease more seriously than anyone, when he'd been diagnosed during high school. More seriously than he did, he'd often thought. Although perhaps they took it seriously for different reasons.

Eve worried, while Madden simply wanted to know who'd anonymously saved his life.

"No luck finding out the identity of my donor," he said, frowning into the tent. "I'll keep trying, though. They have to come out of the woodwork eventually."

She nodded for a handful of seconds. "I'm ready to go in now."

Slowly, they turned in tandem to face the opening, Madden nodding for her to precede him, then following close behind, rejuvenating the part of him that had always needed to be her protector. Standing at her back.

Eve and Madden stopped on the quiet side of the tent where everyone had left half-eaten food and empty champagne glasses behind to converge on the dance floor. They stood quietly, their sides warmed by each other, watching Elton dance and eat a gigantic slice of cake at the same time Skylar dutifully moved from group to group, accepting well wishes.

"You were thinking about leaving without coming in, weren't you?" Madden said.

Her lips twitched. "Parties aren't really my thing. Or yours. I don't exactly see you out there doing the robot."

"You just missed my dance battle. The place was going mental."

"Oh, really?" Eve pursed her lips. "Someone had to be filming. I'll ask around."

"See that you do."

She smiled up at him in a sly, mysterious way that was new. As if, perhaps, she'd finally become aware of her appeal. As if she'd been told she was beautiful. By who, though? And lord, why did the idea of someone else calling her beautiful make his throat burn so badly?

Maybe it was that spiky flash of jealousy that brought Madden to a decision. Or maybe his need to stop hiding his interest in Eve was a desire that had been taking root for a very long time, against his will. Whatever the catalyst, that night, under the roof of the tent, Madden had a long-awaited reckoning about Eve. He grew determined to do *something* about her. To finally kick aside the age roadblock and find out why he'd been so dedicated to her from day one, unable to get her out of his head. To find out why he considered her feelings and well-being above anyone else in his entire life.

It was high time to solve the mystery of Eve.

"I could show you, instead," Madden said. "Dance with me."

If he blinked, he would have missed the panic that scrambled across her face. "You're asking me to dance?"

"Aye, before someone else does."

She breathed a laugh. "You've been gone too long. No one's going to ask."

A muscle yanked in his chest. "There are a lot of foolish men in this town, but they can't all be fools."

That threw her, a line appearing between her brows, as if she was trying to decide whether or not he'd paid her a compliment. "Maybe not. But I wouldn't want to dance with any of them, anyway."

"Good."

That earned him a startled, measuring look. "Good?"

Cautiously, he threaded their fingers together, his pulse picking up at the contact, premonition rolling up the column of his spine. "That's what I said."

Needing a moment to gather himself, Madden turned and guided her toward the farthest end of the dance floor. Away from the hosts. Away from the spotlight.

And then he offered his arms to Eve for the first time, tugging her inch by inch with his grip on her wrist, holding his breath while letting her come closer part of the way on her own. She fit against him like they'd been cut from the same mold and he struggled not to make the sound forcing its way up his airways. *She's here. I can hold her this way now.*

"Crash into Me" by Dave Matthews Band was playing and the scattered notes matched their first few steps, because they were both nervous and dealing with the sensation of touching, of looking into each other's eyes *while* touching, but they were moving in a rhythm by the start of the second verse, his right hand on the small of her back, his left one clasping her hand, resting it against his shoulder.

"So if you're not bothering with the fools of this town, what are your plans, now that you've sprung the halls of Cumberland High?"

While looking at the notch of his Adam's apple, Eve slow blinked, as if she liked the sight, and the muscles below his waist slowly drew tight.

"Oh, um." She appeared to mentally shake herself. "You didn't hear?"

"Hear what?"

"My father decided to retire and move closer to his brother in Texas. He's selling the house and giving me and Ruth a nest egg to do whatever we want." She wet her lips. "I convinced him to leave me the club, instead of selling it too."

Madden's gut sank to the floor. He'd never liked her spending time at Cat Fight. Not because he looked down on the establishment or her association with the place, but he didn't like her around grown men with sex on their mind. In fact, he hated it with every fiber of his being. Eve got enough judgment for being the daughter of a strip club owner, though, so he'd grown practiced at guarding her from afar and holding his tongue. "He did?"

"Yes," she said, with a classic Eve chin raise. "But I'm going to turn it into something different. Something that feels more like mine. A burlesque club." Her slowly building excitement held him captive. "It's going to be a daring and eclectic speakeasy straight out of another time. Smoky and mysterious with hidden corners and jazz. Stage entertainment." Eve looked Madden in the eye, her smile slipping. "I don't want to run from who I am. I want to *own* it. Be unflinching about my legacy in this town, but . . . make it my own. You know?"

He suddenly and violently resented the time he'd spent away from her, this brave and unique human being. He'd spend his life deep in regret that he'd missed milestones in her life. Changes he should have been there to celebrate with her. "That's incredible, Eve. You'll do it. You'll do anything you set your mind to—and for the right reasons. You. What makes *you* happy will always be right."

She accepted that with a ducking nod. "I've had so many offers to buy the property. This town can't wait to get rid of the strip club, but . . . part of me wants to show them they can't drive me out. No matter how hard they try, I won't give in or conform." She shrugged a bare shoulder. "Still think I'm opening a burlesque club for the right reasons?"

"You're not applying for sainthood, love," he said, leaning in to speak against her temple. "Everyone has something to prove. I wouldn't judge you for that."

A breathy pause. "Thank you."

Madden hummed, barely able to keep his eyes open, she felt so good tucked against him.

As the music played, Eve melted closer, too, her breasts grazing, then pressing to his upper abdomen, the fronts of her thighs flexing against the fronts of his. And he looked her in the eye while their hips settled close, every ounce of his willpower being poured into not applying pressure to her lower back, herding her in too tight. They looked at each other long and hard, getting used to the up close and personal contact, the humming current connecting their bodies, hers softening while his did the opposite.

"How long are you in town?" Eve asked in a half whisper.

His brain was so consumed by the sensation of their shapes locked together in a way he'd never even dared to think about before, Madden couldn't remember his flight details right away. "Two days. I'm going back Sunday night."

"Oh."

Did she sound disappointed?

He could extend the trip. Miss a couple practices. He'd do it.

But first, he had something to get off his chest.

"Eve, I've been wanting to say sorry to you for a long time. Over what happened the day of my aunt's funeral."

"Nothing happened," she said quickly, squeezing his hand.

"You wouldn't have left otherwise," Madden insisted. "I looked for you everywhere."

"I knew you would," she murmured, almost to herself. "I'm sorry for splitting like that. I didn't want to be found."

He accepted that with a deep breath. Understood. "Please don't disappear on me like that again."

Eve looked up at him with a teasing squint. "An Irishman discouraging a good old-fashioned Irish exit? Your ancestors will be appalled."

"I'd like to see you while I'm here."

There it was. His interest had been spoken. Out loud.

There was no mistaking what he meant either. Not while he was holding her like this, their mouths only a handful of inches apart, both of them very obviously attempting to moderate their breathing, the final notes of the music muffling the world around them.

"Madden . . ."

"Eve," he said, with a calm he didn't feel. "I missed you."

"I missed you too," she said, then seemed startled over letting the sentiment slip free. "As a friend."

"Are you sure that's all it is now?" He lowered his head a hint more, relieved when her pupils jumped to expand. "I'm not. I never was. You never fit into any single category, no matter how hard I tried to put you in one. Friend, aye, but also . . . the first person I think about when I open my eyes. The time was never right before, but, love—"

"Eve! You're here!" Skylar exclaimed, bounding up beside them.

Madden had no plans to let Eve go or stop dancing, but he had no choice when she practically dove backward out of his arms, her face turning crimson. "Sky," she choked out, gesturing to the tent surrounding them. "Oh my gosh, it's beautiful in here."

"My mom is extra, but we love her, anyway." Skylar looked between Madden and Eve. "I don't think I've ever seen either of you dance in public. I'm honored."

"You should be. It's your party." Eve's throat worked, her gaze evading Madden's. "You . . . and Mad should dance. He's a great partner."

"Oh." Skylar laughed. "Um, only if you're up for it, Mad."

Denial crested in his gut and he ached to have Eve back in his arms. To continue their conversation. To challenge her claim that this radioactive thing between them was friendship and friendship only. But what was he going to do with Skylar watching him expectantly? Tell the girl he adored like a sister no? At her graduation party?

"Of course, Sky," he managed, trying to disguise the frustration.

And before he could blink, Eve vanished, like she always did.

CHAPTER FOUR

Present Day

Madden hadn't slept the last two nights, putting him in a fine mood to confront the woman who'd been his infatuation since high school, followed by a first meeting with his new major-league baseball coaches. But in all fairness, what could go wrong that hadn't *already* gone wrong?

Eve stood in front of him in shorts that would drive a man of the cloth to a life of sin, hip cocked, waist-length blond hair unbrushed and every inch of her gorgeous, making no move to put on a robe and end his suffering. Instead, she stood there with an eyebrow raised, obviously not accustomed to him being so high-handed, but by god, his patience with Eve was running out.

It had been just over four years since he'd allowed his feelings for Eve to transform from friend and protector to something more. Much more. An additional heartbeat, one might say. Since that graduation party her senior year, where he'd made his intentions clear to no avail, he'd continued to return to Cumberland every summer and Christmastime, praying this would be the time Eve finally gave him a chance.

She never did.

Was he delusional to keep trying? From the outside looking in, perhaps he was. Then again, it was impossible to describe what happened between Eve and Madden when they were in the same room. To put it plainly, the ground shook.

And goddammit, she felt it too.

He wasn't so delusional that he couldn't look at the woman he'd studied relentlessly and not see the yearning. It existed. And it only got stronger. So he returned and he returned to Cumberland, waiting for her to be ready. One such attempt had taken place at Eve's Gilded Garden two weeks ago. Madden had gone to look her in the eye and gather the proof of her feelings. The proof that allowed him to keep going. He'd expected to find her in the office or managing the establishment from behind the bar; he'd found her onstage, instead.

Preparing to take off her clothes.

To say he'd had an overreaction would be an understatement.

At least he'd thought so. Until she revealed her reason for performing—a way to drum up some business by inciting the gossip that had plagued her since birth.

Madden stood by that overreaction now.

"You've been what? The *Yankees*?" Even in the midst of his frustration, he couldn't keep from savoring the way her amber eyes lit up like the sun itself, her hands flying to her mouth to catch a gasp. "You're going to be catching for the actual New York *Yankees*?"

He inclined his head.

If his own excitement remained suspiciously absent, Eve's was more than sufficient to replace it. Not that he wasn't grateful for the opportunity to play professionally. So many of his teammates throughout the years would never get the chance. This contract was the reason he stood in front of Eve now with something to offer. His love for the game, however, had always been mired in . . . discomfort.

When Madden arrived from Ireland at age sixteen, baseball was totally new to him. He'd learned the game—and specifically the art of catching—to fit in. To appease his pushy as hell friend, Elton. To belong in a way he hadn't back home.

But oftentimes, baseball tended to make him feel fraudulent. Could the sport be any *less* Irish? He'd left his family behind and now his heritage, as well. It was so easy to hide behind a catcher's mask and a chest protector, he almost resented the ease with which he'd slipped out of his old life and into a new one. As if the past never happened.

It had, though. The burden on his shoulders was the proof.

Still, when Eve now walked straight into his chest and wrapped her arms around his neck, her smoked peach scent clobbering his senses, every grueling game day, practice in the rain, and moment spent second-guessing himself was worth the soft feel of her, the watery laugh against his shoulder.

"That's amazing. Oh my god, *that's so amazing.*"

"What's amazing?"

Eve released him abruptly, and Madden had to clench his fists to prevent himself from drawing her back. "Madden is going to play for the Yankees," Eve breathed.

Twin expressions of disgust looked back at him.

"Ew," said Landon, simply.

"Fuck the Yankees," Lark spat.

"Lark!" Eve half gasped, half laughed. "We don't use that word!"

Landon broke into a giggling fit. "Where is our toast?"

"Yeah." Lark looked around at everyone's faces, obviously encouraged by the stir she'd caused. "Where is our fucking toast?"

Eve had to turn around, her sides shaking as she laughed into her crooked elbow. "Lark, one more time and there's no dessert for a week."

"What the—"

"*Lark.*"

Madden turned, as well, trading a glance of shocked amusement with Eve on his way into the kitchen, where he flipped open the breadbox and removed the plastic sleeve of sourdough, disposing of the blackened first attempt at toast from the toaster with a quick sign of the cross that made Eve's eyes sparkle. Before she got ahold of herself, at least, and sobered.

"The bus is going to be here in five minutes." She clapped her hands. "Clothes. Shoes. Now. We'll eat the toast on the way to the bus stop."

With the kids finally grasping the time crunch, Eve meandered into the kitchen beside him, bending over to take the butter out of the fridge. Those long, smooth backs of her thighs forced Madden to bite the inside of his cheek, his eyes drawn there and held, powerless to do anything but appreciate what he saw. Christ almighty. He'd lived in two countries and played ball in a dozen states and he'd never, ever laid eyes on a woman who came close to the bright, natural beauty of Eve. The name suited her well, didn't it? He'd spent years being tempted by her, though he'd only ever had the privilege of giving in to that temptation in his mind.

She caught him staring and averted her eyes, quickly setting the butter down on the counter. In other words, not interested. And that was fine. That was her choice to make. Madden was well used to being Eve's friend and loving her from a distance.

Two nights ago, however, he'd found out something that gave him a dangerous reason to hope that Eve might be willing to explore a relationship deeper than friendship. He was almost too terrified to find out if that hope had merit, but there was no time to sit about wondering. New York expected him tonight, meaning he was operating with a limited amount of time to do one not-so-simple thing.

Find out once and for all if Eve had feelings for him.

Or if the hunger he glimpsed in her on occasion was all in his head.

"I can walk them to the bus stop, if you're not ready to change out of your pajamas."

The toast popped up. Tongue tucked into her cheek, Eve plucked out the slices and buttered them quickly, cutting them in half and depositing them on separate napkins. "You're kind of crabby for someone who is getting signed by the Yankees."

Madden let that statement stand. "Do you need help packing lunches?"

She shook her head and turned to face him, propping a hip on the counter. "Already in their backpacks. Should I prepare myself for a serious conversation?" Without taking her eyes off him, she handed off the toast to Lark and Landon as they trooped to the door. "If you're here to apologize for carrying me offstage over your shoulder at my very first burlesque performance, I do not accept."

"I still haven't decided whether or not to apologize for that."

"Really?" She laughed through a frown. "I highly recommend it."

Madden was making the morning harder on himself, which wasn't like him at all. Without pointing it out, he knew instinctively she was noticing the same thing. He was the quiet guy who liked to mind his business and observe. Easygoing. But this gut feeling that a lot was at stake had put him on edge, along with the lack of sleep. And maybe, yeah, maybe he had reached the point where being around Eve and never knowing where they stood had grown overwhelming. Painful, even.

"I'll walk the kids down and be back," Eve said quietly, retreating from whatever she saw in his eyes. "Backpacks on, you two."

In four long strides, Madden caught up with Eve at the door, looking her in the eye while he removed her hoodie from its peg by the door and wrapped it around her shoulders. "There's a nip in the air."

"Is that so?" she asked on a shallow breath, looking at his chin. Then his mouth, her pupils expanding.

Confusing him. Always confusing him. She couldn't put more distance between them without moving to bloody Antarctica, but when they touched, when they got close, she was like leashed electricity in his arms. She had to feel that, right? Feel *something*?

"I'll be right back," she said haltingly, sidestepping out of his reach, looking back over her shoulder as she hurried after the kids. Madden dragged both hands down his face on his way to the front windows that overlooked the street, planting his hands on the frame and hunching over, trying to recover from the contact.

Knowing he wouldn't.

He watched her progress to the bus stop—and he didn't like what he saw when she got there. A group of mothers conversed in a huddle and they made no move to include Eve when she arrived, even as their kids welcomed Lark and Landon enthusiastically. Eve stood off to the side until the bus arrived, her expression blithe. Uncaring. She had to notice the furtive glances and eye rolls, though, didn't she?

This was how Eve had grown up. On the outside. Trying to live a normal life while locals submitted op-eds to the newspaper about the disgraceful strip club on the outskirts of town. Cat Fight had long been her father's livelihood. A place where Eve did her homework and helped program the lights, the music. It was the establishment that put food on their table. It was also the establishment that had driven her mother away while Eve was still young, the woman no longer capable of bearing the shame being heaped onto her head on a daily basis.

Unlike Eve, her older sister, Ruth, couldn't withstand the judgment without a coping mechanism and she'd turned to drugs. Though it wasn't until Madden had discovered the children with Eve two weeks prior that he realized how serious Ruth's addiction had become.

Knowing better than to be caught watching Eve in a vulnerable moment, lest she lock him out even more, Madden made sure to be sitting on the couch by the time she got back. She toed off her slides by the door but kept the hoodie on and sat down across from him on a leather ottoman, tucking her hands between her knees. The red tint on her cheeks gave Madden the urge to bring up the women at the bus stop. With an effort, he suppressed it, along with the impulse to reach out, grip her knees, and drag her close until they were nose to nose, breathing each other's air.

"What did you want to talk to me about?" she asked.

This was it. His opportunity. And he couldn't help but feel like a farmer trying to block a rabbit from the exit. If she wanted to find a way out, she would. She'd dart through his legs or run a figure eight and confuse him while she fled.

And if she knew his ultimate plan was to marry her—soon—she'd probably base jump without a parachute from the second-floor window.

First things first. You can't rush a miracle.

"A couple of nights ago, Skylar and I had an interesting chat," he started.

Her back straightened abruptly, her chest moving up and down. "Did you?"

"Oh, I'd say so."

Eve picked at a string on the hem of her shorts, grew agitated and stopped. "What did you talk about?"

"I'm more than happy to tell you." Was she holding her breath? She seemed to be, but he couldn't be positive. Hope could be playing tricks on him. Hope that she cared for him a lot more than she'd been letting on over the years. "We decided to go for a drink in town. As friends. But she called the night off in the parking lot, because she incorrectly believed we were on a date. And she didn't want to hurt Robbie."

Robbie Corrigan was Skylar's new boyfriend.

A hockey player with a past as colorful as his hair.

"You *weren't* on a date, though?" Eve asked, shifting.

"No." Madden shook his head and said it again. "No. We were not."

Her throat looked to be stuck in the swallow position. "Oh."

"I was taking her for a pint so we could talk about *you*, Eve."

She quickly tucked some hair behind her ear. "Why . . . why me?"

"You know why." Madden had begun making progress in her direction. Slowly. One step at a time. "I am not and I have never been interested in Skylar. I think of her as a sister. But when she brought up this notion of us being on a date, I got to thinking, Eve. Things started occurring to me."

"Such as?"

"Such as . . . does Skylar think of me as more than a platonic brother type? Prior to meeting Robbie, of course."

"I don't know," Eve blustered, as if she'd never pondered such a possibility.

Madden wasn't buying it.

"See, I think you *do* know, love. She's your best friend." He was close now. Close enough to see the pink blotches that formed on her neck when she got hot or nervous. "Has Skylar been carrying a torch for me all this time? Answer honestly."

"If that were true, I w-wouldn't j-just betray her confidence like th-that," she sputtered.

"She's with someone else now. It's serious."

"What if it falls through?" she responded, worrying her lip.

Madden thought of the way Robbie, the wild-tempered, brick house hockey player, had reacted to finding out he'd taken Skylar out on a "date." Madden was lucky to be standing there with all his teeth. "You didn't spend your spring break watching them fall in love the way I did. I don't reckon it'll fall through."

"What if it does?" Eve persisted.

"And then she goes back to liking me. That's what you're worried about." Madden's chest muscles knitted together and tugged. Hard. He'd always had a sixth sense when it came to this woman, but he'd missed something important, hadn't he? Yeah, it seemed so. "Eve, answer me honestly. Have you been avoiding this thing between you and me, because your best friend had a crush on me?"

She was already shaking her head. "No. What? No." Then, she seemed to play back his statement, her expression verging on alarm. "What thing between you and me?" she whispered.

"Now who's gaslighting who?"

The tension grew thicker in the small, sunlit living room and he let it, because damn, it felt good. Not tiptoeing around what he'd always known. What he'd known since the night of that graduation party. They were meant to be a lot more than friends.

"Madden . . ." Eve wet her lips. "I've gotten used to not having you."

Christ, his heart almost screamed out of his chest. There it was. The closest thing to a confession she would offer. It might as well have been the keys to heaven. He could work with that. "Get un-used to it," he rasped, reeling over the proof he'd been right. His gut, his head, his chest. All right, all along. "Why would you put your own wants aside for so long, Eve?"

"Because she's a better choice," she said dully, slumping slightly as if something had finally been dislodged from her throat.

Madden's irritation dropped like a volume knob being twisted to zero. "A better choice? Than you, Eve? I don't understand."

"Go to New York, Mad. Please."

He'd pushed her today more than he ever had before. But he had nothing to lose at this stage and couldn't fathom another four years of pining, so he pushed a little more. "Tell me you feel something for me and I'll go."

When several seconds passed and Eve said nothing, he started to lose faith that she'd answer him. Then, salvation. "I don't remember a time when I didn't," she whispered, laying a hand over her eyes. "But I can't give you what you're looking for. I'm not . . . right. For you. For *this*. We're *friends*, Madden." She dropped her voice to a pleading whisper. "Next time you see me, let's pretend this never happened, okay?"

"Fuck that." Madden charged forward, picking her up in his arms and holding her tight. So tight while her breathing changed. Went from quick and erratic to deep, the side of her face very slowly pressing into the crook of his neck. He stayed that way, holding Eve with her feet several inches above the ground, dust motes swirling around them, and he could have stayed that way forever. "I'm not going anywhere. I'm a fucking rock and you can't dig me up. You'd have to dig forever to find how deep

I've buried myself when it comes to you, Eve. I am not going to budge no matter what happens." Setting her down and walking away—for now—was the hardest thing he'd ever done, but he'd known Eve long enough to know he'd pressed her enough for one day. "I'll be back, love," he vowed on his way out.

And he would.

He always would.

CHAPTER FIVE

Two weeks later, Eve sat at one of the ornate Gilded Garden cocktail tables, surrounded by silence, her gaze fixated on the empty stage without really seeing it. A clipboard rested in her lap and it held five résumés for dancers. Today were auditions.

The Gilded Garden already employed a few off-and-on dancers, hired before she'd ever opened the doors to the public, but the performers weren't as inclined these days to travel from Boston or New York City, thanks to the lack of clientele. Ten tickets sold wasn't much of an incentive to drive between two and five hours, understandably.

It was time for Eve to admit she'd been foolish. Opening a burlesque club in a small town in Rhode Island? Mistake. A big one. Instead of selling her father's strip club and splitting the money with her sister, she'd convinced Ruth to allow Eve to use the money to demolish the interior of the establishment that had caused her so much grief growing up and turn it into something she could be proud of.

Ill-advised. Silly. Shortsighted. Arrogant.

Self-indulgent.

Four years ago, Eve couldn't see the forest for the trees. She'd been obsessed with rebranding her family name. Proving herself a businesswoman to all the people she'd attended school with who asked her, every single day of her life, when she planned to join the family business and take off her clothes for cash.

Stripping was a legitimate job. The women she'd known growing up had families, bills to pay, or, hell, they just enjoyed the art of getting mostly nude. Nothing wrong with that.

That being said, now she had Ruth's twins to consider and burlesque was the more socially acceptable form of entertainment, compared to stripping. Or so she'd thought. People in town didn't seem inclined to make a distinction between the two.

Still, burlesque and the lounge she'd built to showcase it were simply more Eve's style than Cat Fight. *Only let them see what you want them to see.* Isn't that the epitome of who she was? And the Gilded Garden represented that. It was her way of saying, *Screw you, I didn't run away from this place and my reputation, I rebuilt it stronger. With more style.*

But maybe . . . no one cared.

Even when *she'd* gone onstage to perform a few weeks ago, hoping to draw some local interest from people who make it their business to see others get humbled, the turnout hadn't been that remarkable. Had she really thrown her heart and soul into something that didn't matter? Had she built a monument to her childhood trauma, simply for herself to worship?

The fact that the club was six months from going under said yes. She had.

Eve's phone vibrated on the table.

"Oh lord," she muttered, recognizing the number on the screen. Lark and Landon's school was calling. "Hello?"

"Hello, is this Eve Keller?"

"Yes. Speaking."

"Great. I've got Landon here in the nurse's office complaining of a stomachache." Some whispering took place in the background. "Landon says he switched sandwiches with Corey W. at lunchtime and he thinks he's allergic to turkey."

The first time Eve got a call from the school about her nephew, she'd almost split her head open leaping out of the shower to answer the phone, assuming blood had been spilled or he'd had some sort of mental breakdown over his mother's sudden absence. Nope. It was always something like this. Yesterday he'd gone to the nurse because his fingers looked weird. "Could you keep him there a little while and see if his stomach stops hurting? Maybe some soda water would help?"

"That sounds like just the thing." Based on the smirk in her tone, the nurse recognized Landon was trying to pull a fast one. "I'll keep you posted."

Gratitude nested in Eve's breast. The school nurse was a real one, nice from day one. It was a testament to Eve's experience that someone being kind to her in this town landed so hard. "Thank you."

No sooner did she hang up with the nurse than a young woman walked into the lounge.

Eve sat up straighter, liking her vibe. She was on the short side and kind of disgruntled looking, but she had a cool rockabilly style with chopped black bangs and a vintage scarf tied around her neck. She was wearing a pair of high-waisted pants and suspenders, complete with a cap-sleeved white T-shirt. Cute. Original. But maybe not the best choice if she planned to audition.

"Hi." Eve stood up and extended her hand. "I'm Eve. Thanks for coming. Did you bring music?"

"Uhh." The new arrival's step slowed. Looking confused, she dug her phone out of her pocket. "I mean, I have Spotify . . ."

Unprepared. Not off to a great start, but Eve wasn't in any position to be picky. "Great. Just pull up your song and I'll tell you how to connect to the Bluetooth. Do you need to change your clothes before the audition?"

"Oh." A slow blink from the girl. "I think we have our wires crossed. I'm not here to audition." She scratched her eyebrow. "I don't even take my clothes off in front of a mirror, let alone a crowd."

Crowd was a stretch. Seven people had attended last night's performance.

Eve dropped like a stone back into her chair and blew out a breath. She should laugh it off and give the girl directions to the interstate or the nearest Starbucks, depending on why she'd come in here, but she didn't have the wherewithal to be cordial or friendly. Her energy had slowly been waning since Madden walked out of her apartment and it appeared to finally be sapped.

Not good.

When she'd had time to breathe, the magnitude of what happened that morning hit her like a two-by-four. Madden had finally figured out her longest-standing secret. He'd called her out for keeping him at a distance because of Skylar's megacrush. And sure, of course her best friend being in love with Madden had a lot to do with Eve keeping him at arm's length. Over the years, however, it had become a lot more than that. Her reasons for ignoring her feelings for Madden had multiplied.

I'm a fucking rock and you can't dig me up.

The grind in her chest was so intense, Eve didn't even have the capacity to react when the nonauditioner sat down across from her, blocking Eve's view of the stage. "You okay, bitch?"

Eve looked up sharply. "Do you need directions? Or maybe an ass kicking?"

A smile bloomed across the girl's mouth. Pretty. She was very pretty.

She'd look even prettier outside. Driving away.

"I don't need directions," assured the girl.

"Not even to the exit?"

Rockabilly girl bit her bottom lip. "Damn. I kind of love you. Are you always this mean? Please say yes."

"Yes."

"Dreams do come true. I'm Veda." Veda, apparently, pulled over a chair from another table and used it as a footrest, crossing her booted ankles on top of it. "I'm here with a proposition." Eve raised an eyebrow at the footrest situation and Veda promptly put her feet back on the floor. "Sorry, I overcompensate when I'm nervous."

"Why are you nervous?"

"Are you serious?" Eve didn't know where this was going, so she crossed her arms and waited for Veda to explain. "You're kind of famous around here. The hot burlesque club lady who walks her kids to the bus stop with no pants?"

It took an effort to keep her expression neutral when her stomach nearly jumped into her mouth. "That's ridiculous. I wear shorts. And a hoodie. It's just a long hoodie that probably makes it look like . . ." She trailed off with an incredulous headshake. "Why am I having this conversation?"

"You're well known around here, so yes, I'm slightly nervous. That's the point I'm trying to make."

"Fine." Eve picked up the clipboard to examine the top page. "What else has you so jumpy, babe?"

"My proposition."

"Which is?"

Veda ran her thumbs upward beneath her suspenders. "You

have a lot of land out back of this place. It's just sitting there, unused. Do you have plans for it?"

As if she could see through the wall, Eve glanced in the direction of the acre that lay empty behind the club. Once upon a time, her father had used the space as overflow parking, but Eve sure as heck didn't have an overflow problem now. In fact, she'd barely thought of the empty land in two years. "No plans at the moment."

"Not going to lie, I was hoping you'd say that." Veda scooted closer to the table, flattening her palms on the surface. "So, I'm in a band—"

Before Veda could go any further, sunlight invaded the club, followed by a series of clicking footsteps. Whoever had arrived was in heels. "Well, praise the lord. Someone came prepared to audition."

"That felt targeted," Veda responded, her eyes trained on the entrance to the performance area, along with Eve's. But unlike Eve's, they widened as a woman sauntered into the room in leather pants, a cape . . . and pasties, complete with tassels.

"You can cancel the other auditions," drawled the newcomer, who appeared to be in her early fifties, though her light brown skin belonged in advertisements for antiaging cream. "Rhonda has arrived."

Eve's lips twitched "Hi, Rhonda. Do you have music?"

"Nope. I dance to whatever is playing in my head."

What little energy Eve had left flatlined. "Okay. I need a drink."

"Question." Rhonda sauntered over to the table, hands on hips, perusing her surroundings as if she was mentally redesigning her new kingdom. "What are the performance parameters? Can I flash a little bush?"

Veda slapped a hand over her mouth.

Eve didn't so much as blink. She'd more or less been raised in a strip club. Sat backstage and listened to the performers recap their conversations with the customers and, on occasion, overheard those exchanges firsthand. She'd been present for it all. "There are no hard rules, although in the spirit of burlesque, we encourage the performers to keep something to the imagination."

"Even if I flash it, I'm staying fully covered. I haven't seen the inside of a waxing studio for the better part of a decade." Rhonda waved a handful of acrylic nails at the clipboard. "Check my references. They're airtight."

Eve flipped to Rhonda's résumé and scanned. "Your most recent job experience is from nineteen ninety-one."

Rhonda's expression lost all trace of amusement. "Eve, right?"

"Yes."

"Trust me, Eve. I can put butts in these seats."

What did Eve have to lose at this point? Fine, she had four more auditions today. And fine, Rhonda wasn't who she'd expected to walk through the door. Well, maybe that was a good thing. What Eve had done so far hadn't worked. And despite Rhonda's lack of recent work in the industry, Eve refused to let age factor into her decision whether or not to give Rhonda a chance with some stage time. Burlesque was about creativity and humor, not what society deemed perfection.

"Can we get a quick preview?" Eve asked.

Rhonda squinted. "I don't take my clothes off, unless I'm getting paid, but I'll give you a little taste."

"That's all I ask."

Rhonda took out her phone, following Eve's instructions for connecting to the Bluetooth. "I Wanna Be Loved by You" by Marilyn Monroe filled the performance space a second later and the music did nothing short of inhabit Rhonda's body. She shimmied around the tables, granting eyelash flutters to the empty seats, stopping every few feet to twirl her pasties in time with Marilyn's breathy croon. Hip bump, hip bump, she strutted down the center of the floor like she was coming to take somebody's man.

"All right, Full Bush Rhonda," Eve called, smiling. "I'll give you a shot."

Rhonda, visibly pleased, approached Eve and Veda while sweeping her cape back over one shoulder. "You won't be sorry."

"I have your phone number here—I'll text you with call times. Please bring your own performance music. Or at least know what you'd like us to play."

"'Thriller' by the king of pop, please. Slowed-down version."

"Wow. Sexy. Okay." Eve massaged her eye sockets as hard as possible. By the time she dropped her hands, Rhonda had left the building.

"That was incredible," Veda breathed.

"Oh, look at that," Eve said, making a note on her clipboard. "You're still here."

"As I was saying about the open land in back—"

Eve's phone rang. The school again. "Hi?"

"Ms. Keller. Can you come get Landon? He threw up."

Alarm jolted her in the seat. "He did? Like, for real?"

"Watched it happen."

"Shit. I'm coming." She found herself unable to move. "Wait, where do I take him? Home or . . . the hospital?"

"I think urgent care might be best?" the nurse answered patiently. "Get him tested for the flu. His temperature is running a little high."

"Okay. Okay, thank you." Eve hung up the phone, unsure of what to do first. She had four more people coming to audition. Then she had to open the club at eight. If Landon had the flu, would the babysitter want to be exposed? And one huge, ugly detail was pressing in on her from all sides. What was it going to cost to take Landon to urgent care? Lark would probably come down with the bug, as well, right? Double whammy.

"Uh . . ." Eve held the clipboard to her chest and stood, feeling far too wobbly to have an audience, even of one. Oh, and it was so telling and terrible the way she suddenly ached to have Madden there. His blue eyes would steady her nerves and she'd stop shaking. He wouldn't overstep, he'd just wait there like a giant safety net, which was exactly what she needed right now. To know things were going to be okay, even if they would never be perfect. "We'll have to do this another time. My nephew is sick at school. I have to go get him."

Veda stood and pushed in her chair, but she was focused on Eve. "Do you need help?"

"With what?" Eve bit off, trying not to regret her tone.

"Anything. I'm an unemployed musician. I have a lot of free time." Veda gestured to the clipboard. "Maybe I could audition these folks?"

"I'm way too much of a control freak for that." Eve laughed, high-pitched and without humor. She speed walked to the door, while Veda jogged to keep up with her. "Look, unless you know anything about sick kids, I don't think you can help me."

"I have two little brothers, actually. Or, they *were* little." She shivered. "One of them has a soul patch now."

Outside the club, Eve quickly locked the door. "I don't think it would be responsible of me to leave two kids with someone I just met." Desperate. *You're desperate.* One night of the club being closed and she'd have no chance of paying this year's property taxes. "Do you have references?"

Veda visibly thought for a second. "You know that real estate agent lady whose face is all over the benches in town? Alexis Asimov?"

Of course Eve had seen those benches with the angelic, smiling blonde in a power suit. "I do, actually."

"That's my sister," Veda said. "You can call her."

They stopped in front of Eve's car bumper. "Wow. You look nothing alike."

"Thank you."

No time to analyze that response. Eve scanned the parking lot. "Where is your car?"

"I took the bus."

Eve hit the button on her key fob. "Get in. We'll call your sister on the way to the school."

They'd driven for a full minute before Veda turned in her seat and said, "I'll watch your kids for free tonight if you listen to my proposal for the outdoor space behind the club. You know, when the sky isn't falling?"

Did it ever *stop* falling these days? "Done."

CHAPTER SIX

Eight Years Earlier

Some bloke—Andrew, was it?—tossed Madden a baseball on his way down the corridor of Cumberland High, slapping Madden on the back as he passed. Madden forced a smile and nodded at his new acquaintance, even as that slap reverberated through his entire body, an echo he had no desire to feel. He remained stalled midstep a moment, reminding himself the slap had been a friendly one, before getting moving again.

Two weeks into being enrolled as a junior at Cumberland High and the other students were obviously still getting used to seeing him there, based on the way they stared as he walked through the rows of lockers. His accent had been imitated around a thousand times. Nothing was familiar. Not the food, the constant high-fiving, or the impractically frantic pace of an American school day. But he'd chosen this, hadn't he?

He'd chosen to stay.

When the morning arrived to return to Ireland, he'd calmly gotten out of bed and walked into the kitchen where Aunt Fiona stood making tea and solemnly asked her to please not send him home. The request had been difficult to make. Madden knew better than to ask for more than what he absolutely needed. Expecting more than what he'd been allotted was selfish. *He* was selfish. Hadn't he been told that often enough?

His aunt had taken one look at his white face and nervous breathing and poured a second cup of tea. He could still hear shadows of that conversation, alive in the house.

"We're not really related, Fiona. I'm a . . ."

A long sip of Barry's Gold. "You're a what?"

"A bastard," he managed, his first time saying the word aloud. Far from his first time hearing it. "My mother was pregnant with me when she married my father." Fiona's brother. "I'm not his, it's easy to see. They're fair-haired and green-eyed, the opposite of me. Maybe if it wasn't so obvious we're from different men, he wouldn't be so humiliated. Maybe he wouldn't . . . take that humiliation out on me."

She'd set her cup down with a rattle. Remained in silence for nearly a full minute. "Does he lay hands on his wife?"

"No," Madden assured her. "He leaves Paul and Sinead alone too. But me being there . . . it's unacceptable to him, Fiona. The sight of me eats him alive and it causes problems in the house. I'm the poison—"

"You are not poison," she hissed, her keel uneven for once. "My father once said the same to me because I rebelled as a teenager. Married someone they didn't approve of and then he gloated when it didn't work out. Made me feel like I couldn't do anything right. I'm in this country because I believed myself to be the poison infecting my own family. Now that I realize it was just a lie I was sold to make a small man feel better about his own shortcomings, it's too late to go back." She turned in her seat. "You are welcome here, in this house of accused black sheep, but don't make the same mistake

I made. Allowing yourself to be run off when you've done nothing wrong but exist."

Madden carefully considered what his aunt said. Perhaps she was right. But he'd been living with the belief that he was wrong for too long to change his mind. He didn't want Paul and Sinead and his mother to weather a storm that wasn't their own making.

They would be happier in his absence. Without the anger he alone seemed to incite.

"I need to stay."

That was it. She nodded and registered him for school that same afternoon.

In almost every way, being in Cumberland was better.

When Madden was at Aunt Fiona's, at least. The quiet fell and he could breathe in a way he couldn't have imagined back home.

In school, however, blending in became very difficult.

Fate had landed him in a house next door to Elton Page, who'd quickly ordained Madden a baseball player and introduced him to his vast network of friends, who also played baseball every bloody chance they got. Madden had never watched the sport before coming to Rhode Island. Now? Every pair of trousers he owned bore dirt stains on the knees. He'd planned on filling in *one time* for Elton's friend at a scrimmage, then bowing out. Trying out for a proper sport, like football. Or soccer, as they called it here.

Then he'd been introduced to the catcher position.

He'd liked the mask.

The silence and repetition of being a catcher.

Perhaps the sport itself would never be something he chose—the noise and grit and intensity of it reminded him of home, and he didn't want to be reminded of that—but he could bear with it from behind the cage. In the background. Observing. Surviving. So he continued to play baseball in this foreign place, playacting like he belonged with a rowdy group of kids with almost freakishly wholesome home lives, trying his goddamn best to blend in, because if he faked belonging long enough, maybe one day he would.

The warning bell rang for fourth period and Madden picked up his pace slightly, needing to get to earth science, so the teacher wouldn't use Madden's lateness as another opportunity to tell a story about his senior class trip to Ireland in 2001. Jesus, he probably would no matter what.

Madden rounded a corner of the empty hallway, drawing up short when he saw her.

Eve Keller.

The serious blond girl he'd met in Elton's kitchen two weeks prior. He didn't interact with her much in school, due to him being a junior and her a freshman, but they were often at the Page household at the same time, whether in the backyard after classes or colliding in the kitchen. They didn't speak much directly. It was hard to get in a word with Elton and Skylar's nonstop lambasting of each other. Eve and Madden were mainly observers, but in an odd way, their spectator status was what gelled them.

A traded eye roll or a quiet, sarcastic comment exchanged under their breath. They'd fallen into a quiet sort of . . . companionship that neither one of them had acknowledged. It just was. And he felt less alone because of it. Still, he'd only been in Cumberland two weeks. Not long enough to consider himself close to anyone.

Which was why he'd found it so odd that the morning he'd asked his aunt to let him stay, Eve's face had popped into his head.

He'd been oddly relieved at the chance to see her again.

Though it was very hard to explain why. Even to himself.

Madden was sixteen. Eve fourteen.

Too wide of a gap for him to consider her . . . romantically, right? Yet he thought of her, nonetheless. When they brushed gazes in the school corridors, an invisible force kicked him in the gut. Pursuing someone two years younger was fucking creepy and he wouldn't allow himself to go there, even mentally, but the way she'd been so bold about announcing her father as the strip club owner . . . that defiance tugged at his chest.

He found himself wanting to ask Elton about Eve.

Is she okay?

He wanted to ask that question, in particular.

Because he knew what a person standing on shifting sand looked like.

He'd seen it in the mirror.

Now he watched as Eve tried to avoid two male students, only to have them step into her path, blocking her from passing. If someone overheard their laughter from down the hall, they might have deemed it harmless, but coupled with their actions, Madden could only pick up on the sinister notes in those twin laughs. Especially when he caught the profile view of one of them and clocked the leering expression. Aimed right at Eve.

Worse, these two were clearly older than her. Closer to Madden's age.

"Dance for us and we'll let you pass." An elbow to his friend's side. "Or do you even know how to shake it without a pole?"

"Come on. One little flash, Eve. Should be no big deal for you."

Disgust sent Madden's stomach plummeting to the sticky linoleum floor. This was what she'd been referring to that day they met in the kitchen. *Ask me if I'm going to work the pole one day. I'm sure you're dying to know. Everyone asks. It's fine, really.*

Christ, the girl was *fourteen* and this was her everyday reality? Not anymore.

"Eve," Madden said, walking into her line of sight and giving her the most reassuring look he could muster while his blood was boiling, "go to class, love."

To be clear, Madden hated violence, but in a strange way, he'd grown resigned to the existence of it. After all, there were three kinds. The type of violence that was perpetrated on the weak and defenseless. An unacceptable, abusive brand of violence he was too well acquainted with. He found the second and third types acceptable, however. Self-defense and defense of the underdog.

Eve was clearly the underdog in this situation.

"I'm fine," Eve said, sounding out of breath, her books smashed to her chest.

"Of course you are," Madden felt compelled to say—and the sharp way she lifted her chin to study him with something like renewed respect said it was the right thing. *She doesn't want to be rescued.* "I just need to speak to these two for a moment."

"Fine." After a brief hesitation, she sidestepped the pair, her shoulders sagging in visible relief when they didn't block her a second time. "You're, um . . . going to be late for class," she remarked when she drew even with Madden, but he could tell it was her way of thanking him without having to do it out loud.

"It's okay." He jerked his chin in the direction she was heading, reminding her it was okay to leave. "My teacher is chill, as you Americans like to say."

Eve tried to replace the fear on her face with a wry smile, but it didn't quite work. Still, Madden had to train his eyes on the ground so he wouldn't acknowledge how that smile made her even more extraordinary. *She's only a freshman.* "I'm glad he's chill," she muttered, adjusting her books with a swallow. "You don't need to interfere, though. I can handle them. I've been doing it for a long time."

Madden had to concentrate on not punching a locker. "Then I reckon it's time you took a break," he said, attempting to remain calm. "Does Elton know about this?"

Eve's lips were stiff when she answered. "He doesn't know how bad it is. And I don't want him and Skylar to know." She hesitated, as if trying to wrestle back the next part, prevent herself from saying it out loud. "I like the Pages . . . and I don't have a lot of friends. I don't want my only ones to write me off as a hassle."

Madden wasn't accustomed to displays of affection, but he recognized the urge to hug Eve in that moment. Somehow, he managed to refrain, though the impulse never quite left him. Ever. "You're worth a lot more than a hassle. And we're friends now too."

"Friends," she repeated, hope dawning. "Um—"

"You going to give him a lap dance, Eve?" snickered one of the boys.

Her cheeks flamed red.

Madden's vision blanketed with the same ruby color.

"Eve, as your friend," he bit off, "I'm telling you to go to class."

She sighed, averting her gaze, but not before Madden saw the light sheen in her eyes and it made his chest feel like twisted metal. "Are you my protector now, or something, Madden Donahue?"

He didn't even crack the slightest smile. "Yes."

Something was exchanged between them under the fluorescent

hallway lights, but he couldn't quite put his finger on what. A grudging allowance to let him be somebody to her, maybe, before she sped off toward class. Madden waited until she was safely inside her classroom and the hallway was empty before he dropped his books to the floor, took the assholes by the collars of their shirts and pounded them up against the row of lockers, satisfied when their eyes bulged out.

You weren't expecting that, were you, motherfuckers?

"Don't say another fucking word to her," he growled through his teeth. "Not *about* her either. Not even to each other. Or I will beat you both to a pulp. Do you understand me?"

This wasn't the last time Madden would issue a warning on Eve's behalf.

Their high school was a big place with equally big mouths and a lot of bravado.

But when he'd called himself her protector, he'd meant it.

That promise didn't have an expiration date.

# CHAPTER SEVEN

Present Day

Madden stood in front of the mailboxes in the vestibule of his new apartment building, keys in hand. After his meeting with Yankees management, they'd arranged for a real estate agent to show him some options. He'd taken a three-bedroom on the Upper West Side instead of choosing one of the downtown bachelor lofts he'd been shown, which seemed to surprise the agent, but thankfully he didn't comment.

What would Madden say, anyway?

I want to be prepared in case Eve and the kids ever come to stay.

After two weeks of no communication with his elusive infatuation, that far-fetched dream made little sense, even to Madden.

Dropping the heavy baseball equipment bag from his shoulder, Madden unlocked the mailbox, pausing before he swung open the slender brass door, issuing a prayer that this time there would be a letter from the New England Donor Council informing him that his donor was ready to be identified. That they were open to meeting him or at least accepting some form of thanks, be it a phone call or an email. Every day that passed without expressing his gratitude seemed to make it deeper and more urgent.

He opened the mailbox door.

Nothing but a takeout menu for the falafel joint down the block.

Clearing his throat hard, Madden locked the mailbox once more, nodding at the smiling older man in the peacoat who opened the inner entrance door that led to a small, carpeted lobby with elevator doors.

"I hope you had a productive practice, sir."

"You don't have to call me sir," Madden muttered as he passed. "Like I said."

The doorman hummed. "I don't know if I mentioned this, but I'm a Mets fan."

"You mention it every time I enter the building."

"Ah. Sorry about that." The man tapped his temple. "Short memory."

"Huh."

Madden tucked his tongue into his cheek to hide his smile from the doorman while the elevator doors snicked shut, but his amusement dropped like a stone as soon as his reflection looked back at him from the polished steel doors. Professional baseball wasn't what he'd expected. To be honest, he hadn't spent a lot of time thinking about the hours, the expectations, the physical toll, and how all that would differ from the AAA level.

On the heels of messy trades, bad press, and demanding fans, a lot of the pro players seemed to have developed a cynicism. Unlike his AAA teammates, the pros were guarded and calculating. The pitchers liked things done a certain way and that meant his signals were often being ignored or criticized in practice. And honestly, he was struggling to find the motivation to try and break the tension. To make an effort with his teammates and learn the peculiarities of each pitcher, so they could connect on the field.

He'd always played the sport to belong.

For a long time, that sense of belonging had been enough to overshadow his niggling resentment for the sport. This sport that had so easily given him a new identity. Poof. No longer the black sheep. No longer the bastard, scourge of the household. In baseball, he was renewed, absorbed into the fold.

Now, far from the comfort of camaraderie, the Madden he'd left behind became harder to ignore. An unresolved version of himself that wasn't so content with hiding, going with the flow. Letting the past fade into nothing.

The part of himself that had been numb for so long was experiencing signs of life again. More and more, while on the field, he found himself wanting to . . . fight. Speak up. Stop living in the background. To claim the sport, instead of the sport claiming him.

Madden unlocked the door to his apartment and stepped inside, dropping his equipment bag just outside the kitchen to his right. After rooming with two AAA teammates in Florida, having so much space to himself disoriented Madden for a moment until he got his bearings.

Two weeks without speaking to Eve. His jaw seemed to tick in time with that thought. Two weeks was too long. He'd given Eve some distance so their conversation could settle, but it was time to check in on her.

Madden sat down on one of the boxes he'd yet to unpack, extending one leg so he could slide his phone from the pocket of his sweatpants. Her name was number one on his speed dial, before Elton. Before anyone. He liked this acknowledgment that she was number one to him in this way, a way he could see with his own two eyes and not have it be a dream, even if he was the only one who knew.

Swallowing over the anticipation of hearing her voice, he dialed. Three rings.

Then, "Mad. Hi."

A rush of heat nearly took him down. "Hello, Eve." There were voices in the background. Was she breathing a little hard? "What's going on?"

"It's like you knew to call."

He stood up. "Is everything okay?"

"Yes. Uh." There was a patch of silence, followed by a door closing and a noisy fan coming on, as if she'd closed herself in a public bathroom. "It's just that Landon and Lark are sick. They have the flu. In the *spring*. I thought he was just trying to get out of class—he tends to do that. No joke, he once said his desk was haunted. But they tested him, and Lark to be safe. Both of them are positive."

He could already hear Eve pacing—and he'd heard enough. Madden picked up his equipment bag and walked straight back out the door. "What is this costing you?"

"That's for me to worry about."

"Eve."

She was silent a moment. "I'm glad you called. You always sound so composed and practical and together." Dazed laughter. "It's calming to know that's possible."

"After how we left things, I'm not together. But I will be, for you." Against his ear, he listened to her breathing change. "Where are you now, love?"

Her exhale bathed his ear and Madden pretended she simply enjoyed the endearment. That it soothed her in some way. "I'm at the clinic with my new babysitter, Veda. She's going to watch the kids while I open the club tonight." Eve's voice caught, ever so slightly, and Madden almost lunged through the elevator doors before they finished opening. "I'm a little overwhelmed, but I'll get everything under control," she said, in an uncharacteristic admission that she was struggling. That was enough to make him move faster. "How is New York?" she asked, obviously trying to change the subject.

"It's not Rhode Island. It's not where you are."

A pause ensued. "Madden," she warned. "Don't come all the way h—"

He ended the call before she could finish launching her protest.

CHAPTER EIGHT

Eve closed the door behind her departing bartender, turned, and pressed her back to the cool wood, sighing the evening from her lungs. Her employees hated being left at the Gilded Garden alone. Something about the low lighting, sultry music, and 1930s-themed decor gave a haunting impression. Eve, however, didn't mind being the last one out. If there were ghosts living among these walls, they were better behaved than humans.

She checked the time on the phone in her hand. Just after midnight. The kids would be long since asleep. Tonight had been slow at the club, an unfortunate recurring theme lately, so she'd had ample time to check in on Lark, Landon, and her apparent new babysitter, Veda. After starting antibiotics this afternoon and being given some over-the-counter medicine to relieve their symptoms, her niece and nephew were on their way to recovery. No temperatures as of nine o'clock, thank god.

Veda needed to leave soon. That gave Eve a smidge of time to herself.

And she knew exactly how she needed to use it.

Humming along with the swing music that filtered in from the performance area, Eve pushed off the door and sauntered down the hallway, freeing her long hair from the clip she'd used earlier to create a twist on top of her head. Sank her fingers into the tumbled-down mass and rubbed out the kinks and soreness of her scalp. When she reached the audience seating, a half circle of tables and chairs, her pulse started to flutter in her wrists and throat, a mixture of excitement and nerves bumping around in her belly.

She stood center stage in the blue spotlight and closed her eyes, letting her imagination conjure up a crowd of people, well dressed and stirring with anticipation. Their eyes tracked her every movement and she made a meal out of each and every one, starting with her heels. Giving the crowd her profile, she staggered her legs and slowly bent forward without bending her knees, slipping off one shoe, then the other, setting them neatly to one side. But when Eve straightened and settled her fingertips on the buttons of her sweater, that's when her blood truly started to pump.

The members of the audience were faceless, but it was the imagined change in their energy, a growing eagerness on their part, that made her stomach ripple with butterflies. Made her hips and breasts feel like weapons at her disposal. A means to entice.

One by one, she released the buttons, but instead of opening the black wool of her cardigan, she gave the audience her back and slowly, slowly, slipped the material down to expose one shoulder. All she heard now was the music of her own blood, the pumping rhythm of it, how the tempo sped up when she shimmied the garment down to her wrists and let it drop, leaving her center stage in a bra and high-waisted skirt.

They'd have to wait for more, though.

They were rapt, dangling from a string. Watching her. Afraid to blink as she swayed from the stage into the dining room and perched herself on one of the front tables, leaning back in an arch and shaking out her long tresses to the low, slow boom of bass. She lifted the fingers of her right hand and dragged them down the curve of her throat, lips tilted in a wicked smile, the front snap of her bra between her index finger and thumb.

Eve flicked the snap open but used both hands now to keep the silk cups together, preventing them from opening. Uncrossing her legs, crossing them again with the opposite thigh on top, moving her shoulders to the music, knowing they were all holding their breath, silently begging to see her breasts. And that projection of hunger gave her a melting sensation between her legs, prickled her skin from toes to scalp, made her thrum.

Everywhere she thrummed.

She wasn't the only one.

MADDEN HAD TO be dreaming.

What the hell had he walked in on?

Eve was sitting on a table in the empty lounge, her sweater and shoes discarded on the floor, her opened bra being held together by delicate fingers while she moved with the music, a flirtatious smile on her mouth. Eyes closed.

Speak up. He needed to announce himself.

If he had the ability to speak, he would have. Immediately.

But he could only stand at the mouth of the hallway, arrested by the mind-blowing sight of Eve performing a striptease for no one. Although it seemed to be . . . for her. Her chest rose and fell on heavy breaths, proof she was enjoying herself. She uncrossed her beautiful legs, as if to give the slightest peek between them, and Madden's throat went fucking dry, his pulse noisy and erratic in his ears, his chest.

Hungry eyes devoured the parts of Eve he hadn't seen in way too long. Since last summer when they'd gone swimming in the Pages' backyard. He'd seen her in a bathing suit then. A high-waisted vintage deal that reminded Madden a lot of the skirt she wore tonight. The delicate curve of her spine, the breadth of her hips, the wild waves of her hair when she wore it down. The tight swell of her ass. All those ingredients that composed Eve . . . he knew them better than he knew himself.

When she slipped off one side of her bra, but quickly covered her breast with the palm of her hand, Madden made a sound in his throat, guilt over his stiff cock taking hold. In total, he'd probably been standing there in the shadows for less than two minutes, but that was too long. He needed to make her aware of him before she removed the bra completely.

"Eve." She gave no sign that she'd heard him. "*Eve.*"

The other side of her bra slipped off, leaving her in that tight skirt with her hands cupped over her tits, and it physically hurt to walk at that point, but he started to pick his way through the chairs and tables, no choice but to get closer and be heard.

"Eve," he barked.

Was it a tragedy or a revelation the way her hands left her breasts, baring them, her palms closing around the edge of the table for stability as she screamed.

"Madden?"

"I called your name," he said, hoarse, turning around like a gentleman ought to, but not before seeing her high, lush tits, in full. Those rosy, pebbled nipples. The flush running up her neck and down the center of her torso. Eyes heavy lidded, bottom lip swollen from self-inflicted bites.

Aroused.

Eve was *aroused.* From taking her clothes off in front of an empty room.

The mystery she'd always represented deepened. He was simultaneously turned on by the knowledge of what made her breathe so hard . . . and galled to be only finding out now.

"I-I told you not to come here," she rasped, followed by the sound of her bare feet hitting the ground, the snap of her bra reengaging. A flash of blond to his right told Madden she was retrieving her sweater from the stage. "Dammit, Madden."

He didn't respond.

All his concentration funneled into a grip on his willpower, also known as the one thing stopping him from throwing her back up on the table to see if she'd uncross her legs for him, as smoothly as she had for the nonexistent audience.

Patience sapped, he glanced back at her over his shoulder. The sweater was back on over her bra, but she hadn't engaged any of the buttons, leaving a swath of her upper stomach on display along with her cleavage. He wasn't going to say it out loud, but good god, she might as well still be topless for the effect she was having on him.

Eve fumbled with her phone where she'd left it on one of the tables, her fingers tapping on the screen a few times before the music stopped playing.

Silence dropped like a velvet curtain.

They were both breathing hard.

"What was that, Eve?" Madden said, turning around fully.

A flippant shrug. "What was what? I'm short on dancers these days. I need to know what I'm doing in case I ever have to fill in."

Madden laughed, the low incredulous sound echoing off the stage. "I was against you performing before, but now that I've seen what it does to you? No, I don't reckon I'd like anyone to see you like that."

"Like what?"

Slowly, he wove around the single table that sat between them, noting the way she stared at his chin, instead of meeting his eyes. "Hot, love. Turned on."

Her breath hitched. "I don't know what you mean."

"Yes, you do." When she closed her eyes, Madden stepped into her space, stopping just short of their bodies touching, no idea how she'd react if she felt how hard she'd made his dick. But the pleasure he got from pressing his mouth against her ear made up for the pain. He'd take all the pain in the world to spend any length of time this close to her. Close enough to smell her smoky peach perfume, close enough to hear her breathe. "What do you like about taking your clothes off in front of a room? You can tell me."

"I don't know," Eve whispered after several seconds.

His lips brushed side to side against her ear. "Are you sure?"

She reached back and gripped the edge of the table behind her. As if she was in danger of losing her balance. "If you tell anyone—"

"Eve, you know me better than that." Madden took a chance, settling his hand on her hip, beneath the flap of her cardigan, his thumb brushing the smooth skin of her stomach, the rush of southward heat making him burn inside his clothes. "Why would I tell anyone a goddamn thing about you when I want to be the only one who knows?"

"Madden," she said on a gasp, on the verge of pulling away.

He pressed his thumb gradually into her hip abductor. "Tell me."

Eve closed her eyes for a moment. When they reopened, they were more arresting than he'd ever seen them and that was saying a lot. "It's empowering. To me. Being . . ."

"Being?"

"On . . . display like that. Being wanted. The . . ."

"Lusting."

Her stomach hollowed against his hand, as if the word itself had inspired some relief. Or an increasing lack of it. He couldn't be sure, but he wanted to be. "I guess."

"You guess or you know?" he pushed in a low voice against her temple.

"I know."

Christ.

Eve had an exhibitionist streak. He hadn't seen that coming. At all.

If he hadn't driven here tonight, he might never have found out.

What the hell was he going to do about it, though? This was the closest she'd ever let him get to kissing her, touching her, and he suspected the reason for that was he'd found her in a vulnerable moment. She *needed* to be touched.

"Have you done anything to . . . explore it?"

"No. This is enough."

"Is it?"

"No."

That endearing confession had Madden chuckling out of pure affection for this woman. This woman he'd seemingly been chasing unsuccessfully since the beginning of time.

And he'd be chasing her until the end of time unless he got creative.

It wouldn't be right to use the information he'd just learned to his advantage. But here was the thing about Eve Keller. To be there for her, to effectively help her, one had no choice *but* to get creative. That's how it had always been. And whether she wanted to admit it or not, she needed help now. Madden would use whatever he had at his disposal to make life better for this woman. End of story.

"Eve."

"Yes?"

He gave in to fulfilling half of tonight's fantasy by picking her up by the waist and settling her butt on the closest table. "I dropped by tonight for a reason."

It took her a moment to speak, her gaze slipping down to his hands where they grasped her waist. "Dropped by? You drove almost four hours."

"Believe me, love, it was fucking worth it."

Eve shoved at his chest, but the assault was half-hearted.

In fact, she appeared to be hiding her pleasure over the compliment.

"Go on."

"Go on telling you I'd pay every penny in the bank to see the show again?"

"No." Her color deepened. "Go on, tell me why you 'dropped by.'"

"Oh, that." Madden wanted to remember this moment for the rest of his life, so he dropped the teasing tone and lifted her chin in his hand, waiting for her to lock in on him. "I came here to propose, Eve."

CHAPTER NINE

I came here to propose, Eve.

Eve reacted as Madden predicted she would, although it took her a while to catch up. He liked to think their proximity had something to do with the muddling of her thoughts. When she blinked several times and her posture lost any hint of casualness, though, Madden braced, knowing he was in for a battle.

"What did you say?"

"You heard me, loud and clear."

"You came here to propose what?"

"Marriage."

The pulse at the base of her neck was going a mile a minute. "I'm not *that* amazing topless." Eve laughed, obviously still under the impression Madden was joking.

Or hoping so, anyway.

"You bring me to my fucking knees topless, but that's beside the point."

His serious tone of voice made her swallow hard. Cornered. She was cornered and didn't like it, so Madden forced himself to take a step back that allowed her to scramble off the table to her feet. "Mad, this isn't funny."

"Eve, when have you ever known me to joke about you?" She clearly didn't know how to respond to that—or didn't want to—so he continued, searching his memory bank for all the bullet points he'd formulated during the four-hour drive. Thinking wasn't an easy feat with her so close, however. Close and bewildered and ready to bolt.

More than anything, he wanted marriage to this woman to be real.

Now that they'd cleared up the fact that her best friend's crush had rendered him off-limits for years, he wanted to take the time to date her, be her boyfriend, take whatever feelings she had for him and nurture them into love. But with Lark and Landon dropped into her lap, they didn't have the luxury of time. If Madden wanted the opportunity to help, he needed to appeal to Eve's common sense, instead of her heart.

For now.

Just for now.

He'd find a way in later, once her immediate needs were covered.

"My contract with the Yankees . . ." Madden started. "Look, my salary is on the low end for catchers in the league, seeing as I've only been brought up from the minors and haven't proven myself, but even so, it's lucrative. And it comes with health benefits." Her face lost a touch of color and he couldn't decide why. Had she been expecting a more romantic reason for his proposal, even if that very thing would have spooked her? God, he hated that possibility, but it was too late to turn back now. "I want to give you access to those benefits. For the kids. For you."

"Marriage is kind of an extreme solution, wouldn't you say?"

"No."

"Well, you're wr-wrong," Eve sputtered. "It is."

"Eve." He approached her, cautiously, taking note of her white knuckles that held the cardigan tightly to her breasts. "I've made no secret of the fact that I feel more for you than friendship, but at the very least, we have that. So let me help you as a friend, if nothing else. You won't owe me anything. I'm not doling out charity here."

"You're proposing a practical marriage. A marriage of convenience."

Madden hid his negative reaction to those descriptors. "Yes."

Eve nodded for several seconds, until it turned into shaking her head. "I appreciate the offer. I appreciate you thinking of me and the kids, but I can't do that."

"Why?"

There was a reason. A heavy one. He could see it swimming in her eyes, but she pressed her lips together tightly and didn't let it out.

"Maybe a marriage of convenience is too straightforward for you," he said slowly, no choice but to let his feet carry him forward, toward Eve.

"What does that mean?"

"It means you're a little complicated, love."

A blond eyebrow went up. "Are you expecting an apology?"

Madden clucked his tongue. "Jesus, no. I love your complications. Don't ever apologize for them. But they exist." The territory he was approaching was unfamiliar, but a woman like Eve required bold moves. For so long, he'd stood and allowed her to keep him at a distance, patiently waiting for her to admit she wanted him. That approach had gotten him nowhere. He'd still have patience with her. As much as she needed.

But he wouldn't sit back and observe anymore.

"You said dancing for an empty room isn't enough for whatever it is you're feeling. What would be enough?"

"I don't know."

Madden eliminated the distance between him and Eve. Stopped in front of her. And when she didn't back away, he lifted his hands to hold the sides of her face. "I'll help you find out."

At once, her eyelids seemed to weigh down, but she fought through that visible response, trying to focus on him. "What do you mean by that?"

"I mean . . ." He lowered his mouth to her ear, dropping his voice to a whisper. "You're a bit of an exhibitionist, aren't you? You could explore that safely with me."

Several breathless seconds ticked by. Then, "W-while we're also *married?*"

"Like I said, complicated."

"That's putting it lightly." Eve matched his whispering tone. "I'm pretty sure a wife with benefits is just a wife."

"If you go by the classic definition."

"You're trying to appeal to the side of me that rebels against the status quo."

"Am I, Eve?" He rubbed his open mouth against her ear, gratified when her breath caught. "I must have been paying very close attention to you all these years."

"Seems so," she said, tilting her head just slightly. An invitation.

Madden wasted no time suctioning his mouth down the side of her neck, grinding his teeth together when she shivered violently and pulled away, her gait unsteady as she took several steps, putting a table back between them.

"Madden, I can't marry you. I can't do that."

Holding in the hurt was not an easy feat. Still, he kept his voice steady. Weighted with patience he didn't feel. "I don't suppose you want to tell me why." When she only looked down at the surface of the table, a groove between her brows, he suspected he'd gotten as far as he could for one night. "Right. Just promise me you'll think about it."

Eve's eyes closed. "I can't."

She wouldn't even give him the slightest consideration?

His Irish temper was a rare thing. When it bubbled to the surface out of sheer frustration, he knew it was time to take a step back.

"Are you finished here for the night?"

"Yes."

"Grand. I'll make sure you get to your car."

Eve nodded. Hesitated. Then set about turning off all the lights and collecting her purse from the office backstage. Madden waited by the door, exiting behind her when she breezed past. Watching her lock the front entrance with a quick twist of her wrist, he noticed that, at some point during the last few minutes, she'd attempted to button her cardigan, but she'd hastily married the buttons to the wrong holes, making the ends of her sweater uneven.

Madden didn't mention the mistake as they walked side by side to the driver's side of her car, but once they arrived and she opened the door, tossing her purse across the console into the passenger side, Madden's mouth moved all on its own.

"Your buttons are uneven."

Eve looked down and winced. "I did it on the fly."

"Come here and I'll fix it for you."

There was a single lamppost in the parking lot of the Gilded Garden and it stood at a distance, shining enough light to show that her cheeks had turned pink. A war waged itself in her eyes and he counted himself lucky for that. Maybe Eve didn't want to be in a romantic relationship with him, but she couldn't completely hide the attraction. The emotion she carried for him.

Eve nodded once. Sniffed.

Heavy throbs worked their way through Madden's cock as he stepped forward, looking Eve in the eye while he pulled her away from the car. "What . . ."

He turned her around to face the empty parking lot and the tree line that created its perimeter, the lamplight spilling across her cheek, her neck . . . and when he flicked open the buttons one by one from behind, opened both panels of the cardigan and exposed her breasts to the night air, the soft illumination spread across her shoulders too. The sliver of her collarbone that he could see when he tilted his head.

"What are you doing?" she asked, haltingly, making no move to cover herself.

"Feeling my way in the dark with you, love." He slung the cardigan over his right shoulder, the way he would a towel in the locker room, before sliding his fingers into her hair at the back of her head, tugging downward in a way that forced Eve to arch her back, whimpering over the fact that she was now offering her breasts to the stars. The moon had turned her hair to silver, nearly. "Do you like that?"

A few ticks of silence passed, but eventually she nodded. "I . . . yes."

With his free left hand, Madden reached around to the front of Eve and gripped the hem of her skirt, lifting it several inches in his grip, up, up, until her panties were visible to the empty parking lot. "Do you like that too?"

Eve was breathing too hard to respond, her body sagging back against him.

Trembling.

Lord, if he was the kind of man who took advantage of another person's weak moments, he'd walk her around to the hood of the car, bend her forward, and rip her panties down to her ankles. But he wasn't that kind of man. And he especially wasn't that kind of man when it came to Eve, the girl he'd loved for fucking years.

No, hunger and temper were not a good combination, so Madden reluctantly drew the hem of her skirt back down, breathing in and out the scent of her hair while he buttoned her back into the cardigan, his fingers itching to massage her tits. Pet her nipples.

Not now. Not yet.

"Text me when you get home. I'll be staying at my aunt's tonight, if you need me," he said directly against the crown of her head, instead, his tone like sandpaper. "Okay?"

"Okay," she said quickly, and thank god she needed another three seconds to pull away, her struggle giving Madden hope as he watched her drive out of the parking lot.

# CHAPTER TEN

Eve knew she was dreaming. She was locked in one of those half-asleep, half-awake type of deals—and desperately holding on to the overnight world her imagination had built. Because in her imagination, there was no reason to say no to sex with Madden. There was no reason to say no to anything. And her body had been highly, *highly* keyed up since last night when Madden watched her dance topless, followed by several prolonged touches. Nearness to his hard, sculpted mouth.

When he'd yanked up her skirt in the parking lot, this dream that was more of a fantasy, if she was honest with herself, had been inevitable.

Eve's legs squirmed in the sheets of her bed now, because in her feverish imagination, Madden didn't stop at flashing the parking lot her panties, he pulled them all the way down to her ankles, smoothing his huge catcher's hand over her bare butt cheek, squeezing and lifting it roughly. With his hot mouth riding up and down the column of her neck, he turned her, throwing her up against the side of the car, his hands everywhere, stroking over her breasts, molding her hips, pinning them to the car roughly with his lap when she wiggled to tease him, growling praise into her ear.

Who's my good girl?

In the predawn light of her bedroom, Eve moaned into her

closed mouth, her fingers busy in her panties, her middle and ring fingers rubbing circles against her clit, an abundance of moisture making her slippery. More slippery than she could ever remember being, because oh god, she could still feel his hands on her body from last night. Could still see the lust in his eyes before she covered up her bare breasts.

How long had he watched her dance?

What if he hadn't spoken up and she'd ended up in nothing but panties?

Eve's neck arched, her mouth opening in a silent O, heels digging into the mattress as she sank two fingers inside herself, slipping them back out slowly and stroking that swelling part of herself while tension increased in her belly.

"Come on, come on, come on," she whispered.

Back to the parking lot. Madden had her flattened to the side of the vehicle, a hand moving against her backside, the other one unzipping his pants. That's when a car pulled into the parking lot, a black Mercedes with tinted windows. Idling. No one got out, it just remained there with headlights on, pointing directly at Eve and Madden.

"Show everyone who you spread your legs for," he said into her neck, his accent thicker in his need. Then he covered her mouth with his left hand and rammed himself deep, right there in the twin spotlights, grunting his approval at the feel of her. *"So tight."*

Eve rolled over to orgasm, whimpering as quietly as possible into the pillow, humping the heel of her hand once and grinding into it, the relief like a downpour from above, her muscles constricting and relaxing, before going through the cycle all over again, her toes stretched and straining. *Fuck, oh fuck, oh fuck.*

As soon as the waves of bliss abated, she rolled over once again and stared up at the ceiling, the sheets clinging to her clammy skin, trying to catch her breath. As always, when the faceless audience made an appearance in her dreams, she felt conflicted. On one hand, she didn't believe women should ever feel shame for their sexual fantasies. Without her own sexual experience to draw from, all she *had* were fantasies. They were safe. Especially when they were contained inside one's own head. But much like that recent evening when she'd prepared to perform burlesque for the first time, the motive was what gave her pause.

She'd told Skylar and Madden and even herself that she was performing onstage to bring in more of an audience. Locals who would pay to see her fulfill the destiny of taking off her clothes onstage, the way they'd always predicted. And while that had *something* to do with her decision to perform, that wasn't the full reason.

Something inside her liked being . . . coveted. Objectified.

Problem was, she didn't know how much of her childhood at the strip club played into this. Was her fascination healthy? Was it okay to explore or would it lead to Eve confronting her early introduction to sex?

Eve's weekday morning alarm went off and she sighed, reaching over to tap the dismiss button. If the kids weren't sick, she'd be getting them up for school right now. Today, they needed lots of rest and fluids, plus the antibiotics. When they woke up today, there was a good chance they'd already be feeling better, thank goodness.

I've got this.

Allowing herself a few extra minutes in bed, Eve scrolled through her emails, deleting advertisements and moving invoice reminders to her work folder, to be dealt with later.

When? It was anyone's guess.

Her fingers paused on the screen when she came across an email with the subject heading: *You Have New Test Results.* Sent from the urgent care where she'd taken the twins.

Her pulse started to thrum a little faster when she opened the attachment and saw the word *asthma.*

"What the . . ." She sat up in bed, reading from the beginning.

Presence of wheezing in the patient's lungs. Follow-up appointment with pulmonologist recommended. Asthma likely present.

Asthma. Landon had asthma.

Had her sister been aware of this? What did this mean?

How dangerous *was* this condition for her nephew?

Eve got out of bed and pulled on a robe, doing her best not to overreact. "Pulmonologist. Okay." She'd just started googling local results for pediatric pulmonology when there was a knock at the door of her apartment, and for a split second Eve was dead positive it was her sister standing out in the hall—and she had no idea how to feel about that. Dread over losing the kids and their presence in her life. Relief that she wouldn't have to figure this scary shit out alone. Dread, relief, dread.

"Who is it?" Eve called, approaching the door.

"It's me. It's Veda."

Eve stopped in her tracks, frowning . . . yet, still decidedly more relieved than she'd been when suspecting the knocker was her sister. "Oh." She opened the door and stepped back to let the young woman inside, smiling absently at her saddle shoes, high-waisted jeans, and polka-dot tube top. "Did you leave something here last night?"

"Nope, I'm just being the go-getter my parents always wanted."

Eve stared at her blankly.

Veda let out a small huff. "I'm here to present my business idea, bro. I was going to drop it on you last night, but you seemed tired and distracted."

Understatement. "That I was."

"Any better this morning?"

"No, but there's coffee for that. Have a seat." Eve scrubbed at her face on her way into the kitchen, hitting the button to heat up her single cup brewer, taking two mugs out of the cabinet while Veda hopped onto one of the stools at the breakfast bar. "You mentioned your parents. Do you live with them?" Eve asked.

"Much to their dismay, yes. I'll be the last to leave."

"How many siblings do you have?"

"Three. My younger brother is in his first year of college at Tulane. The middle one is backpacking through Europe, as we speak. And my older sister is the real estate queen I mentioned last night."

"Right, the one with her face on the benches."

"Yup. I can't even go to the store without being reminded I'm the slacker sibling."

Eve snorted. "Slackers don't get up this early."

"Actually, I haven't gone to sleep yet." Veda covered a yawn. "My friend had a late gig in Providence. I made it in time for the last set."

"Damn." Eve stared down at the steaming coffee as it filled the mug. "I'm only twenty-two and somehow you're making me feel old."

Veda hooted. "All right, I'm going to shoot my shot. Are you ready?" She shook out her hands as her coffee mug was set down in front of her, along with the milk jug and some sugar packets. "You've got that acre of space behind the club, right? It's sitting there, unused. But what if you could turn it into something that would offer a whole new revenue stream?"

"Big words for seven a.m." Eve blew on her coffee, which she took black. "Go on."

"Like I said, I had to drive to Providence last night for a gig. We don't have any music venues around here. And there are plenty of musicians in Cumberland and the surrounding areas— you just don't see us because we're all sleeping in our parents' basements. Not to mention, everyone is looking for somewhere to go on Friday and Saturday nights. As of now, there are only two options in this town. Bar one or bar two. Sad, right?" She wet her cherry-red lips. "We could put an addition on the back of Gilded Garden. For shows. And maybe have an outdoor venue option as well, for summer nights." Veda shifted in her chair, excited by her pitch. "Picture blue lights in the woods, the low pluck of my bass. We'll put down pavers for the tables and chairs. Like a half-moon patio. A stage. The bar could be inside, but have a walk-up window to serve the outside customers. Realistically, the venue would only open two, maybe three nights a week, but you'd have that space to rent out for parties. Or whatnot." Veda paused for breath. "I can't read you. What are you thinking?"

Eve hid the dreamlike expression that was trying to take command of her face. Remodeling the Gilded Garden and decorating it to create a timeless escape had been her favorite part of the last four years. Because she'd been building *toward* something. Something she'd dreamed would be a success. Had that happened, though?

No.

Eve sipped her coffee. "I like the idea, Veda, but I don't have the extra capital to make it happen right now. We're talking six figures here." It hurt to expose a weakness out loud, but she liked this girl and wanted to impress on her that she wasn't getting a brush-off. "The club . . . is still finding its footing."

"I gathered that after you hired Full Bush Rhonda." Veda thought for a second. "What if I crowdsourced it? Like a GoFundMe?"

Eve was already shaking her head. "I don't like asking for handouts."

"We could frame it as a separate venture. I don't mind being the face of the charity case. It wouldn't be the first time. Ooh." She dug her phone out of her back pocket. "That rhymed. I need to put that in my notes. I write songs for the band, you know."

"What is the name of your band, by the way?"

Veda grinned. "The All-Nighters."

"Fitting." Eve sighed while pacing her kitchen slowly, from one end to the other. Dammit. Veda's idea was in its infancy, but it was a good one. And it could bring in a whole new—and younger—clientele to the burlesque club. "Let me think about it." Madden's face materialized in her mind, his jaw set, eyes following her every movement. "I've had a lot of proposals in the last twelve hours."

Veda paused. "You have another proposal for the backyard space?"

What was it about this girl that made Eve less guarded? "Um, no. A marriage one."

"Wow. I can't even get matched on Tinder." She stared at Eve. "This is a legit marriage proposal we're talking about?"

"Yes."

"Is he hot?"

Why water down the truth? "Extremely."

"Is he a criminal?"

"No."

Veda blinked. "Sounds like a resounding yes to me."

Eve drained the last of her coffee. "It's complicated." She chewed her bottom lip, visions of an outdoor dance floor floating through her mind. "Why don't we make an appointment with the town inspector to make sure we're zoned for an outdoor space and find out what the requirements are. It doesn't hurt to find out. We'll see what they say and take it from there. But no promises. Sound good?"

"Yeah." Veda ducked her head, seemingly to hide a smile. "Yeah, sounds perfect."

"I'll text you with the details." Eve put her mug back beneath the brewer. It was a multiple cup kind of morning. "Right now, I have to find a pulmonologist for Landon."

"Why?" Veda paused on her way to the door. "Does someone have asthma?"

"Landon, apparently."

"I've had asthma my whole life," Veda said, going through her phone. A second later, Eve's phone dinged with a text message. "That's my doctor. She's a little bit of a drive, but she's good with kids."

"Okay, great. Thanks."

Veda opened the door and let it swing shut. "I'll be back later to babysit," she called through the closed door. "But you're paying me this time."

"Roger that," Eve said, dryly, pressing the button on the coffee maker for the maximum number of ounces. "Guess she's here to stay." Waiting for her next cup to brew, Eve opened her laptop on the breakfast bar and started doing some research. The deeper she got, the heavier the weight in her stomach became.

An out-of-pocket pulmonology appointment could be six hundred dollars if Landon required tests—which he would, if he hadn't been diagnosed previously. Inhalers. Backup inhalers.

Follow-up appointments. This was going to be expensive. She'd sell everything she owned to get the kid the medical treatment he needed, but he also needed a roof over his head. Both those things would stretch Eve's funds to the limit.

Asthma could only be the beginning too. Other conditions could present themselves in him or his sister, right? Kids broke arms. They swallowed magnets and goldfish. A trip to the emergency room could break the bank. Already, the school trips and class dues, extra food, clothes were adding up. Throw in medical costs?

No way around it. Eve needed insurance for them.

They needed security.

A brief search told her a family plan, using the club as her employer, could be well over a grand every month. Holy shit. How did people afford this? Was everyone just struggling and keeping quiet about it?

Eve closed her laptop and picked up her phone, weighing it in her hand. Not only the device, but the decision she was about to make. Normally, there would be nothing on this green earth that would induce her to take this megalevel of help from someone, but she couldn't wait until she was drowning to reach for the lifeline.

And if she had to reach for someone, it would always and forever be Madden, wouldn't it? She wanted desperately to be pragmatic about this decision, but it was easier said than done when her pulse was going haywire at the prospect of being his wife. Madden Donahue's wife. A secret dream she'd been harboring since age fourteen. Even if they were marrying for security, what if she pretended otherwise? Just for a moment.

When Eve closed her eyes, the inundation of images almost buried her. Madden standing at the altar. Eve dozing in the crook of his arm while waves rolled up lazily on the shore nearby. Him raking up fall leaves in a front yard. Their eyes meeting across a table set for the holidays. His hair silvering. Laughter. Peace.

She opened her eyes on a gasp, demanding the twist in her chest to abate.

Usually, when she let her fantasies get the best of her, Eve used Skylar as the oar to paddle her to safety. Never mind her other reasons for denying the romantic feelings between herself and Madden. Her friendship with Skylar was at stake. She'd leaned on Skylar's crush so many times that it had become a habit. One she apparently hadn't quite broken, because she was dialing her best friend before she could stop herself.

"Eve!" Skylar answered midway through the second ring. "I was just thinking about you! How are the kids? How are *you*? I have a million questions, but I'm running out the door to practice."

"Sorry, bad timing—"

"Rocket," a very deep, very male voice called in the background. "Don't forget your cleats are in my back seat."

"Oh, um. Right. I'll probably need my cleats for practice . . ." Skylar mumbled, suspiciously breathless. "Don't ask me why they're in Robbie's back seat."

"I'm afraid I must," Eve said on a rush of breath, her eyes stinging at the sound of her friend so happy. Surprised to find out . . . she wasn't surprised at all. Not after the way Skylar had spoken about Robbie with such tenderness the last time they'd seen each other. Deep down she'd known their relationship was special, hadn't she?

Accepting it was harder.

"What can I say? He likes a girl in uniform." Skylar sighed. "And out."

Their laughter mingled on the line. "Things are going strong with Robbie, then?"

"Yes." Eve had never heard Skylar's laugh so carefree before. "Yes, they are."

Eve closed her eyes and swallowed the fist-size lump in her throat. Part of her didn't want to ask the next question, because she already knew the answer. Already knew in her bones that Skylar had moved on from Madden. And that meant what now?

The only obstacle was Eve.

Eve wet her lips. "It almost sounds like the torch you've been carrying for Madden is . . ."

"Extinguished. Yeah." Something passed between them in that moment and Eve got the suspicion that Skylar might have finally realized Eve had been carrying a torch of her own. Thankfully, Skylar didn't say it out loud, because Eve wouldn't have known how to handle that revelation, in addition to everything else. "He's an amazing guy, you know? He's just not my guy."

"Yeah." *He can't be mine either.* "Listen, I don't want to hold you up. Go to practice and we'll talk soon."

A minute later, Eve straightened her spine and texted Madden. *Can we talk?*

CHAPTER ELEVEN

Madden moved aside the old lace curtain to look out the window, warmth trickling down into his stomach when he realized Eve was giving herself a pep talk in the car. Night stood on the verge of falling, so her features were in the shadows, but he could see her mouth moving. Could sense her resolve, though he could only predict what she had to be resolved about. Saying no to his proposal?

The warmth in his stomach soured and Madden let the curtain drop, raking a hand through his hair and taking up a post on the other side of the room. Leaning a shoulder against the wall to wait for Eve to be ready.

Tonight would mark the first time she'd ever been in his aunt's house—Fiona hadn't been one for visitors—and although his aunt had passed, this was still, very distinctly, her house. Waterford crystal candleholders in the center of the coffee table. Rosary beads hanging from the doorknob. Lace pillowcases that matched the curtains, sewn by herself. Madden couldn't bring himself to change a single thing. Couldn't make this house his own or sell it to anyone else. No. He left everything as it was, preserving the legacy of the woman who'd saved him.

Aye, his aunt Fiona had quietly given him sanctuary from the turmoil he'd grown up with. She'd survived her own, once upon a time. They might not have been blood relatives, but they'd been cut from the same cloth, Madden and his aunt. Beyond the first time, they didn't talk to each other about their trauma. The comfort was unspoken. She'd offered him love through deeds, such as hiring an immigration attorney to take them through the lengthy process of obtaining a green card, which he hadn't achieved until his first year in college.

Madden wouldn't describe his relationship with Fiona as close. It was more they'd shared a silent, mutual place to heal. She treasured the privacy of her home above everything, and while he'd often wondered what had led to that need for constant calm, he never questioned her out loud or invited over his friends.

He simply left it.

Madden pushed off the wall when he heard a car door slam out in the driveway.

A hesitant knock on the front door got him moving. He stood in front of the threshold a moment, his gaze trained on the wooden *Fáilte* sign above the door and he said a quick prayer, asking his ancestors to lend him some of their luck, then he opened it to Eve standing on the stoop, gorgeous in a pair of jeans and a snug white T-shirt, tucked in tight, as if he needed any more encouragement to stare at her tits and remember last night.

How she'd looked topless in the parking lot, glowing in the lamppost light.

You'd do well to keep your head on straight for this.

Right.

"Eve."

"Madden."

After taking a moment to absorb her, he stepped back. "Come in."

She tucked her long, loose hair behind her ear, before stepping inside, passing close enough to Madden that it almost seemed like she was having mercy on him by doling out a bit of her smoky peach scent. God, what he'd give for the freedom to back her into the door and kiss her hello. How was it possible their mouths had never touched and yet, he missed kissing her so badly? It was as though half of his soul had been stolen before he even knew he had a soul to begin with.

"The kids are with their new babysitter?" Madden asked, closing the door behind Eve.

"Yes. Veda." She set down her purse on the console table but kept her phone in hand. "I'm starting to think she might be my guardian angel. She kind of fell into my lap." Eve chuckled. "Two days ago, I didn't know she existed and now she's in my top five contacts. Weird how that happens."

For Eve, this was rambling. Madden loved her sharing any part of her life with him, but he didn't love knowing she must be nervous. "She must be special if you've seen fit to trust her."

"Yeah, she is." She opened her mouth and closed it, shaking her head.

"What?"

"She's trying to convince me to open a music venue behind the club. We have an appointment with a town inspector tomorrow. This is on the heels of hiring a woman named Full Bush Rhonda. I may need a vacation."

A laugh rumbled in his chest. "Being open to new things is healthy. A totally practical marriage, for instance."

"Is that your best shot at a segue?"

"How'd I do?"

Her lips twitched. "Not bad. If only I was ready to talk about it." Eve sauntered backward a few steps, keeping her eyes trained on him as she moved deeper into the house, no idea she was going in the direction of his bedroom. And he imagined what it would be like, coming home from a night out with Eve, her seducing him farther into the house, both of them stripping clothes off in their haste to make it to the bed. "So . . . this is your aunt's house. I've only ever been in the garden."

A pang caught Madden in the sternum.

He remembered Eve in the garden, outside his window, along with Elton and Skylar. Knocking. Wondering why he wouldn't come swimming. Worried about him. Before any of them knew his kidney disease was the culprit for his lethargy and pain. Before Eve had forced him into going to the hospital.

Madden rubbed the scar on his lower right abdomen absently. "Aye, my aunt needed the quiet. We were alike that way. I don't mind some noise now, though." He shrugged a shoulder. "Playing ball, I suppose I had no choice but to get used to shouting again."

He didn't mean to say *again*. It had just slipped out.

But the stumble caused Eve to quit her perusal of the house and look at him, a question hovering in her eyes that she didn't voice. His difficult upbringing had been alluded to throughout the years, but when Eve or his friends asked about it, he'd taken a cue from his aunt and let the silence speak for itself. There was no sense giving them that burden to carry, was there? He knew firsthand how heavy it was. "I'm so glad you found your aunt, Mad."

"Me too," he said, with a firm nod. "Although I think if she'd invited you in for tea, she would have enjoyed knowing you, Eve. She was only set in her ways. It had nothing to do with . . ."

"With my father owning the much-maligned strip club?" Eve winked at him. "It's okay, Mad. I never assumed she was judging me. Or barring me from the house."

"I wouldn't have stood for it." When she only stayed silent, Madden cursed under his breath. "I'm sorry, I don't know why I brought this up."

"It's good that you did, actually." Her smile was tight. "My reputation in this town has a lot to do with what I came here to say."

Madden frowned. "How so?"

Eve circled the living room once, reminding him of a restless cat checking her new surroundings for threats, before perching on the arm of the couch. She waited until he'd followed and come to stand directly in front of her before speaking again. "Well . . ."

She shoved her steepled hands between her knees and he had to bite his cheek to resist the urge to grab them, warm them between his own. Damn, she looked anxious.

"Eve, you can say anything to me."

"This is hard. I thought I had everything figured out. I'm supposed to have everything figured out."

"You had no idea your sister was going to leave the kids with you, Eve. You couldn't have seen that coming. You've had no choice but to adapt."

"Yes, I hear that. I agree. But it's more than just the kids. I was so superior, thinking I'd open this club and make bank. Show everyone I didn't only have staying power, but that I could take my pride back. And it's just been . . . um. Kind of a wake-up call to find out that my trauma only mattered to me. Those people were capable of cutting me off at the knees and moving on. They didn't feel any of it and they never will." She swallowed. "I'm starting to think I did all this for nothing."

A tide of denial, outrage rose in his midsection. "Eve—"

"Hold on, let me just finish."

Madden bit his tongue. "All right."

It took her a moment to get up and running again. "There's nothing I can do to change everyone's perception of me and I've learned to live with that, but, Madden, if that ugliness touched you, I would not be able to live with it."

Somehow, despite his years of studying Eve Keller, he didn't see this coming.

Not even a hint of it on the horizon. And he could see now he'd been shortsighted, his eye on the immediate goal. Blind to Eve's insecurities that she hid so well. So well he almost forgot they existed sometimes. Well, here was the proof.

"I'm . . . going to marry you, Mad." She looked up at him with a face full of gravity and he was so caught off guard by having his ultimate wish granted, he nearly went end over end into the atmosphere. "But only if it's a secret. I don't want anyone to know. Not because I won't be proud as hell to be your wife, but because . . . because I'm not . . . you remember the way Skylar was treated for being friends with me? These moms won't talk to me at school pickup. I'm not doing that to you. You're in this whole new world of professional sports and media attention . . ."

Madden's anger caught up with his euphoria, storming through it. Not anger at Eve. Anger at everyone else. The entire world. "Eve, I don't give a right fuck about anyone's opinion. Let them talk. Let them say ignorant things about a woman who'd raise her niece and nephew at the drop of a dime, no questions asked. Who'd stand by her father when the whole town campaigned to throw him out. You're better than any of them. Than anyone." His hand cut the air in half. "I won't keep you a secret."

"This is my hard limit. It stays a secret." Eve stood up, sucking in a breath when Madden lunged into her space, stopping just short of touching her. But Jesus, he might as well have been for the effect their proximity had, her lids dropping like sandbags, her nipples hardening against the white cotton of her shirt. "Secrets don't stay secrets very long, Madden. Because of that, I think we should put a time limit on this."

He pressed a kiss to her forehead, plus a second one before drawing back. "Do you now?"

Eve hummed, desperately trying to keep her attention off his mouth. Did she think he couldn't read her returned attraction? "Yes. If I can't get the club to a place that is lucrative in the next six months, then I'll have to sell. Either way, at that point, I'll have the extra money to take care of Lark and Landon. Give me until then, then we can . . . divorce."

Madden could have argued. Could have explained to her that, no, nothing about them would be temporary and ask why she couldn't simply accept that, but he stopped himself. He stopped and gave the turning point between them some critical thought.

He'd gotten what he wanted today.

Eve had agreed to marry him.

He had six months to convince her to stay married to him. For real.

Six months to calm her fears that their connection could drag him down in some way. Which was bullshite, if he'd ever heard it. Not to mention, he'd welcome any criticism or judgment with open arms if it meant having Eve.

Six months.

"Fine," he forced out. "Six months."

Eve's eyes widened slightly, as if surprised not to receive an argument. "Six months in secret."

"Semisecret," he qualified. "We'll need a witness when we marry."

"Right." She chewed her lip. "Not Elton."

"Yes, Elton." Madden smiled, aching over being in this reality where he casually discussed marrying Eve Keller. "He'll keep quiet."

Her skepticism was plain. "Fine, but I get to tell one person as well."

"Skylar?"

Eve hesitated.

"Eve." Madden shook his head. "She's over me, love. Trust me."

"Yes. I . . . know. It's just hard to imagine anyone getting over you." In the wake of that unexpected statement, he almost suggested they go track down an officiant right that very second. Could she tell she'd left him winded? "Can I have two people?" she asked.

Madden inclined his head. She could tell a million. The more, the better.

"Thanks. I'll tell Skylar. Soon. I just want to do it in person. For now, I'll tell Veda, since she already knows you proposed." Eve put her hand out for a shake, even though there were mere inches between them, so her hand could barely fit. "I guess we have a deal."

"Not so fast, love. What about the rest of it?"

She frowned in confusion. "The rest of it?"

"Aye." He brought his mouth down to hers, grazing their lips together only slightly, but that featherlight touch and her subsequent shaky inhale was enough to grip his balls with need. "Go on. Pretend like you forgot."

One shaky breath. Two. "Oh, you're talking about the . . . benefits thing?"

"In fact, I am. Though I'm not fond of the word *benefits*."

"What would you call it?"

He hadn't thought of a proper description, but only one word occurred to Madden and he said it against her temple. "Fulfillment."

A tremor passed through her. "Friends with fulfillment."

"Friends," he scoffed gently into her hair. "Right. Married for six months. In secret. And when you need fulfillment, you get it from me. Do you accept those terms?"

"You're so confident you can fulfill me?"

Not the slightest hesitation. "Aye, love. Watch me."

CHAPTER TWELVE

A firm press of heat bore down on Eve's tummy, making everything southward turn to jelly. Only two men had ever aroused her like this. Madden. And the Madden in her imagination. The one she'd been sleeping with for years. But this marriage could only be temporary, so her exclusive attraction to Madden wasn't a good thing. "I don't know, Mad. Hooking up when we're planning a divorce in six months could get messy."

"I've wanted you in bed for years and you wanted me too. Isn't that right?"

Still getting used to voicing her feelings for him out loud, it took her a moment to hum an affirmation.

That hum was enough to make his chest rise and dip dramatically. "And we haven't given in, because your best friend fancied herself in love with me."

"Uh-huh."

"That didn't stop the wanting, though, Eve. Didn't stop me dreaming about what you'd feel like underneath me. For years. We're already messy," he breathed against her mouth. "What's a little more?"

"You have a point," she managed, her voice threadbare.

Eve's hands rose of their own accord, slowly, framing the sides of his face. His breath held while she thumbed the bristle of his jaw, the sculpted curve of his bottom lip. It was so, so silent and still in the house, impossibly quiet, except for the accelerated rapping of their hearts. He was letting her take the lead, letting her decide when the kiss finally happened, after a millennium of wondering what it would be like, but his tether wasn't a long one, made obvious by the hands that fisted in the hips of her jeans, sliding her to the end of the couch arm, into the safe haven of his well-muscled body, so that she had to tilt her head back to look at him. To maintain the touch of their lips.

"Put me out of my misery, Eve." His voice shook.

"I'm getting there," she whispered, pitching her head slowly to the right, memorizing the spellbound look in his eyes before closing her own, focusing on touch. On the warm restraint of his breath bathing her mouth. The way his hair wrapped itself around her fingers as if welcoming her home. The power of him, waiting there, waiting to be tapped.

And finally, she did.

She teased open his lips with her own, stroking her tongue inside. Just once.

Madden released a hoarse sound, but he waited for the next move, his grip tight, so tight, on the denim covering her hips. She licked into him again, two more times, nearly moaning over the low, hot pulse between her thighs, that drugging tug of muscle cutting her patience in half like a machete.

"Madden," she managed, before going deep with the next play of her tongue, their breaths escaping like the hiss of a punctured tire, her fingers twisting in his hair to pull him down—and he went, a man at the end of his rope, yanking her to the very, very end of the couch arm, lurching closer to loom above Eve while their mouths feasted, his thighs bracketing her knees, his stance making her feel dainty and trapped in the most delicious way.

And speaking of delicious, Madden was the definition of that word. He kissed like he was determined to feed her, like he could abolish her hunger with slick, carnal rides of his mouth over hers, the heat of his thick body reaching through her clothes, sensitizing, eliciting a whimper from her mouth. Her first ever whimper?

"Eve." He tilted her head back and raked his open mouth up her jaw. "Christ. Worth the wait doesn't even begin to cover it."

They raged back into the kiss, but the storm was building to a category five now. Sirens were going off in the back of Eve's mind, his forearm gathering her hips closer to his own, angling them while he claimed ownership of her mouth from above with hungry pants, and lord, oh lord, her thighs were so close to dropping open and inviting him to rub himself in the place where she got wetter by the second.

This was their first kiss, though.

Were they moving too fast or was this combustion inevitable?

"Madden," she said, struggling to breathe.

"What do you need, Eve?"

"I don't know."

"Don't you?" He nipped at her mouth and she could feel the knowledge in his touch. Could see the memory of her dancing topless right there in his eyes. "Say the word and I'll take you to the backyard. I'll strip you naked and get started fucking the last four years out of my system. There's no chance anyone will see us." He fisted her hair, drawing it to one side so he could suck and bite the skin of her neck. "But someone might hear you begging me for more, though. Someone will know my gorgeous girl took her panties off to allow me a ride."

That . . . taunt? Promise? Dip into her psyche? It made splotches of light bloom on the insides of her eyelids, the walls of her sex squeezing and releasing rhythmically, searching for him, but her hands moved first, ripping his T-shirt upward, off and over his head, revealing that sturdy chest with the cross tattoo in the center of his pecs. A smattering of hair. The ripest muscles she'd ever laid eyes on in real life.

A five-inch-long scar running down the left side of his abdomen.

Her own stomach flipped over in response.

"You want the possibility of being seen, being caught, watched, I'll give you that. You trust me to do that?"

Trust didn't come easy for Eve, if at all, but she trusted Madden with most things. With this. Exploring the part of her she'd denied satisfaction for a long time. And she didn't really have a choice but to nod, tilt her head back, and let him suck marks onto her neck and throat, because all her fantasies had been with him.

"Out back, then?" he growled.

"I think so, yes."

"You think so." His jaw flexed. "If this is moving too fast, love . . ."

She didn't have a single ounce of doubt that he could handle the delay of gratification like a man. "It's moving very fast."

"God, I know. Okay." Madden pulled back, panting, his strong hands cradling her head. In her periphery, Eve could see the extended zipper of his jeans, the outrageous curve of his length straining inside the denim. How he could be so worked up and yet speak to her so gently was this man in a nutshell. A quiet storm. "Let's just take a deep breath here." His chest puffed up and down. "We're not about to rush this."

What followed was a moment very different from the urgency and madness of the kiss. A quiet calming of pulses and haywire breaths. A seeking of comfort. Madden kissed a path across Eve's hairline, down her cheek, before sipping at her mouth.

"I can give you what you want. I wanted to prove that." His thumb traced her jawline. "Have I?"

Her head nodded by itself. "Yes."

A low sound of pride in his chest. "We're settled, then?"

Dang, her lips were swollen. "Friends with fulfillment."

"Uh-huh." He dropped his forehead against hers, his energy growing a little frustrated. Or anxious, maybe. "I have to be back in New York tomorrow morning." His eyes burned with promise. "But I'll be back in three days to marry you."

Holy shit, this was happening. Eve looked at him, then asked, "Why does that irritate you?"

Blue eyes searched hers. He replied, "It's only the three days that irritates me. I'm afraid you'll change your mind."

"I don't plan on it."

The tick in his jaw said he wasn't reassured in the slightest. And wow, the impulse to be late opening the club, to stay and do whatever she could to ease his mind, startled Eve. She couldn't fall into the trap of making this relationship too . . . romantic. Too sweet.

That wasn't her.

And that kind of starry-eyed romance wasn't in the cards for them.

"Guess you'll just have to wonder," she murmured with a smile she hoped was mysterious, sliding out from beneath his shirtless body. "See you soon, Madden."

As soon as her feet touched the ground and she stood, her liquefied knees gave out.

Madden caught her before she could drop like a stone, his

chuckle ruffling the hair at the crown of her head. "Consider me reassured."

Ducking her head so he wouldn't see her blush, she speed walked for the front door. "My feet were asleep."

"Whatever you say, love."

Eve was halfway to the club before she realized she was smiling.

CHAPTER THIRTEEN

Seven Years Earlier

Something wasn't right.

Eve, now a sophomore, watched Madden from across the swimming pool, her narrowed gaze hidden behind a pair of black, cat-eyed sunglasses. Elton was telling Madden about his plans to ask out one of their mutual classmates, while absently tossing the ball into Madden's waiting glove. Elton didn't seem to notice Madden's grimace every time he trapped the baseball in his leather mitt or the strain around his mouth when throwing it back.

Eve noticed.

She noticed everything about Madden.

How could she do anything but notice him when he shadowed her at school, a gorgeous savior trying not to be noticed unless he was needed? His unique way of intervening whenever someone harassed Eve both relieved her and perturbed her. Could she handle these goons on her own? Yes! Obviously. But, well . . . sometimes, in a period of weariness, she could breathe easier knowing she wasn't alone. That he'd come, without fail, and be the voice she couldn't find.

Other times, she resented Madden intervening because it made her feel helpless.

Dependent on his protective nature.

But . . . he seemed to understand that. And he wasn't offended by her occasional lack of grace and gratitude. *God*, that was nice. To have someone stare into the face of her complicated attitude without flinching.

When Eve really sat down and dissected what Madden meant to her . . . she got overwhelmed. And so, she tried extrahard not to. Especially because of Skylar and her unabashed adoration of the man who'd become her stepbrother's best friend.

But if Eve had to whisper the truth to the universe, she'd say Madden was the boy she pictured in her mind's eye when she imagined her first kiss. Her first time having sex, too, his eyes steady on hers while he moved above her in a slow rhythm, their fingers twined together on either side of her head. On those days when he walked her to Cat Fight to make sure she arrived safely, gruffly reminding her to lock the office door in her wake, she stared at that door and wondered if he was staring back from the other side. Hoping and dreading that he might be, because what could she do about it?

Madden was the closest she'd ever come to trusting another human being. Maybe . . . maybe she even did. Trust this equally fierce and gentle man completely. With her very life.

Wasn't that terrifying?

Bottom line, she noticed everything about Madden.

And he'd lost weight.

His usual robust frame had weakened in front of her very eyes over the last month. He'd declined to eat when the Pages invited him to stay for dinner. One lap in the pool earlier that afternoon had left him short of breath. Pale. Did no one else notice? Even his performance behind home plate hadn't been as stellar, his throws seeming . . . labored.

"Just going to use the bathroom," he said to Elton now, interrupting his friend midsentence. "Tell me the rest when I come back."

Elton threw up his hands. "How can you stand the suspense?"

When normally Madden would have come back with a quip, his jaw only clenched. He patted Elton on the shoulder and walked toward the house, his gait abnormally stilted.

Eve chewed the inside of her cheek for a moment, then made her decision. She reached over and popped out one of Skylar's AirPods. "Going to run inside and grab a water. Do you want anything?"

"Orange juice, please," responded Eve's best friend, before she raised her voice and shouted across the pool, "If Elton didn't drink it all!"

Elton shot her a middle finger.

Skylar returned with two.

Just your typical afternoon with the Page siblings.

Eve pushed her sunglasses onto her head and crossed the yard, opening the sliding glass door to let herself into the silent house. Doug and Vivica Page were out training for a half-marathon, leaving her alone in the house with Madden. A situation she craved *and* avoided at the same time. But intuition tugged at Eve's consciousness, begging her not to avoid him today.

Something is wrong.

Eve turned down the hallway leading to the bathroom, stopping short, her ears ringing at the sight of Madden hunched over, his forearm braced on the wall to keep him standing.

"Mad," she said, unable to keep her voice free of alarm.

He straightened, but didn't turn around. A large, but withering silhouette in the late-afternoon dusk. Her heart started to canter.

"What's wrong?"

"Nothing, love."

"I know something is wrong. You can tell me."

"How can I?" His hand came off the wall to press against his lower back. "If I don't know what it is."

With a swallow, Eve moved in his direction . . . and for the first time, she understood his protectiveness toward her. How quickly it could manifest. Because the need to protect him flooded her in a deluge, so swift her legs became unsteady beneath the weight.

She stopped beside Madden, examining his profile. "You haven't been yourself."

He closed his eyes. "I'm sorry."

"You . . . you don't have to apologize," she choked out on a humorous laugh. "Let's just figure out what's wrong. What are your symptoms?"

"Besides feeling like absolute shite?"

"Be more specific than shite."

A beat passed. "They're going to be wondering why you're in here."

Normally, Eve would care about that. If Skylar clocked her spending too much time with Madden and how that would make her best friend feel. That consideration rode on her back like a clinging monkey. But not right now. Everything got shuffled to the wayside when his labored breathing started. They were only standing still.

"Tell me, Mad."

He closed his eyes. "Pain. A lot of pain in my back and sides. These massive headaches. Sometimes I can't catch my breath. Like now."

Eve had never felt more fifteen in her life.

More wistful for adulthood. Knowledge.

This is serious, whispered a voice in the back of her head. *This is bad.*

"We have to go to a doctor."

Madden had already begun shaking his head. "No. I'm just training too hard."

"That's not what it is," Eve said, adamantly.

He strove for a jovial tone and didn't pull it off. "Are you worried I'm not going to be able to protect you as well?"

"No, I'd never worry about that."

"I do." His gaze slowly found hers. "I worry if I go to the doctor and find out something is wrong, I won't be there to look after you, love."

That kicked the breath clean out of her lungs. "Is that why you haven't gone?"

He said nothing, confirming her suspicion.

Denial collided with urgency so quickly, she got dizzy. Didn't know which to deal with first. "We have to go. We have to tell someone."

"No."

Eve played the only card she could think of. The one that was right there, staring her in the face. Whatever it took to get him help *now*. Immediately. "If you get worse or something happens to you, who will protect me then? Who will protect me without making me feel weak and pathetic, Madden, because you're the only one who can pull it off . . ."

He was pulling her into a tight hug, then cutting her off. Kissing the crown of her head. And she almost wheezed over the contact, the warmth and safety of Madden Donahue. A good man, already at seventeen. An honest man.

But who was protecting *him*?

"Everything okay?" Skylar called from the kitchen, followed

by the sound of the refrigerator opening. Though they were still out of sight, Madden reluctantly dropped his embrace and stepped back, leaning against the wall once more, obviously out of necessity. "Oh, there's orange juice!"

Eve fought for composure, reached down deep for bravery, and called, "Skylar, can you go get Elton, please? Tell him to come here."

A brief pause. "Is everything okay?"

Madden didn't even try to prevent her from revealing his struggle at that point. That's how she knew they'd reached a critical stage. Someone needed to act.

"Madden needs help," Eve called back, barely keeping the hitch out of her voice.

A single beat passed, then Skylar's footsteps echoed on her way into the backyard, two sets approaching a moment later.

The four of them drove to the hospital in Elton's truck, Madden beside Eve in the rear cab, their hands clasped tightly together out of sight. A gesture of comfort. Friendship. Solidarity.

If them holding hands was anything more, now was not the time to examine it.

But as they pulled up to the emergency room and Eve gave his hand a final squeeze, before exiting the truck and running ahead to explain the situation to reception, she vowed there *would* be time. If something was seriously wrong with Madden, she'd do whatever it took to be the reliable safety net he'd always been for her, without her having to ask.

No matter what it took.

CHAPTER FOURTEEN

Present Day

Madden watched the sun disappear behind the wall of the stadium, but it blinked back into his eyes as soon as he stood to throw the latest strike back to the pitcher. The game had gone to extra innings and his thighs were beginning to ache from being in the crouched position so long, but he performed the necessary mental math, nonetheless, ordering himself to stay sharp.

The next batter strutted up to the plate while taking practice swings, "Fein" by Travis Scott blasting from all ends of the stadium. So far this season, at least one player on every team had this as their walk-up music, but Madden could admit, it was effective. The crowd was on their feet behind him. Madden blocked out the stomps and raised voices, however, and recalled the batter's style, along with the pitches that were landing tonight.

Answer: not many.

The pitcher Ruiz's moment in the spotlight was fading, his career on a downswing.

Meanwhile, the bloke at the plate was in the midst of the best season of his life. Madden had a feeling Ruiz wanted to walk the batter and hope for a double play on the next at bat. But considering the batter hadn't gotten on base once tonight, Madden figured he'd be impatient. He'd swing at the first decent pitch, they'd have their final out and take the win.

Madden signaled for a breaking ball.

The pitcher spat, shook his head.

After a hesitation, Madden dropped the sign for a slider.

Another denial.

Madden punched his glove, put it up. Waited.

Throw what you want, then, motherfucker.

As predicted, Ruiz walked the batter. But instead of a double play on the next at bat, the batter clocked one out of the park, scoring two runs and effectively ending the game.

"Son of a bitch," Ruiz bellowed fifteen minutes later as he walked behind Madden into the locker room, throwing his glove against the row of lockers. "How about giving me a decent signal out there?"

Madden searched for some extra patience and couldn't come up with any. He'd played on several baseball teams since coming to the States and he'd never met a bigger group of prima donnas in his life. His pitchers refused to admit even the most obvious of mistakes, searching for any reason to believe they were still the wizards of baseball they'd been called throughout their careers.

That compelling need he'd had more and more lately—to speak up, to stop playing it safe in the background—grew stronger than ever. Maybe the sudden burst of self-assurance came from Eve agreeing to be his wife or the fact that his hard work on the field had been rewarded with opportunity.

Whatever the reason, he was tired of being quiet. Tired of making himself inconspicuous so everyone would be comfortable, the way he'd done growing up.

"You might want to check the tape, man," Madden bit off. "It was your decision to walk him."

Ruiz turned around. "What the fuck did you say?"

Madden stared at him without flinching.

"Jesus. Is this guy really the best we could do?"

"Yeah, I am," Madden responded, his delivery low and precise. "And you know why? They busted the salary cap signing a bunch of overpriced fucking crybabies."

He expected the punch.

Honestly, he might have even wanted it.

Only one day of stressing that Eve would back out of the wedding already had him sleep deprived and pacing the edge of an invisible cliff. Madden knew she needed to make doctors' appointments, but she continued to hold off on connecting their names, which had him anxious. Missing her too. God, the missing of her was like a hot rash on his skin.

As the fist connected with the right side of his face, Madden wanted to regret inciting the man. After all, he needed this position with the Yankees to support Eve and the kids. But the pain felt so familiar, it took him right out of his stress. He'd been hit many times before and survived. It wasn't a healthy thing that the reminder of what he'd survived could calm his jumpiness, but there it was. The truth.

Maybe I didn't simply survive. Maybe I earned the right to be here.

Maybe I don't have to feel like a fraud hiding behind a mask anymore.

Madden thought of his aunt's words: *You are welcome here, in this house of accused black sheep, but don't make the same mistake I made. Allowing yourself to be run off when you've done nothing wrong but exist.*

Madden's eyes flew open at that, his jaw and cheekbone stinging from the punch.

Several players had inserted themselves between Madden and Ruiz, corralling the pitcher on the other side of the locker room.

No one was bothering to hold Madden back because he hadn't budged an inch under the blow.

"Damn, the rookie can take a punch. You have to give him that."

"Don't have to call us out like that, man," someone said in his ear. Chandler. The shortstop. "I'm only a crybaby on days that end in Y."

Madden made eye contact with every player, in turn. "I said what I said."

Chandler backed off, hands up in surrender. "Respect."

MADDEN COULDN'T SHOWER, change, and get out of there fast enough. On one hand, he wanted to rewind the last fifteen minutes and stay silent. Making waves in the locker room could only jeopardize the stability he was hoping to provide Eve, and god, he couldn't have that. But the part of Madden that had been quiet and agreeable for so long, saddled with the guilt he'd been carrying since birth, felt like he'd taken a deep breath of fresh air by being heard. Using his voice and feeling as if it was relevant. Worth hearing.

Desperate for a distraction, Madden slid his phone out of the side pocket of his equipment bag where it sat in the passenger seat of his truck. And he called Elton.

"Hey," his best friend answered. "Fucking Ruiz. You made the right call. You can lead a horse to water, but you can't make him drink. Is that how that saying goes?"

"Something like that." Madden eyed himself in the rearview. "Had a little dustup with him in the locker room. Should be sporting a shiner by tomorrow morning."

"No shit? He hit you?"

"He's better at pitching," Madden said dryly, his fingers tapping on the steering wheel, a prickle of nerves tightening his scalp. "Do you think Eve will mind that I've got a black eye on our wedding day?"

"Nah, I doubt it." A long pause, followed by something being knocked over in the background. "Wait, what? Did you say *wedding day*?"

"I did." Pride stuck in Madden's throat so firmly, he had to wait for the obstruction to clear. "In two days' time. As soon as I can drive back to Rhode Island."

Elton laughed incredulously. "Two *days*? I'm so lost." A silent sputter ensued. "Have you been seeing her behind everyone's back? You have to be leaving out ninety percent of the story."

"All you need to know is she's marrying me." Madden's fingers went still on the steering wheel. "But we're not telling people, so it needs to stay between us."

"What? I already group texted everyone in my contacts."

Madden's spine snapped straight. "You didn't."

"Nah, I'm just messing with you."

He slumped back into the driver's seat, left hand to his pumping chest.

Elton was silent a moment. "Anyone with two eyes could see there was something between you and Eve for the longest time. I figured you two decided it wasn't worth the risk of losing the friendship. What changed?"

Madden considered telling Elton that Eve had avoided anything romantic with him for so long because Skylar had been nursing a crush, but he liked Skylar too much to give her brother that kind of ammunition to use against her. And he would.

Besides, Eve's reluctance to give him a real, authentic chance wasn't solely about Skylar anymore. Eve had been ostracized and mocked in Cumberland for so long, she now believed herself a liability. Madden swallowed the rising tide of anger on Eve's behalf. Anger at himself for not being capable of shielding her from the hatred.

"I'm marrying her for financial security. She's got the kids now." Jesus, saying the rest made him vulnerable, a place he did not like to be, but he needed to offload to someone. "But I wouldn't mind it being real."

"Wouldn't mind it?"

"Prefer."

"Prefer?"

"I'd sell my soul for her. Are you happy now?"

"When am I ever happy, my dude?" Elton coughed. "What about her? Is she strictly business about this?"

"Yes," Madden said. His physical relationship with Eve was nobody's business but theirs. He didn't even want another man thinking of Eve in terms of who she was sleeping with and when. Not even Elton, who treated Eve like a second sister. That was Madden's business and his business alone. "There's no way you can make it to Rhode Island for the ceremony, right? Are you on the road?"

"We're home for the next three games." Elton paused while he presumably checked the schedule on his phone. "Can you wait a week?"

Hell no. Three days was a stretch. "Absolutely not."

"Okay, turbo. Let me talk to the coach about missing practice. It's not every day my best friend gets hitched in a top-secret ceremony." He made a disappointed sound. "There isn't even time to throw you a bachelor party. What is the point of having a best friend?"

"I wouldn't have allowed you to throw me one, anyway."

"Of course not." Elton sighed, but there was a smile in the sound. "I'll text you once I've talked to Coach."

"Grand. And Elton, remember, we're not telling anyone about this."

"How am I going to explain to my parents why I'm in town?"

"Tell them you're homesick."

"Real talk, I wouldn't be lying. My balls sweat enough in Florida to fill a kiddie pool." He carried on, as if that imagery didn't have Madden on the verge of dry heaving. "Eve said you could tell me about the marriage?"

"Yes. She's telling one person too. That was the deal."

"Is she telling Skylar?"

"Not yet," he hedged, not sure how to tell Elton that his stepsister had been crushing on Madden for the better part of a decade. "I think Eve would rather wait and tell Skylar in person. She's telling Veda, this new friend slash babysitter of hers. I think she's coming to the wedding."

"Veda. Is she hot?"

"She's too young for you."

"Does she have a sister?"

"Doesn't matter. You're coming here to be my witness, not get laid."

"Fine. Jesus. If it happens, though . . . it happens."

"Okay, I have to go. Maybe see you soon. Not sure I want to anymore."

They shared a laugh and hung up, Madden checking his phone calendar for the date, as if it had changed since the last time he looked.

Two more days, Eve.

CHAPTER FIFTEEN

Eve stared at the marriage license where it sat on the dashboard of her car, reflecting up into the windshield. She was getting married today and it didn't feel real. For one, the courthouse was walking distance from a Krispy Kreme and that didn't feel very wedding-like at all. Although maybe it made total sense to get married beside the donut joint, since this union would be the fast food of marriages. Quick and functional.

A practical option.

Why were her palms sweating, then?

She cranked the air-conditioning, pinching the loose neckline of her white jumpsuit and flapped the material to create a breeze. So many things about this wedding didn't feel right. Skylar should be there, but Eve couldn't bring herself to come clean to her best friend just yet. How would that conversation play out?

I'm marrying Madden for the kids. For the insurance.

Skylar was a borderline genius. She'd see right through Eve.

Old habits die hard and Eve had been pretending not to be infatuated with Madden for so long, the truth was buried deep in her belly beneath a ten-ton boulder. Either Skylar would pick up on the undercurrent of Eve's feelings for Madden and look back at the last eight years through a lens of dishonesty.

Or, worse, Skylar might feel guilty for standing in the way.

Eve didn't like those options.

I'll tell her. Soon.

She pulled down the overhead mirror and checked her lipstick. She'd gone with vivid plum for the occasion, her hair in a loose braid. God bless Veda for showing up at the apartment this morning and doing a cartoonish double take, because it gave Eve some extra confidence. They'd left the apartment together with the kids and dropped them off at school, before driving fifteen miles to a courthouse with enough distance from Cumberland to keep tongues from wagging.

As of now, Veda was inside the Krispy Kreme "getting dinner," because once again, the erstwhile musician had pulled an all-nighter.

Judging she had approximately three minutes until Veda returned to the car, Eve plucked her phone out of the cupholder, fully intending to google a place to have lunch after the wedding, but she found herself dialing her sister instead. Ruth wouldn't pick up. Eve didn't expect her to, because they didn't allow unlimited phone calls in the rehab facility, and anyway, Ruth needed this time to focus on herself.

Still, there was something about her imminent nuptials that inspired a need to reach for family. She and Ruth had never been confidantes. Never shared giggling secrets past their bedtime or bonded over the boredom of too-long family road trips. They'd more or less kept to their own devices growing up, communicating wordlessly when necessary if their father was having a bad day, after their mom had finally left after years of threatening to go, and he needed space. Or if one of them was getting the cold shoulder in town, they might share a knowing eye roll. They were simply different people with opposite ways of channeling sadness, frustration.

But apparently a shared past—and now the twins—had bonded them enough to make Eve want to hear Ruth's voice right about now.

Three rings. Four.

A generic manufacturer greeting, followed by a beep sounding in her ear, prompting her to leave a message.

"Hey." Eve stopped to smooth the bumps out of her tone. "Hey, it's me. I just thought I'd call and tell you . . . I'm getting married. I'm not supposed to tell you that. I'm only supposed to tell two people, and you're not one of them. But yeah. Married. Me. And, um . . ." An unexpected gust of pressure blew the words out of her. Why? Because she was about to embark on something scary and felt the need to confess and enter the union with a clear conscience? "It's Madden Donahue that I'm marrying. I'm sure you remember him. I fought with Dad for three days straight until he signed the consent form to determine if I was a match when Madden was diagnosed with kidney disease. Remember?" she said, semi-jokingly. Finding out she was a match was the foremost memorable moment of her young life. "Hard to forget all that paperwork, followed by a week in the hospital. Although you didn't mind it so much because you got custody of all my low-rise pants afterward." The backs of Eve's eyes prickled and stung just saying those words out loud. Even if no one was listening. This message would probably get ignored. But the admission lifted a grand piano off her chest. "I've loved him for a long time, which is why I can't . . . like, I can't keep him. Or love him publicly. If anyone understands, it's you. We both grew up in this town. And the world is just a bigger version of Cumberland, isn't it? Can't escape who we are. I don't want to. But I won't make him defend me all the time. Or, god, what if he started to regret me—" Eve stopped and cleared her throat.

"Anyway, the marriage is temporary, but six months with him is better than nothing, you know? I can live on memories. I can do hard things."

Eve hung up, right as Veda exited the Krispy Kreme in a red polka-dot dress, off the shoulder—last night's clothes, apparently—double-fisting glazed donuts. The musician circled around the back of Eve's car to stand outside the driver's-side window.

"You sure you don't want one?" Veda called through the glass. "They're fresh."

"I'm good," Eve responded, giving her a thumbs-up.

That thumbs-up remained suspended in the air when Madden's truck pulled into the parking lot, two spots away from them. The ignition cut out, but he made no move to exit the vehicle, he and Eve staring at each other through their respective windows, her stomach flipping like an Olympic gymnast doing a floor exercise.

Finally, he got out of the truck and Eve couldn't help it. She sighed out loud. Thank god she was alone inside the car, because multiple cool points would have been deducted for the wistful whoosh of appreciation over Madden in a suit. Black, of course. Crisp white shirt underneath. A navy-blue tie to match his eyes. Some extra care had been taken with his hair, too, the lot of it tousled back into a windswept look.

Somehow, the black eye only heightened the potency of the man.

"That's the guy?" Veda shouted through the window. "Are you kidding me?"

Eve smacked the glass. "Indoor voice, babe."

"Sorry," Veda replied, taking a bite of one of her donuts. "But like . . . *yeesh.*"

Get out of the car. Eve's legs were slow to cooperate, but she finally got out, brushing the wrinkles out of her jumpsuit, just in time for Madden to reach them. And he wasn't alone. Elton had also arrived and swaggered behind Madden in a pin-striped suit and a derby cap.

"Oh good, the Peaky Blinders are here," Veda drawled, observing Elton's approach.

Skylar's brother drew up short. "Wow. This must be Veda." He doffed the cap and bowed with a smirk. "This acquaintance is off to a fine start."

"Sorry, that just popped right out of my mouth." She held up the shiny confections. "I blame the donuts."

Elton raised an eyebrow at the pastry in her hand. "Are you going to finish that?"

"Yes." Veda laughed, as if the question were ridiculous. "Get your own."

"Where did you find this girl?" Elton asked Eve, while pointing his hat at Veda. "A 1940s pinup girl convention?"

"Fifties." Veda sucked the glaze off one of her fingers. "Nineteen fifties."

"Oh, okay. Let me file that under information I don't need." Elton shook his head at the younger woman, a deep groove between his brows, before visibly wrestling his attention away. "Hey, Eve," he said warmly, coming forward to kiss her on the cheek. "I just want to say that I called this pairing. You and Madden might have had everyone else fooled, but not me."

"Okay, Elt," Eve said dryly, no longer able to ignore the burn of Madden's gaze on the side of her face, the slope of her neck. Everywhere. She took a deep breath and looked up into the most dramatic pair of eyes on the planet. "Hello, future husband."

A corner of his mouth jumped, but when he spoke, his expression was sober. Serious. "Hello, future wife."

One minute in his presence and Eve's stomach muscles were already tighter than a drum. "You look—"

"You look—" he said at the same time.

Eve laughed quietly, watching the tips of his ears turn red.

"Dare I ask how you came by that black eye?"

"I told you waiting three days to marry you wasn't going to be easy on me, love."

While Eve did everything in her power to recover from that statement, Madden ticked his gaze between Elton and Veda. "Would you please give us a moment alone before we go in?"

"I don't know," Elton hedged. "What if she drags me back to her time machine?"

"Me?" Veda replied. "You look like you just got back from defending your turf in Birmingham."

Elton laughed. "Fine. That was pretty funny."

If Eve had blinked, she would have missed the pleasure that crossed Veda's face. Pleasure she quickly hid under casual boredom as she extended a half-eaten donut. "You want the rest?"

"Do I?" Elton said, in a flawless Cockney accent, rubbing his hands together.

Veda snort-laughed, handing over the donut, and off they went, side by side into the courthouse, trading names of their favorite bakeries in and around Cumberland.

"I can't tell if they're going to be enemies or friends," Eve mused out loud.

"I guess we'll find out."

I CAN'T BELIEVE I'm about to marry this woman.

Words wouldn't do Eve justice. She looked beautiful in the

white jumpsuit, the neckline low and dipping between her breasts, her hair soft and wavy, pulled back from her face. Resplendent. That's the only description Madden's brain supplied.

Goddamn, what he wouldn't give for a wedding night.

He'd have that lipstick smeared all over her chin and cheeks before the door closed behind them. "I have to be back in New York by tonight," Madden said, not bothering to hide the regret in his tone. "I wish I didn't, but I need to be on a flight to Milwaukee in the morning."

"That's okay. Really."

"Is that the marriage license?" he asked, nodding at the paper in her hands.

"Oh." She seemed to have forgotten she was holding it. "Yes."

"Can I see it?"

Eve pressed her lips together and handed it to him, both of them standing in the midmorning hum of traffic as he read their names on the page together. The document giving him permission to become Eve's husband. She couldn't know the impact it was having on him, the knowledge that she'd taken the time to apply for the document, carried it with her. All to marry him. Could he tell her without sounding ridiculous?

"Thank you," he said, finally. "For . . . taking care of that."

"You're the one doing me a favor, Mad. You realize that, right?"

She didn't get it. He'd make sure she did. In time.

"I brought you something," he said.

A long pause ensued. "You did? Like, a gift?"

"Yes."

Her chest dipped. "But I didn't get you anything. I didn't know we were doing that."

"Stop. I don't need a thing." He folded the marriage license carefully, tucking it into the inner pocket of his suit jacket. Then he reached down and took her by the wrist. "Come on. It's in my truck."

Eve allowed him to pull her along, the little wisps of hair around her face fluttering in the spring breeze. "Can't you wait until I have something to give you too?"

"No."

She gaped. "Why not?"

Madden didn't know how to explain, so he didn't. Instead, he opened the second cab of his truck and took out the gold eight-by-ten frame he'd propped up in the footwell. He started to explain, but he didn't have the words untangled yet, so he simply handed her the framed sketch and watched.

Watching Eve. His favorite pastime.

"It's me."

He nodded.

"I've seen this before . . ." She traced a fingertip over the image, which depicted Eve sitting on a tree swing in a party dress, smiling. Not just any smile, though; it was somehow mischievous and loving, all at once. It was, in his opinion, the perfect smile. "I've seen this picture in one of Skylar's photo albums before, but I never knew where it came from." She looked up at Madden. "You took this picture?"

"Aye." The back of his neck felt warmer than usual. "I found someone online who takes a photograph and turns it into a sketch. It was going to be a Christmas gift last year, but ah . . . I don't know, the timing didn't work out." She'd been avoiding him, as usual, but he wasn't unwise enough to point that out on their wedding day. "But after what you said about people and their preconceived notions about you, I got to thinking maybe

I'd give it to you now. That's how I see you. A little guarded, a lot full of life. Protective of the people you're looking at, but not willing to let them know too often, because the secret would get out, wouldn't it? That you're tough as fuck, but you're sweet and soft too. That's how they would see you if they were smart enough to look. That's all."

"That's all," she echoed, dully, blinking up at him with an emotion he couldn't name. Or maybe couldn't let himself hope for. "Madden, I-I don't know what to say."

"You don't have to say anything, love." He huffed a low laugh. "I take that back. You could tell me you like it."

Eve looked up at him for so long, he started to wonder if he'd asked for too much. "If my apartment was on fire, it's the first thing I would grab on the way out." She swallowed twice, a light sheen in her eyes. "Besides the kids. I guess," she said on a wobbly laugh.

Pride and relief rocked Madden back on his heels. "Right, then." On second thought, "If we could avoid any mention of your apartment catching fire from now on, I would appreciate it, Eve."

More blinking. "I'll just go put this in my car."

"Grand."

A moment later, Madden watched Eve place the framed sketch in her trunk and when she straightened again, he was standing in such a position that her back met his chest and she gasped, the sound scraping right down his belly. The braid that ran all the way to the small of her back was too much of a temptation not to wrap it around his fist and tug until her face was tilted toward the sky. "It might not be tonight, Eve," he said, biting her neck, firm but gentle. "But there will be a proper wedding night."

She hummed, gave a jerky nod. "Yup. This is messy, all right."

Madden pressed a smile into her temple, slowly releasing her braid and taking her hand, twining their fingers together. "Shall we go make it worse?"

Or better, depending on who you asked.

"After you," Eve breathed, accepting his hand and letting him walk her toward the courthouse.

CHAPTER SIXTEEN

Seven Years Earlier

Autosomal dominant polycystic kidney disease.

That's what they'd diagnosed Madden with. Blindsided, he'd sat and listened to the doctor explain the rare, genetic condition that had caused a healthy seventeen-year-old's kidney to enlarge and stop filtering blood properly. And perhaps with the pessimism that came with being Irish, he'd fully expected to be dead by now. But only two days before he was set to begin dialysis, the doctors had informed him of the donor. Someone planned to carve an organ out of their own body to be transplanted inside his. It didn't make sense.

Why would someone do that for him?

Why didn't they want to be named?

Madden came very close to rejecting the offer. The doctors, nurses, even his friends had questioned his sanity. They'd assured him the opportunity might not come around again, and Jesus, he'd thought, *Who is going to look after Eve?*

Everyone else would be fine without him. Skylar and Elton had their lovely, if freakishly fit parents. His aunt enjoyed her solitude and had only offered to let him stay because he didn't disturb her peace or expect her to get involved with his daily life. Phone calls with his siblings and mother had grown more infrequent lately, their lives getting busier and, he suspected, speaking with him only dredged up the darker times they wanted to forget. Perhaps Madden's father had even instructed them to keep communication minimal.

But Eve. Who was watching out for her while he was laid up in bed? Her father wasn't a bad sort, but they weren't close. Same with her sister.

"Where is she?" Madden asked for what seemed like the four-thousandth time. "Where is Eve?"

It had been four days since the surgery and he loathed the weakness of his limbs, his bones. The lethargy that was slow to dissipate, though it would. They'd assured him it would. But Eve hadn't been to see him once.

Skylar and Elton, who stood at the end of his hospital bed, exchanged a shrug, Elton looking unconcerned. Skylar, however, had a furrow between her brows, as if she didn't understand Eve's absence either. "She hasn't been in school. When I texted her, she said she's just been sick. It must be a pretty bad flu." Skylar seemed to force a smile. "She asked how you're doing, though. I told her you came through with flying colors."

"Let's focus on the important stuff," Elton said. "The doctor says five more weeks until you can start throwing a ball again."

"Gently," Skylar stressed.

Elton waved that off. "Don't worry, though. You'll be back in peak condition for the summer league. I hear the scouts show up to the games. Try and snatch up some last-minute talent. You've still got a shot."

"Grand," Madden muttered. He wanted to press the issue about Eve. Someone needed to go check on her. A week without school? Was she afraid to go without him there to keep the arseholes at bay? If so, he needed to get the hell out of this bed. Sooner than later. He was useless here.

"Could you hand me a shirt?" Madden asked Elton, pointing to the small hospital room closet. Slowly, he turned and slung his legs over the side of the bed, ignoring the sharp discomfort in his lower right side, the unforgiving weakness of his muscles. *Have to get stronger.* "I'm going for a walk."

The Page siblings froze. "I don't think you're supposed to leave yet, Mad," said Skylar. "Let me get a nurse."

"I'm going."

"Is this a food thing?" Elton asked, eyebrow raised. "I can bring you some takeout."

"It's not a food thing. I just need to get out of here—"

The hospital room door opened on a slow creak.

Eve stood on the other side.

Relief hit Madden like a wooden bat to the chest.

All right. Okay. There she is. She's fine.

In an oversize sweatshirt and a messy ponytail, she looked worse for the wear. Paler than usual. Smaller than usual? Or was he just disoriented?

"Goddamn, Eve," Elton said. "You look like shit."

Skylar smacked him in the shoulder before turning to her friend. "Dude. You're alive." She bounded forward to usher Eve into the room. "You must have been supersick to miss all the action. They sliced Madden open, moved some stuff around. But look at him now, he's good as new."

"So it seems." Eve gave Madden a half smile. "Sorry, I didn't want to get you sick when you'd just been through surgery. I would have visited." He managed a nod to let her know it was okay, which seemed to relax some of the tension in her shoulders. "How do you feel?"

Confused. Frustrated. Grateful.

And since she'd arrived, he no longer wanted to claw off his skin. "Better."

Her throat worked. "Good." In a familiar movement, she lifted onto her toes and dropped back down, a signal she was getting ready to run. "Well—"

"I wouldn't have come to the hospital, if not for you, Eve," Madden said, needing to get the sentiment off his chest, where it had been sitting for weeks. "At least not as early as I did. Thank you for that."

"Yeah," Skylar said, giving her best friend a side hug. "How did you know something was wrong?"

"Too much *Grey's Anatomy*, I guess." Eve laughed. And did her face get whiter, along with the sound? "It's no problem, Mad. Glad everything worked out."

"Who do you think the anonymous donor is?" Elton asked the room at large, his expression cagey. "It's probably our baseball coach. He's *that* desperate to get you back behind the plate."

"I don't know who it is," Madden said. "But I'm going to find out."

Skylar wasn't engaged in the conversation. She was looking at Eve, who, to his horror, swayed on her feet. Thankfully, Skylar propped her up before Madden could dive out of the bed to catch her. "That flu must have kicked your ass," Skylar said, visibly worried. "You're, like, zoned out."

"I know, right?" Eve shook herself. "Probably should have stayed in bed one more day. I'm fine, though."

"Drive her home now, Elton," Madden said, feeling helpless.

Elton smirked. "I'm going to allow you to order me around

this once, since you just had major surgery, but don't make it a habit."

Madden stayed silent, watching the trio leave the room.

Something scratched at his subconscious, a parallel attempting to draw itself, but his brain fog didn't allow the thought to complete. He was out of bed a moment later, preparing to do battle against his mental and physical fatigue, motivated by something he didn't dare name.

# CHAPTER SEVENTEEN

Present Day

"You may now kiss the bride."

The officiant probably had no idea those six words impacted the two people standing in front of him so much. Eve could feel Madden brace, like he'd been hit by a strong wind. Flutters of various sizes and shapes traveled up her midsection and ran in chaotic loops around her throat and wow. Wow. She couldn't help but be glad this wasn't their first kiss, because at least she knew it would scramble her senses.

Forewarned is forearmed, wasn't that the saying?

Besides, Madden wouldn't kiss her in front of everyone the way he kissed her when they were alone in his grandmother's house, right?

Nah.

Eve took a deep breath and faced her husband for the first time.

How did he want to play this?

They probably should have discussed the kiss beforehand. A prolonged peck seemed to be the norm, even for couples who were planning on the long haul. Real couples, unlike them, who were simply uniting for a while.

That's how I see you. A little guarded, a lot full of life. Protective of the people you're looking at, but not willing to let them know too often, because the secret would get out, wouldn't it? That you're tough as fuck, but you're sweet and soft too.

Madden's speech from the parking lot made back-to-back U-turns in her brain. Part of her wanted to chalk his evaluation of her up to luck. Ha ha, lucky guess, champ. But no. No, he'd been studying her even closer than she realized, and the fact that he was still standing there, despite knowing her flaws, made Eve's knees feel loose and shaky, vulnerable in her entirety.

Especially when he reached for her hip and gripped it, like he'd done it a thousand times before, drawing her forward at the same time he invaded her space, his mouth dipping down to find hers and fusing them together, his palm sliding into the valley of her waist. Then around to the small of her back to pull her even closer. Flush with his body. Meaning she had no other option but to tilt her head back so far—and he caught it, the back of her skull. Cradled it in his free hand, fingers splayed. Opening his mouth over hers while his other hand slipped just an inch lower to the beginning swell of her bottom. Stepping closer, even though there was no more space to eliminate.

Mouth slanted over the top of Eve's, Madden kissed her like no one was watching.

She didn't expect the carnality of it or to feel the graze of his tongue against her own, so a rough sound slipped out of her, before she could catch it, her hands flying to the lapels of his jacket, fingers curling into the material to hold herself up.

It might not be tonight, Eve. But there will be a proper wedding night.

This kiss was the physical version of that statement.

And she didn't want to acknowledge this, but the fact that they weren't the only ones in the courthouse while this man tasted her mouth was breathing life into the part of herself she always kept hidden. The part of herself that was restricted to fantasies she only allowed herself to have while lying in bed by herself at night.

Abruptly, Madden stopped kissing her, but he kept her head cradled in his palm while he settled their foreheads together, searching her eyes.

"If this goes on any longer, I'll never be able to leave."

"And you must." She sounded like a buzz saw. "There's no choice . . . right?"

His lips twitched against her mouth. "No, but I'm glad you're wishing otherwise."

Eve tried to sound breezy. "Am I?"

"You having fun with my pecs, love?"

Eve dropped her gaze and blinked, discovering her wayward hands were caressing the thick double hill of Madden's pectoral muscles, massaging them through the front of his dress shirt. "Just helping you warm up for the game," she muttered.

"Game's tomorrow."

"That's why I'm being so thorough." She started to drop her hands, but he caught the right one, bringing her wrist to his mouth for a kiss, right on top of her erratic pulse.

"That does it. I need a drink," Veda announced.

"You guys know we're still here, right?" This, from Elton.

"I'm here too," said the officiant.

Eve took a giant step back, attempting to fix her hair while Madden watched her in all his characteristic stillness. Observing. Memorizing.

"We're supposed to get a certificate, I believe," Eve prompted the officiant, her fingers clumsy in their attempts to fix her braid.

"You should get a *medal*," Elton pointed out. "Who kisses like that at a wedding?"

"We do," Madden answered, calmly.

Veda shook her head. "My situationship never kisses me like that."

"He should." Elton seemed to startle himself with that comment. "I mean . . ."

The younger woman turned slightly to face Elton. "You mean . . . ?"

Elton looked long and hard at Veda before clearing his throat. Hard. "You don't happen to have an older sister, do you?"

Veda's shoulders drooped, but she appeared to force a smile. "I do. You'd love her." She fluttered her lashes a little maniacally. "Everyone does."

Oh boy, Eve thought. *Oh boy.*

"As soon as we sign the certificate, I have to get on the road," Madden said in her ear, distracting her. "I'm going to call the family liaison while I'm driving, so they can get whatever documentation you need for the insurance."

The reminder of the insurance was good. Well-timed.

She'd almost forgotten why they were really there.

"Thanks, Madden," Eve said quietly, a few minutes later, as the foursome piled out of the courthouse, Veda and Elton suspiciously quiet.

"You don't have to thank me," Madden said.

"Sorry, my gratitude stands."

His nod was reluctant, but his eyes held a promise as he climbed into his truck. "I'll be back soon, Eve," he said, before closing the door and starting the engine.

Madden pulled out of his parking spot to reveal Elton on the other side of the truck, getting ready to enter his own vehicle.

"I'll be in town for the night, if you need anything," he said, winking at Eve. "Congratulations."

"Thanks," Eve said dryly. "Come to the club for a drink if you're bored."

"I'll see if I can convince my sister to come too." Veda pushed through a smile.

"Great," Elton said, after a beat. "Will your situationship be there?"

"I don't know! Maybe!"

"Okay!" Elton jerked open the door of his car with a smidgen too much force, smiling back at them with a full mouth of teeth. "See you later, then."

Veda and Eve stood side by side in the parking lot, long after both men's vehicles had disappeared from view.

"It's been a weird morning," Veda remarked, sounding a little tired.

"Yeah."

"We should go to iHop and grub."

"That's the best thing you've ever said to me."

"Oh yeah?" Veda turned her grin on Eve. "I haven't given you your wedding present yet."

"Wedding present?"

Veda rolled her lips inward to wet them. "I know it's premature, because we haven't heard back from the inspector yet, but sue me, I'm an optimist."

"I don't like where this is going."

"Deal with it. I just watched you make out for a full minute with an Irish god and have no current plans to get laid."

Eve's tummy muscles cinched up like a pair of handcuffs. "Fine, that's fair."

"He wants to impregnate you. You realize that."

She fanned herself as discreetly as possible. "Stop sidebarring."

"Fine." Veda squared her shoulders. "I started the GoFundMe for the Jam Jar at the Gilded Garden. That's what I'm calling the music venue for now, by the way." She rubbed her hands together. "We've already raised thirty thousand bucks."

Disbelief had Eve's mouth falling open. "Thirty *thousand*?"

"I told you. Musicians have rich parents who want them out of the house!"

And while Veda commenced dancing the Charleston, belting out "We're in the Money," Eve heard her new friend's singing voice for the first time.

"Holy shit."

CHAPTER EIGHTEEN

Eve stared dumbfounded at the entrance of the Gilded Garden as more and more customers arrived. The tables were almost completely full and it had been so long since that happened, she wasn't prepared with enough waitstaff, so she'd had no choice but to jump in and play hostess, guiding people to their seats in front of the stage and taking drink orders.

"What is going on?" the bartender whispered at Eve as she picked up another round of espresso martinis.

"I have no clue," Eve murmured, piling drinks onto her tray. "And I'm not questioning it either."

"Do you have someone new performing?"

"Yeah, but . . ." Eve shook her head as another laughing group of college-aged students piled into the lounge. "Full Bush Rhonda didn't mention having a following like this. She hasn't performed since the nineties."

The bartender did a double take. "Excuse me? Full Bush who?"

"You'll see," Eve said, weaving through the throngs of cus-tomers to drop off the martinis. She remained another twenty minutes to help the waitress fill orders, before ducking through the blue velvet curtain leading backstage. There, she found Rhonda sitting at one of the performer vanities, awash in a row of Hollywood-style lightbulbs, putting the finishing touches on a very dramatic cat eye. "Rhonda."

"Yes?" drawled the older woman, touching her tongue to the corner of her mouth. "What can I do for you, honey?"

Eve's lips quirked at Rhonda's smug tone. "These people are all here for you, aren't they?"

She patted her hair. "Told you so."

"Rhonda, none of these people were alive the last time you danced."

"Bitch, you can't let me have my moment?" Rhonda said on a burst of laughter, elbowing Eve in the hip playfully. "I've got nine grandkids, all college age or older, and they did their damn . . ." She wiggled her fingers in the air. "Social media magic. You're welcome."

The rising hope in Eve's chest was tentative, but . . . it felt good. She hadn't experienced one of those feelings in a long time. "Are your grandkids here too?"

"Some of the girls, yes. It was a tougher sell to the boys, but they're going to take me out for dinner tomorrow instead."

"That's probably for the best."

Rhonda hummed, distracted by a clump on her eyelash. "I've always danced for the ladies, anyhow. There's always a face or two in the crowd that just transforms when they see how much I love my body, flaws and all. I like to think they go home and look in the mirror a little differently. With more gratitude for what they've got."

"That's beautiful," Eve said, meaning it. Tucking it away for later, so she could reflect on it some more. For her, burlesque had always been about seductiveness. Teasing. The decadence of the slow reveal. But there was more to it. More to consider. "You're on in half an hour. You ready?"

"Born ready!"

Eve scooted back through the curtain, bobbing and weaving

to avoid getting clocked by stray elbows, returning to the bar with her tray at the ready, quickly kissing a newly arrived Elton on the cheek. "I could barely get a parking spot," he shouted over the noise, taking off his black ball cap and tossing it on the bar as he took a seat. "Is it always like this?"

"No."

Elton nodded with approval at the packed lounge. "Guess I'm in for a treat."

Eve smiled. "You have no idea." Checking the time on her watch, she was reminded that more than one event was taking place tonight. "Do you know the score of the Yankees game?"

"Are you serious? I get alerts in real time." He winced. "They're losing. Three to one. But it's early."

"Yeah. Is Madden happy there?"

"Why don't you ask him?" He dropped his voice to a stage whisper. "You're his wife."

She flipped him the bird. "I would. I will. It's just . . ."

"You're both the strong, emotionally stunted silent type?"

"You get more annoying with age, you know."

He grinned, though it dipped slightly as he glanced back over his shoulder toward the door. "So is the rockabilly donut queen coming with her boyfriend, or what?"

Eve didn't show a reaction, but she found it very interesting that Veda had spent a lot of time at iHop dropping sly inquiries about Elton and his romantic history, which Eve had been compelled to be honest about. Elton had always been the type to commit fast and hard. Too fast and hard. He wanted exactly what his parents had. An established place in the community, permanency, respectability, kids, square footage.

Considering Veda was still in her party phase and didn't show any signs of slowing down, any mutual interest in each other could end . . . badly.

"Yeah, she's coming. With the situationship and her sister."

"Nice. Nice." He popped his neck. "How old is she again?"

"The sister?"

"Uh. Veda."

Oh brother. "Twenty-one. Too young for you."

"I'm not interested," he scoffed, leaning sideways to order a beer from the bartender. Then, "But out of curiosity, how is that too young? I just turned twenty-five."

"She's a different kind of young, Elt."

"Right," he said, brow furrowing. "Maybe the sister."

"Maybe the sister."

The door of the Gilded Garden opened and in walked a trio that could not be more mismatched. Veda was arm in arm with a boy who looked like a paid *Grease* extra, right down to his leather jacket, Elvis haircut, and the toothpick dangling from his mouth. Beside them was a real estate agent. Even if Eve hadn't seen her face on half a dozen benches throughout Cumberland, she'd know this woman was into selling houses. She had on a blue blazer, pleated pants, and ballet flats. Her smile was bright and welcoming. Hair tastefully waved and spilling around her shoulders.

In other words, Veda's exact opposite.

Eve watched Elton's gaze bounce from the sister, Alexis, to the *Grease* extra's arm, which was crooked around the back of Veda's neck, tugging her close as they advanced toward the bar. In the end, Elton's eyes stayed on Veda, a telltale muscle ticking in his cheek.

Red alert.

"Hey, guys," Veda said, seemingly avoiding eye contact with Elton. "This is my . . . friend and bandmate? Slightly more? I don't know, but his name is Smith." She hesitated, seeming kind of nervous, but she finally looked at Elton. "And this is my sister, Alexis. Alexis, this is Elton and Eve."

Elton stood slowly, jerking his chin at Smith. "Hey."

Smith fished the toothpick out of his mouth. "Hey."

"This space is just a dream. You've done wonders with it, Eve," Alexis effused, cutting the odd tension, before coming forward, tucking her purse neatly beneath one arm and extending a hand toward Elton. "It's nice to meet you. Alexis."

Elton pried his attention off Smith and Veda, making a visible effort to focus on the young woman who couldn't be more his type if she tried. "Hi, Alexis." He tipped his head at the bar, swallowing. "Can I buy you a drink?"

Her pearly whites were on full display. "Sure!"

It made no sense that Veda appeared crestfallen when she'd been the one to show up with Smith. Not to mention her sister, who she'd brought specifically to introduce to Elton. But there it was. Veda watched Elton and Alexis launch into an easy conversation, her body language that of someone who'd just been trampled.

Eve would have to sort through the odd undercurrent between Veda and Elton later, though, because the Gilded Garden was at maximum capacity for the first time ever.

"Enjoy yourselves," Eve said, gesturing for everyone to take the remaining seats at the bar. "I have to help the waitstaff and give the performer a five-minute warning."

NINE MINUTES LATER, Eve couldn't even call drink orders over the cheering—and the praise was well earned, because Rhonda *cooked*.

She emerged from behind the blue curtain in a floor-length robe adorned with peacock feathers—presumably fake—and fluttered her falsies for a good thirty seconds to absorb the applause. She then crooked her finger at the busboy, whispering something in his ear, to which he nodded, with a grin on his face. Eve's eyes widened considerably as the busboy got down on all fours, acting as a footrest while Rhonda proceeded to peel back one side of her robe, demurely, making a meal out of stripping off her thigh-high fishnet stockings one at a time.

Gradually, skillfully, the robe came off one rolling, shimmying shoulder. Then it slipped off the other, the duster slithering to the ground before Rhonda bent forward, ass to the crowd, giving them just a flash, before she was back under the robe, midspin to face the audience once more, the music picking up tempo. Using the busboy as her voluntary footstool again, she propped a pointed toe on his shoulder and leaned back, arching, reveling in the purposeful movement of her ample cleavage.

Remembering what Rhonda had said backstage, Eve scanned the crowd and, indeed, saw several young women transfixed by Rhonda's confidence. Her enjoyment of herself, her body, what it could do. This was important.

Although every constructive thought in Eve's mind fled when Rhonda faced the crowd fully and finally ditched the robe . . . living up to her nickname and then some.

A beat of silence swept over the crowd. Then they absolutely lost it.

Veda bounded up beside her. "Dude."

"*Dude.*"

"Do we even *need* the GoFundMe now?"

It wasn't lost on Eve that Veda had started using "we" with regularity when referring to the triumphs, woes, and potential future of the Gilded Garden. Oddly, she didn't mind it so much. "Yes, we do," Eve said, sending Rhonda a thumbs-up. "I'm in a lot of debt."

Veda nodded right through that revelation. "Not for long."

Eve slow-clapped. "Give it up for Full Bush Rhonda."

"A living legend."

CHAPTER NINETEEN

Madden picked up a stuffed bear from the shelf of the rest stop convenience store, turning it over in his hands. Did five-year-olds still like stuffed animals? Maybe a coloring book and crayons would be a better option. Growing up, he'd had a filthy, ripped-up football—*soccer* ball, they called it here—and that ball had been his constant companion. He'd kicked it against every wall in his neighborhood, used it as a chair while he ate his supper, slept with it at the foot of his bed.

When he'd started playing baseball upon landing in Rhode Island, he'd thought about that filthy football, flattened somewhere in a trash heap, and mentally apologized for betraying it, silly as it sounded. Long story short, he'd never had toys.

Though his siblings, the legitimate ones, were given plenty.

Unable to swallow the obstruction in his throat, Madden swiped another teddy bear off the shelf. A blue one and a brown. They could have their pick.

He paid and got back on the road, immediately transitioning to the fast lane. His eagerness to see Eve was likely to get him pulled over and slapped with a speeding ticket, but he couldn't convince himself to slow down. A week had passed since their courthouse wedding and he'd replayed that first kiss as her husband every time he closed his eyes. He'd nearly rubbed himself raw knowing the next time he saw Eve, he could very well take her to bed as his wife, if she allowed it. How many times had he imagined twining their ringed fingers together over her head and driving himself deep while their mouths reunited?

He'd lost count somewhere around a thousand.

Madden took his foot off the gas pedal upon realizing he was doing ninety.

Who could blame him with a woman like Eve waiting on the other end of the drive?

Morning fog still sat low in the valleys he passed, the sun just beginning to peer through the greenery on both sides of the New England highway. She'd know he'd left New York at four in the morning—and he didn't care.

Good. Let her know how badly he wanted to see her.

ABOUT AN HOUR later, Madden stood outside Eve's apartment door, teddy bears in one hand, flowers in the other. White orchids. They were funeral flowers, aye, but they also had the kind of old-fashioned glamour he associated with Eve. With her club.

A soft rain had started to fall outside, just beginning to dampen the asphalt surface of the parking lot when Madden got out of the car. Now it picked up little by little, pattering on the roof of the building and muting the light in the hallway. As such, her face looked even softer than usual when she opened the door in her gray silk shorts and white tank top. She wore her hair in one of those sideways buns with little pieces sticking out. Feet bare.

He was turned inside out in seconds.

"Madden."

His grip tightened around the cellophane wrapping of the bouquet and they both heard it, his reaction to hearing his name in her voice. And the sudden press of need in his stomach wasn't only the unbearable hunger to get between her legs he'd been living with for years, it was a hell of a lot more. The week away on the road had been grueling and now comfort stood in front of him in the form of Eve, her eyes tracking his mental state in a sweep, the way they always had. God willing, they always would.

"Eve," he said thickly.

"Long week?"

Briefly, the echoing shouts from the locker room invaded his mind, before he silenced them again. "Yes."

She turned sideways to allow him inside and he went, their bodies brushing slowly as he moved past her, the contact making her eyes close, Madden leaning down to unrepentantly sniff her hair. "I love orchids, you know," Eve said gruffly, taking the flowers out of his hands, continuing into the kitchen with hypnotic sways of her hips and, Jesus, the way his fucking blood pounded watching her go. "So dignified and graceful. Smooth and unblemished on the outside, hiding the most interesting parts of themselves."

"I had a feeling you'd like them," he managed, using his boot to nudge the door closed. "It occurred to me you didn't have flowers at the wedding, so . . ." Madden paused in the act of removing his jacket when he saw the framed sketch he'd given her a week prior hanging on the living room wall. Pride rolled through him in a golden wave.

"I might not have had flowers, but I had that," she said, darting him a vulnerable look while placing the orchids in a vase of water. "Um. Why was it such a long week? Apart from having to squat and hold up a glove for five hours every night."

His lips jumped. "Someone has to keep the umpire company."

"Guess so," she murmured, coming around the kitchen island to hover in the living room. "Do you want to sit down?"

Madden gave a nod and joined Eve in the living room, both of them standing in front of the couch, him in jeans and a long-sleeved shirt, boots. Her in those little pajamas. Why was the stark contrast of their clothing making it so hard to concentrate?

Because if he got on top of her, she'd feel next to naked.

Hard on fragile.

They started to sit down beside each other on the couch and, god, that pleased him, the fact that she didn't try and sit outside of his reach. Before she could find her seat, however, she popped back up. "I didn't even ask if you wanted coffee—"

"Eve." He caught her wrist before she could dash off. "Why are you nervous?"

"I don't know," she said, huffing a laugh. "I think because . . ."

Madden used her wrist to tug her closer, until Eve stood in front of him, then released it in favor of running a knuckle up the inside of her thigh, gratified when goose bumps popped up on her arms, her belly hollowing briefly. "Because there's a good chance we're going to consummate this marriage this morning?"

She released a rocky breath. "Yes." Her tongue emerged to wet her lips. "I thought I'd have some warning before you came back. This isn't exactly wedding night worthy."

"Is it not?" He shifted on the couch to frame her hips in his hands, squinting one eye as if evaluating the outfit. "Short, tight. Doesn't require a bra. Easy to take off. I'm having a hard time finding the downside, love."

"It's not . . . special occasion wear."

"You *are* the special occasion, Eve." He leaned in and kissed her stomach. "We'll move this at your pace. I'm just as happy to sit here and talk."

"No, you're not," she scoffed breathily.

"What?" He pretended to be wounded. "I love a good conversation."

"Stop telling lies. I used to wonder if you'd taken a vow of silence."

"That's only because I was listening to every single word coming out of your mouth." Madden took advantage of Eve's stunned reaction, snagging her wrist again and pulling her down onto his lap sideways, grinding his molars together when her ass landed on his groin, so full and tight. "For now, we talk," he said, reclining into the cushions, bringing her with him, his eyelids drooping when she slowly laid her head on his shoulder. "How were the kids this week? All better?"

"Yes, although Landon has a lingering cough, so he's needed his inhaler a lot. You should see the paperwork I had to fill out so the school nurse can give him his inhaler. You'd think we were signing a treaty with France."

Madden chuckled. "But it helps him?"

"Yes. So much. Lark wants one now too. She thinks it's cool." Eve lifted her left hand and he held his breath as she hesitated, before finally tracing the crew neck collar of his shirt. God have mercy. He'd sit like this for the rest of his life, a willing victim of her touch, the taut cheeks of her ass firm on his cock. "Rookie mistake, by the way, giving them different color teddy bears." She gestured at the bears he'd brought in. "One of them will become the ultimate bear for no reason and they will go to war over who possesses it."

"Ah Jesus." Her laugh vibrated through him. "You'd never know I had two younger siblings, would you?"

Her mirth faded. "You've never really talked about them," she said, after a moment. "What are their names?"

The living room turned momentarily fuzzy around him. "Paul and Sinead. I haven't said their names out loud in a long time."

Eve must have noticed the involuntary tensing of his muscles, because she lifted her head from his shoulder to look at him. "Do you speak to them?"

"Not much anymore," Madden said. "In the beginning, I tried to keep in contact with them and my mother, but once I sensed it was easier for them to go without speaking to me, I more or less left the ball in their court. The calls thinned out after that."

"How could it be easier not to speak to *you*?"

Her incredulity was like a balm to his wounds. "I think . . . or at least I hope the home was a better place to be after I left. That hope is the reason I never went back." His gaze skimmed over her hair. "One of the reasons, anyway."

The fingertips that had been tracing his collar moved down to the center of his chest now and paused there, as if feeling for the sudden racing of his heart. "Was your home such an unhappy place growing up, Mad?"

Everything inside him wanted to change the subject. Or lay her down on the couch and distract her with sex. But there was something about holding Eve this way—protectively, securely—that made Madden feel in control. No matter what he said, no matter what horrible images his brain conjured up, Eve would be there, safe. He was keeping her such.

"My siblings and I have a different father. My mother . . . she was pregnant with me when they married, right. My da didn't come to find out until after the wedding that I was another man's child. It changed him, or so I'm told. Apparently, he used to be a kind man, though I don't know if I believe that. Something my aunt told me made me wonder if his temperament ran in the family. But at least it was directed at me, not my siblings."

"He wasn't kind to you," she said, quietly, her chest rising and falling.

"No, love."

A full body wince from Eve. "I see."

He rubbed her back to ease the distress. "The . . . his aggression was only ever focused on me. When I stayed in Rhode Island, I told myself I was taking the reason for his hatred away. It needed to be done. But . . ." He pulled her closer, his eyes closing of their own accord when she pressed her face into his neck. "For a long time, I felt like I'd quit, instead of fighting. Like I'd abandoned myself and who I am. My family. Hid across the ocean from a man who was the real coward. Hid behind the plate."

"You were never hidden to me. To anyone." She opened her mouth and closed it, emotional pain on her face. "You were an important addition to this place."

His throat felt heavy. "Maybe I've slowly started to believe that. Hindsight has me realizing how much I tried to blend into the background here, the way I did back home." He thought of the tension in the locker room throughout their week on the road. "I'm wanting to speak up more and more, though. What if . . . I have something worthwhile to say? Someone has to fix what's broken with the team and that was never my job, my inclination before, but what if it is now?"

"Follow your instincts." Eve nudged the side of his neck with her nose. "And if yours need more time to bake, then follow mine. *Everything* you say is worthwhile. Always has been. Always will be."

Madden didn't know how to express the wealth of gratitude spinning inside him, so he gave up a heavy exhale and tried to tell her with his eyes. "I didn't come here planning to say all of this. It must be the rain. I think about home more when it rains."

Eve took her time sitting up in his lap, rolling their foreheads and settling their mouths together, breathing in and out. With their lips holding that position, she lowered the straps of her tank top, pulling the garment down just enough to expose her firm set of tits with their pebbled nipples. Touching the tip of his tongue with her own, she lifted his hand and placed it on her bare breast. "Maybe next time it rains, you'll think of me, instead."

And then his mind went blessedly fucking blank.

CHAPTER TWENTY

Eve didn't consider herself a nurturing person. She valued those people tremendously. They were the volunteers helping during a natural disaster. They were the nurses who'd cleared up her confusion about asthma. They were kindergarten teachers and caretakers. On the flip side, she loved a few people very fiercely, if quietly, and didn't count herself among the ranks of those who cared for others.

The impulse to soothe Madden in that moment was as foreign to her as holy matrimony. As foreign as having a husband walk through the door, give her a bouquet of perfect-for-her flowers, and ask how she'd been. All she could say was . . . Something strong and unrecognizable compelled her to expose herself physically to him, as if trading one vulnerability for the kind he'd shown.

Resting their lips together, she placed his warm, extralarge hand on her breast, heard his breath stutter at the contact, and licked the seam of his mouth, making the barest contact with his tongue, but, whoa mama, that was enough to send a roll of thunder all the way down to her sex and grip her flesh with anticipation.

"Hold on," he said, the words muffled by their almost-kiss. "Let's talk awhile more. I want to be sure this isn't out of sympathy."

"It's not," she gasped when his thumb brushed over her sensitive nipple.

"I don't know why I told you all that now—"

"I'm glad you did."

Intense blue eyes searched her face, as if for proof. "Why?"

"I like knowing things about you." Okay, apparently, she was going for way more than physical vulnerability this morning. With their breaths picking up and blending, Eve couldn't seem to remember why she shouldn't say anything and everything on her mind. "I feel closer to you after you told me about your family. It's not sympathy. It's . . . intimacy."

The brackets around his mouth softened just slightly. "You're sure?"

Briefly separating their lips, Eve turned to straddle Madden, scrubbing her palms up and over his broad shoulders, beginning to feel drunk on the freedom she had to touch this man. Not Skylar's crush. Just Madden. Her husband. A man she wanted to be honest with.

As much as she could, anyway.

"There might be a teeny tiny feeling of . . . wanting to soothe you because you had to talk about something that upset you. There might even be some . . . need to reward you for being honest with me."

Madden was already shaking his head. "Eve—"

"What's wrong with letting me have it, though?" she whispered, tilting her head slowly to the right and licking into his mouth, tasting his heated groan, feeling the rising thickness of his shaft against the seam of her shorts. "We both want this, no matter what it's about." She slid her knees wider on the couch and rocked forward, watching his pupils dilate to the size of dimes. "Don't we?"

"Fuck me, Eve. You have no right being so goddamn sexy." Before she could issue a flirty rejoinder and watch his eyes go black again, Madden turned them sideways, pressing Eve's back to the couch and pinning her there, fitting his hips right where they belonged. Between her thighs. "I'd rather make you forget your need to soothe me."

She lifted her knees and shifted, teasing, while biting her lip. "How are you going to do that?"

"Showing you I don't need soothing."

"Everyone needs soothing once in a—"

Madden grabbed the back of his collar and hauled off his shirt, tossing it toward some unseen destination, because she couldn't look away from the raw strength suddenly staring her in the face. The rugged beauty of him already had her around the throat, but then his hand added even more pressure, his palm sliding up between her breasts and closing gently around her throat. "You kiss your husband hello next time he walks through the front door," he said, leaning down to deliver a kiss so thorough, her fingers dug into the edge of the sofa. She was left gasping by the time it ended, her lips swollen and tingling. "That's the first thing you do, love. That's how you greet me. If I only get this mouth for six months, I'm going to make good fucking use of it."

"I don't feel the need to soothe you anymore," she panted, not wanting to move or breathe or do anything to disturb the decadence of being pressed down by his weight and told what is what. "I'm over it."

"Good." He marauded her mouth again, his tongue moving with blatant, erotic ownership, his thumb stroking the hollow of her throat, reassuring her and flustering her at the same time until she was whimpering, an aggressive ache spreading between her legs. "But, Eve? Eve."

"Huh? What?" Who was that woman talking? She sounded *frantic.*

"You're going to get *my* mouth for six months too," he rasped, that possessively confident hand turning her head left so he could stroke his tongue down, downward over her collarbone, his lips ending at her stiff nipple; without hesitating, he covered her with his mouth, her tits firm in his hands while his mouth savored, worked, licked over the distension of her with a precision that had her gasping and burying her fingers in his hair.

"Oh my god," she moaned.

"One week into this marriage and you already know getting topless for me is going to win any argument." He licked across to her other breast, his brows drawn together tight as he lapped at her nipple slowly, kissed it, then delivered a vicious drag of suction that made her back arch off the couch. "Smart girl," he said when he finished twisting her into a pretzel. "I've been obsessed with these tits for fucking years. Now you're going to come from having them sucked."

"Not possible," she gasp-laughed. "No."

He released her right breast, sliding his hand down between them, waiting for her to nod before he delved his long, blunt fingers inside her sleep shorts and gripped her sex through the cotton material of her panties, rubbing until her folds were separated between the gentle but firm touch of his fingers. "Jesus Christ, if your pussy can get this wet, I reckon you can do anything."

Was praise her thing? *Is praise my thing?*

Her eyes were literally in the back of her head, chest heaving, her sanity hinging on his full, massaging strokes between her thighs, the character of which was so cocky, so unlike his personality, that the shock of his skills was going to blow her fuses. And the likelihood of that increased tenfold when he started splitting time between her mouth and her breasts, giving them equal hungry attention, slanting his mouth over hers with a vengeance one second, licking and suckling her the next until . . . until it started to happen, a hot quickening at the equator of her body, the prickle of goose bumps raking up her skin like an assault, her skin flashing hot and cold, hot and cold, gold flashbulbs snapping at the edges of her vision.

"Okay, it's really happening," she gasped, ordering her core not to flex on instinct, but to let the orgasm crest naturally and prolong itself. Tricks of the single girl trade. "You weren't lying. Don't stop."

"Never, love."

She'd take issue with her whiny tone of voice later and how it sounded ridiculous in the presence of Madden's perfect baritone, but right now Eve had something brewing in her belly, fierce and twisty and agitating—and when she looked down at her shiny nipples and saw him bare his teeth at them, the pleasure sped up and imploded, rocketing her hips upward, her inner walls bearing down, buckling, a scream churning out of her, both knees shaking on either side of his waist. Every part of her shaking, the smell of sweat and sex and soap heavy between them, his gaze riveted by her body as it writhed through the worst/best agony, committed by him.

"Madden . . ." Weakened by the thorniest, most unique climax in recent memory, she turned into a puddle of bones on the couch. "What . . . *what?*"

He loomed over her, propped on one elbow, his expression almost thoughtful as he watched her huff and puff through her recovery.

"How do you not look cocky right now?"

"Should I?"

"Yes."

He hummed, a line snapping in his jaw as he slowly ground his bulge between her thighs, then punching his hips forward once, twice, the friction against her sensitive sex making her want to grab his butt and keep him there. "Catch your breath, Eve. I'm going down on you now."

Panic made a slow slice through the fog, like the bow of a ship. *Going down on you.* He'd . . . he'd have to take off her panties for that. In the light.

He'd see the scar. He'd know.

Madden was already sitting back, his eyes glittering with intention in the dull morning light, the dainty waistband of her panties pinched between his fingers. How would she ever explain that scar? He'd react badly for so many reasons. Because she'd never told him. Because she'd made herself vulnerable to long-term health risks. But most of all, if Madden saw that scar, there would be no convincing him to end this relationship at six months. His commitment to her would be lifelong and she wouldn't do that to him.

Stop him.

"Wait. No." Despite Eve's lethargy, she sat up and ordered herself to soften the alarm in her tone. "No," she murmured, climbing onto her knees—and it didn't require any effort to sprinkle seduction into her movements, because he was thick and gorgeous and pissed he wasn't giving her oral sex right now. Put that at the top of his list of good qualities. "You have to let me recover first," she said, closing the short distance between them on her knees and running her nails down his hard chest, leaning in to kiss the dip between his pecs, dragging her mouth sideways to breathe hot air against his nipples.

"Eve . . ." Madden was starting to breathe harder. "Let me get a goddamn taste."

The raw vibration of need in his voice almost made her give in, damn the consequences, but she bit him playfully, instead, her fingertips teasing circles low on his abdomen. "Let me get mine," she said softly, sipping kisses on the swell of his chest, his jaw, his shoulders, all while her fingers danced over the heavy ridge behind his zipper. "Show it to me, Mad."

A sound dragged up his vocal cords, his stomach muscles bunching in a way that looked almost painful. "Eve."

"Show it to me so I can suck it," she whispered, stroking him through his pants, her grip firm, her thumb tracing base to head, teasing him there, before massaging back down to the root. "Are you going to make me say please?"

He bit off a groan, a sheen of sweat building on his chest. "I'm the beggar in this relationship, love. I'd beg for you until my dying breath."

Eve's chest grew heavy and she nodded, dropping her face low to rub it against the protrusion between his thighs, dragging her open mouth side to side, witnessing the growth of him right in front of her eyes. As her fantasies usually included two elements— Madden and some light voyeurism—her gaze couldn't help but slip over to the window across the room and notice the slight gap between the curtains.

Someone could easily look in if they wanted to.

The thought alone was enough to infuse her with heat, her fingers working to free the button of his jeans—

"Caught you looking at the window, Eve," he managed between rasping breaths.

The tips of her ears tingled hot. "Me? No."

Madden made a skeptical sound and caught her jaw in his

hand, lifting her up until their lips melded together, the growth of his beard scraping the softness of her cheeks and chin as his mouth rode over hers, seeking and hungry. "Trust me to give you what you need," he said, taking her mouth again, again, again, until she almost begged him to stop the torture and fuck her. As hard as he wanted, however he wanted. Plainly put, she'd never been so lost to lust in her life. Nothing mattered but the next stroke of his tongue, the next position of his hands, the radiant heat of his body.

"I do trust you," she gasped.

Madden nodded and rose from the couch, bringing her with him. He guided her across the room to the spot directly in front of the window and knelt her down.

Then he yanked open the curtains.

In spilled the muted, stormy light across both of them as Madden unzipped his jeans, the tendons shifting and popping in his forearms. Meanwhile, Eve was trembling, her tank top around her hips, soaked through her panties, mouth swollen . . . reeling from the impact of what was taking place. Sure, her apartment was located on the second floor and the rain was blurring objects on either side of the window, but there was an identical building across the parking lot and their windows faced hers. If someone was watching, they would see her kneeling in front of Madden, half dressed.

"Mad . . ."

"Is this what you need?"

Her body was too keyed up and defenseless to make words. To make sense. Yet at the same time, in this submissive position with an audience—be it real or imagined—she felt more powerful than she ever had in her life.

She nodded vigorously.

Madden used the back of his wrist to swipe sweat from his forehead, hesitating to gather himself before fisting his shaft and bringing it out of his jeans, showing it to her, long and engorged in his palm. Pumping it top to bottom in his grip. "Is this what you need?"

"Yes."

He stepped closer and rested the smooth head against her mouth. "Good girl. Show everyone how well you suck your husband off."

Eve pretty much blacked out. That's how she would remember it later. The last thing she recalled with her human brain were those eleven words, prior to her animal brain taking over, her fingers scraping his jeans down to his ankles, along with his black briefs, the salt and weight and texture of Madden in her mouth. Finally. God, he was huge. And generous with his approval, moaning her name any time she did anything. Anything. Flicked her tongue across his damp slit, took him so deep her lips brushed his balls, blinked up at him. He praised it all. He shook through it all. Eve couldn't remember if she even stopped to breathe, she was so eager to be a good girl, to lose herself in this moment where she was an object of hunger. A means of pleasure. It was freeing, exciting, erotic. It was the hottest experience of her life. Everyone watching was envious of Madden. Wanted a turn they would never be allowed. Only in their dreams.

"Love. Love, I can't hold on to it anymore."

"Give it to me."

"Say that again," he rasped, panting. "But call me your husband."

"Please, I want my husband to give it to me."

Eve barely finished breathing those requested words when Madden's hips jerked, a choked sound left him, and she covered him with her suctioning mouth, whimpering at the simultaneous power and weakness of him, how susceptible he was to her touch, the salt washing down the back of her throat, the sinew of his thighs straining underneath her palms. All of him. All of him, every part was perfect, but the fact that she was trying to express that truth was probably lost on Madden, because he was too busy praising her.

"Eve. My god. My god. Eve. You don't know the pain of needing to fuck this mouth. You're so beautiful. Work me. Fuck, that's it. Work it all out of me. *You're so fucking beautiful.*"

When her animal brain winked off and her human one came back online, Eve was in a heap on the floor, struggling to breathe while Madden zipped himself up above her. How had this happened? How had giving someone else head knocked Eve on *her* ass? What in the world was going on here?

She stopped caring when Madden got down on the floor and lay beside Eve on his side, studying her face while his right hand molded her ass, his touch firm and possessive.

"Can I go down on you now?"

"*What?*"

Her phone rang.

CHAPTER TWENTY-ONE

Madden paused in the act of tying his shoelaces, his fingers suspended while he watched Eve run around her bedroom. He simply couldn't concentrate on both things at the same time, and frankly, he might never be able to concentrate on anything for the rest of his life after that blow job.

He'd had women on their knees before, but it had been a long time. Since those first two years in college, to be exact. When Madden left for college, Eve was still sixteen and he was doing his god's honest best to pretend his infatuation with her didn't exist. He'd had a blur of hookups in those first two years of college trying to drive her out of his head. That first visit home after her graduation, though, he'd almost begged her for forgiveness, even though they weren't in a relationship. Even though she'd shown no interest in one.

They'd never even spoken to each other in a romantic sense before that night.

He'd asked her out and gotten turned down flat. But he hadn't gone near another woman since they danced in that tent on the Pages' front lawn. Once he admitted to himself that Eve was the end game, he didn't look back, right, or left. Only forward.

Four years of cat and mouse had ensued, him trying to have contact with her in any way, shape, or form. He'd fucking *pined* for her. Lusted day and night. Missed her like hell. At times, he'd even felt flashes of resentment, confusion for being kept at arm's length. Not even a friend did that, let alone someone he had a very clear connection with.

Now? He thanked god he'd waited.

No one in this world compared to Eve.

His stomach was still in fucking knots from kissing her. She was wild, sensual. Sexy beyond description. Honest, funny, vulnerable, adventurous. His.

The occupant of his entire heart.

"What exactly happened with Landon at school, Eve?" he called, wanting to hear her voice. "Did I hear something about a chef's hat?"

"Yes. He refuses to take it off." She hopped on one foot past the door of her bedroom while donning a pair of socks, and Madden tilted his head to watch the shake of her bare ass cheeks, apparently not gentleman enough to look away. "He's locked himself in the bathroom because someone dropped the hat into a puddle at recess. The teacher cleaned it off and left it to dry in the staff lounge, but he wants it back and he's not taking no for an answer."

"I see."

Eve stopped in her doorway, now wearing a pair of short, red athletic shorts and a half-tucked T-shirt. "Why are you putting on your shoes? You're not coming with me."

"Why not?"

"People might see us together."

"The deal was that we didn't tell anyone we're married, love," he said calmly. "Not that we wouldn't be seen together."

She frowned and disappeared again, returning a few seconds later drawing a brush through her long hair. "You don't think people are going to wonder why you're coming to deal with a school-related issue with me?"

"Well, as you know, I don't give a fuck."

"But I do."

The panic molding her features was going to be the death of him. "You can tell the teacher or whoever is watching so closely that we've been friends the better part of a decade and I'm visiting from out of town."

She chewed on that, but it didn't seem to check any of her worry boxes. "Will you please stay in the car?"

Madden's jaw nearly fused together. "Jesus, Eve."

"It's for your sake, not mine. Please."

That statement bodychecked him in the heart. "This place and its people don't deserve you," he growled. "Not the other way around."

"I know you mean that, Mad. But I still want you to stay in the car. Please. This is stressful enough without worrying I'll . . ." She dropped the brush to her side, closed her eyes for a beat. In a quieter voice, she said, "It's also that I don't want you there if someone makes a weird comment or turns their nose up at me. I'm used to it. But you would have to say something, and I don't need to be defended."

Come back to New York with me.

Madden wanted to say that out loud, so badly. Maybe he would have, if the burlesque club wasn't still in its infancy. If Eve didn't have Landon and Lark to look after. He'd risk her getting spooked in exchange for offering her a chance to get away from the stigma that had been attached to her in Cumberland.

"I'll stay in the car," he said, instead, because he didn't want to add to her stress. She had enough reason for that already. "One guess what I'll be thinking about while I wait."

Eve frowned. "Baseball?"

"One more guess."

In the kitchen now, she dug through her purse. "Lunch?"

Madden walked in her direction, coming up behind her in the kitchen and gripping the island on both sides of her body. "Wrong again." He dropped a lingering kiss on her shoulder. "Your phone rang before I had a chance to say . . ." His lips moved higher, up the side of her neck. "I'm not the same man I was before you got on your knees for me. Fuck, Eve. Just . . . *fuck*."

A shiver passed through her. "So, you're going to be thinking about blow jobs while you wait."

"No, love. I'm going to be thinking about returning the favor."

"Oh." When did her apartment become such a sweatbox? "First of all, please pass on this obsession to every man. The world would be a much happier place."

"I'm only obsessed with eating *your* pussy." He reached down and cupped her sex, giving it a firm squeeze. "I'm not passing that on to anyone."

"Um." She gulped. Audibly. "You probably shouldn't fluster me when I'm about to meet with a pissed-off kindergarten teacher. I need to be clearheaded to negotiate a hostage crisis."

"Sorry." With a final tightening of his grip, he let her go, sliding the keys to his truck out of his pocket, holding them up. "I'll drive while you pull yourself together."

"So generous of you." Eve giggled, and the sound delighted him so much, he pressed her tighter to the island and tickled her side with his free hand. "Madden!"

"Sorry." He kissed the side of her face, letting his mouth roam down her neck, razing her with teeth as he went. "I love hearing you laugh."

"You're the only one who can get it out of me." She turned between him and the island, running her fingertips up the center of his chest, driving them straight into his hair. As she clutched those strands, everything below his waist tightened in response. "You're the only one who can get a moan out of me too," she murmured, going up on her toes to slowly lick the hill of his Adam's apple.

Madden dropped his keys. "Eve," he said raggedly, seeking her mouth, his hands reaching for her thighs so he could yank them up to his hips.

She dodged him with a flushed smirk, snatching up his keys and twirling toward the door. "Don't worry. I'll drive while you pull yourself together."

He chased her down the hallway, their laughter echoing through the building.

APPROXIMATELY FIFTEEN MINUTES later, Eve stood in front of a fire-engine-red bathroom stall door with a crispy new chef's hat in her hands, courtesy of the local pizza shop they'd swung by on the way over. She'd expected to feel a punch of nostalgia walking into the elementary school she'd once attended, but nothing felt or looked familiar. Surely everything hadn't always been so . . . miniature? Her surroundings were tiny, right down to the soap dispensers and trough-style sink.

Landon's teacher had her back pressed against the door, presumably to keep other students from entering while Eve talked Landon off the ledge. The woman's fingers flew over the screen of her phone, her eyes ticking to Eve and back down to whoever she was texting. *It's about me.*

She's gossiping about me with her local friends.

That girl who owns the burlesque club is here.

She looks like she just got out of bed.

You should see what she's wearing.

Guess I should be glad she's wearing anything at all.

Perhaps Eve's assumptions had everything to do with her current surroundings and nothing to do with reality, but throw in the woman's smug welcome and Eve felt somewhat . . . exposed. As though everything she said would be broadcast around town, dissected and evaluated. Which is why she'd always kept her mouth shut in class or at school functions growing up. The most innocent statement out of her mouth never failed to be related back to the strip club, nudity, boobs. Every time.

You're not in high school anymore.

The teacher is probably just texting her boyfriend.

Probably. But Eve still found herself torn between relief that Madden had stayed in the car and the sudden wish he'd come into the school with her. The ache for his supportive presence surprised her as much as it scared her. She'd always done hard things on her own. Now would be no different. The future would be no different either.

That's how it had to be.

Eve looked down quickly, keeping her gaze trained on the brim of the chef's hat.

"Hey, Landon?"

Silence. Then, a sniffle. But no further response.

"I brought you a new chef's hat. Want to see it?"

More sniffles. "No."

Eve reared back a little. "Why not? It's the same as the other one."

"I want the *other* one."

"I'm sorry. It got wet and it ripped." When Landon didn't respond, Eve sighed, opened her mouth to suggest they get ice cream later. Anything to incentivize him. But she stopped short when she heard the quiet, yet distinct click of an iPhone camera. Had the teacher taken a picture of her? Cold sweat spread beneath Eve's clothes, her knee-jerk reaction to call the woman on her behavior, but she didn't want to make the moment worse for Landon. *Focus on your nephew.* "Want me to crawl in there with you, kid? We'll stay in there forever. You can be the mayor of toilet town and I'll be your trusty assistant."

Was that a tiny giggle she heard?

Eve's chest expanded with hope. "We'll have big parties. BYOP. Bring your own plunger."

Fine, that joke was probably lost on the five-year-old, but it had to land with the teacher, right? Wrong. The woman still hadn't looked up from her phone.

Any mother in the same position wouldn't have been treated like this.

It was just her.

That certainty now sat in her stomach, heavy but familiar.

The feeling of not being respected.

Eve swallowed, trying and failing to stave off the inferiority. They'd been in the bathroom for five minutes and she was no closer to getting Landon to come out. "Why is that chef's hat so important to you, Landon?" she asked, changing tactics.

The silence drew itself out for so long, she wasn't sure he was going to answer. But then, "I used to wear it. To help my mom cook."

"Oh," Eve breathed, winded. Of course, the hat had special meaning to Landon. He'd been asking to wear it to school for weeks. Why hadn't she asked why before now? Had she been so caught up in her own bullshit that she couldn't see what was right in front of her? Wetting her lips, Eve turned to the teacher. "We're going to need that hat, please."

The woman lowered her phone. "It's wrecked, honestly. We couldn't salvage it."

Eve nodded. "Still. We need it. I'm happy to go get it myself."

"Out of the trash?"

"Yes."

"Fitting," mumbled the teacher as she pushed backward through the bathroom door. Eve's blood flushed cold, then hot, hating that sickly feeling of embarrassment she spent so much of her life trying to avoid. She wanted to follow the teacher into the hallway and remind her that, sure, she could laugh or run her mouth as much as she wanted when it came to Eve, so long as she treated Lark and Landon with the same love and respect as the other children. Was she? After the woman's total lack of assistance or empathy, Eve doubted it. Lark and Landon were two more people in her life not getting the treatment they deserved . . . because of her. "Hey," she blurted, hating the quaver in her voice. "Let's go get your sister and have a ditch day."

"What's a ditch day?"

Eve thought on her feet. "Well, the first order of business is fixing that goddamn hat. Where there's a will there's a way."

"Really?"

"Yup. And . . ." Eve rubbed at her chest. "Maybe, if you're up for it, we could cook something at home. I know cooking with your mom is special and it won't be exactly the same, but I can sub in until she gets back."

The latch on the stall slid open, the door creaking open slowly to reveal the tear-streaked face of her nephew. "We cook meatballs."

"Okay. Do you want to cook meatballs with me? Or leave meatballs for Mom . . . and make something different with me?"

Thoughts whirred behind his eyes. "Something different, I think."

"Cool, man. One problem, though."

"What?"

"I can't cook. Will you teach me?"

This time, he definitely giggled.

Eve laid an arm across his little shoulders and escorted him toward the door. "My friend Madden is hanging out with me today. Can he help us too?"

Landon looked up at her. "The baseball player?"

"Yes."

"But he's a Yankee."

"We like him despite that."

"I guess." Her nephew's brow furrowed. "Can we play baseball after we cook?"

For some reason, the imagery of that cozy, family-esque scene caused Eve to panic. "Uh, maybe. We can ask him. I don't know if he has any equipment with him, but . . ."

"Skylar's house has some," Landon said.

"That is true." She squeezed his shoulder. "We'll see."

They'd only taken two steps into the hallway when Landon's teacher came into view, the sodden tatters of his chef's hat pinched between her thumb and index finger. Landon's prized possession resembled a paper place mat from Denny's that had been left out in a hurricane.

"Shit," Eve muttered, before forcing a smile onto her face as the teacher handed her the chef's hat she'd unwisely promised to repair. "Just needs a little spit shine, right, Landon?"

He threw up a fist. "Right!"

"I'm needed back in class," said the teacher, her expression pinched. "Landon, do you want to head back with me?"

"Nope," her nephew responded. "We're ditching."

"Well"—Eve held back a laugh—"I just remembered he has a doctor's appointment . . ."

Landon's face fell. "*I do?*"

Eve put her hand over his mouth and ushered him toward the attendance office. "Lark has one too," she called over her shoulder to the now openly scowling teacher. "If you could send her out, please?"

Ten minutes later, her niece and nephew skipped alongside Eve toward the parking lot. While she had waited for Lark to join them in the attendance office and signed out both kids for the afternoon, she'd shot off a quick text to Madden to let him know plans had changed.

The kids came first, and Eve sensed they needed a diversion. Some spontaneous fun.

Now she could see the outline of Madden through the windshield of his truck and the sight was so welcome, the pulses in her neck and fingertips fluttered, the sun above extra warm because he'd be sharing it with her, with them—

A man strode past on the sidewalk and did a double take. So did Eve. Because she knew this man. Steve Kirk. One of her tormentors from high school. And one of the only people who could shrink her down to the size of a flea. Was he a teacher here? Or had he come to pick up his kid early, same as her? Just passing by?

"Eve Keller. Is that *you*?"

She winced but kept walking, hoping and praying he would see the kids and leave her alone. "Hi, Steve."

"You never rescheduled your performance. I keep checking the website."

Eve shrugged, her skin starting to pipe hot.

Ahead of her, the car door opened and Madden got out, standing to his full height, his narrowing gaze trained on Steve, causing memories from high school to come rushing back in rapid order. This was not good. In fact, considering the kids were present and they were outside an elementary school, a potential confrontation was a terrible possibility. Steve, however, didn't notice Madden's presence. Which is probably why he continued to run his mouth.

This is why.

This is why I wanted to come alone.

This is why I spare people I love.

"Like I told the waitress at the lounge, forget the stage," Steve kept going. "If Eve ever decides to make house calls with her little act, I'll be her best customer."

Madden moved in a flash. One second, he stood beside the driver's-side door, the next he was in front of Steve Kirk, staring the man down from a good six inches higher, the front of the man's shirt twisted in a shaking fist. "Get the kids in the car, Eve," he said, sounding strangled.

Eve jolted into action, her heart hammering in her throat as she hustled the kids toward the truck, babbling to them about cooking and baseball, hoping to distract them from whatever was taking place between the men twenty yards away on the sidewalk. Thankfully, they seemed totally oblivious to the tension among the adults, more concerned with their upcoming adventure.

Eve buckled the sister and brother in, closing the door behind them just in time to hear Madden say, "I warned you years ago about leaving her alone, didn't I? Did you think I forgot? I didn't.

Maybe I shouldn't have assumed a piece of garbage like you could evolve. Or grow the fuck up. That's my mistake. Yours was speaking to her like that." He twisted Steve's collar until his gasps were silenced and his arms started to flail in panic. "If the kids weren't watching, you'd be having your jaw wired shut this afternoon. I'd be doing the world a favor. When I let you go, you better use that first breath to apologize to her."

Madden loosened his grip and Steve sucked down oxygen with a wheeze.

"I'm sorry, Eve. I'm sorry."

"I sincerely hope you're not here to pick up a daughter," Madden finished. And with that, Madden threw him away like trash, causing the man to stumble backward several feet before righting himself. He looked around, fixing his hair, more concerned with being humiliated than his own behavior. Meanwhile, Madden appeared to be debating the wisdom of chasing the man into the wild blue yonder.

"Mad," Eve called, jogging toward him and inserting herself between one of the best men she'd ever met—and the worst. "I get the anger, believe me, but you've done enough."

Madden's chest rose and fell like he'd just lapped the block. "I want to kill him."

"I know."

"Come to New York with me, Eve," he said in a growled rush. "Get away from this."

Shock made her eye sockets tingle. "What?" she said slowly. "You know I can't."

He seemed to snap out of his trance then, tempering himself as she watched. "Right." His jaw popped. "Right, I know."

"I'm used to it." Eve tried to laugh, but the words wobbled out like jelly.

Wrong thing to say. Madden lit up with temper all over again.

"Hey." She went up on her toes and forced him to look her in the eye. "That's not what I meant. I meant . . . it doesn't faze me like it did in high school."

Madden searched her face. "You don't have to lie to me."

Then he did something she didn't expect. Didn't see coming.

He wrapped her in a bear hug. Lifted her against his body so securely, she could have let herself go limp and it wouldn't have made a difference. She sucked in a breath and shifted on her toes, as they were the only part of her body connected to the ground, fighting against the lethargy that stole over her, even as her brain demanded she reassure him again that she was fine. *I'm fine!*

But what if I'm not?

Madden didn't seem inclined to release her any time soon and her eyelids took that as an invitation to droop—and when that happened, New York painted itself on the backs of her eyelids, buzzing and flashy and vast and loud. Just for a moment, she allowed herself to picture herself walking into a doorman building, hand in hand with Madden, a million miles from the claws that had been dug into her skin since childhood. Free to go anywhere, do anything, with friends or anonymously. Out of the quicksand.

The vision started to feel so good, too good, that Eve's eyes shot open with alarm.

"The kids are in the car," she murmured breathily, wiggling until he freed her. Refusing to acknowledge the knowing look heating her back as she speed walked to the truck. "Let's go make a disaster out of my kitchen."

CHAPTER TWENTY-TWO

Madden sat on the bumper of his truck, hands clasped loosely between his knees, his head lifting when Eve's car turned into the parking lot of the middle school. He'd spent the afternoon in Eve's kitchen with the kids making Spam and cheese omelets, followed by brownies, Lark and Landon delightfully making a mess while Eve sat at the kitchen island trying to mend the ruined chef's hat.

He could still see her, head bent over her task, holding her breath while trying not to tear the fragile paper even more, blowing a hair dryer on a low setting to take out the excess dampness. Using a tiny tube of Krazy Glue to seal the torn sides back together and fluffing the paper to return the hat to a semblance of its own shape.

She'd explained to him why the chef's hat meant so much to Landon.

To think the woman trying so hard to resurrect a paper hat for her nephew had to endure abuse from the community that should be supporting her during a difficult time . . . it was torturing Madden. Leaving tomorrow morning would be like walking over a sea of broken glass, because one thing he knew for sure, if something similar to the Steve Kirk incident happened while he was gone, he'd never know about it. She would keep it to herself.

How much was this woman keeping to herself?

Madden waited until Eve pulled into a parking spot before standing, taking the bag containing bats, gloves, and balls out of his truck bed, settling the strap over his shoulder. After they'd cooked long enough to set off the building's smoke alarm twice, the kids were covered in muck, so she'd asked him to pick up some equipment from the Pages' while she cleaned them up. They'd planned to meet at the local middle school in an hour.

Now Eve and the twins crossed the deserted parking lot in his direction, backlit by the beginning of a purple-red sunset. She reached down to absently stroke Lark's ponytail, seemingly unaware of the look of pure hero worship the little girl gave her in return. Landon ran full speed ahead at Madden and yet time slowed down, this scene playing out in another time and place in his mind.

Eve meeting up with him, their kids in tow, no plans for the rest of the night, except to be together under the endless Rhode Island sky.

Someday.

Someday, please.

"Have you been here long?" Eve called, her step slowing as Landon collided with Madden's thighs, wrapping his arms around them. "We, um . . . found brownie batter in some very interesting places."

Lark tittered. "Landon had some in his *ear.*"

"He was just trying to block out the sound of the fire alarm, wasn't he?" Madden put his hand out for a high five, nodding when Landon's palm connected. "Smart lad."

"I want to hit first when we play baseball!" Lark shouted.

Landon slumped very dramatically, before popping straight again. "I'm second!"

"Sure, we're getting ahead of ourselves. You have to start with the basics."

"A game of catch, right?" Eve interjected. "That's how you started."

"You remember that day?"

"The day we met?" She pursed her lips, shrugged, though her eyes were twinkling. "Sort of."

"Don't be telling them lies, now, Eve. You remember it right down to the brand of crisps everyone was eating." He pretended to think for a second. "Doritos."

"They were Fritos, actu—" She cut herself off, shaking her head at him. "Uh-huh. I see what you did there."

Madden couldn't hide his grin. "Knew you remembered."

"Maybe I just have a head for details." Eve sniffed, smoothing her white athletic skirt with both hands. "Should we start with catch, then?"

"Catch sounds good. Let's hit the field."

They spent the next half hour teaching Lark and Landon the mechanics of throwing and catching. It was a good thing Madden had the foresight to bring softballs, instead of smaller, harder baseballs, because there were *a lot* of misses. At first. Lark got the hang of it first, opening her glove and moving it into position, doing a dance every time she trapped the ball without letting it drop. Landon took a while longer to start catching with some consistency, but once he did, his confidence tripled and he was smiling, already asking when they could play catch again.

"I have to leave early in the morning for New York." There was a mandatory practice tomorrow night, before they hit the road for a three-game stretch in Arizona. "But I'll come round again to play catch with you, don't worry."

"Me too?" Lark shouted, lobbing the ball to Eve.

"Of course," Madden said.

The twins traded a broad smile.

Eve smiled too, watching them, and god help Madden, there was a wound inside him that had been there so long, he'd forgotten it existed. The need to be a good big brother. To be the one who taught Paul and Sinead how to play sports. How to cook or even sneak out of the house successfully. He'd never gotten that chance because their father had quietly ordained him other. Not one of them. Until they'd all started to believe it.

The enthusiasm from the twins, the fact that they seemed to like being around him, sealed up that wound ever so slightly. Maybe . . . he'd get a second chance.

Madden was distracted from that hope by Eve, who fished a bat out of the bag and rested it on her shoulder at a jaunty angle. "Shall we show them what Aunt Eve can do?"

"Uh-oh." Madden warmed. "Go on, kids, run to the outfield and stay alert. She's a slugger."

"Don't inflate their expectations," Eve admonished him, taking a few practice swings. "My best friend is a D1 softball player. You pick up a few things."

"More than a few things if I recall."

"We'll see if I've still got it."

There was no way Madden was letting Eve out of his sight when she was being playful in a skirt and holding a bat. The image would probably be with him for years to come, the way she poked a stray hair back into her ponytail and tapped the bat against the insides of her sneakers, all while the kids dashed into the outfield giggling, Lark turning a cartwheel with the baseball glove still on her hand.

Eve's stance was perfect as he remembered.

God, was it perfect.

But Madden wasn't idiot enough to let an opportunity pass when one presented itself. That would be thumbing his nose at fate. As an Irishman, that was unacceptable.

"Needs a little work," Madden said, jogging from the mound to the batter's box. "Let me help you, love. Just a touch."

"What?" Eve looked down at her bent knees, genuinely perplexed. "What am I doing wrong?"

"Ah, loads."

"Really."

"Really." Madden dropped his mitt and slid up behind Eve, pressing his lap to her gorgeous arse, his arms extending around from his position behind her, gripping the bat right above her hold. "Nearly had it, but you want to be choked up to about here."

"Okay . . ."

Once she'd done as she was told, Madden dropped his left hand to her thigh, right where the white hem met her bare skin, squeezing, sliding a quartet of fingertips down to her knee, taking hold and adjusting it slightly. "Cheat this leg out a little more."

"Madden, the kids."

"They're doing cartwheels, love. Let me get a fucking fix."

"Okay."

He walked into her, drawing her back at the same time, his mouth breathing hard into the crook of her neck. "Beautiful woman. If we were alone, I'd make you walk the bases with your shirt and bra off. Then I'd put you just like this, just like this, and pump my cock where it belongs, that little skirt jacked up around your belly."

She whimpered. "We have to stop."

"I know. Okay." He kissed the back of her neck. "Your stance is perfect now."

It gratified him to hear the hitch in her breath. "Pretty sure it was before."

"Aye, but you won't catch me admitting it."

Eve laughed breathlessly as Madden strode back to the mound, measuring his breaths—in, out—until he got his need back under control. As much as was humanly possible when Eve Keller walked the earth, anyway.

"Pitch underhand," she reminded him, her cheeks flushed from more than the sun. "And go easy. I might be rusty."

"You? Never."

Proving him correct, she smacked his first pitch deep into centerfield, inspiring squeals of delight from the kids. And unabashed appreciation from Madden as she ran the bases, turning her own cartwheel into home plate and sending Lark into peals of laughter.

Watching the perfect moment play out, Madden had two burning questions.

One, how the hell was he going to leave her again in the morning?

And two, would she allow him to get close enough that he might have a shot of never having to leave her again?

Before Lark and Landon moved in, the phrase "screen time" wasn't a common one, at least not in Eve's vocabulary. Now those two words were a magical incantation uttered at the end of the night, after dinner and bathtime, the milkshake that brought the kids to the yard. All Eve had to do was hold up the iPad, the twins came running, and they did not move until their hour was up.

"Wow," Madden said, from his lean against the doorjamb of Lark and Landon's bedroom. "What do they watch on that thing. Cartoons?"

"Sometimes." Eve yawned on her way out of the room. "Mostly

they watch kids their own age opening mystery toys. It feels like a cult, but I need my free hour."

Following her down the hallway into the kitchen, Madden laughed under his breath. "I'm only surprised you don't use it more."

"It's tempting."

Speaking of tempting, Madden fell solidly into the category tonight. No, he *was* the category. Towering, attentive, and covered in the day's dust, he took up so much space in her kitchen. Depleted the air of oxygen, too, if her suddenly winded state was any indication, and yeah. He'd really shown up for her today. Turned out, accompanying her on errands, defending her honor, and giving the twins an unforgettable ditch day made him the most tempting of all, especially considering he'd driven over four hours to get her naked and didn't get what he wanted. Not a single complaint either.

Eve took a wineglass out of her cabinet, arching an eyebrow over her shoulder at Madden to wordlessly ask if he wanted some, but he shook his head no. She could feel his gaze climbing the backs of her thighs as she poured and then his hands were there, too, his mouth settling on her shoulder while he gripped her thighs, rubbing up and down roughly, robbing her of breath in an instant. The longer his touch traveled up and down her thighs, the more heat wandered south, making her wet, and when the path of his hands started to cheat a little higher, disturbing the hem of her white skirt, she had to set down her wine and hold the counter for balance.

"Madden."

"Yes?"

"I don't think I can. With the kids here? Not yet. I don't want them to hear something or feel weird about someone spending the night without me having a chance to explain."

"I get it," he said, moving her braid out of the way to kiss her neck, rake his open mouth over her ear. "Turn around and let me fuck your mouth awhile, at least, love."

"Okay," she breathed, knee deep in the kiss, before she'd fully turned around, Madden's body backing her into the cabinet, rattling them, his hands molding her hips like he was going to be tested on their exact shape. His palms rode up her belly and started to go higher, but he hesitated. "Don't worry, they're not moving until the hour is up," Eve said. "A nuclear bomb wouldn't budge them."

With a gruff rumble of hunger, his hands closed over her breasts and squeezed just the right amount, not hard, but not soft, while his tongue worked her mouth. Fucked it, just like he said he would, neither one of them wanting to come up for air, waiting until the very last second, breaking to replenish their lungs loudly, then colliding once more. Wreaking havoc on each other, Madden's growing stiffness a very real presence against Eve's belly. Remembering the length and weight of him in her mouth that morning, she pulsed in response, her body needing desperately to feel that strength from the inside.

"I want it so bad," she gasped, when they broke for air. "Oh my god. I want you. Why are you doing this to me?"

"I've kept my hands off you for years. This is what a breaking point looks like."

Her head fell back and he zoned in on her neck and throat, abrading her with his teeth, drugging suction that she could feel in her nipples and belly. Between her legs. "Maybe if we're really quiet . . ."

He attacked her mouth with a low moan, this giant, professional athlete who never got flustered suddenly a vibrating mass of muscle, his hands shaking where they scraped roughly against the valleys of her sides and up to her breasts, his mouth slanting and taking everything she had. "Eve," he said, pausing his assault, his warm breath pelting her mouth.

"Uh-huh," she managed, distracted by the thick swell of his pecs, which seemed to expand under her touch.

"I'm struggling," he said against her mouth.

"How?"

"I want our first time to be done right, the way you deserve." Madden pressed closer, letting her feel his erection. "I also want to ask you to walk me to my truck, so I can give it to you hard and fast in the parking lot, god help me."

Madden watched Eve's face as he said those words—and she held nothing back, so he had to be aware his idea turned her on.

She hid nothing. Not her yearning. Nor her trust in him.

"Yeah, I know you like that, love," he said thickly, reaching beneath her skirt to grip her pussy, muffling her gasp with his own lips. "This is gold to me, but I can treat it dirty too."

"Parking lot," she breathed, nodding. "Good."

They broke apart with an effort, Madden pacing to the other side of the kitchen with his hands on his head, while Eve straightened her clothes, running trembling fingers through her hair and attempting to regulate her voice. As soon as she was somewhat calm, she left the kitchen and went back down the hallway, stopping in the doorway of the twins' bedroom. "I'm just going to walk Madden to his truck. I'll be right back. Okay?"

Victims to the blue light, neither one of them responded, the high-pitched voice of their YouTube heroes echoing around the room.

Eve turned and crept back down the hallway. Was this bad? Was she being irresponsible? She probably wouldn't have the objectivity to be sure until tomorrow, because her body was in a state of high alert. Up ahead, Madden stood leaning against the front door with his arms crossed. Even from this distance, she could see the sweat beading his upper lip, the not-so-steady rise and fall of his chest. He claimed he'd been waiting years to get his hands on her and now that she'd let her need for him run free, without trying to lock it down or hide it, she could admit it was the same for her.

She'd waited so long. Too long.

This was what her breaking point looked like too.

When she reached Madden, she took her keys off the console, plus her phone, saying nothing as he opened the door and followed her out into the hallway. She locked the door behind them, paused to make sure she didn't hear any little footsteps, then moved toward the stairwell, followed by Madden. Something about him walking behind her, not saying a word, his energy raw and restless, was such a turn-on she could barely walk a straight line. At the glass front door of the building exit, she turned the handle, walking out into the light rain, the droplets doing nothing to cool the fever of her skin.

She'd only taken a few steps into the parking lot when Madden snagged her wrist from behind. "I'm parked on the other side."

"Okay."

Wild, absolutely wild, that they'd stopped their frantic make-out session a full five minutes earlier, but they might as well still be trapped in the midst of that frenetic kiss. One glance at Madden's reckless eyes and Eve could see it was like that for both of them. Seconds later, she was proven right when they turned the corner that made up the edge of the building, entering the far end of the parking lot.

Much like the parking lot of the club, pine trees lined the far end, behind them stood the building. The lights of some residences were on, some off. Only a few cars were parked on this side, because it was farthest from the entrance, but there was a rear driveway often used to enter the lot. It wasn't unreasonable to think someone could pull into the dark parking area while they reached for each other in the shadows of the building, but that didn't stop them. With the crickets chirping around them and soft rain blowing on the wind, Madden backed Eve against the side of the brick building, demanding consent from her mouth from above and she freely gave it, letting him in. Letting him take.

Begging him for what they both needed.

Or what she assumed she needed, anyway. A frantic quickie wouldn't be the drug of choice for most virgins, but she'd been exploring her body long enough to know what it wanted, what it could stand. That she probably hadn't been a virgin in the technical sense for a long time and, god, desperate, sweaty, rough . . . those were the facets of her fantasies that brought her to the brink.

"Hard and fast," she exhaled between sweeps of his tongue.

"You don't need to remind me what we decided," he rasped, his possessive hands finding her backside beneath her skirt, kneading her cheeks while looking her in the eye. "Are you on anything or do we need a condom?"

There was trust here. They didn't need to give details. "We don't need anything."

Lust rippled across his features, leaving them slack and starved. "Praise fuck. I just want to feel every part of you," he breathed, his right hand sneaking around her hip and coming up between her thighs, feeling and testing the juncture of her thighs like he owned her flesh. "Are these panties built in?"

"Yes."

He tore the swath of fabric with a determined twist of his fist. "Been wanting to do that all fucking day."

Before Eve could catch her breath from the panty rip heard around the Northeast, she was pinned between Madden and the building. Being around this man growing up, she had been too young to know what sensuality looked like, but she'd never miss the signs again. Not with this man. Madden was predatory in a way that was all green flags, because she encouraged it, and he pounced on whatever she offered, her mouth, her neck, the V of her thighs when she wrapped her legs around his hips and he surged between, exhaling a curse while he humped her into the brick once, twice.

"Hard and fast," he whispered in her ear. "Are you sure, love?"

"I'm probably going to die if you don't."

"Next time, nothing short of an act of God is keeping me from licking your pussy. Do you understand me, Eve?"

This was unbelievable. She could actually feel the gathering of her own wetness and he wanted to ask important questions? "Please. I don't know. Please."

Keeping their foreheads pressed, eyes locked, Madden reached between them and unzipped his jeans, blocking a grunt with his teeth when he brought his shaft out in a fist and drew the head slowly, so slowly through her wet flesh. "You have to be our lookout, love," he said, raking his mouth side to side over the top of hers without kissing it, like she whimpered for him to do. "I'm going to be too distracted with pounding you to know if anyone is coming."

Eve's flesh drew in so hard on itself, she almost cried out in pain.

She needed to close her legs and bear down to avoid the awful-wonderful pulsations, but his hips were in the way and she was damp, so damp, so warm.

Having sex in the open, nothing but the drape of the eave's shadows to hide them, was illicit, but . . . it was also care, wasn't it? Madden was fulfilling her fantasy, as promised. He'd listened and taken her seriously, and now, now he was giving her in spades what she'd needed for so long. Giving her the illusion she'd dreamed about so much better than she could have instructed him or hoped for.

"I d-don't think anyone is coming," she stammered, taking hold of his broad shoulders, her hips moving in a slow circle on top of the shaft he held right there, right there against her entrance, ready to fill her for the first time.

Eve's first time, period, not that anyone needed to know that but her.

"Madden."

"I know, love. I'm trying to calm down so I don't come from the first feel of you."

"Oh." That admission caused lust to bite at her nipples, turning them into hard little aches, and because she felt so sexy, she used one hand to jerk down her neckline, along with the cups of her bra, partially freeing the top half of her breasts and her pointed nipples—and staring at them with famished eyes, he pumped the full length of himself inside her with a strangled yell, holding so deep she felt him everywhere, his body keeping her flat against the brick wall while he panted shallowly into her neck.

Wow.

Her fantasies . . . and her toys . . . hadn't done this feeling justice. Madden's body was inside her body. His hands were clutching her ass cheeks, the hair of his thighs tickling the insides of her knees. The cords of his stomach were in a rough flex against her belly, and most importantly, *his body was inside her body.* The intimacy of that was so welcome, so perfect, Eve didn't mind the breathless stretch of flesh, the slight bit of pain that faded more with every second that passed, his big body sandwiching her between it and the wall.

"Eve," he said through his teeth. "Didn't I . . . get you wet enough?"

She was too busy marveling to understand the question. "What?"

"You're very fucking tight, love." He moved his hips and shuddered. "Fuck. Won't it hurt you if I go hard?"

"No," Eve said, kissing his chin, rocking forward and twisting her hips a little, causing his breath to escape in a hiss, a burn of discomfort rising and ebbing just as quickly, leaving nothing but the full, blessed pressure behind. "Don't forget fast."

"Eve . . ." He studied her face with a drawn brow, as if some intuition demanded he question her further, but his body got the better of him and looking at her face, groaning at the shake of her half-exposed breasts, he started to thrust. Small, powerful punches at first that made her teeth clack together, the pace picking up gradually, his length pulling farther out, farther out, so he could use his grip on her butt to hold her still to receive his thick drives. The full, hot occupying of her sex.

Madden looked her in the eye and fucked her hard up against the building, in full view of the parking lot or anyone who might drive up, walk by, or look out their window. The possibility of being seen made Eve's skin prick with excitement, tension budding and tugging below her belly button; his intense focus on her face coupled with the visible thinning of his control made her feel lusted after. The strength of him could easily overpower her and yet, in these moments, Madden was nothing without the warm haven between her legs. He couldn't survive without the pleasure she gave, her thighs spread almost lewdly, breasts bouncing in time to his hip movements.

He might be dominating her, her legs vulnerable and flopping on either side of his hips with every full-body surge, but Eve was exultant. A queen and a sexual object, all at once.

"Does that feel good—" Eve started.

"Don't talk," he choked out. "Don't say a word."

"Why?"

"I can't handle your voice on top of this cunt." Madden growled into a series of smacking pumps, his lack of restraint so riveting, so animal in nature, she didn't want to blink and miss anything. "You're going to get yourself kidnapped straight to New York with this thing."

"By who?"

"*Me*, Eve. Me. Don't you feel how fucking hard I am?" His right hand flew up from her backside to frame her jaw firmly, their panting breaths mingling between them. "Jesus, I'm afraid to ask, but you've never been with a man like this before, have you? Tell me the truth."

Her mouth dried up. "Why, does it matter?"

"Eve," he growled, his tone unrelenting.

"Fine," she whispered, the hand on her jaw giving her no choice but to look him in the eye when she really wanted to bury her face somewhere and hide, the vulnerability of the moment so heavy, it thickened her voice like cake batter. "I never trusted anyone but you. Never felt safe with anyone but you. I had t-to wait for you."

He made a sound she'd never heard before. A sound she'd never heard anyone make and one she couldn't describe. And she'd never seen this man shed a single tear, not even in the hardest moments during his illness, so the layer of moisture in his eyes felt like the world was ending. "Eve, I—"

The rumble of an engine to Eve's left was followed by a dual approach of headlights, approximately fifty yards away. An old car rolled into the parking lot playing "Rock Lobster" by the B-52s, the sound muffled by their rolled-up windows, and Madden cursed darkly, pressing her tighter to the wall, which sank his impossible hardness as deep as it could go, and baring his teeth over the top of her sobbing mouth. "Don't move."

"I can't."

"Am I hurting you?"

"The opposite," she gasped.

He still had that mysterious sheen in his eyes, but he seemed distracted by whatever had caused the show of emotion. Distracted by the connection of their bodies, which he ground together now, his head falling back on a shaky exhale, Eve jolting at the new, forced angle that kept them hidden from the parking lot, the thickest part of his arousal rubbing relentlessly against her clit.

A car door slammed on the other side of the building.

Two loud voices carried on the wind, making the new arrivals seem close. So close.

"Don't stop," she whimpered.

"There's a good girl," he groaned, his breath hot on the crown of her head. "There's my beautiful wife telling me how to make her come."

"Oh god."

The voices got louder.

He fucked her harder.

Stamped his mouth over hers, just in time. Just in time for a concrete wave to mow her down, winding up her insides like barbed wire around a fist, then freeing her, letting her whip out into an open, unfamiliar space while this man, this man who made her weightless, held his drive deep between her legs, his entire rock-hard frame shaking like a leaf while she whined and kicked through the orgasm, the door slamming at the front of the building, the voices cutting off, and no sooner did that happen than he was plowing into her two, three, four final times and erupting, letting loose a sensation she couldn't have imagined accurately if she tried. The white-hot flood, the sudden full-body tremble of him, her own sense of fulfillment watching Madden take his own.

"Love, my love, my love," he muttered into her neck, rolling his face around, his arms banding around her to hold her tight to his body, like he'd never let her go. Ever.

That should have been a sign of what was to follow.

They slowly came down from the high peak of their own creation, the breaths slowing over the course of a couple of minutes, the sprinkling rain cooling their feverish skin. His mouth lingered in places like her cheek, her temple, pressing hard kisses while his hands moved, fixing their clothing. Stroking her bottom and apologizing in between presses of his lips for being rough, for the bruises she might have in the morning.

His movements were sweet and caring. So much so that Eve wasn't expecting the look of pure determination blanketing Madden's features when he finally stepped away from her, tucking a stray piece of hair behind her ear.

"Deal's off, Eve. I want more than six months."

Those words didn't sink in until after he twined their fingers together and started walking, five steps, ten . . . all the way to the front of the building, where he kissed her hand and let it go.

"Good night." He leaned down and slanted their mouths together, just one, thoroughly devastating kiss that could have developed into another trip to the shadows if he hadn't stopped, moving slowly, reluctantly out of her reach. "I'll be back soon."

His earlier words came back to her in a rush.

Deal's off.

I want more than six months.

"Wait," she called, panic burdening her chest. "Deal's on!"

"*Off*," he roared back, slamming the driver's-side door shut, starting the engine, and driving off into the night while she stood with her jaw on the worn welcome mat.

What the hell had just happened?

CHAPTER TWENTY-THREE

Holy shit, this was really happening.

Eve had expected delays, red tape, asses to kiss. But somehow, the town inspector had not only approved the rear yard of the club for a designated outdoor space, but their contractor's plans had been approved.

And thus, they'd broken ground on the Jam Jar.

Did going pedal to the metal on the addition scare her? Yes. But she didn't have time to debate the pros and cons when she was digging her way out of debt. Although, with the influx of customers, thanks to Full Bush Rhonda and her influential grandkids, the Gilded Garden was edging its way out of the red. Eve's gut told her to trust Veda's vision and that's what she was doing.

Some might call her leap of faith shortsighted, but she'd been a girl with a dream and a dollar once too. It wasn't a coincidence she and Veda had found each other.

Eve shifted her travel mug of coffee in her hands, trying to swallow the sense of being invaded. Not easy when a construction crew was leaving a path of dusty footprints on the pristine oak floors of the Gilded Garden. Lumber made itself to the rear acre balanced on hefty shoulders, a table saw whirred outside beneath the low canopy of trees. An expansive plot had been dug and was being reinforced with steel rebar and mesh, awaiting a concrete pour—the spot that would one day be a patio, while other members of the crew worked on the stage.

Veda waved at her from across the chaos, but her usual smile was missing, which appeared to be due to her boyfriend. He'd traded his vintage tough guy look for paint-splattered jeans and the company T-shirt, though he still had a bandanna hanging from his back pocket. He made an irritated gesture at Veda and she closed her eyes, appearing to take a deep breath, before walking away to join Eve.

"Hey," Eve greeted her.

"Hey," Veda said, forcing a chipper tone. "Crazy how this was just an idea in my pretty little head and now it's a construction zone, right?"

"I agree that it's crazy." When normally Veda would have laughed or made a self-deprecating joke, she slumped a little, instead, so Eve rushed to qualify her statement. "Crazy in a good way, I mean."

"Yeah," Veda said with a nod, obviously trying to sound bright. "Speaking of ideas, I had another one I wanted to run past you. The GoFundMe is still bringing in donations—we're nearly at forty thousand. But I thought . . . what about a live fundraiser? You don't open the club on Sundays. We could do it then, so it wouldn't interfere with the schedule."

Eve cataloged Veda's excited energy and wanted to be supportive, but her mind immediately conjured up an auction or a bake sale. "Hmm. What are you picturing?"

Veda framed the stage with her raised hands. "The All-Nighters would play a gig, but we'd also have burlesque performances in between sets. Sort of a way to fuse the two—music and performance art. Merged into one venue. We'll ticket the event and put a portion of it toward the reno. You could use a chunk toward the bills."

She shrugged. "I think people will be more inclined to donate if they can see the renovation in progress. Roped off, of course. What do you think?"

"I think you're brilliant, actually," Eve said honestly, staring at the stage and envisioning a whole new scene. Rockabilly burlesque. Somehow the marriage of the two was the perfect fit she'd never considered until now. "I'll schedule staff and dancers for Sunday, if you can handle the band."

"Consider it handled," Veda said, rocking back on her heels.

"Now." Eve hooked an arm through Veda's and tugged her into the unlit lounge, out of earshot of any construction workers. "Come on. Let's go sit in my office, so you can tell me what's been bothering you."

Veda blew a raspberry. "You already know it's a man. It's always a man." They wound their way through the seating area to the backstage space, continuing through the door of Eve's office where she flipped on her brass desk lamp. "I'm really starting to think they're not worth the hassle, honestly. Mood killers, every last one of them."

For the millionth time since he'd left her in a confused, gelatinous state in the building parking lot, Eve thought of Madden. He definitely hadn't killed the mood *that* night. No, he'd read her mood and matched it. He'd . . . oh my god. Given her the peak sexual experience of her life. Granted, she'd been a virgin, but she'd grown up in a strip club and currently owned a bar, which meant she heard *a lot* of gripes. Women lamenting their lack of a spark in the bedroom with their partners or disappointed with hookups that had seemed so promising. She was wise enough to know it was rare for a woman to be so satisfied she walked around in a zombie state, the way Eve had been doing for the past week.

Deal's off, Eve. I want more than six months.

Some enlightened part of her wanted to scoff at Madden's parting shot. She'd waited for Madden to be her first time and now he was placing too much importance on a hymen. How silly.

But . . . it wasn't silly.

Because waiting for Madden had been about a lot more than "saving herself" or "staying pure." No, she didn't buy into the belief that a woman had more value if she was untouched. In Eve's case, however, the years of waiting were partly out of fear. The number of times in her life she'd been objectified and spoken to with disrespect had led to a wariness of men. Of their motives. What would happen if she put her faith in one of them?

Madden, though.

In his presence, she was free of fear. Of doubt.

Eve felt his protection and respect and love. And she didn't want to settle for less.

So she'd waited.

"Okay, woman, you're zoning out on me again," Veda said, waving a hand in front of Eve's eyes. "Please stop. It's actually terrifying the way you're suddenly staring at something in the corner." Veda looked over her shoulder and whimpered. "Is it a ghost?"

"Not a ghost." Eve waved a hand. "Sorry."

"Don't be sorry; tell me why you're staring into the ether."

"I can't."

"Sometimes you take the whole mysterious vibe a little far, you know that?" Veda slumped back in her chair, crossing her legs unceremoniously. "Fine, I'll start. Smith is cockblocking me. Vocally speaking."

Eve sipped her coffee. "I need you to elaborate."

Veda swallowed, her fingertip tracing a circle pattern onto her knee. "The All-Nighters are recording a demo and he won't let me sing on any of the tracks. Nothing but backing vocals, anyway." That finger was now stabbing into her knee. "It's a battle every time I want to add one of my original songs to the set list. Or do anything but showcase *him*. I get what he means about the band sticking with its original vision, but . . . I don't know. I'm just starting to feel more and more stifled. Creatively."

Dump him.

That's what Eve wanted to say.

Eve had heard Veda sing—she had pipes for days. If this guy was trying to prevent an audience from hearing that, he was afraid of being outshone. Period. That advice might come on a little too strong, however, especially from Eve, who'd never even attended one of their shows, so she took a roundabout tack.

"What do the other band members say?"

"The band was already formed when I joined. They're all childhood friends, you know? All dudes. They're not going to vote against him."

Eve hummed. "What is the response when you sing at shows?"

"People like it, I think." Veda shrugged. "Maybe they're just being nice."

"They're not just being nice," Eve said firmly. "You're talented, Veda."

The other girl sniffed. "I'm no Full Bush Rhonda."

"Who is?" Eve deadpanned. "Look, keep fighting to be on the demo. Keep fighting to sing at shows. If it's important to you, it should be important to him. Period."

"Wow. That's so real," Veda said, sounding kind of hollow. "Sort of like Madden marrying you so the kids can have health insurance?"

Eve thought of Madden handing her the framed sketch outside the courthouse. How he'd spent hours cooking with the
kids, teaching them how to play catch. "Yes . . . like that," she
managed.

Veda leaned forward. "I knew you were acting like a stoned
ghost hunter over the Irish dude. The second I brought him up,
you got that faraway look in your eye."

"No, I didn't," Eve scoffed, not used to being called out. "I'm
thinking about the construction. I'm running numbers and—"

"Stop lying." Veda slapped a hand off the edge of the desk.
"He banged your brains out, didn't he?"

Eve rolled her eyes, perched her mouth on the spout of her
coffee mug. "Veda."

"Please. I'm losing faith in men. Tell me one of them knows
what he's doing. Tell me one of them isn't just an entitled little
bitch that expects everything and gives nothing."

"Technically, I'm your boss and that makes this conversation
inappropriate."

"Then temporarily fire me, bro. Give me the dick digest."

Eve was really good at keeping secrets, especially her own, but
this odd euphoric feeling had been held prisoner inside her for a
week and it weirdly wanted out. And yeah, maybe she did want
to verify Madden was one of the good apples and perhaps inspire
Veda to demand better from Smith in the process. "Fine, you're
fired. Temporarily." Eve put her hands over her eyes. "He . . .
um. He listens. He pays attention."

"Stop. I'm already about to come."

"Like, extremely close attention. When we were . . . *you know.*
I swear I couldn't breathe or blink or move a pinkie finger without him . . . reacting to balance me. Like his instincts are tied to

mine. I don't know how he did it, but he made me feel dominated and free at the same time. I couldn't feel my legs afterward. I still can barely feel them."

"Wow," Veda whispered.

"Yeah."

"I thought you were just going to tell me he has a big one."

Eve drew the line at detailing Madden's physical attributes, but she gave Veda a telling look. The other girl crossed herself in response.

"Next you're going to tell me he's obsessed with going down on you." Veda laughed. Eve kept her expression neutral. No need to rub in her good fortune. Even if it was temporary. "Do you worry about him being in New York?" Veda then asked after a few moments, her expression genuinely curious. "I mean, in terms of women and how they tend to gravitate toward pro athletes. Do you worry about that?"

The thought hadn't even crossed Eve's mind. There was no rule against him pursuing other women during their six-month arrangement. She simply knew Madden wouldn't. "No. I'm not worried." She narrowed her eyes. "Do you worry about Smith?"

"Are you serious? He's a musician. I worry about him meeting other women when he's sleeping." Veda sighed. "It's slim pickins out here, bro. Not all of us can lock down a stacked athlete. Just you and my sister."

"Oh." Now, this was interesting. Not wanting to spook Veda, Eve pretended to scan some of the paperwork on her desk. "Have Elton and your sister seen each other again since we introduced them?"

"Yeah, I think once. And they've been texting." Veda's leg started to bounce up and down, somewhat violently. "Like, there is literally no better match, right?"

Eve gave a noncommittal sound.

"She wants to settle down. Yesterday." A long swallow shifted Veda's throat. "Just like Elton, right?"

There was no way around that truth. "Yeah. For as long as I can remember, he's been a serial monogamist. His fatal flaw is getting too committed too fast. It's led to him getting his heart broken more than once."

Veda hadn't blinked in a full minute. "Really?" After an extended silence, she shook herself. "Yikes."

"You're not the settling-down type?"

"No," Veda said vehemently. "Well. I mean, eventually. But that's not my *dream*."

"What is your dream?"

No one had ever asked her about her aspirations—Eve could see that truth in the way Veda's chin jerked up at the question, eyes vulnerable. "I want to perform, yeah, but . . . in my own place, like this one. I want to be the place musicians come to be discovered."

Eve processed that, her affinity for Veda growing. "I think that says a lot about you. That you want to put out a stepladder for other people, instead of climbing it yourself and leaving everyone else behind on the floor."

Veda tried to suppress the pleasure that flooded her features but didn't quite succeed. "Thanks." She exhaled and changed the subject back to Eve. "Madden is obsessed with going down on you, isn't he?"

Thankfully, Eve's phone rang, saving her from having to answer the question.

"Oh." She held up her phone so Eve could see Elton's name scrolling sideways across her screen. "Speak of the devil."

Veda's leg finally stopped jiggling.

"Hey, Elton," Eve answered. "What's up?"

"Hey." He was silent for a moment. "Is that construction I hear in the background? You're really doing this, aren't you?"

"Yup. Me and Veda."

He took two breaths. "Yeah. How is she and toothpick boy?"

"Good with lumber, actually," Eve said smoothly. "Do you think he makes his own toothpicks?"

"Do I care?" He coughed. "Veda. She's . . . good, though?"

"Uh-huh."

Veda frowned, obviously confused by her inability to hear Elton's side of the conversation. "What did you call about?" Eve asked.

"Right. Me, Robbie, and Sky are going to the Yankees game on Saturday to watch Madden. I sweet-talked him into getting us into one of the team boxes." He paused. "Mad sent extra tickets. I'm guessing in the hopes you'd come."

That casual speculation made breathing harder, but Eve kept it together while looking at the calendar on her desk. "You want me to go . . . three nights from now?" Yeah, wow. That excited leap in Eve's chest told her she really wanted to attend, but leaving town was impossible. Not with the construction just getting underway and two kids at home. Impossible. "I can't. The kids . . ."

"I can babysit," Veda said, sitting up straighter. "Whatever it is, go."

"Veda is there?" Elton fairly shouted in her ear.

"Yes, she's volunteering to babysit, but—"

"No, my parents will babysit. Sorry. I left that part out—I asked them before I even called you." He paused. "Actually, one of the tickets was going to be for Alexis, but she can't go. Does, uh . . ." He coughed. "Does Veda want to take the ticket?"

It took every last one of Eve's facial muscles to hide her smile. "Do you want to go to a baseball game on Saturday?" she asked Veda, lowering the phone. "That would put it right before the fundraiser. Might be too much?"

"Me? He wants *me* to go?"

Leave it to Veda to skip over the practicalities, like sleep and time management.

"Put me on speakerphone," Elton demanded. Eve did as he asked, only wishing she had a tub of popcorn for the show. "What do you mean, *'me?'*?" he asked Veda, sounding extra-grouchy. "You've never been to a baseball game before?"

"And that surprises you? What would I even wear?"

"I'll bring you something."

"Something of *yours*?"

"Yeah."

"Fine." What an interesting shade of pink Veda's face had turned. "I-I mean, if Eve is going and everything. I guess I'll go too."

Part of Eve saw this impromptu trip for the bad idea it was. Going to his game to surprise Madden was a total wife thing, wasn't it? She should stay in Cumberland, distract herself with the last-minute fundraiser and Jam Jar expansion, take care of the kids and wait for their six-month verbal contract to end—whether Madden wanted it to or not.

On the other hand, she'd be there with friends. Childhood friends.

Skylar.

Oh lord, if she saw her best friend, she'd have no choice but to finally come clean about being married to Madden. Yes, Skylar had a new, serious boyfriend, but after protecting Skylar's feelings for so long, Eve couldn't help but feel a tiny bit like a traitor.

But damn, she really wanted to watch Madden play. To celebrate him at the pinnacle of his career. Even at the price of a difficult conversation.

"Eve," Elton said.

"What?"

"You're coming. We'll meet you at the entrance to the VIP suites."

"Oh. VIP?" Eve reared back a little, exchanging a wide-eyed glance with Veda. "Fancy."

Elton chuckled. "You're married to a Yankee. Start acting like it."

Eve hung up, shooting Veda a wince. "Is it irresponsible to go live it up in a VIP suite when I'm barely covering the club's expenses this month?"

"Pshh." Veda waved off her concern. "We've got one fundraiser kicking ass and a second one planned for Sunday. Plus, Full Bush Rhonda is performing tonight. Those bills are as good as paid."

"Right . . ." Eve's phone rang again. Seeing it was Rhonda calling, she tapped the option for speakerphone. "Hey, Rhonda. What's up?"

"Eve," said Rhonda, her tone the verbal equivalent of wringing her hands, "I don't think I'll make it in tonight. We can't find my new puppy. We're looking everywhere."

Eve and Veda exchanged a doomsday look, Veda whipping out her phone to check the time. *She's onstage in five hours*, she mouthed to Eve. "Oh no. Um . . ." Eve could bring in one of the new hires, but they all lived a good distance away and many of them had second and even third jobs. It would be a long shot and they wouldn't bring in the same crowd. There was only one option—find the dog. "Rhonda, how about Veda and I grab the kids from school and come help you look?"

"Oh! That would be amazing."

"Send me your address."

RHONDA "FULL BUSH" Nieves was, apparently, loaded.

From the sidewalk, Eve and Veda stared up the grand, sloping lawn currently being showered by the sprinkler system, toward the affluent colonial lit from within. The setting sun cast a golden glow on the lush surrounding gardens, making the home resemble a New England postcard.

"My car is going to get towed in this neighborhood," Eve said with a sigh.

"Do you think she'll adopt me?" Veda let out a low whistle. "Imagine the basement. A musician's dream, for sure."

Their jaws unhinged when Rhonda opened the front door in a cashmere leisure set and waved, signaling she'd join them in a moment. As they watched, a man who resembled a young Antonio Banderas came up behind Rhonda and wrapped her in a bear hug from behind, saying something into her neck that made her giggle.

"Maybe this is my sign to stop waxing," Veda remarked, sounding pensive.

Eve bit back a snort.

Rhonda and the man who appeared to be her significant other joined them on the sidewalk, Rhonda kissing Veda's and Eve's cheeks, sending a pinkie wave to the twins. Her canoodling partner gave the group a slow, debonair wink as he passed, sauntering a few yards away to light up a thin cigar.

"Thank you so much for coming to help us, ladies," Rhonda said. "This is my boyfriend, Sebastian."

Sebastian winked at them a second time but said nothing, continuing his slow saunter down the sidewalk, wreathed in pungent smoke.

"He doesn't talk much," Rhonda said, smiling. "I find silence an admirable quality in a man. Tell me I'm pretty or shut up."

"What is your life?" Veda demanded to know, stomping a foot.

"No, really," Eve jumped in. "Satisfy our curiosity. You obviously don't need a side hustle, Rhonda. What are you doing working for me?"

"Staying young." She shrugged a sensual shoulder. "Keeping everyone guessing. Reminding myself to love this body, even as it ages. And at the end of the day, I just like people cheering for me. Is that a crime?" Rhonda squinted up at her lavish house. "The last time I danced, I was a single mother putting myself through night school. Landed a job with a tech company after I graduated. That job was boring as hell, but it put my kids through college. Now I get to stay home and play dress-up with my dogs. And Sebastian."

Eve and Veda laughed.

"Speaking of your dog, do you think we should split up into two search parties?" Eve asked. "You two head in one direction, me and the kids will head in the other?"

"When do we get to see the dog?" Landon called from the back seat.

"I'm petting it first," Lark sang.

"Aunt Eve said we're petting it at the same time," her brother said through his teeth.

"That's right, Landon." Eve turned toward the kids and vigorously rubbed her hands together. "We have to find the puppy first, though, don't we? Are you guys ready for an adventure?"

"*Yeah!*"

"*Yes!*"

"I knew I could count on you two." Eve crouched down to put them at eye level. "And you know, when we find this dog, we have to celebrate. What do I always say about celebrations?"

"They suck unless there's ice cream."

"That's right." Eve turned to face Rhonda. "What is the dog's name, so we can call for him?"

Rhonda hesitated, her attention straying to the twins. "She's a teacup poodle, you see . . ."

Eve raised an eyebrow.

"Her name is Pocket Rocket."

"Of course it is," Eve deadpanned.

Veda doubled over laughing.

And so, minutes later, Eve, Landon, and Lark walked through the prestigious Thornwood Estates of Lincoln, Rhode Island, calling for Pocket Rocket.

"This is definitely going to be my show-and-tell on Monday," Lark announced.

"Great," Eve said, shining the flashlight on her phone beneath a parked Mercedes. "Can't wait for that phone call."

"What phone call?"

"The one from your teacher to tell me how well you're doing." Being the only adult in on the truth made her miss Madden. A lot. She'd only had one single day of him helping with the kids and already, his absence was so much more . . . profound. *He would have known exactly where to look for this dog.* He'd have been so casually confident helping them in the search, answering the kids' questions without having to overthink.

He'd be holding Eve's hand.

Who knew she'd ever miss having her hand held so badly?

Madden's steadying touch would reassure her right now, when she felt kind of . . . wobbly. Why did she have two kids out in the dark looking for a dog named for a portable vibrator? Didn't children need more stability than this?

She had to be doing this wrong.

"Aunt Eve?"

"Yeah, Lark?"

The little girl stopped to perform a spin. "Can we do this every day?"

"Oh, um . . ." Eve glanced down at the twins, warmth spreading in her chest at the identical grins staring back up at her. "I don't know if we want the dog to get lost every day, right? We want him to stay inside where it's safe."

"But this is fun!"

"Dog hunt!" Landon growled. "You make everything fun, Aunt Eve."

A boulder hit her in the chest. "Really?" She shook herself. God, that sounded needy. "I mean, yeah. It is fun. It's fun because we're together, right?"

The twins smiled at each other. It was only fleeting.

But it made Eve feel like she was doing something right.

An urge to text Madden rose up swiftly, but she didn't have a chance to follow through because when they came upon the next car, also a Mercedes, they stopped in their tracks at the faint sound of yelping.

Lark and Landon gasped. Then they looked at Eve for guidance.

Okay. Maybe I've got this aunt/guardian thing handled. As well as I can.

Eve got down on her knees and shined her flashlight beneath the car. "Pocket Rocket?" she said, hoping the owner of the closest house wasn't listening. "Pocket Rocket, your rescue team has arrived."

The smallest dog Eve had ever seen came scuttling out, shaking its one-inch tail and snarfing, his little nails clicking happily on the ground.

"Can we get a dog?"

"No. But we can get ice cream."

Chants of *Pocket Rocket* echoed down the manicured block, slowly transitioning into the twins in a barking competition. With the tiny pup cradled to her chest, all Eve heard were two happy voices and the beginning of a feeling.

Contentment.

Temporary, sure.

The kids weren't hers to keep forever.

Neither was Madden.

But the feeling exceeded her expectations.

Made her want to dream about forever. *Just* dream.

CHAPTER TWENTY-FOUR

Madden brought the chest guard down over his head, shifting it into place. His helmet went on next. Leg guards. Forty-five minutes to game time and he needed to be on the field, warming up. Most of his teammates were in the tunnel now, although some of them lingered behind him in the locker room, including Ruiz, today's pitcher and the motherfucker responsible for the black eye that had finally returned to normal.

Without Ruiz on the field, Madden had no reason to be out there himself. Hard to warm up as a catcher without someone to throw the ball.

Glancing back over his shoulder, Madden noted the pitcher didn't seem inclined to budge any time soon, lest he lose his staring contest with the floor. Madden opened his mouth to ask the veteran if he was all right, but the man's forbidding energy had him closing it again, reaching for his phone to kill a few minutes while the pitcher got his head together.

Kill time.

Right.

He went straight for his Eve folder. Pictures of his wife. Anything to remind him why he was sore and exhausted and returning to this hellhole of a locker room, day in and day out. With their losses mounting and the press calling for a restructuring of the coaching staff, morale was at an all-time low. There was none of the camaraderie and jokes Madden was used to in the locker room setting. Just a lot of bitching and mouthing off.

Before he could swipe to his Eve folder, a text popped up from Elton.

Surprise, it read. With a picture attached.

Madden tapped immediately, his heart knocking loudly against his ribs at the photo displayed on his screen. Elton was holding up the phone, taking a group selfie that included him, Robbie, Skylar, Veda. And Eve.

Eve was there. At his game.

Madden fumbled the phone, the device bouncing off the locker to the ground and skidding a couple of feet. "Fuck."

"That bodes well for the game," Ruiz drawled.

"Throw the ball well enough and I'll bloody catch it."

Ruiz ignored the jab for once, pointing to the phone, which was still on the floor with the selfie on display. "Who is that?"

"Some friends. They're in one of the boxes," Madden grumbled, crouching down to scoop up the device. "My wife is there too," he tacked on, for some reason. Maybe he just loved saying *my wife* in his head and couldn't stop himself from seizing the opportunity to say it out loud too. This man wasn't going to give a shite and he'd repeat it to no one, because Ruiz had proven to be nothing more than a narcissist who thought the entire world revolved around him.

"You're married?"

Madden did a surprised double take. "Yes, but it's . . . complicated. I'd rather not—"

"Guys, did you know Donahue was married?"

"Nah," responded an unseen teammate.

A couple of locker slams. "Where you been hiding her?"

"I'm not hiding her." On the other side of the locker room,

a couple of official Yankee reporters lingered, comparing notes. They didn't seem to be paying attention to the conversation, thankfully, but that could easily change. "Would you mind keeping it down?"

"You don't want people to know you're married?"

Now one of the reporters' heads popped up, splitting his interest between Madden and Ruiz, giving Madden no choice but to take a spot on the bench beside Ruiz. "I'd rather keep my personal life to myself," Madden said in a low voice. "That's all."

"Don't worry, man. No one gives a shit about catchers."

"Thanks."

Ruiz sighed. "Ah, I'm only fucking with you."

"It's becoming a pattern."

"Well. You're an easy target. It's nice to be able to hit a target these days, you know? Any fucking target." Ruiz tapped the tip of his glove against the inside of his knee. "Starts used to be so easy. I knew what was expected of me and I executed. My ERA was two my second year in the league. *Two.* Soon as it started to slip, everyone around me lost faith." He shook his head. "I had no idea my personal faith was so tied up in theirs. Can't even find it anymore. Can't even find the fucking point of this."

Sure, Ruiz was talking about himself. Not exactly shocking. But he'd never gone this long without blaming someone else for his performance and that was worth noting. Normally, Madden would walk away now. It wasn't his place to counsel anyone. What could he possibly offer by way of wisdom? He didn't feel like keeping quiet anymore, though. Didn't feel like blending into the scenery. Maybe . . . he had something of value to offer here. More constructive than calling Ruiz an overpriced crybaby this time.

"To be fair, your whole life, you're working toward being a

professional. Then it's about winning championships. Leaving a legacy behind. But once you've secured that, once they've put that crown on your head, some of that drive is . . . diminished."

"Good talk." Ruiz wiped away a fake tear. "I'm feeling so inspired."

Madden sighed, but he didn't let the sarcasm deter him. "Why did you play? In the beginning."

"What else? The promise of greatness."

"You've achieved greatness now," Madden said. "Let's say you allow yourself to stop chasing that. What else is there?"

"Nothing." Ruiz opened his mouth, closed it, looking at Madden curiously for the first time. "Why do you catch?"

Madden hesitated, never having voiced the truth out loud. "The goal at first was to be accepted in a new place, to blend in with new people. To observe from behind the mask. Although I've resented the sport for a long time for those exact reasons. The mask kept me quiet. Hidden. Like I was . . ."

"Growing up," Ruiz finished for him, with an astute squint.

Madden nodded in affirmation, staring straight ahead. "Anyway, now a lot of this is for her. The sport gave me something to offer her and . . . I guess that broke up the resentment. More and more, I'm seeing baseball with fresh eyes."

"You're talking about your wife."

My wife. "Yes."

The veteran sighed. "That's admirable, man, but, dude, playing the game has to be for you too. You have to want to win. Guess we're both a little lost."

"I'm finding my way, slowly but surely." Madden observed the pitcher in his periphery. "Do you want to win?"

"Yeah. But . . . I don't *need* to win. It's not do or die anymore.

I'm too . . ." He searched for the right word. "*Comfortable. I think that's the problem.*"

"You're comfortable being a has-been."

"*Easy*, Irish," Ruiz said. "Words hurt."

"Sorry." Madden's lips jumped. "Who do you think about when you're on the mound? Who do you want to see first after a win?"

"Haven't you heard a word I said? I'm playing for *me*."

Madden shrugged. "Then go out there and imagine twenty-year-old Franklin Ruiz is watching you from behind home plate. Play for him." He was surprised to see Ruiz set his jaw as he considered Madden's words, the light of competition filtering back into his eyes. "Within reason, Ruiz. You've got a whole team to consider too."

Someone came into the locker room and gave a two-minute warning before they took their field, prompting Ruiz to stand. "Is that your way of telling me to stop going rogue on the mound and start listening to your fucking pitch calls?"

Madden didn't even blink. "Yes."

They shared their first laugh.

"Fine. Let's do it your way today, Irish."

"It's about goddamn time."

EVE DIDN'T EXPECT the immense pride that inchwormed its way into her chest watching Madden assume his position behind home plate. This was the big show. She'd put his ascension to MLB in the Huge Deal category. She'd known he'd reached the pinnacle of his career, but to see it in real life? To watch his face captured fleetingly on the giant screen, his hat backward—hot—that hand she knew so well clutching the catcher's mask to pull it down over his face . . . she could barely breathe around her pride in him.

Every person in the stands was occupied, organ music pumped through the loudspeaker, interspersed with the announcer's voice. Men sold beer in the aisles, little kids sat in the crowd with gloves on their hands. This was entertainment. The highest level of baseball. And it was so very far from Cumberland. From what Eve knew.

"I'm already bored," announced Robbie, Skylar's professional hockey player boyfriend, proceeding to be shoved simultaneously by Skylar and Elton. "I'm kidding!" he said, laughing. "How could I be bored with all this free food around?"

The hulking redhead wasn't joking. Eve had already eaten a shrimp cocktail, two filet mignon steak skewers with fingerling potatoes, and a mini carrot cake. Now she stood by the giant wall of glass overlooking the field with a flute of champagne in her hand, the air-conditioning making her wish she'd brought a sweater, instead of opting for a navy-blue strapless sundress. The last thing she'd expected was to be cold on a warm spring day.

Or to be surrounded by so much wealth in the VIP suite.

Men in expensive suits and their tastefully accessorized wives were at ease in these posh surroundings, absently accepting personalized cocktails from the waiter. Taking up space. They didn't think twice about dropping their Chanel bags on the sleek white leather sectional and striking up an animated conversation—and Eve envied that. Aspired to that kind of comfort in her own skin. As it was, she still had her own black envelope clutch wedged tightly under one arm and she'd positioned herself out of the way.

Who does she think she is?

That's what everyone in Cumberland would say if they saw me here.

"Dude," Veda whispered, appearing at Eve's elbow, just in time to help her avoid a serious case of impostor syndrome. "This box is *noice*. A bitch could get used to this."

"I know." Eve glanced over her shoulder at the sterling silver buffet. "I'm trying to wait an appropriate amount of time before I have my second and third dessert."

"Fuck that math. I've had four."

Eve started to ask which of the minidesserts she should go for next, but Elton sauntered up beside Veda with a frosted pint of beer in his hand. "The shirt looks good on you," he said to Veda, referring to his old Brown jersey that he'd brought from home. Being that Elton was taller and broader, she'd opted to tie the sides of the button-up around her stomach, showing off the embroidered waistband of her high-waisted jeans. "I can confidently say it has never been worn like that."

Veda preened. "I add a little dazzle wherever I can."

"You . . . yeah," Elton muttered. Eyes glued to Veda's face, he took a long pull of his beer. "Do you know the rules of baseball?"

She shook her head. "All I know is we want the team in pin-stripes to win."

Elton smirked, using his beer to indicate the two blue rows of seats on the other side of the glass wall. "Come sit with me. I'll explain as we go."

"Oh, um." Veda hesitated. "Should we . . ."

"What?"

Twin spots appeared on Veda's cheeks. "Is it weird to sit together alone if you're sort of dating my sister?"

Elton's throat muscles worked. "No. We're friends, you and me. Right?"

"Friends." Veda brightened. Everywhere but her eyes. "Right, yeah, I know. Besides, in what world could I steal a man from Alexis?" She let out a hearty laugh. "You're probably explaining the rules of baseball to me to earn points with her, right? Don't worry, I'll make sure to put in a good word, slugger." She looked at Eve, whispering, "Oh god. Am I still talking?"

"Afraid so."

"Quick," Elton said, handing her his pint. "Drink the rest of my beer before you make this any weirder."

Veda drained it in ten seconds and handed him back the empty glass. "Thanks." She snuck a slow smile up at Elton. "You have terrible taste."

His scrutiny of Veda's features went on a second too long. "I don't know my taste anymore," he murmured, holding the cold pint glass to his temple.

"I'm talking about beer, Elton," Veda whispered. "You have terrible taste in beer."

"Right." Apparently, he was having a very difficult time looking at anything but Veda, but he managed to set down the pint glass and steer her toward the exit that would take them out into the stadium-style seating area. "Back to baseball. There are nine innings . . ."

As the conversation between Veda and Elton faded away, Skylar slid up beside Eve, giving her a little hip bump. "Hey."

"Hey, babe," Eve responded, cataloging the changes to Skylar's appearance since the last time she'd seen her, about a month ago. With her eyes holding a permanent sparkle and her dark brown hair in a wavy tumble, the girl looked incredible. "What is going on with my brother and that rockabilly girl?"

"Oh, he's dating her sister, Alexis, a local real estate agent in Cumberland who is precisely his white picket fence and two-point-five-children type, but he's obviously crazy for Veda, who pulls all-nighters, lives with her parents, and shivers at the thought of marriage."

"Whoa."

"Tell me about it." Eve winked at Skylar. "Moving on. Hockey looks good on you."

"I'm going to let you give me conversational whiplash because we have way too much to talk about and I don't know when we'll be alone again." Her best friend breathed a laugh. "Hockey feels as good on me as it looks." She seemed to lock eyes with Robbie across the suite. "I didn't see him coming. He's . . . *wow*. You know?"

Eve warmed. "Tell me more."

"I mean, it's superearly," Skylar qualified. "We've only been seeing each other for a month, but . . ."

"When you know, you know."

"Yeah," Skylar breathed, pressing her palms to her cheeks and lowering her voice. "I fell asleep at my apartment after practice yesterday and he just showed up, all frowny and griping. He packed me a bag and carried me downstairs where the Uber was waiting. Took me back to his place and—"

"I can guess what happened next."

"No. I mean, well, *yeah*, but not until the next morning. He just wanted to sleep beside me." She let out a burst of air. "I'm in love with him."

Eve's chest swelled—and it almost burst wide open when she looked over at Robbie and saw him mooning at Skylar like a lovesick puppy. "I can tell, Sky. I'm so happy for you."

"Thanks." Skylar rolled her lips inward, wetting them. "But . . . there's something I need to speak with you about. Concerning Madden?" She looked down at the ground for a moment, as if piecing her thoughts together. "When everything was developing between me and Robbie, we hit some speed bumps and I ended up going for a drink with Madden in the middle of it all. I mistook it for a date, but Madden very tactfully told me it wasn't. He only asked me for a drink to talk about you, Eve. All those years I had a crush on him and . . ." She reached out and squeezed Eve's shoulder, her features rife with chagrin. "He was locked in on you the whole time."

Breathing was difficult—which was ridiculous, considering Eve had known on some level that Madden had wanted her a lot longer than a few weeks. To hear that he'd said it out loud to her best friend, though, rocked her back on her heels. "Is that what he said?"

"I think his exact words were 'It's always been Eve for me.'"

"Oh," Eve said choppily.

Skylar pulled her into a hug and Eve went, resting her chin on Skylar's shoulder. "Eve, I promised him I would talk to you about accepting his help. You need health insurance for the kids and—"

"I married him," Eve blurted, her heart rate speeding up as the announcer started to call the opening lineup for the Yankees. Wow. Her usual modus operandi was to keep her lips zipped about her business. Was Veda rubbing off on her or was she feeling guilty for keeping something so big from her best friend?

Too late to turn back now.

"We're married. But only for six months," Eve rushed to add. "Well. Five and a half now, I think."

Slowly, Skylar reared back, her jaw dangling in the vicinity of her ankles. "Why didn't you tell me?"

Adrenaline had Eve's pulse racing. She almost gave some dumb excuse about having been so busy, she didn't have a chance to call, but Skylar deserved better than that. Way better. "I guess . . ." She swallowed hard and looked her friend in the eye. "You wanted him for so long, it still felt like I was stealing him."

Skylar blinked rapidly, her gaze dropping to the floor. When she focused on Eve again, there was a fine layer of mist in her eyes. "I think maybe I was stealing him from you all those years. I was the one standing in the way."

Denial weighed down on Eve's chest. Not denial of the truth. Denial of seeing her best friend looking anguished, Eve being the cause. "Skylar—"

"Eve." The pitcher reached out and squeezed Eve's forearm. "Let's call it like it is."

"Okay." Eve let out a slow breath. "Now that I've seen you with Robbie, I'm not worried anymore. I know you're happy."

"And now you get to be happy too." Skylar gave her one more squeeze, for good measure. "Now. Tell. Me. Everything."

Approximately six minutes later, Skylar hadn't said a single word. Or blinked once.

And Eve hadn't even *mentioned* the parking lot sex.

She had, however, confided that the six-month rule and secrecy had been instituted to protect Madden's reputation. By keeping it separate from hers.

"Eve," her best friend said in something of a warning tone.

"Skylar," Eve responded, suspiciously.

"I know you're not a fan of unsolicited advice."

Eve sipped her drink, winking over the brim. "No lies detected."

"Normally I respect your boundaries, but you're just going to have to grin and bear it this time." Skylar took her by the shoulders and shook slightly, sloshing the champagne in Eve's glass. "Don't let other people's opinions affect your decisions. Especially when those opinions are small-minded and ignorant."

Did she take her friend's advice seriously? Yes, of course she did.

But Eve had lived under the weight of disapproval for a long time.

She didn't even know how to begin shedding it.

Or what she would do if she ever managed to leave the condemnation behind.

Was it time to start wondering?

THE TOP OF the ninth inning was when things got hairy.

One, the game was tied 4–4, their opponents were up to bat and had a man on third.

Two, Veda and Elton hadn't budged from their spots in approximately three hours and their sporadic bursts of laughter could probably be heard down on the field.

And three, Eve was pretty sure Robbie and Skylar were fucking in the bathroom. Skylar had spilled lemonade on her shirt ten minutes ago, Robbie had come to the rescue with club-soda-soaked paper towels, and they hadn't emerged since.

Eve was definitely fifth wheeling and she didn't mind that one iota, because she didn't have to pretend to focus on a conversation, as opposed to the true passion that had developed during the game: staring at Madden.

This wasn't the first time she'd ever been to one of his games. No, she'd been to dozens of high school games and once or twice, she'd road-tripped with the Pages to watch him play for Brown. She hadn't had a chance to catch one of his minor-league games, though she'd planned on it. But this—*this* was cinematic.

A flatscreen showed the game in the suite, so she could hear the announcer calling the game. Had a bird's-eye view and a close-up of Madden when he took off his mask to argue a call with the umpire in the fifth inning, his black hair shaggy around the sides of his backward hat, eye black swipes high on his cheeks. Every time he stood to throw back the ball to the pitcher, Eve had to breathe through her nose, to say nothing of the full-body sweat she encountered when he threw out a runner stealing second, his mask falling behind him in the dirt, blue eyes snapping with concentration.

God, her husband was hot.

She was very invested in this game too. Perhaps to the untrained observer, this was any other baseball game, but Eve could see something in Madden's eyes that she hadn't expected after talking to him about his issues fitting in with the team. She saw optimism. When they'd gotten their third out at the end of the third inning, he'd even traded a smile and a fist bump with Ruiz, the pitcher.

Now the closer had taken over and wasn't having quite as much luck.

The Yankees needed one more out, but even Eve recognized the face of the player at bat. That had to mean he was good, right?

Even Skylar and Robbie must have sensed something important was happening, because they were out of the bathroom—a little flushed, to be sure—all of them splitting looks between the field and the television.

Two balls, two strikes.

The pitch came in.

Clonk. The ball zoomed past the pitcher, bounced once, and got snapped up by the shortstop.

Elton stood up. "Oh shit," Eve heard him say, through the glass—and a second later, she understood why. The runner on third was sprinting for home, toward Madden, who was guarding the plate, his glove up and ready to receive a rapid-fire throw from the shortstop.

Madden caught the ball and put down his shoulder, just in time for the runner to collide with him at full speed, knocking him hard to the ground. So hard that a cloud of brown dust went up. Eve dropped her purse, unable to breathe, pressure building deep in her eye sockets while she stared at the television, waiting for Madden to move.

Was the entire crowd dead silent or had her ears stopped working?

The cloud of dust settled. Madden held up the ball.

He hadn't dropped it. *Yankees win.*

Pandemonium erupted, the intensity of which Eve had never experienced in her life and maybe never would again. Elton and Veda came barreling into the suite, wrapping Skylar, Robbie, and Eve in a group hug, everyone screaming and jumping at once.

At least, until they noticed there was a medic being called to home plate.

The five of them watched in horror for ten excruciating minutes as a man stood over Madden, blocking the view of him from the camera. The low drone of the announcer's voice was the sole sound in the suite until a buzz started somewhere in the vicinity. It took Eve several beats to realize it was her phone vibrating.

She looked at the screen. Unknown number.

"Answer it," Elton said, squinting at her phone.

Eve tapped the green icon. "Hello?"

"Is this Eve Keller?"

"Yes. This is she."

"I'm Hank Jones, one of the family coordinators here with the Yankees. You're down as the emergency contact for Madden Donahue."

A heavy jolt in her middle. "I am?"

"Yes. I'm sure you're following the incident at the game. His injury doesn't appear to be serious, but his shoulder took a hefty blow. They're transporting him to Mount Sinai as a precaution for a couple of x-rays. Wanted to let you know."

Eve didn't know whether to be relieved or horrified, but her body seemed dead set on the latter. Madden in the hospital. It was all too reminiscent of those scary months during high school when she cried herself to sleep every night, terrified she was going to lose him. Apparently, she was housing some leftover trauma, because her knees wouldn't stop shaking. "Thank you for calling."

"You got it."

Eve hung up and looked at the group, who seemed to be holding their collective breath. "They're taking him to the hospital as a precaution. His shoulder took a serious hit, so they want to do x-rays, but otherwise, he's okay." Standing there made her feel useless. "Should I . . . go? Or would I just be in the way?"

"Go," Elton said. "You're probably the only one they'll let in to see him."

"Why?"

Elton's lips twitched, but he didn't respond out loud.

Right. She was Madden's wife. The hospital would allow family.

"Never mind." Eve ran a set of fingers through her hair, looking around for her things. What had she brought? *Your phone is in your hand.* "Oh! Wait, I'm Veda's ride back to Cumberland."

"Got it covered," Elton assured her. "I'm heading home to see Mom and Dad for a night or two, anyway. Veda can ride with me."

Eve didn't have time to dwell on the electrified air sizzling between Elton and Veda—she was growing more restless by the second and had to get moving. With a kiss on everyone's cheek and promises to keep them updated via text, Eve was out the door.

CHAPTER TWENTY-FIVE

God, I fucking hate hospitals.

Madden gritted his teeth and suffered through another round of prodding by the team doctors, attempting to disassociate, the way he'd done during too many rounds of medical tests at age seventeen. Impossible. For one, there were too many executives in the room relaying the doctors' diagnosis to the media, the front office, and lord only knew who else needed to know real-time information about his bruised rotator cuff.

"For the discomfort, Mr. Donahue," one of the nurses said, handing him a little paper cup with white pills inside. Madden handed it back straightaway.

"No, thank you," he said, as politely as possible, sweating bullets. Too many lights, too many masked faces and voices. Too many goddamn machines. The scene was an echo of his least favorite memory, taking him back to the days of dialysis. When the future was unknown and strangers looked at him with sympathy, unable to tell him when the weakness and pain would come to an end.

"Are you sure?" asked the nurse, his eyebrows winging up to his hairline. "That was a pretty hefty collision."

"I'm sure." Madden remembered all too well the feeling of nausea that often went hand in hand with the more intense pain relievers. When the nurse simply stood there looking at him,

Madden replayed the man's comment. "You saw the collision? Were you watching the game?"

"No, but the replay is everywhere on social media right now. You're the pride of New York." He chuckled. "They're calling you Bad Madden. It's not the best nickname in history, but it's one that will probably stick, so you better get used to it."

Bad Madden?

Jesus.

"When am I getting the hell out of here?"

The nurse seemed thrown off by the question. "You've only been here for forty-five minutes."

In Madden's opinion, that was forty-five minutes too long. Dammit, why had this happened today of all days? Of course he got injured during *the one game* Eve attended. Now, instead of seeing her after the game, he was stuck in a narrow bed with scratchy sheets, listening to team trainers confer with one another about the fastest rehab plan to get him back behind the plate.

Had Eve already gotten on the road back to Cumberland?

"Is there any family you'd like us to call?"

Yes. Please call my wife.

"No." He cleared his throat of the need to request the one person he wanted to see. There was no need to inconvenience her over a minor scrape. "No, it's not worth the bother. Just a bruise."

"You're going to have a purple map of the world on half of your upper torso, Bad Madden. It's a little more than a bruise."

"Please don't call me that."

"It's going to stick," sang the nurse as he departed.

Madden sighed, dropping his head back on the pillow and resigning himself to being stuck. Another twenty minutes passed before the nurse returned.

"You have another visitor."

Most likely a member of the coaching staff. Or yet another press liaison.

"Great," Madden muttered, not bothering to open his eyes.

"Blond girl. Kind of . . . Grace Kelly hot?"

His lids flew open at that, his pulse stumbling over itself. *"What?"*

Not Eve. It couldn't be Eve. She'd come all the way to the hospital to see him?

"They're making her wait in the hallway until someone leaves the room." The nurse jerked a thumb over his shoulder. "With all the Yankees personnel rubbing elbows in here, we're at capacity."

Madden used his good arm to sit up. "Get them out. Get her in."

"Uh—"

The surprise had rendered his tongue useless. "That's my . . . she's . . ."

"I hope you're going to say sister, because I'm pretty sure two doctors are already planning a proposal."

"That's *my* wife," Madden growled, rushing to add, "But . . . don't announce that she's my wife, all right? Just bring her in."

"You got it, Bad Madden." The nurse turned to the room and clapped his hands. "Out into the hallway. All of you. The reigning king of New York needs his privacy."

"I think king of New York is a bit of an exaggeration," Madden muttered, craning his neck to try and catch a glimpse of Eve through the rectangular window in the hospital door. God help any doctor he caught hitting on his wife. They'd be trading places with him in this bed.

"It's not an exaggeration, actually." Someone stepped forward with a laptop. "I'm Josh. I'm the social media manager. Not only has the clip of the collision, followed by you holding up the ball, gone viral, but there's already a remix of the announcer's voice saying Bad-Bad . . . record scratch . . . Bad-Bad Madden." His fingers flew over the keys. "Here, let me play it for you."

"Please don't."

"He has a visitor," the nurse informed everyone with an embellished wink. "A very special one."

Madden ground his molars.

The fact that Eve had to wait even a minute, instead of being ushered right in, was going to make his head explode. She'd come. She'd already traveled from Cumberland. Now she'd probably gone through traffic hell to make it from the Bronx to the hospital.

And still, no one had moved to leave the room.

"Either she comes in here or I'm going out there," Madden said, already swinging his legs over the side of the bed, more than prepared to walk.

"Whoa, whoa, whoa," everyone said at once. "Lie down."

"Don't aggravate the shoulder. We need you in Pittsburgh next week."

"Let him have his special visitor," snapped the nurse, followed by more clapping. And finally, finally, the suits started to file out of the room, leaving it blessedly empty.

A steady beep had become background noise in the hospital room over the course of the last hour, but when Eve appeared in the doorway, that beep got faster and seemingly louder? "What in the hell is that?" he asked, sounding a little winded, because dear god, too many days had passed since he'd seen her last and she looked incredible in that dress. A dark blue one he hadn't seen before. It molded to her body from her tits down to her hips, then it kind of flowed out just past her knees. She'd twisted her hair up, but she must have done it on the fly, because little pieces had fallen out, free to brush her neck, exactly like his fingertips and mouth needed to do.

"Um . . ." Eve didn't blush very often, but she was now. Why? "I think that beeping is coming from your heart monitor."

Without missing a beat, Madden ripped off the round white stickers and their connecting wires from his chest, rendering the room mostly silent, though the number of voices in the hallway could only be muffled, not quieted completely. "It has always done that when you're around," he said, ignoring the burning of his earlobes. "Now you know."

Eve's features softened, her chest dipping and rising, yet she remained glued in place by the door, her purse clutched to her stomach.

Deal's off. I want more than six months.

Those words were like a stick of dynamite crackling between them.

Maybe that demand had been a mistake, but he'd make it all over again. He simply wasn't built to let this woman go. Eve wasn't merely in his blood, she'd become his blood itself. She ran in his veins. His inner thoughts often presented themselves in her voice. Eve lived inside him. And maybe Madden had some barbarian blood, too, because the crank of possessiveness had turned another revolution when she admitted to waiting for him. Admitted to not trusting anyone else with her body. She felt this too.

"How are you feeling?" she asked, finally setting her purse down on a chair, folding her hands at her waist, and walking toward the bed. "You freaked all of us out."

"I'm fine. It's just a bruise." Although, damn, his shoulder was beginning to feel pretty stiff and raw. "Sorry about all the drama. The trainer asked me to stay down at the plate until they could determine if anything was broken."

Eve nodded. "Elton knew what was coming as soon as the guy started running toward home plate. I think he might have psychic powers."

"Nah, he just knows me. I don't budge." Madden gave in to the impulse to reach out and take her hand, pulling her closer. "Not on anything."

"You don't waste any time addressing the elephant in the room." They both watched in fascination as their palms fused together, followed by the slow threading of their fingers. "What ever happened to small talk?"

"We've never made small talk. That's not us."

"Can we try?" Eve took a measured breath. "I don't do nerves very well."

Madden's thumb paused in the act of swiping right to left against the pulse of her wrist. "What's wrong with your nerves?"

She gave him a meaningful look. "I don't love hospitals, I guess. I didn't like the first time you were in one and I don't like it now."

"Ah, love." They stared at each other for long moments, remembering. "I'm fine, I promise. Who has the kids?" he finally asked, his voice quiet.

"The Pages," she said, making an effort to surface from the past. "They'll be Olympians by the time I pick them up."

"Or shell-shocked from the freakishly competitive environment. One or the other."

"That's also a possibility." She grinned, studying him, her gaze lingering on the thick bandaging and ice on his shoulder. "You're kind of good at baseball. Did you know that?"

"I was just showing off for my wife."

The pulse he rubbed with his thumb went skittering. "I hear she was impressed."

Damn. The amount of pride he felt over that probably amounted to a sin. And speaking of sinning, he had a lot of it on his mind, even with a busted shoulder. "Impressed enough to spend the night with me?"

"So much for small talk, huh?" Eve glanced toward the door and back at Madden, visibly wrestling with something. "When I was on my way here, I got a second call from the family liaison. He told me to enter at the rear of the hospital to avoid all the cameras."

Confusion landed, followed by the sinking sensation of dread. "Cameras?"

"It's one of those internet wonders, you know." She huffed a laugh, but her eyes held a touch of anxiety. "You're a lot more famous now than when you woke up this morning."

"I don't want to be famous."

"I don't think you have a choice." Eve reached out and traced the contour of Madden's brow, as if she was memorizing the texture of him. "They're going to want to know everything about you. It's going to take barely any digging at all to find me."

"*Good.* Let them."

She was already shaking her head. "I know you want more than six months from this marriage, but maybe it's for the best if—"

"Don't finish that sentence," he rasped.

They stared at each other in stony silence, the distance between them scant, but it might as well have been a mile—and Madden desperately needed that gap to be narrowed. *Desperately.* Who knew standing his ground at the plate today would be the thing that drove Eve away? To Eve's way of thinking, her reputation and profession would taint his own and there didn't seem to be anything he could say to convince her he didn't give a shit. Not even if he said it a million times and meant it with every fiber of his being.

Stall.

He could only think to stall and pray this whole Bad Madden thing blew over.

"Come home with me tonight." Despite the pain in his shoulder, he sat forward, curling his hand around the back of her neck. Massaging her nape. Gratified when her pupils expanded, her breath quickening at his touch. "I won't have you driving home alone in the dark."

"I'll be fine."

"Come here."

She hesitated. But when he made it clear he was willing to put himself through pain to get closer, she rushed to perch on the edge of the bed. God forgive him, he took advantage of her being slightly off-balance, pulling her face down to his until their mouths were only a half inch apart.

"Sleep in my bed with me." Madden twisted their lips together, not kissing, just dragging. Breathing. "The only decision we have to make tonight is which shirt of mine you're borrowing. If you need one at all."

Eve rubbed the side of her nose against his, almost absently, as if she wasn't aware of the nuzzle. Or couldn't help it. "Nothing will make me forget what's at stake."

He sipped at her mouth. Once. Twice. "We'll talk about this when we're not somewhere that makes us both uncomfortable."

"Fine," she whispered, her palm skimming down his chest now. "I'll spend one night, but only because you're hurt and someone should be with you."

"You're coming to be my nurse, are you?"

Their lips moved damply on top of each other when she nodded. "Uh-huh. I'm going to wipe your brow and pat your hand comfortingly. Just like in the movies."

"Nurses don't usually sleep in the same bed as their patients."

"I suppose I could take the couch."

"The hell you will."

The victory of getting Eve to agree to sleep at his apartment didn't overshadow the fear of what could possibly lie ahead, but their closeness distracted him, to say the least. He'd successfully stalled any rash decisions. For now. He'd work on the rest as soon as he got discharged from this fresh hell known as a hospital.

"Come get in bed with me right now. We can practice for later."

"I don't know if you noticed, but there are two dozen people foaming at the mouth to get back in this room and talk to Bad Madden."

"I'm already sick of that nickname," he groused.

"Too bad. You earned it." Eve started to stand, but she gasped when Madden caught her around the waist with his good arm and tugged her on top of him, farther and farther up his body until she straddled one of his thighs and their mouths were even.

"Jesus Christ. Can't I have one real kiss, woman?"

She struggled to push herself up without touching his injury. "You had your chance, Mr. Donahue."

"I was warming you up." Madden bent the knee between her legs, an action that pressed his thigh up tight, so tight to her pussy, shuddering over the warmth he found there. They stayed like that for long moments, Eve pulsing against his flexed thigh, her hips riding up an inch, back an inch, just once, her teeth sinking into her full bottom lip, the effort to restrain herself visible. "A week is too fucking long without you, Eve. In every way.

Not just being inside you. But goddamn, a few hours is too long for that, let alone a week." He moved his thigh. "Tell me you missed me."

"I missed you."

"Kiss me like you missed me."

She didn't hesitate, maybe she couldn't, as she arrowed for his mouth, her lips opening over the top of his with a whimper that balanced his growl perfectly. *She* balanced every uneven part of him in a split second, his taciturn soul relaxing because what could be wrong with the world when this gorgeous, stubborn woman in a sundress was on top of him, taking great pains not to touch his shoulder, but aye, she was getting wetter against his thigh. He didn't have to feel it with his fingers to know. He could sense her need in the way she kissed, as if she'd been starving for a week and now, she'd been offered a feast.

That's what they were to each other.

A mutual feast.

He just needed to keep reminding her until her arguments ran out.

Madden was calculating the wisdom of sliding his hand up her dress and playing with her from behind through her panties, because surely the skirt would hide anything he was doing to her, but that's when he heard the voices approaching. And he froze.

Those voices were too familiar. He heard them day in and day out.

In the locker room.

On the field.

"Love."

She mewled her way down to his throat, sucking his skin.

"Love," he panted. "We have to stop. The team is here."

"What?" she asked, raising her head and looking adorably befuddled, a rarity for his badass Eve. "Who is what?"

Christ, her tits were nearly falling out of her dress. "My teammates. They're not going to let anyone keep them out, if they want to come in. They lack anything resembling a boundary." He sat up with her in his arms, wincing. "Let's pull up your dress."

Eve was still in a fog, so Madden performed the task for her, one-handed.

The voices drew closer now and that finally seemed to penetrate Eve's haze.

"Oh! Your team?" She scrambled off him, but her state of disarray couldn't have made it more obvious what they'd been doing. Her hair was sideways and half free of its clip, her mouth rosy and swollen. "Should I go?"

"Don't even think of leaving my sight."

"When did you get so pushy?"

"Since you threatened to divorce me early while I'm in a hospital bed."

He regretted the outburst as soon as her face started to lose color. "It sounds terrible when you say it like that."

"It's terrible no matter how you say it," he said quietly. With every ounce of the conviction he felt. "And it's not happening."

They only had five seconds to glare breathlessly at each other before the door was kicked open, slapping off the opposite wall and sending a meal tray crashing to the floor.

Ruiz stood at the front of the pack, holding a bouquet of roses. "Bad Madden, you Irish brick house motherfucker. Ice that shit and get back to *work*."

"Planning on it."

"Planning on it," Ruiz echoed with an attempted brogue.

"This dude is crazy. Hey. Brought you some flowers—" The pitcher was advancing into the room, but cut himself off when he noticed Eve standing in the corner. Still looking like she'd come within inches of being ravished. "As I live and fucking breathe. Is this Mrs. Donahue?"

Eve shot Madden an incredulous look, flushing to the roots of her hair. "I'm Eve." She waved at the dozen or so men who were trying to pile their way into the room to get a look at her. "Oh boy. Hi, everyone."

"Hi, Eve," came a chorus of baritones.

If Madden was annoyed at being stuck in a hospital bed before, the ordeal had just become untenable. His instinct told him to surround Eve, protect her from everyone's curiosity, so that's what he was going to do. Without another thought, Madden ripped off the blood pressure cuff, followed by the flimsy sheet, before climbing to his feet, gritting his teeth over the brief lack of equilibrium.

"Whoa." Ruiz tossed the roses onto the counter. "Lay back down, man."

"Madden," Eve said, coming forward and attempting to guide him back to the bed.

He drew her up against his uninjured side instead. "I'm fine."

Ruiz turned and looked at the rest of the team. "Coach! Get this warrior off the injured list. He only needs one shoulder." The pitcher leaned around Madden to make eye contact with Eve. "Your man got me back on track tonight. I haven't pitched the lights out like that in five damn years."

"Finally pulled your head out of your arse and listened, is what happened."

Every player in attendance howled, but none of them found the comment more amusing than Ruiz. "Something tells me we're not done brawling, Donahue." He put his hand up for a fist bump, which Madden cautiously returned. "But I think we're going to be all right, man. You're blunt as fuck and kind of weird, but I like you."

"Thanks."

Ruiz laughed, exchanging a high five with the player closest to him. "We're about to go celebrate, but we wanted to stop by and see you first. Get better, man. Like I said, we've got work to do."

Madden nodded, surprised to find an odd sense of . . . belonging with the group of men in front of him, which he'd come nowhere close to experiencing at the professional level until that moment. They weren't a bonded group of friends, they were individuals with big personalities and complicated paths to the pros, but maybe the individuality worked for him. Maybe this worked better for him than blending to fit. "I'm not going anywhere."

"Good," Ruiz said, sincerely. "Bad Madden. Bad Madden."

The Yankees' starting lineup chanted their way down the hallway to the elevator, their voices carrying until all three groups had piled into the empty cars. When the quiet was all that remained, because even the executives were in a hush now, visibly moved by what they'd witnessed, Madden found Eve looking up at him, at first thoughtfully, then with understanding. Pride.

"Let's go home," he said.

CHAPTER TWENTY-SIX

Mental note to self: Never drive in Manhattan again.

The ordeal of retrieving her car from the pay lot, then double-parking among a sea of honking vehicles to pick Madden up at the front entrance and now circling Madden's city block trying to decipher humanity's most confusing signs to determine if a spot was valid or she'd get her ass towed? Eve thought, *Never again.* Not that Madden seemed to mind sitting in her passenger seat, smiling to himself as she cursed and got stuck behind delivery trucks, rickshaws, and yellow cabs.

"If I lived in this city, I would be homicidal."

"No, you'd just adjust to taking Ubers or the subway."

"Is that what you do?"

Finally, she found a metered spot that she'd only have to pay for until seven p.m. And tomorrow was Sunday, meaning no meters were in effect. *Hallelujah.* "Unless I'm going to the stadium, I just walk everywhere," Madden said.

"I can picture that," Eve murmured, resting her hand on the back of his seat and maneuvering in reverse into the space, her body all too aware of Madden's proximity in the small car, those blue eyes tracking down the front of her dress, his palm swiping slowly down the thigh of his sweatpants as if to dry it. "I . . . can picture you out walking by yourself in your overcoat, looking all serious and thoughtful."

His lips twitched. "It's too many people for me. I'm usually just trying to finish my errand and get back to my apartment as fast as possible."

"Not a city person."

"No."

Eve turned off the engine. "There's a chance you could be here for a while. Or be asked to move to an entirely new city at some point." She set about collecting her things from the car—phone, keys—dropping them into her purse. "You could have a long time left with the league. Over a decade."

"If I'm lucky."

"I have it on good authority that Irishmen are pretty lucky."

Madden's eyes ran an appreciative lap around her face, that palm drying itself once again on the leg of his sweatpants. "I can't say I disagree."

This man's directness was going to be the death of her. He hadn't been lying when he said they'd never been good at small talk. They always ended up in the deep end of the conversation within minutes. And Eve preferred the way they communicated, but this . . . spending the night together, being his emergency contact, informing the nurse station at the hospital that she was Madden's wife, the whole team being aware of his marital status? They'd broken new ground. What happened to her determination not to turn too much soil?

"Let me come around to your side and help you out," she said, pushing open the driver's-side door. "You've been enough of a hero for one day."

"Now, love, I don't want a fuss."

"You're getting one." Eve shut the door before he could protest again, waiting for the oncoming traffic to zip by before circling around to Madden's side, growling at him when she found the door already open, his feet planted on the sidewalk. "You know, you're the only person I know who is more stubborn than me."

"I'm glad you noticed," he said, gripping the roof of the car with the hand of his good arm, gritting his teeth and hauling himself out before she could help. "I like you knowing I'm going to keep showing up."

"Like a bad penny," she quipped, although he was towering over her now, grizzled and messy from his ordeal, so the joke came out sounding kind of breathless.

"No, Eve." Without looking, he closed the passenger door behind him with a neat little slam. "Like your husband."

Small talk? I don't know her.

Eve swallowed the legion of butterflies unleashed by the word *husband* and turned in a circle, scanning the high-rises blocking the night sky on all sides. "Which one is yours?"

He jerked his chin. "One block that way."

"Okay." She locked the car, testing the handle once, then they fell into step beside each other, the pedestrian noise growing louder as they passed a pub, several patrons outside smoking or making calls. The mood was drunk.

"Oh my god," yelled a guy in a Yankees jersey who promptly threw down his cigarette and stomped it out. "It's Bad Madden."

"Shit," Madden muttered, taking Eve's arm and steering her past the crowd at a quickening pace. "It stuck."

A chant of the nickname started in their wake, more and more people spilling out of the bar to watch them advance down the block.

"Give them a little wave," Eve cajoled, struggling to keep up with his long strides. "It'll make their night."

Sighing, Madden turned slightly and nodded at the bar patrons over his shoulder, sending them into an absolute meltdown.

"Was that so hard?"

"I'm never going outside again."

Eve bit her lip to stifle a laugh. "I guess we're ordering you takeout tonight."

Madden guided her beneath a long red awning, muttering a greeting to the doorman as they entered the building. "You're not hungry?"

"Have you witnessed the stacked buffet in the VIP suite? I'm not going to be hungry until Monday." Eve nearly sighed out loud over the vintage chandelier that hung in the lobby, the persimmon-colored carpet that stretched from one end to the other. The gold light fixtures. The half-moon checkerboard floor in front of the elevator. "I like what you've done with the place," she murmured, as they stepped into the elevator and the door closed. She watched as Madden tapped the button for the twenty-fourth floor, a little alarmed to find his hand unsteady. "Is your shoulder hurting?"

"It's fine." The car moved upward at a rapid pace, but she couldn't tell if it was the elevation or the way Madden watched her that caused her stomach to feel weightless. "I'm just always picturing what it would be like to bring you back here, and now . . . here you are."

Eve held her breath, then exhaled. "Bet you didn't picture yourself with only one arm."

"No, I did not," he said, chuckling and sounding kind of . . . nervous. "I haven't done much with the apartment yet. I don't know, it feels odd to settle in when the city doesn't feel . . ."

"Like home?" The elevator door opened and Madden gestured for Eve to precede him, which she did, her pulse leaping when he settled his left hand on her hip, squeezing to nudge her down the left corridor. "Where feels like home? Cumberland?"

"Definitely more like home than Manhattan, but it's my aunt's home. That's how I've always thought of it. Florida felt temporary too." He produced his keys, unlocking the black door with a gold G above the peephole. "I've no nostalgia for Ireland, as hard as I've tried to recall the good parts of it, because there are some. A lot, actually." He paused. "I'm not sure where I'm meant to put roots down."

They stood in front of the door, making no move to open it, even though it was unlocked. "Cumberland is starting to feel less and less like home to me, lately," Eve said quietly, as if imparting a terrible secret. "It feels like a betrayal to say that and I don't know why. It's a town that's never wanted me back."

She could hear Madden's hand flex into a fist, an audible squeeze of tendons, and she reached over and covered it with her own. He said, "You're wanted here. With me."

"I know." Maybe it was the sudden, intense need to lighten the mood after his hospital trip or maybe she genuinely felt a little giddy, a whole night in front of her in this strange land called Manhattan. So far from real life and all her responsibilities, the moment seemed like a dream. "Let's play house tonight."

Madden did a double take, but his expression warmed. "Go on."

She'd set a record today for blushing and now she was breaking it. "This is home for the night. We both belong here. We've put down roots and . . ."

"We're husband and wife, home after a long day, dying to put on pajamas and relax." He raised an eyebrow. "It's not that far-fetched if you think about it."

"I guess it's not."

Madden nodded at the handle. "Shall we, love?"

It was a visceral thing, shedding the Teflon she wore as a

second skin. Was it being outside Cumberland's borders that made it possible? Or being with Madden? Or . . . both? "We shall," she said, her smile unfettered as she pushed open the door. And gasped. "Oh, Madden. The *view*." Eve walked inside, dropping her purse on the closest surface, coming to a stop in front of the glass door that opened onto a small rectangular balcony. "I'm completely turned around. Is that New Jersey or Brooklyn?"

"New Jersey," he said behind her, the dead bolt sliding into place.

"I mean . . ." She fluffed her hair. "Obviously, I already knew that, because this is my home and I'm here every day."

"I already love this game."

Eve crossed back through the functionally decorated living room toward Madden, framing his face in her hands. "You didn't get to shower after your game, honey. Do you want to take one now?"

His chest dipped so low, she thought it was caving in. "I know I must smell like death, I just don't want to miss a second of you being here."

"But I'm always here," she said, feigning confusion.

"Right." He tilted her chin up in his left hand. "You look like you could use a good wash yourself."

Eve gasped.

Madden winked at her.

"Is my husband trying to get me into the shower?"

"Aye," he rasped, his breath shallowing.

Reaching back, she lowered the zipper of her sundress, bringing it down until the material started to slip, past her hips and onto the floor, leaving her in a black strapless bra and matching high-waisted panties. More than anything in this world, she wanted to get completely naked in front of him, but that wasn't possible.

She'd have to make it work in a way that kept her secret hidden.

"Who am I to disappoint Bad Madden?" she said, taking his hand and leading him to the bathroom.

CHAPTER TWENTY-SEVEN

God almighty, he loved her like this.

This was the Eve he'd long suspected she hid under the cool, controlled surface and what a fucking privilege that she'd chosen to take off her mask for him. If he'd done something, anything to make her feel safe enough to lay down her armor, he'd consider it a life well spent.

In theory, showering wasn't a sexy undertaking when a man had to wrap his bandage in plastic and avoid the shower spray, but as he stood there with a towel wrapped around his waist at one end of the bathroom, watching Eve bend forward in a bra and panties to test the temperature of the water, Madden concluded this was already the best night of his life.

"Okay, honey . . ."

Honey, she was calling him.

Jesus, Mary, and Joseph.

"The water is exactly how you like it. Which I know, as your wife," Eve said with a sparkle in her eye, her voice a little muffled by the shower spray. "You're going to stand in the tub while I wash you, sort of like a dog."

"You're saying all the right things, love." A smile burst across Eve's face without a hint of hesitation and Madden never, ever wanted to leave that bathroom. "Should I . . ." he started, gesturing to his clothes. "Strip?"

"Yes, please," she purred, coming up in front of him to help take off his T-shirt, very carefully, her forehead lined with concern as they navigated his bruised shoulder. He didn't realize she was holding her breath until they dropped the garment to the floor, and she let it out in a gust, her relief obvious as she slipped her finger beneath the waistband of his sweats and briefs, pausing before she could lower them. "I can't help but notice you wouldn't let me help you out of the car, but you're willing to let me help take your pants off. Very telling."

"I believe that's called splitting hairs."

"Is it?" She laughed the question, but her mirth dissolved quickly when she tugged his pants and briefs down to his ankles and came face-to-face with how his cock felt about her lack of clothing. "Bad Madden, indeed."

Madden didn't recognize the sudden pressure in his throat. Did he have the urge to laugh or cry? He wasn't the best at letting other people take care of him, but he was compelled to drop his walls, same as her. Allow himself to treasure the chance to be at the mercy of this woman. He closed his eyes, because he could barely handle the sight of her kneeling and untying his shoelaces, the brush of her fingertips on his ankles sending waves of warmth up the insides of his legs and tightening his balls.

She dragged those same magical fingertips up the front of his body as she rose, running a single digit along the heavy length of his dick. "Let me wash you?"

The plea in her tone made him dizzy, so he focused on the little mole that sat on her shoulder. "I'd only let you do something like that."

"That's good," Eve said, taking Madden's wrist and guiding him to the modern, sharp-edged tub, stepping inside in her strapless bra and panties, bringing him inside with her before turning them and shutting the glass door that was already fogged, closing them in a hot, misted, and private environment that he'd never look at the same again. "Because I'd only do it for you."

"That's good." He managed to echo her words, barely, due to the water running over her body and soaking the bra, those sexy, waist-cinching panties, plastering them to her wet hips, that mound he ached for between her thighs. Lord, he'd never given a second thought to the features of the shower, but the multiple vertical nozzles built into the walls were a blessing now, because they were both dripping in seconds. Eve had totally abandoned worry in front of him, showing no sign of stress or hesitation, just letting her hair dampen, the spray painting her body with water from four different directions, while she poured body wash into her palms and rubbed them together. Madden's stomach knit up like a drum when she rested those sudsy hands on his shoulders, scrubbing his neck, his chest, even thumbing his ears.

Maybe he'd died at home plate today and this was heaven.

How else could he explain the way she cleaned him, head to toe, like she was born knowing his body and the effect of her stroking palms over his knees, nipples, abdomen, down his buttocks and in between, looking him right in the eye as she did it.

"I was thinking . . ." she said, leaning in to sip shower water off the middle of his chest. "We should definitely put Christmas lights on the balcony rail this year."

We're playing house.

She wanted to play house.

And all while his brain was in the process of going offline, handing off the reins to his downstairs brain, because yeah, Eve's hands were perfect, so bloody perfect, leaving his erection hanging there, untouched and throbbing, while she circled around behind him and worked shampoo into his hair. But Madden stifled his groan of the word *tease* and focused on the world they were living in their minds.

Maybe if he was convincing enough, it could be their real future.

"Christmas lights. I like that idea." He tried not to moan over her fingernails on his scalp. "We'll pick a color no one else has. Purple, maybe. And when I fly into LaGuardia after being on the road, I'll be able to pick out our apartment from the sky."

"Everyone on the plane will wonder who buys purple Christmas lights."

"And I'll just smile to myself. Because I know it's us."

She pressed a smile against his spine, and in a state of total bliss, he searched for a way to keep the game going. "We're not one of those dinner party couples, are we?"

"God, no. But we make up for never hosting because we always bring some obscure dessert from the cool, experimental downtown bakery. Like matcha rice pudding. Everyone rolls their eyes at us for being city people, but we have the last laugh because we come home to no dirty dishes."

"And we never have to shovel the snow. But we tip the super generously." Madden turned around because he couldn't stand not seeing her face anymore. "Although someday, I wouldn't mind shoveling the snow again."

Eve nodded, following his line of thought while shower water trickled down her cheeks, the makeup smudging around her eyes. And if he had a camera in that moment to steal the image and make it immortal, that photo would be the next one he framed for her, because she was magnificent in her relaxed, playful state. "You'll retire, naturally, and . . ."

"And what?"

She took a moment to breathe. "And Lark and Landon will be

in college by then, so we'll just . . . go anywhere we want. Maybe Wyoming or South Dakota."

"Definitely somewhere I can shovel snow."

"And I'm a new face to all our neighbors. I'm just Eve. New in town. No one knows anything about me. 'She's kind of serious, but she does her part for the neighborhood.' That's what they'll say."

"And her husband kisses the ground she walks on," he added, even though his throat was burning over the wistful wish she'd just made. For a clean slate. What he wouldn't give to hand her that wish on a platter, even if he hated the fact that she needed one. Everyone else should have to change. Not his wife. "Her husband decorates the whole house in those purple lights every year, because it's tradition."

She slipped her hands up his wet chest, tracking her progress with glassy eyes. "Deep down, we're still those annoying city folks who never host the dinner party."

He pressed his mouth to her temple. "We like our privacy."

"Yeah," Eve whispered, lifting onto her toes to rub their mouths together, her fingers finally, finally, cupping his erection, running her palm all the way down to his balls and massaging their way back up. "Most of the time."

Madden's pulse was already pumping a thousand miles an hour, but the implication of the words *most of the time* brought him back to the parking lot a week earlier when he'd fucked his wife against the side of the building, because a little risk of exposure fulfilled her needs and his job was to make that happen. Every goddamn time she asked.

Without taking his mouth off Eve's, he reached over and slapped off the shower.

His shoulder could have been blown off by a shotgun that

afternoon and he wouldn't have felt the pain in that moment. There was only getting inside his wife and in the immediate interest of that, he ripped the plastic bag off his shoulder, using his one good arm to lift her out of the tub, leading her out of the bathroom.

She didn't ask where they were going. And the expression on her beautiful face when he pulled her out onto the balcony into the warm spring night was so trusting, Madden had to swallow the words *I love you* and, Jesus, they were heavy and got stuck in his windpipe, even as he sat down on the one reclining deck chair that had come with the condo, Eve gasping for air as she came down on top of him, straddling his lap, their mouths fusing in a frenzied, moaning kiss, her silk-covered pussy pressing down in just the spot and gliding front to back. *Fuck.*

"We can only fuck out here if you're going to be quiet, love," he said, gripping a section of her hair and holding her steady so he could look her in the eye. "Eve?"

"I'll be quiet. I'll be quiet," she babbled, mascara under her eyes, her long blond hair stuck to her cheeks and shoulders. Disheveled. But her gaze was so clear when she looked at him. There was lust, aye, but there was knowledge there, too, that her request for risk had been heard loud and clear. That he wasn't a man who only talked the talk, he walked the fucking walk too. And it got her hot. "You're going to relax and let me do the work tonight," she said, reaching back to unsnap her bra.

The sight of her bare tits made Madden's vocal cords sound rubbed with dry sand. "I won't relax until we've been married six months and one day."

Something flickered in Eve's eyes. "Tonight, we are. Tonight, we're the purple Christmas lights couple," she said, pressing the high globes of her tits to his chest, angled in a way that wouldn't disturb his injury, her tongue slipping into his mouth in a slow French kiss. It went on and on, neither one of them willing to stop and draw oxygen, drawing only on each other, her wet thighs shifting around his hips, excited, her cunt flexing and rubbing on his hardness. And when a plane flew overhead, she whimpered into his mouth, the kiss kicking into a frantic pace, Eve reaching down to shift aside her underwear, leaving them on but allowing soft to welcome hard. Welcome the slick friction of their nearly joined sexes. "We've been married two years. Long enough to make the lights a tradition," she whispered, breathing erratically against his mouth, jacking off his cock now, the tip already buried in the warmth of her creases. "You know I like to play nurse when you're injured, and you let me. You secretly love it."

Every color of the rainbow flashed in front of Madden's eyes when Eve pushed his tip into her heat and dropped down, her ass smacking off his lap with a closemouthed cry.

Motherfucker.

This woman was perfection.

Being inside her was the epitome of being spoiled.

An indescribable indulgence.

And on top of her body fitting his like a glove, she was in a dirty mood.

"You secretly love having your dick ridden," she leaned down to whisper, her hips already moving in hot little writhes, her pussy tight enough around him to have his left hand flying out to grip one of the slats of the balcony rail, holding it in a white-knuckled grip and begging himself to last. "It's almost good enough to get injured on purpose, isn't it, honey?" she said, rubbing their noses together while she wrecked him.

Wrecked him.

His sides puffed in and out, his cock being treated to a slippery rhythm she composed on their behalf, her stiff nipples dragging through his damp chest hair as her hips rode, her enjoyment so clear, so unfettered, he could only watch her parted lips and glazed eyes in awe, her thighs opening and sliding, almost like she was army-crawling with the lower half of her body, her pussy starting to spasm; and she only moved faster, faster.

"Do you like that?" she said in a halting whisper, sitting up to play with her tits, kneading the supple flesh and teasing her nipples into buds that had him salivating. "Do you like being bare inside your wife?"

"*Love*," he managed, bearing down on his lower body to prevent himself from spilling. "You're going to make me bust."

That admission made her tremble. "But do you like it?"

"I fucking love it. Don't stop." His cock gave an ominous throb, his lower spine pulling hard. Hard. "Oh god, don't stop."

"Shhh." Watching his face closely, Eve pumped her hips faster. "Someone will hear you. They'll know I'm on top of my husband, making him moan."

"Exactly where you belong." Madden lifted his hips and held, grinding. "Right where I should have put you that night we danced at graduation. You were mine even then, Eve. And if you'd crooked your little finger at me, I'd have taken you behind the tent in your white dress and shown you how true that was. How true it'll always be."

The glow in her eyes was a crossroads of lust and regret. But he wanted to banish the latter and live in the now, the togetherness of them. To hell with the impropriety of it all, she was his number one priority and the only thought in his head was Eve's pleasure as he lifted his hips, again, again, and fucked her from below with vicious upward drives, bouncing her until she wailed, loud and long, the sound carrying god only knew how far until Madden jackknifed and stamped their mouths together, the contact of their tongues ending them both, the girl fairly melting in his lap, her hips jerking, her head falling back on her shoulders as she clenched around him viciously, pitching them over the edge together.

"Mine." He ripped the word hoarsely against her neck.

Seconds later, she slumped into his embrace, whispering, "Unequivocally."

CHAPTER TWENTY-EIGHT

Madden and Eve didn't go to sleep until three in the morning.

They were having too much fun.

To Madden's everlasting shock, Eve found crackers that weren't expired in the cabinet and paired them with marmalade from the fridge. They sat in the center of his bed with Eve in a borrowed T-shirt that said "Protect Your Nuts" and depicted a catcher in position behind the plate—a birthday gift from Elton, obviously. Madden himself was bare-chested in sweatpants with a fresh ice pack wrapped onto his shoulder and he sat, stupefied by his own luck, as the most beautiful woman on the planet knifed the sticky orange substance onto crackers and fed them into his mouth, his bedroom feeling less like a temporary crash zone and more like a haven for the first time.

He'd half expected Eve to clam up after they had sex, too much vulnerability on display for one night. Thank god she hadn't. With her hair in disarray and her face free of makeup, she fucking glowed, her smile coming so easy that his conviction that Eve should be with him—and out of Cumberland, kids and all—only grew by the minute. And there was no chance he'd say that out loud and risk shattering the perfect evening, but damn, his bones were feeling it. How the hell was he going to let her leave in the morning?

"I know you stumbled into baseball by accident. After all, I was there the day it happened." She flashed him a half smile. "Before that, what did you want to be when you grew up? When you were little, I mean."

"A grocery bagger."

Her laughter said his answer had caught her off guard and the rare lightness of the sound made him dizzy. "For the money or the apron?"

"The gossip," Madden scoffed, as if that should have been obvious. "My first memories are my mum taking me to the shops and finding out everyone's business from the man who bagged the ingredients for supper. Mr. Leary was petty as sin and everyone knew it, too, but they continued to tell him their secrets in exchange for somebody else's. I thought he was more powerful than the president of Ireland."

Her eyes were wide as saucers. "Do you remember any of the gossip? What was the best/worst thing you heard?"

"I once found out two of my primary school teachers were shagging and I pretended to be sick the next day, I was so anxious about seeing them." Watching Eve giggle into the crook of her elbow, Madden couldn't control his smile. "The little bits of hearsay were the best, though. Like the two elderly men in the neighborhood feuding because they supported rival rugby teams. One of them tipped over the other's grocery cart right there in the store—this is all coming from Mr. Leary, mind you, so it could be an exaggeration—but anyway, the man felt so ashamed about knocking over the cart, they had to call a priest down to the shops to absolve him. They still went back to feuding the next day, but it was smaller things, like sniffing aggressively at each other in the pub."

"Not the aggressive sniffing," Eve gasped, her eyes sparkling with tears of mirth. "Do you think Mr. Leary is still there?"

"I don't know," Madden said honestly. "If not, I hope at the very least they retired his apron."

Eve sat looking content for a moment. "When I was a kid, I wanted to be Vanna White. You know, the lady who turns the letters on *Wheel of Fortune*. Not because of the gowns, although I coveted that wardrobe." Eve shrugged. "But mainly because she was always smiling. I thought she had to be the happiest woman alive. She really only had to smile for half an hour a day, though. I didn't grasp that until I was older and I think it only made me envy her more."

Madden wanted desperately to pull Eve into his lap and hold her, because he didn't know the right words for the revelations she was bestowing on him, like little glimpses into the place she'd always been so cautious to allow anyone, even him, but he wanted to keep her relaxed. Free of pressure. Laughing. If this spell was broken in the morning, he wanted her to remember she was happy here with him. "Eve."

"Yeah?"

"I adore you, but it would have killed you to smile even for thirty minutes a day."

She was eating a cracker when he said it and she had to cover her mouth to keep it from ejecting along with her laugh. "They call me Vanna Spite."

His deep rumble filled the room. "Frowns not gowns."

"Stop," she wheezed. "Game show dreams: dashed."

"Something tells me you'll recover from the disappointment," he said dryly.

She grinned at him so long his chest started to hurt. "Were you hazed as a freshman on your college baseball team?"

Madden didn't bother trying to hide how happy it made him to have her curious. About him. To be showing it so openly. "I was, but not in any horrifying or illegal ways. Dirty jockstrap in my locker. Vaseline in my glove. Things like that."

"Boys are so weird. Did you haze the freshmen, too, when you became an upperclassman?"

"That's not really my style, love."

"I know." Eve paused in the middle of putting marmalade on a cracker to study Madden under her lashes, before continuing. "They probably idolized you."

He squinted at her, genuinely curious. "Why would they idolize me?"

"Because you have a moral code and nothing shakes it. You're solid and unwavering and good. I can imagine you in the locker room, sighing heavily and letting everyone else spin out."

"Did I ever tell you about the time I had to wait three days to marry my wife? I got so impatient I called my teammates overpaid egomaniacs and got a right cross for my trouble?"

She leaned forward to feed him a cracker and he bit in while looking her in the eye and smelling his soap on her skin, deciding he'd never been treated to a finer meal. "Even the calmest among us has a breaking point," she said quietly, sitting back with flushed skin, probably due to the fact that he couldn't hide his wonder and appreciation.

Eve thought nothing shook him? Madden wanted to bring up the fight he'd almost gotten into a week earlier with that son of a bitch who'd suggested she make house calls, but he didn't want to remind her of that. Even thinking about it made his scalp prickle with anger, so he could only imagine how the memory would make her feel. "You don't lose your cool very easily, either, Eve. What's your breaking point?"

A beat of silence passed while she chewed a cracker. "Apart from a threat to the kids, I don't think there's anything that could make me *show* that I'm at a breaking point." She wet her lips. "But that wouldn't mean I'm not cracking on the inside." She paused. "That doesn't mean I haven't cracked a million times on the inside."

"You can show me the cracks anytime you need." Not reaching for her in that instant sent a ripple of pain through his shoulder, he tensed so quickly. "I'll hold you together until you can manage it yourself."

Eve's smile was a little bittersweet. "You might not realize it, but I've shown them to you more than anyone over the years. Probably because you showed me your own."

For the first time that night, she withdrew slightly, as if realizing she'd revealed too much, gathering up the box of crackers and the plate holding the knife and marmalade, walking across the bed on her knees to set everything on his side table. "I think it's time to switch to heat on your shoulder. They gave you that heating pad at the hospital, right?" Madden struggled for a moment with letting Eve care for him, but ultimately dipped his chin. She said, "I'll grab it. Do you want another ibuprofen?"

"No, love."

She stood at the foot of the bed now, looking so sweet and unguarded in his oversize shirt and bare feet, the urge to wrap his protection around her was growing. "Do you want anything at all?" she asked.

Madden shook his head no, but that was a lie. He just didn't recognize it until Eve had left the room and the life, the magic, left along with her. Maybe it was the strange quality of the day, but he was suddenly in need of proof that Eve being there wasn't all in his imagination. He stood abruptly, unwrapping the plastic holding the ice pack on his shoulder, letting it drop as he followed her into the living room, his stride slowing when he saw she was sitting cross-legged in the dark, going through the hospital bag.

Not a fantasy. Real.

He leaned against the wall outside the bathroom and watched her, the moonlight turning her hair silver, highlighting the curve of her cheek.

I can't believe that's my wife.

The combination of lust and idolization was a potent one. It made his heart feel like a big, unwieldy thing, while his body primed itself. Made his breath short and coldcocked him with yearning. Just by looking at her. She'd probably never know the extent of how deep his obsession with her ran, would she? How could he even begin to describe it to her?

He couldn't.

His body ached to show her, though.

And so when Eve padded back in the direction of the bedroom, Madden intercepted her in the dark. Swallowing her gasp, he continued the thorough assault of her lips, her tongue, and her neck in the hallway, framing her face in his hands, worshipping her with slanted strokes of her mouth as they stumbled, his back meeting the wall first, before he surged forward to the other side of the hallway, taking her mouth like she'd signed over ownership with a signature on a dotted line. Pressing her to the wall this time.

"I lied. I do want something."

"I only need one guess what it is," she said, whimpering when he reached beneath the T-shirt to hold her bare pussy in his hand, her whole body liquefying between him and the wall.

"Can we fuck again, Eve?"

His bluntness made her thighs cinch shut around his hand, trembling. "Y-yes. Yes."

"You look like an angel." Madden dropped his forehead to hers, looking her in the eye while he strummed her clit with his thumb, but finding her so wet, he pushed his middle finger inside her, slowly, slowly, enjoying the shocked pleasure that overtook her features. "You don't like being treated like an angel, though, do you?"

"No. Not at all."

"Good girl being honest with me," he muttered, the abandoned kiss she offered him and the dampness that resulted encouraging him to add a second finger, twisting those digits gently, wet fucking her at a warm-up pace, his body surging forward to pin her more securely when her back arched off the wall on a ragged moan. "Be a little more honest now," he rasped into her neck, locking his fingers in deep and squeezing her sex in his grip, kissing her sobbing mouth once, twice. "What's going to make this come?"

"Madden. Please."

"You want to be craved, even if I'm the only man satisfying his craving."

"Yes," she whispered, his intuitiveness apparently making her hot, because she pulled down the waistband of his sweatpants, her hands stroking over the swell of his backside, her nails digging in and pulling him close, so close.

"Do you trust me?" he asked.

"Always. Yes."

Madden pulled Eve off the wall and walked her backward toward the bedroom, his fingers never stopping their exploration between her thighs. Not until they reached the edge of the bed and he dragged his fingers out of her tight heat. With her standing in front of him sucking in gulps of breath, he picked up his phone and opened the camera app, not hitting record, but engaging the flash and shining it at her legs. Giving her the illusion of recording was easy, knowing he'd rather die than allow her image anywhere on the internet. Making her believe he might, though? He could do that. He could do anything if it gave her pleasure. "Lift up the shirt and show me something sweet, love."

Eve's lips were parted and swollen, her eyelids heavier than sandbags, turning her even sultrier, his girl so gloriously turned on by the flash on her naked thighs, she was nearly shaking. "Okay," she whispered, lifting the hem just enough to show the wet split of her pussy, before it was gone, her hands fisting in the material and pressing to her juncture, her chest beginning to heave faster, faster.

"Goddamn, that was so pretty. Next time, we'll give them a close-up." She inhaled and whimpered at the same time, those fists pushing in closer, as if she couldn't help but supply herself with much needed friction. "Turn around now and let me film. That's why you left your panties off, isn't it, Eve? To tease everyone?"

She almost couldn't manage to face the bed, her legs had become so visibly weak, but she managed, bending forward and supporting herself on both hands, her sides heaving while Madden tossed the hem of her shirt up to the middle of her back and shined the light on those full cheeks, smoothing his hand over them, massaging, running his thumb up that tempting split in the center.

"Fuck," he ground out. "Can't believe this is finally mine."

She was chewing her lip when she looked back over her shoulder at him, shivers racking her frame. "Let me feel it. Let me feel how much I'm yours."

Now it was Madden's turn to be unsteady, no choice but to toss the phone down on the bed beside Eve so he could take possessive hold of her hips, tilting them into position while at the same time, he nudged apart her ankles, his right hand dropping to his cock to stroke it against the soft flesh of her backside, his breath catching in his throat when he saw she'd picked up the phone and flipped the camera, holding it up so he could watch himself enter her from behind, his features tightening with heat, Eve's jaw falling open, her eyes locked in on him even as she moaned, her hips circling to take him deeper.

She dropped the phone after his first drive, their skin smacking loudly in the dim bedroom, the southern region of his stomach already protesting too much of her perfect pressure at once. Madden pushed deep and stayed still a moment, taking deep breaths to control himself, his mouth pressed against the side of her face. "Christ, there is nothing like the feeling of you around me." He pulled out, then thrust deeper, groaning. And without thinking, he gave her the fantasy she'd kept to herself so long that he wouldn't allow her to cloak it in darkness anymore. Not with him around. "Who wouldn't want to get this tight little thing on film? We'd make millions off it."

Eve jerked underneath him, cried out his name, and climaxed, her orgasm a swift and vicious twist of her inner walls, the hoarse echo of his name turning him on until he got lost, forgetting anything resembling rhythm and bucking into her from the back, her spasms and the angle of her hips urging him on until he broke, stiffening over the pliant curve of her body and dying a blinding death, his body singed by the excruciating pleasure.

They took a full two minutes to recover after they collapsed on the bed, their shallow breaths eventually slowing as they turned toward each other, Eve cuddling up into Madden's good side, tucking her face into his salty neck. "You're the only one who *gets* me. And you're the only one who gets me." She kissed his jaw. "Just making sure you knew."

"I love you, Eve," he said, the words escaping in a rush of gratitude. Of truth. A truth he'd known for so long, he couldn't remember a time before she'd defined love for him. "Go to sleep now, knowing that. Knowing it'll never change. It's been you the whole time and it'll be you for all the time to come."

Madden didn't need to hear Eve say the words back, because he already knew.

She wouldn't have been there, wouldn't have given him so much trust otherwise.

But he fell asleep dreaming of the day she'd let down her final wall and say them.

CHAPTER TWENTY-NINE

Eve had set her alarm to go off early. She had a long drive back to Cumberland; the twins were still with the Pages and she didn't want to impose on them any longer than necessary. As much as she wanted—maybe even needed—to remain in this blissful purgatory known as Madden's apartment, she had responsibilities to attend to. The sun had barely backlit the sky-scrapers in the immediate distance, so she assumed she wouldn't be alone in bed. And yet, the pillow beside hers was empty.

She stilled in the act of pulling aside the comforter and sheets to climb out of bed, Madden's voice reaching her from outside the bedroom. In the kitchen, maybe?

Who was he talking to?

With a broad yawn, she contemplated giving in to the urge to lie back down and wait for him to return, even if she just got a good morning kiss for her efforts. It would be worth the wait. Every single thing about him had been worth the wait. Recalling the three words he said to her in the middle of the night, her heart felt like one of those jewelry boxes with the spinning bal-lerina, just singing and pirouetting in her chest. She was tender between her legs and covered in whisker chafes . . . and she must be a greedy lover, because she could only crave more of him in-side her. Pressing and stretching and stroking.

Eve rolled over and inhaled his scent off the sheets, unable to suppress the smile that had started to feel natural sometime yesterday. This . . . was happiness. Miles and miles from Cumberland and the hundred-pound albatross around her neck that came with her position in the town. Maybe . . .

Maybe she should start thinking about moving one day.

Not today, of course. Or anytime soon. Just . . . someday.

Those tiny sprinkles of possibility caused relief to explode in her bloodstream, and she turned over on the bed, staring up at the ceiling, seeing images painted there. Ones she shouldn't allow herself to imagine. Not when they weren't possible.

Still, she thought of that house with the purple Christmas lights and her throat seized up with hope. Dangerous hope. When she closed her eyes to picture heaven now, it wasn't the posh interior of a burlesque club, it was them. Lying in a backyard beneath the stars, listening to the crickets chirp. For years, she'd driven herself to improve the club, make every detail perfect, but without having to set foot inside the Gilded Garden last night, she'd been lighter. Freer.

What did that mean?

She'd always dreamed of being accepted by her hometown.

Wouldn't leaving mean giving up on that dream?

Madden's voice rose slightly, and Eve frowned, turning her head to stare at the bedroom door. Was it her imagination or did he sound agitated?

Slowly, she stood and pulled on Madden's shirt, which had lain in a heap on the floor overnight, leaving it wrinkled but still decidedly perfect, because it belonged to him. Then she walked barefoot to the bedroom door and turned the knob, pulling it open without a sound and listening.

"I don't understand why this is anyone's business," Madden said. "This is my personal life we're talking about."

Several seconds of silence followed, though Eve could hear her pulse pick up its pace in her ears. Personal life. Who was he speaking to?

"Jesus Christ, why is everyone making such a big deal out of one single play? I performed the job I was hired to do. End of story. There *is* no story beyond that." A pause. "I don't care if the press disagrees. I wasn't signed by the Yankees to be a media clown. I'm a baseball player. That's all anyone should be concerned about. Not her."

Eve recoiled from the door, a sandstorm whipping up inside her rib cage.

Her.

As in . . . *her*?

What was going on?

"Isn't there a team lawyer who can issue a cease and desist?" She could hear him pacing now, his footsteps much slower than the rapid beat of her heart. "They can't just ransack our lives because the internet decided to take an overnight interest. They'll move on to someone else tomorrow." He cursed. "I swear to God, if anyone harasses Eve . . ."

His pacing stopped. A crashing sound followed from what Eve assumed was Madden's fist slamming into a cabinet.

"Do I know how her job reflects on the organization?" Madden asked in a hushed rasp. "What the fuck does that mean?" He hissed an exhale. "Don't even say the word *prenup* to me."

No. Please, no.

Out of necessity, Eve went on autopilot.

The shock of what she'd overheard was too great to deal with, so she desperately switched her focus to what she could control right now. Getting out of there as fast as possible. Driving back to Rhode Island, picking up the kids, thanking the Pages, getting an update on the construction at the club, preparing for the week. There was so much to do and she was two hundred miles away.

And if she'd heard correctly, she was causing trouble for Madden.

Not just by existing. By existing as his wife.

He'd garnered some attention with his heroic play yesterday and now he was under scrutiny. Which meant, she was. And he'd be guilty by association. Just like Skylar had been in high school. Outcasted because they were friends. Just like Lark and Landon being treated differently at school. Because of her.

"I'm such an idiot," Eve whispered, lurching around the room collecting her things. Panties. Her phone. Everything else, like her purse and shoes and dress, were on the other side of the door with Madden.

"Shit," she breathed, looking down at the screen of her phone.

Five texts from Veda. She'd slept through five texts?

Popped by the club last night and there's a news van in the parking lot. WTF.

A reporter asked if I know the owner of the club. I said no comment. Hilar.

Holy shit. You're on ESPN's Instagram.

HOLY SHIT. You're on the whole internet.

Hey. You should probably call me.

Taking the deepest breath possible when she felt like curling up in a hyperventilating ball on the floor, Eve inhaled deeply and left the bedroom with her chin firm, head high. She didn't make eye contact with Madden. She couldn't. Why had she agreed to this marriage?

What was this going to mean for him?

"Eve."

"Just grabbing my stuff."

"Don't even think about leaving." He tried to block her path, but she had momentum going in her favor and ducked past him, continuing out onto the balcony to find her dress, her shoes. She stripped off the borrowed shirt on the way back into the apartment, yanking on the dress without ceremony while eyeballing the living room for some sign of her purse. There.

As soon as she grabbed it, she'd go.

"Okay. You obviously overheard my phone call. There's some media attention involving us, but we're going to handle it together." When she tried to sidle quickly past him, Madden hooked Eve around the waist and drew her back against his chest. "Stop. Just stop."

Despite the fight-or-flight response burning her alive, her eyelids nearly fluttered closed over the firm, reassuring strength of him. The scent that washed over her, making her think of laughter and messy sheets and crackers and skin. Memories that would have to last a lifetime, because they couldn't make any more. "Let me go."

"No."

Oh god, being held by him was going to cause her to break down. "Madden, I'm sorry," she whispered, racked by a sob of pure devastation. Dread for everything to come. The unknown. "I'm sorry. I'm sorry."

He took a measured breath in and out. She didn't have to turn around to know he was angry. His frame vibrated with the emotion. "I don't consider myself a violent man, Eve, but I would very much like to murder everyone who put this burden of fucking responsibility on you." He turned her in his arms and shook her, but she could only stare at his chin and try not to shatter. "You are a miraculous woman. An amazing woman. And that includes everything about your past, present, and future. *They* are the problem. Not you."

"It won't matter. 'Amazing Woman Marries Yankees Catcher' is not the headline. The headline is 'Yankees Catcher Marries Daughter of Strip Club Owner.' Or 'Failing Burlesque Club Owner Sinks Claws into Yankee Phenom for Health Insurance.' Followed by a whole lot of quotes from the good people of Cumberland about how I've always been a blight on their town." Being careful of his shoulder, Eve wiggled out of his hold. *Get me out of here before I cause any more damage.* "It's okay, I can take it. The fact that you saved the game yesterday makes you a hero. I'll get all the blowback and that's good. That's good."

Madden looked like he could dissolve at any moment. A figure made of salt that had gotten stuck out in a rainstorm. "Eve, you are going to stay here and let me protect you from all this," he said, trying to keep his voice steady and failing. "The kids too. We're not dealing with this separately. We're not separating, *period.* I don't give a fuck what anyone is saying. You're the only thing I've *ever* given a fuck about."

Her heart lurched painfully. "No, I saw you yesterday with your team. I saw you wondering if you could really belong and the answer is yes. You can. You belong doing this and the opportunities are endless for you now. I'm sorry, Mad. There's too much at stake for you. I'm going." Eve hustled for the door and made it out, blowing into the hallway with her shoes in one hand, purse in the other. In the one stroke of luck that morning, a woman had just stepped into the elevator and held the door for Eve, even though she was visibly taken aback by Eve's dishevelment.

"*Eve.*"

Madden appeared in front of the elevator, bare-chested in sweatpants, right before the door closed, missing them by a split second. And she didn't feel an ounce of relief when the elevator started to descend. In fact, she felt sicker and sicker to her stomach the farther she got from Madden, his words rolling like dice around her head. *I don't give a fuck what anyone is saying. You're the only thing I've* ever *given a fuck about.*

He'd thank her one day, wouldn't he?

Down the road, he'd agree distancing themselves was the right thing to do.

Eve closed her eyes and listened to the whoosh sound every time the elevator passed another floor, trying to remember which direction she'd parked the car. If she had enough gas to get home. How much damage had she done by marrying Madden?

"I thought you looked familiar," murmured the woman beside her, holding up a copy of the *New York Post*. On the front page of the newspaper was a truly iconic shot of Madden, flat on his back, holding the baseball in a cloud of dust at home plate, beneath the headline "Introducing Bad Madden." In a smaller picture below, Eve had apparently been seen by a photographer as she left the hospital beside Madden, one shoulder wrapped in ice, the other arm draped across her shoulders. She was smiling up at him more dreamily than she knew herself capable of, Madden leaning down to kiss the crown of her head. She couldn't even read the caption beneath the photo. Maybe she didn't want to.

"I can't believe I live in the same building as Bad Madden," said the woman, eyeballing Eve's bare feet. "I hope there's no trouble in paradise."

Eve pressed her lips together and said nothing, the line of white, illuminated circles blurring in front of her eyes. Finally, they reached the lobby and the woman sped off, most likely due to Eve's pathetic vibes, and after a beat, she entered the lobby too.

Okay. Just need to get to my car.

Flashes went off one by one outside the building, blinding Eve through the glass double doors. At first, she was merely confused by the sudden ripple of voices that increased into shouts, but she slowly became aware of what was happening.

They were there for Madden.

They were there for her.

Shaking, Eve turned her back and searched the lobby for a place to sit down and put on her shoes, no choice but to use the lip of a giant potted plant. She had two options. Brave the throng of reporters who had taken a sudden and alarming interest in their lives. Or go back upstairs to Madden and be convinced to stay. That's exactly what would happen. They would fight and they would end up in bed. And she would tell him she loved him and confide how scared she was—and then he'd be stuck. As stuck as all these people would eventually believe him to be.

Go. She had to go.

Eve stood and squared her shoulders, clutching her purse and phone to her chest.

Just as she reached for the door, prepared to propel herself through the wall of people and cameras, a door burst open to her left and Madden stepped into the lobby, his chest covered in a light sheen of sweat.

"You took the stairs?"

"There's only one elevator," he muttered, his complexion whitening as he took in the gathered media with a dawning visage of dread. "What the fuck?" He pointed a very stern finger at her. "Eve, do not go out there or you'll give me a heart attack."

They stared at each other across ten feet of space.

Run to him. Do it. He'll protect you.

No, you have to protect him or he won't protect himself.

Eve yanked open the door, put her head down, and tunneled through the mass of people.

Madden's bellow echoed in her wake and it occurred to her the scene they were making. A lovers' spat. Airing their marital woes on the New York City sidewalk. It was the worst way to detract from the abundance of attention already being paid to them, but she'd lie low after this. After she escaped.

Behind her, she heard a grunt of pain and recognized the sound as coming from Madden, her heart flying up into her mouth. Madden's shoulder. Oh god, this couldn't be good for his injury. He was going to hurt himself even worse trying to follow her. Why couldn't she do anything right this morning? "Hey," she shouted, backtracking through the crowd, pulling reporters out of the way, shoving cameras without thinking. "Watch his shoulder. *Hey!* Please, watch his bruised shoulder!"

With a collective mutter, the crowd stepped back to give him space. Eve, as well. The tangle of voices silenced little by little until there was nothing but herself and Madden looking at each other from a short distance, their audience waiting in rapt stillness for something to happen. It was impossible not to acknowledge how truly gorgeous Madden looked with his naked, muscular torso, a stark white bandage on his shoulder, his finger-brushed hair, the low-hanging black sweatpants.

A puckered scar on the lower corner of his stomach.

He looked surly as hell, his eyes like twin blue bonfires.

Hard to believe this was the same man she'd played house with last night.

Heck, if she had a camera, she'd be filming him, too, but for now, the paparazzi seemed inclined to let things play out, but what did they think was going to happen?

Nothing, that's what. She was getting on the road where she belonged.

No sooner had Eve turned to go than a familiar hand grabbed her wrist, jerking, causing her to whirl around and lose her balance at the same time. She crashed into Madden's chest, his hand catching her chin to tilt her head back, that mouth stamping down on hers with such possessiveness, she lost her train of thought along with her reasoning skills and sense of survival, allowing him to take her mouth in a determined kiss that caused wires to cross and snap and fizzle inside her head.

Madden kissed her long and hard while the cameras shuttered away, and by the time she realized his intention, the damage was already done.

"You'll get no distance from me, Eve *Donahue*," he rasped against her mouth, keeping her jaw in his hand while delivering a firm, meaningful look. "I can see I'm not going to get through to you today, but I'm telling you right now, in front of God and everyone, you are my wife and that's how you'll stay." He kissed her stunned mouth one more time, hard. "Drive carefully. My heart is your passenger." Turning in a circle, he shouted, "If she doesn't get to her car safely, I'll get myself traded to Boston."

A gasp blew down the block.

And with that, Madden turned and stalked back to the building, nearly ripping the door off the hinges to get back inside. Slowly, Eve walked to her car without incident, although there was the sporadic snap of a camera lens.

And the gradual dimming of what might have been.

CHAPTER THIRTY

Madden unknotted his tie on the way out of his meeting with the Yankees' general manager, letting the frosted glass door shut with a resounding click behind him.

Exactly nothing had been resolved, as he'd been hoping. Now, instead of following Eve back to Rhode Island, he'd lost almost an entire day trying to run interference with the press, to absolutely no avail. The only thing this meeting had served to confirm was what he already knew to be true. New York City sports journalism went big and splashy when they detected the public's interest in a story, the fallout it caused in the personal lives of their subjects be damned.

This morning, when he'd looked out over the mass of cameras and shouting reporters, he'd realized this in a snapshot of clarity. There was nothing he could do to dampen what they considered his rise to fame and the public romanticizing of his and Eve's relationship.

Romantic? They didn't know the fucking half.

But they were actively trying to find out.

He'd hired security for Eve and, thankfully, she'd accepted. At least, that's what he'd been told over the phone by the head of her new security team.

As predicted, she wasn't answering his calls.

Could he really blame her after he'd kissed her in the middle of the avenue? Her one condition for marrying him had been to keep their union quiet. Well, he'd soundly blown the roof off that secret, hadn't he? He'd been desperate to show Eve that he didn't give a fuck about everyone else's opinions. That he'd choose her, stand beside her, every single time. And yeah, his wife being photographed on the front page of the *Post* for everyone to ogle had roused his possessive instincts, because he'd also felt the need to make it crystal clear Eve was under his protection. That she belonged to him.

If Madden wanted that to be true much longer, this attention on him, on *them*, needed to die down.

Unfortunately, public interest had only seemed to grow throughout the morning, footage of yesterday's catch now interspersed with shirtless Madden kissing Eve among the media mayhem. They were calling him Down Bad Madden now, which didn't bother him at all. What troubled him were the pictures of Eve in the VIP box starting to surface, along with headlines that only validated the concerns Eve had had all along.

"Madden's Madam: Catcher Kisses Nudie Club Cutie."

They'd cheapened her. They'd cheapened the art form of burlesque and the club she'd sunk her blood, sweat, and tears into.

And he'd been the one to drag her into the spotlight.

Madden walked out of the building on East 161st Street feeling too much like a caged animal to call for a cab. He remained in the shaded doorway, trying to figure out his next move. Was there one? Or did they just ride out the tide of interest until the press moved on to someone or something else?

At the moment, he was just grateful no one had followed him uptown. The last thing he needed was to get arrested for decking a reporter.

He called Elton, who answered on the second ring.

"Hey, man," answered his friend, his concern palpable.

"Hey. Are you still in Cumberland?"

"Yeah, I'm at my parents' house. We convinced Eve to stay here with the kids for a while, hoping maybe those news vans outside the club would give up and go home."

"Eve is there," Madden breathed, a hint of pressure in his chest alleviated. "Good. Is she . . . okay?"

"She's looking a little shell-shocked, to be totally honest. We had to turn off the television because pictures of you two were popping up during the entertainment portion of the news." He sensed Elton shaking his head. "This craziness couldn't have happened to two more private people. What a kick in the ass."

"Yeah." Madden dragged a hand down his face, his one wish in life to be at the Pages' house in front of Eve at that moment so he could reassure her in some way. Or to just be around her. See her. Hold her. In the hours since she'd left, he'd been operating with the most important half of himself missing.

"What did the front office have to say about it?"

"They act concerned and they claim they're going to make some calls about the intrusion of privacy, but they're full of shit. After a string of low-attended games, they need the attention, good or bad." Madden exhaled his frustration. "All because I held on to the stupid ball. What else was I supposed to do?"

"Dude, that guy plowed into you like a freight train."

"I almost wish I dropped it at this point."

"Blasphemy, but I'll allow it, considering the circumstances."

"The only silver lining is I can't practice for a week. As soon as I get back to my place and pack, I'm heading to Rhode Island."

"That's good. Eve needs you here, whether she admits it or not."

Madden rubbed his forehead. "Whatever you do, don't say that to Eve."

"Nope. I'd like to keep my balls attached to my body."

Madden frowned at the silence that followed, the pacing he heard in the background. "Is everything all right with you?" he asked Elton. "You seem kind of preoccupied."

"Me? Yeah, I'm good." A floorboard creaked and Madden recognized the sound. It belonged to the loose floorboard in front of the Pages' front door. "Fine, I'm slightly preoccupied."

"What's up?"

"Oh, I don't know. Maybe because Veda was supposed to be here an hour ago, but her phone is dead. Get this—I think she might have fallen asleep. In the middle of the day! And do you want to know why?"

"I have a feeling you're going to tell me."

"Because last night, when I dropped her off—at midnight, mind you—she went back out. After midnight! To go watch a friend play a gig. Can you imagine?"

"Okay, first of all, you sound like an old man," Madden responded. "Second, why are you tracking this girl's movements?"

"Because I'm . . . morbidly fascinated by how somebody can live like this," Elton said. "How does she function with no sleep and never more than thirty percent battery left on her phone? It's madness, I tell you."

Madden was beginning to get suspicious. Elton was spending a lot of time worrying about Veda, who he wasn't dating. Could *never* date. Not when their lifestyles were polar opposites. "How's her sister?"

"Who?" At first, Elton sounded genuinely confused. "Oh right. Good. Alexis is . . . great," he muttered. "I have to fly back to Florida in the morning, so I'm taking her out tonight. I think. I haven't followed up with her yet."

"Maybe you should get on that?"

Elton sighed.

"You like Veda."

"Nope," Elton fired right back.

"Deny it all you want."

"Did I mention she's asleep at two p.m.?" Elton asked, scoffing. "She dropped out of college to start a band with her *situationship,* who dresses like *Elvis.* She wears a push-up bra. She's at least ten years from wanting to settle down and I'm—"

"Ten minutes."

"Admittedly."

"How do you know she wears a push-up bra?"

"Forget I said that. The point is, Veda is a living, breathing headache and Alexis is exactly what I'm looking for—" Elton broke off suddenly, his last statement followed by a pregnant pause. "Veda. When did you get here?" Madden's best friend took a heavy breath. "I don't know what you heard, but I didn't mean . . ." Footsteps. "Come back here. I'm sorry."

"Shit," Madden murmured to himself.

"Fuck. I have to go. I'll call you—" Again, Elton stopped talking, that floorboard near the front door groaning in the background. "Hold on, someone is pulling up."

Madden pushed off the building, his pulse playing leapfrog. "Who is it? Media?"

"No." He made a raw sound of disbelief. "Holy shit, Mad. It's Eve's sister."

CHAPTER THIRTY-ONE

Coming home to Lark and Landon was like a balm to Eve's soul.

They'd heard snippets of adult conversations and clips of the news surrounding Eve and Madden, but they were more interested in convincing their aunt to take them to McDonald's for dinner. Some very welcome normalcy.

"Please, Aunt Eve. Please," Lark pleaded.

Landon clasped his grubby hands together. "Please. I have a loose tooth!"

Eve reared back. "And chicken nuggets are good for loose teeth?"

"Yes," Landon said, solemnly, his chef's hat sitting askew on his head. "Toys are good for them too."

"Oh, really? I've never heard that." Eve laughed, though she could hear the strain in her own voice. "Guess we better get some extra."

They ran full speed into Eve, wrapping their arms around her legs and squeezing. Normally, she was a hair ruffler in these types of situations, but she found herself kneeling down in front of the twins and opening her arms, the smell of dirt and crayons going a long way to reassuring her that everything would be fine eventually. Maybe not today or next week, but no matter what happened, these kids would still call her Aunt Eve and think she walked on water. God, that was comforting.

She rubbed circles into each of their backs, pressing her cheek to the top of Lark's head. "Go stuff your things into your backpacks. Toothbrushes, especially. We should hit the road and let the Pages get back to their regularly scheduled program."

"I won't hear of it," Vivica said from her spot in the kitchen. "Not until we know for sure those vultures aren't lurking outside your apartment."

"Vultures?" Landon asked, wide-eyed.

Vivica winced. "Sorry."

"It's okay." Eve took Landon by the elbows and smiled. "It's nothing to be scared of. People who work at the newspapers want to ask me about Madden because he's so famous. Did you see his big play?"

Landon beamed. "Yup!"

"I saw it too," Lark piped up. "That other guy is a dick!"

"Whoa. Language."

Lark pointed across the room to where Elton was pacing in front of the door for some odd reason. "Elton said so."

The bad influence in question held up his hands. "Guilty."

"Good lord, Elton," Vivica chided. "She's never going to leave these precious babies with us again."

"Don't be so sure about that," Eve teased, standing as the kids ran off to collect their things. Or play in mud, whichever struck their fancy. Then in a more serious tone she asked, "How will we know if there are people outside my building?"

"Veda was supposed to swing by and check," Elton said, his tone irritable. "But she fell asleep, and her phone is dead."

"Ah. She must have been out last night."

"Oh sure, just a little five a.m. outing. No big deal. No idea if she's in a safe establishment. Or if there's anyone making sure she gets home all right." Elton waved his hands around. "Let's all just fly by the seat of our pants here, shall we?"

"Are you okay?" Eve asked, raising an eyebrow.

"Oh, I'm just peachy," Elton said sourly, looking down at his phone, then at her, covertly enough that her instincts pinged. That was Madden calling. The knowledge alone that her husband was on the other end of the call made her chest knit up like a baseball glove. Where was he? What was he doing?

Was he still half stuck in the afterglow of last night and yearning to be back there, the way she was every time she closed her eyes?

The proof of his touch lingered everywhere on her body, from the chafed patch on the curve of her neck, courtesy of his unshaven face, to the soreness between her legs. His gruff midnight voice wouldn't leave her ears, sneaking up on her in the middle of lectures to herself. Self-admonishments for getting too cozy. For letting herself dream about a future for her and Madden. For going to the hospital and acting like Madden's wife in the first place when . . .

That's what she wanted to be. Deep down.

Not even that deep down anymore, because she'd allowed hope to ransack her common sense. Now their night of playing house only served as proof of how wonderful a life with Madden would be . . . if only she were a different person.

On the other side of the room, just outside the sliding glass door that led to the back deck, Veda appeared with a pinkie wave and a yawn.

Eve hid the wave of gratitude for her new friend behind a smirk.

Leave it to Veda to show up at the back door instead of the

front, wearing a blue mechanic's jumpsuit and her hair tied up with a bright red bandanna.

Eve crossed to the back door, wordlessly letting in the younger woman.

They started to exchange greetings, but their attention was drawn to the television, where Sherry Shepherd was relaying yesterday's news to a studio audience. "And did you see that Yankees game yesterday?" A ripple of yeses went through the crowd. "Not the baseball game. I'm talking about the game that happened afterward." An image of Madden and Eve French-kissing among a plethora of cameras popped up on the screen behind the host. "Because this Yankee has *got* game. Look at this man unafraid to kiss his woman in public. We've been sleeping on catchers, ladies—"

The television winked off, courtesy of Vivica. "Sorry about that," she said with a wince.

"It's fine," Eve whispered. But it wasn't. In fact, she felt dizzy. That was her picture. On national television. Who knew what kind of details about her personal life were to follow? "I just need a minute."

"Take your time," Veda said, patting her arm. "I'll go annoy Elton."

"Good idea," Eve managed, sitting down on the edge of the couch. She'd been driving for four hours in silence and obviously the story had escalated during that time.

Don't look at your phone.

Don't do it.

Although forewarned meant being forearmed, right? Maybe she should do a quick Google search and find out what was being said. Purely so she'd know in advance how badly this whole nightmare was going to reflect on Madden.

She pulled out her phone and deployed the search engine.

"Madden's Madam: Catcher Kisses Nudie Club Cutie."

This, from TMZ.

Nudie Club?

Madam?

Eve scrolled down some more and clicked on a Buzzfeed article titled "Why Is Everyone Suddenly Talking About the Yankees? We Explain the Down Bad Madden Buzz."

"Oh my god," she whispered as picture after picture appeared on her screen. Not just of her at the game and hospital yesterday, but pictures of the inside of the club, Eve posing with patrons. Where did Buzzfeed get them? They weren't on the club website.

She read further.

> Sources close to the couple say they've known each other since high school, but claim they've been on and off again, because Donahue can't come to terms with Keller owning a burlesque club where she is a regular performer. The club, which was an honest-to-goodness strip club back in the day and a source of much vitriol in the town, was passed down from Keller's father . . .

Eve's stomach sank slowly to the floor.

Half this article wasn't true at all. Were they just allowed to print lies?

She couldn't even tell if this was a worse look for her or Madden.

A sudden hush in the house caused Eve to look around, finding Elton and Vivica staring out the window by the front door.

"Please don't tell me there are reporters here," she said, rising.

The moment Elton turned around and she saw his face, she knew it was something worse than the press, but she couldn't imagine what. What could be worse than bringing this circus to another one of her loved ones' doorsteps?

Please. I can't take one more punch today.

"Eve." Elton came forward with a line between his brows, unexpectedly taking her by the shoulders, alarming her even more. "It's going to be okay."

"What's going on?"

"It's your sister. Ruth is here."

A full-body chill cascaded downward from the top of her head to the soles of her feet. Ruth was here. Ruth was *here*? What kind of condition was she in? Should she be around the kids? Why wasn't Eve given any warning about her return?

Eve realized she'd frozen halfway between the living room and the front door, everyone in the room staring at her. Waiting for a reaction.

Jesus. Pull yourself together.

"Okay," she said, wetting her parched lips. "Okay, I'll just . . . I'll go outside and talk to her. Can you occupy the kids while I figure out what's happening?"

"I'm on it," Veda said.

Even in the midst of her own turmoil, she didn't miss the shadows in Elton's eyes as they followed Veda's retreating back down the hallway. But she couldn't worry about that now. For better or worse, she had a sister to reunite with.

WHEN EVE WALKED out onto the Pages' front porch, her knees had almost buckled from the relief of knowing her sister wasn't only alive and well, but visibly healthy. Hair in a ponytail, face free of the pinched misery that had been there the last time they were together. This was the sister who lived in Eve's memories as a preteen, before addiction sank its claws into Ruth.

Ruth Keller was direct, a little guarded, but a good, loyal person who'd gone through those early stages of life with the same stigma as Eve. Instead of pushing everyone away and driving herself to prove something, the way Eve had, Ruth chose numbness. And then the numbness became normal until it almost killed her.

This time, she'd chosen her kids. Eve couldn't be prouder of the willpower that must have taken. Couldn't be prouder they shared that same stubbornness. After Ruth asked about the kids and Eve assured her sister they were happy, healthy, and full of beans, they sat in silence for a full five minutes before Ruth began to talk.

"I went through with the six-week treatment program," said her sister now, her voice clear. Confident. They sat side by side on the front steps of the Page house, both of them looking at the ground, neither one of them comfortable with the multitude of emotions that came with this kind of reunion. "I can't even describe what it feels like not to have that burden anymore. How clearheaded I feel, like I just broke out of a nightmare."

"I'm glad, Ruth," Eve whispered. "I'm so glad. Good for you. I'm proud of you."

Her sister lifted her hand, hesitated, then reached over to hold Eve's.

All Eve could do was stare at their clasped hands, wondering if they'd ever done that before. If so, the displays of affection must have been when she was really little, because she had no memory of them.

"Eve."

"Yes?"

"I'm the one who is proud of you." Ruth let that statement hang between them. "We were never very close and I regret that, but that didn't stop you from stepping up for me at a moment's notice. I'll never be able to thank you enough."

Oh god, she was going to take Lark and Landon.

Eve could see it coming.

The overwhelming wave of sorrow made her feel so guilty, but she couldn't control it. Not now. Not with everything else going on.

"There's a place down in North Carolina . . ." started her sister, prompting Eve to make a harsh, involuntary sound. Ruth only squeezed her hand tighter, as if she understood what her return was costing Eve. "It's housing for single mothers like me. They help care for the kids, help women get on their feet and find a job—and there's built-in treatment." She blew out a breath. "I need to go, Eve. I want this. I don't want to mess up again, and this is the best way to ensure that doesn't happen. Best way to make sure I can be with my kids. Clean."

Eve nodded vigorously. "I understand. I do."

"They're going to miss you, but we *will* visit. Or you'll visit us." Ruth used their joined hands to turn Eve's face, so they were eye to eye. "The goal is to end up back in Cumberland. I want them to grow up near their famous aunt."

A little jolt took place in Eve's belly. "You saw the news."

"I did." Ruth studied her. "I also got your voicemail from the day you married Madden. I guess I wasn't surprised when you admitted to loving him." Her attention dropped to Eve's abdomen, her scar tingling beneath the scrutiny. "You wouldn't have sacrificed so much for him unless you did."

It hadn't felt like a sacrifice. More like a blessing to reach into the depths of her feelings for Madden and find an offering. To replace the words she couldn't say out loud. "Yes. I do love him very much."

"Do I sense a but coming?"

"No buts. Our love is just a complicated business."

Ruth nodded, remaining quiet for a few extra beats. "Listen, Eve. You're in the middle of something hard and I don't want to add to it, but the timing . . . it's just timing. I was going to take a few days to visit with the kids, make my way back to them slowly, and give you a chance to say a long goodbye." She paused. "But I thought it might be for the best if we kept the twins out of the media limelight you've got on you right now. These people seem kind of aggressive. The last thing I want is to have that limelight include me. You don't need that on top of everything else."

If that didn't prove they were sisters cut from the same cloth, Eve didn't know what did. She wanted to feel resentment toward the legions of people clicking on harmful articles and the slander artists embellishing the truth, but she didn't have the energy. Her ability to fight had all but flatlined in the relief of seeing her sister healthy. In the sadness of knowing her time with Lark and Landon was over. But she needed to make one thing clear.

"You know, no matter what they printed, I'd be proud of you, Ruth. Okay?" Eve took a halting breath. "Never ashamed. Not for a second."

Ruth gave her a watery look. "Same goes."

"Good" was all Eve could muster up. "Should we go see the kids and explain everything?"

"Yes, please." Her sister swiped at her eyes. "I can't believe I haven't held my babies in six weeks."

"They missed you too. Believe me." Eve swallowed hard. "When you get a chance, make some meatballs with Landon. Okay?"

"I can't wait."

Both sisters stood, turned, and walked slowly up the steps. "I might be returning them with slightly dirtier mouths and for that I apologize."

Veda opened the door before Eve got the chance, her interested gaze bouncing between the sisters. "Uh, Eve. I'm sorry to interrupt." She held up her phone, shaking it a little. "Is now a bad time to tell you Full Bush Rhonda called in sick tonight?"

"Full Bush who?" exclaimed her sister.

Eve never got a chance to explain because the twins came barreling out into the open at the sound of their mother's voice, throwing themselves into her waiting arms, each of them promptly bursting into tears of joy. And it was one of the most beautiful sights Eve could remember witnessing and one she would carry with her for a lifetime. But she could also feel a dramatic shift happening inside her.

A perfect collision of grief, relief, and fear.

The pressure of holding it together too long.

The total lack of control of her own situation. The theft of her privacy.

Everyone in this town and now the world believed her to be something she wasn't, and she couldn't do anything about that, could she?

Unless . . .

She could find a way to reclaim her own story.

Take back control.

Show everyone they couldn't dictate her shame if she refused to feel any.

Eve looked at Veda. "No worries. I'll take her spot."

CHAPTER THIRTY-TWO

Eve sat in her car at the very edge of the parking lot outside the Gilded Garden, observing the utter chaos from a distance. A line of people waited to get inside and more were on the way, headlights appearing every other minute at the entrance to the lot. Some patrons were being interviewed by women in sleek pantsuits holding microphones, their cameramen close behind.

She cracked the driver's-side window, catching the faint twang of a stand-up bass coming from inside the club. Presumably, the All-Nighters were warming up, preparing for their big fundraiser performance, but the clientele in line were such a mixture of ages, Eve deduced a lot of them were here to catch a glimpse of Bad Madden's kissing partner.

They were going to catch a whole lot more than a glimpse.

Exhaling through her nose, Eve sank farther into the seat and watched the lights flicker on the Gilded Garden sign, trying with all her might to breathe through the emptiness. After a tearful goodbye, the kids were gone. Just like that. On the road to North Carolina. She'd softened the blow of their abrupt parting by explaining they needed to go on an adventure and report all the cool details to her in a weekly phone call. Thankfully, their excitement over seeing their mom cushioned the sudden separation for them, but Eve herself was adrift. The fact that they could disappear from her everyday life with so much speed proved they'd never really been hers to begin with, right?

Just when it had started to feel like they were. Hers.

Her phone buzzed in her lap, but she didn't bother looking at the screen, her gaze still fastened on the flickering sign. Madden would be calling again. He had to stop eventually, though. A few hours ago, she might have been inclined to answer and talk through the reasons they needed to go their separate ways, but her grief over watching the kids vanish at the end of the driveway had left her lethargic.

Well, if she was going to give the performance of a lifetime, she needed to buck up. The public wanted her flesh and her soul and all her secrets? She'd hand them over in a way *she* chose. In a way *she* controlled. And her performance in front of all these lookie-loos would be the nail in the coffin on her relationship with Madden. Let the customers take their pictures, let the cameras roll. Post her all over the internet. Drive home the fact that she was bad for him. She was bad for everyone.

That she'd briefly thought otherwise during their night in Manhattan was laughable now. Look at the circus they'd attracted. If she remained married to Madden, the attention would only lead to more stories about her. Madden, a good man, would become the butt of a joke by association and Eve couldn't bear it. This marriage needed to be over.

It ended tonight.

Eve yanked down the visor and flipped open the mirror, checking the balance of her cat eyes, running a pinkie finger beneath the red curve of her bottom lip. Her distant gaze alarmed her enough to give her pause, but ultimately, she slipped on her black stilettos and climbed out of the car, inhaling the spring breeze that blew her loose hair back, that same wind ruffling the silver fringe of her skirt. Last, she checked the laces of her black corset top . . . and started to strut.

Bedlam didn't break out until Eve was nearly at the pathway leading to the front entrance, then every head seemed to turn simultaneously, cameras pointing in her direction. Three reporters bounded over and shoved their microphones in her face, asking the questions she'd anticipated.

Will Madden Donahue be in attendance tonight?

What is your exact relationship to the catcher?

Is it true he disapproves of the club?

Why take your clothes off when you're married to a Yankee?

Eve continued to walk, staring straight ahead and not answering a single one of their questions, some part of her knowing they just wanted words to twist. A sound bite. She wouldn't reward them for dragging her and Madden into the public eye, though. At least not like this. She'd give them the payoff of her own choosing onstage.

It wasn't until one of the reporters asked an unexpected question that her step faltered, the oxygen turning icy in her lungs.

"Is it true you donated a kidney to Madden Donahue?"

Was it all in her head the way everything went silent? The woman who'd asked the question had done it quietly, but it caused the other two reporters to whip their heads around, their surprise obvious. Eve's heart kicked into a gallop, then a sprint, her mouth going as dry as cotton. How . . . how did they know that? How could anyone know that?

As of now, it appeared to be a mere suspicion, but how long would that last?

A camera flash to Eve's right broke her out of her stupor and she propelled herself into motion once again, speed walking blindly past the line and bouncer, into the packed club, taking in everything at once with the eye of an owner.

Thank god she'd called in extra bar staff and waitresses. They had the crowd handled. Some patrons were seated, but the audience was standing room only, and she even recognized some faces from town. From the past. Good. Might as well burn her reputation all the way down. She didn't have to worry about fallout on the kids anymore, did she?

Ignoring all the sudden attention on her, Eve traded a thumbs-up with Veda, who was onstage doing a sound check. Eve wove through the tables as quickly as possible, releasing a sigh of relief when the dark backstage area enveloped her. Even that stale hint of ancient musk was welcome. She sat down in one of the tufted performers' chairs and stared at her reflection in the mirror, the reporter's question replaying itself in her head.

Is it true you donated a kidney to Madden Donahue?

That was it. Her final layer of what she could control was gone. Torn away.

How soon until he found out? How was he going to react?

Desperate for something to do with her hands, Eve pulled open one of the vanity drawers and located a pair of long black silk gloves, drawing them on jerkily.

"Eve?"

She turned her head to find Elton was backstage now, approaching her cautiously.

"Hey, Elton. I didn't know you were coming." Her laugh was a touch hysterical. "You're about to get to know me a whole lot better."

"Yeah," he said, scratching his chin. "You're really performing, are you?"

"Yup."

"Look, I'm not the right person to have this talk with you, but my sister is in Boston and you're not answering her calls. Madden is in traffic ready to commit heinous acts of violence to get here. Veda is . . ." He gestured to the curtain. "Out there. So, it's just me and I'm playing big brother, whether you like it or not."

Eve leaned toward the mirror to spread around her glittering eye shadow, which had started to gather in the crease of her eyelid. "Fire away, Elt."

He shifted in his boots. "It has been a wild forty-eight hours. A lot of changes for you. A lot of lies being told about you and Mad—and that's not fair, Eve. But I'm worried all this upheaval is making you perform tonight for the wrong reasons, you know? You want to do burlesque in front of all these people because you enjoy it? Fine. Madden will be pissed off, but he'll get over it. Now, if you're performing because everything is blowing up in your face and you want to add some kerosene, that's a different story."

Being called out so accurately burned. "I've been a pariah since you've known me."

"My family has never seen you that way," Elton said. "In fact, a lot of families in this town see you for the amazing person you are. It's just the law of the land that assholes are always the loudest."

"I know. I know that." Eve took a breath. "You might not understand this, but the only way to salvage my pride is to lean into that image now. I have to own it and show them I don't give a fuck what they think."

"You don't have to do anything. In fact, do nothing. Let the dust settle."

"It's never going to settle for me."

Elton opened his mouth to respond, but the All-Nighters chose that moment to start playing, the sound of deep, plucky bass filtering in through the heavy velvet curtain. Out of necessity, Elton came closer, presumably to continue their conversation. But when Veda started to sing, he stopped in his tracks, looking like he'd been struck by a bullet between the eyes. "Is that . . . that's Veda."

Studying his face, Eve nodded. "She's really good, right?"

Elton took a few steps and turned to lean back heavily against the wall, his chin dropping down toward his chest. "No. She's amazing." He raked a hand through his hair, letting it fall to his side, listening to her croon the chorus, start to finish. "I said something stupid and she overheard it. Now she won't even look at me. I didn't realize how much I need her to look at me until she stopped doing it."

"Aren't you taking her sister out tonight?"

"She's here," he said, sounding numb. "She's at the bar."

"Jesus, Elton." Eve shook her head. "You're the one who needs some advice."

"Hit me."

Eve never got the chance, because the All-Nighters finished their first song with a blistering high note from Veda. And before they could launch any further into the set list, Veda stumbled through the opening in the curtain, Situation Smith hot on her heels.

"What's wrong?" Veda asked him.

"What's *wrong*?" Smith advanced rather menacingly into Veda's space, poking her hard in the chest with his index finger. "You're showing off on purpose." A shove of Veda's shoulder. "You're so fucking selfish—"

Eve was already on her feet, readying to knock the kid's head right off its block, but there wasn't a chance for her to intervene. In the blink of an eye, Elton's hand manacled Smith's throat, ripping him completely out of Veda's orbit. With a sound Eve had never heard come from a human being before, Elton lifted the guy clean off the ground and body-slammed him to the floor, getting right in his face.

"Believe me, I was looking for any excuse to beat the shit out of you. *Any* excuse except you putting your fucking hands on her," Elton said through his teeth. "And you looked so comfortable doing it, I'm not even going to let you off with a warning. You don't deserve one." A right cross caught the musician in the nose, the crunch of cartilage leaving no room for speculation—that nose was broken. His agonized wail was further proof. "Touch her again and I'll break every bone in your fucking body."

For once, Veda appeared to have nothing to say, standing stock-still and regarding the scene before her with an expression of confused shock. Eve moved to stand behind her friend, wrapping an arm around her shoulders from behind. "Oops," Eve murmured. "Looks like you have to finish the set on your own."

Eve's remark didn't get the desired laugh, but at least she'd tried.

Elton stood slowly, shaking out his fist. "Are you okay?" he asked Veda, voice gravelly, his gaze so packed full of yearning, Eve felt compelled to look away to give them some privacy.

"As okay as I can be, I guess," said Veda quietly. "For a living, breathing headache."

Wincing, Elton came forward. "I didn't mean that, sweetheart."

"Don't call me sweetheart when you picked my sister." She huffed a humorless laugh. "Everyone always does."

"*I* didn't pick her, babe," Smith protested from his bleeding sprawl on the floor.

"Shut the fuck up, Smith," everyone shouted at the exact same time.

Smith rolled over onto his side and curled up in the fetal position.

"You set me up with your sister," Elton said, throwing up his hands. "What was that? Some kind of test?"

"I don't know. Maybe I was hoping you'd be different." Veda looked down at her hand, as if surprised to find herself still holding the wireless microphone. "I'm going to pick myself from now on. Because if I don't pick myself, no one will."

"Veda . . ." Elton rasped.

But she was already gone, stomping back onstage with a countdown for the band and belting the opening lyric, which just happened to be "That man's no good."

Elton remained rooted to the ground for a beat, his head tipped forward, then he moved without warning toward the back exit, kicking it open and disappearing into the night. Deeming the sobbing man on the ground harmless, Eve sat down and waited for her turn to take the stage.

CHAPTER THIRTY-THREE

By the time Madden pulled into the parking lot of the Gilded Garden, he was ready to combust. He'd have been there two hours earlier, if not for the congestion on the highway. And when he saw that there wasn't even one available parking spot, his panic increased. Too many fascinated people around Eve. Too many members of the media warring over information, wanting to know more about them and willing to get up close and personal to track down details. Anything they could report to feed the growing public interest.

Even now, he could see cameramen and reporters lurking at the front entrance, barred entry by the bouncer. That was a good thing, at least. To avoid being rushed and questioned, Madden drove his truck around back, through an opening in the trees, and parked at the backstage exit, alighting from his truck as fast as possible before anyone caught wind of his arrival.

Keys in hand, he juggled until he found the right one. The key Eve had given him years earlier and he never thought he'd have to use. Thankfully, it still worked, and Madden let himself into the backstage area.

As soon as he heard the music, he knew he was too late.

It was the same song that played the night he'd walked into the empty club and found Eve dancing by herself. His wife was out there on that stage right now. And did he like her taking off her clothes in front of strangers? Hell no, he didn't. He wanted the seductiveness of Eve to be deployed only on him. Only ever on him. But he was more upset knowing she'd been driven out there by desperation. By the self-destructive need to detonate a bomb and walk away giving everyone the finger.

Including him.

And yet, as he took a position at stage left to watch her, out of view of the crowd, he saw the woman he'd fallen in love with. God, she was fucking glorious in her unsmiling defiance, black silk gloves on the ground at her feet. Standing with her hip cocked in the blue spotlight, she pulled the lace of her corset with a coy flutter of her eyelashes, sending the crowd into a tizzy, the volume increasing as she loosened the black, ribbed garment more, more, before swiftly giving the audience her back and letting the corset tumble down, past her hips to the floor.

She kicked it backward at somebody in the front row with the aid of her sky-high heels, hitting them square in the face. "Oops." She pouted over her shoulder.

She wore nothing now but heels, a tiny silver skirt, and a black lace bra that looked suspiciously sheer from where he was standing. His body reacted to naked Eve the way it had been made to do, his cock swelling a little more with every wiggle of her hips. And yet, his hunger was accompanied by the twist of dread in his stomach, his chest. His ample knowledge of Eve told him this was wrong for her. She was acting out. But what could he do about it without making the situation worse? Her control had been stolen over the last forty-eight hours. He couldn't and wouldn't take any more of it.

A beat dropped midway through the song and Eve moved with it, turning to the crowd and letting them see her in the brief, transparent bra, their whistles and cheers egging her on, and it was hard to know that, despite her mental turmoil in this moment, her underlying desire to be on display was being satisfied.

Eyes closed, body locked in a sensual roll, Eve lowered the side zipper of her skirt, all the way to the bottom, and Madden's mouth dried up, his pulse thickening everywhere because he couldn't take his attention off the beauty of her, peeling open the side of her skirt in the sapphire light and . . .

What was that?

She turned away from the audience again before her panties could come into view . . . and they must have been low-cut panties, instead of her usual high-waisted ones. The ones she always wore and had in every color. But not tonight and . . . Eve stopped on a dime as she faced Madden, her movements ceasing as if her batteries had run out. He couldn't see her face, though; all he could see was the scar running from the lower right side of her belly button, curving kind of like a hockey stick and ending near her pelvis.

Hot and cold flames engulfed his body, the sound of the music turning thin and distorted in his ears. His brain struggled through a violent tide of confusion to make sense of Eve having that scar. A kidney donor scar. He knew. He knew what they looked like, because he'd researched the process extensively, wanting to know what his donor had gone through. Why they thought him worthy. Wanting to understand why someone would save his bloody life and not come forward. Not give him the opportunity to say thank you.

Knowing this stubborn, complicated, and quietly generous woman as well as he did now . . . how in god's name had he never guessed it was her?

His stomach was collapsing in on itself.

What if there had been a complication with the surgery?

She only had one kidney now, his Eve. What if something happened to the remaining one? What if she needed the one inside him?

Madden had no control over his actions and he must have taken a step into view, because suddenly the crowd was chanting his new, ridiculous nickname, but he couldn't see anything or anyone but his wife, his savior. His hero. None of these people would ever know they'd been in the presence of someone who'd sought only to be selfless and gotten nothing but persecution in exchange.

In that moment, he wanted to burn the whole town down.

"No," he heard himself saying, his fingertips tracing the air in the shape of her scar. "No, love. No."

Eve stared back at him with an attempt at defiance, but her chin was wobbling, the blue light turning her eyes into lakes of moisture.

"Why? Why didn't you *tell* me?" he said uselessly, because the music absorbed his voice, but she seemed to read his lips, nonetheless. Not that she responded. In fact, Eve seemed to come free of a trance in the moments that followed, looking out at the spread of faces and drawing into herself, the spell she'd woven now broken for her.

Madden stood there at a loss for what to do. How to keep breathing now that he knew what she'd sacrificed for him. How did someone live under the weight of so much love and gratitude for a person?

My god, the *strain* she would feel if he let it all show.

Just then, the love of his life was struggling, however. He could read her like a book and she'd been interrupted in the middle of making the point she felt compelled to make. Furthermore, it occurred to Madden that his sudden appearance had put a halt to the performance, and he looked disapproving, just as the media suggested he might be.

No, he wouldn't be that. He'd never be that again.

And he wouldn't stand in the way of her taking back her control.

Without examining his actions too closely, simply doing what felt right for Eve, Madden walked farther out onto the stage, moving closer to Eve until she had to tip her head back to look at him.

"Keep going, love," he leaned down to say in her ear. "I'm right here with you."

"You shouldn't be here for this," she whispered.

Madden tipped up her chin and gently notched their lips together. "Lose the skirt."

Her lids fluttered, and he could sense her struggling between two options. What she needed to do and what she thought was best for him. But when he pressed his mouth more firmly to hers and let her feel a graze of his teeth, the former won.

Looking him in the eye, Eve started to sway her hips to the music once again, sending a ripple of cheers and shouts through the audience.

"You're fucking beautiful," he said, rolling their foreheads together. "Don't stop."

"Okay," she said haltingly, but her confidence grew as she absorbed whatever was on his face, a little bit of mischief taking up the insecurity he'd seen moments earlier, and, lord, was he grateful to see it go. "Feel free to join me," she murmured, turning him to face the rapt audience, before taking a slow lap around his body, stopping in front of him with a raised eyebrow.

Madden stripped off his shirt, tossing the garment out into the audience, who were absolutely roaring at this point. Eve wasn't expecting it.

He'd cherish that spark that reentered her eyes afterward for the rest of his life.

With a challenging look, she gave Madden her back, pressing the curve of her butt into his lap and sliding all the way down to the floor, before working herself all the way back up. When the audience cheered their approval, Madden looked down to discover Eve had left her silver, tasseled skirt on the floor.

He swallowed hard.

Had he really earned the care of a woman this extraordinary? This beautiful?

Left in a pair of black low-cut bikini panties, the bra, and heels, Eve ran her hands up the front of Madden's chest and okay, yeah, disgracing himself onstage became a distinct possibility, because goddamn. His wife was sexy and challenging. Unafraid. Especially when she looked up at him and the words "Take off my bra" came out of her mouth.

And Madden obeyed, reaching around to the back of Eve while the cheers rose to a deafening fervor, people stomping on the floor and pounding the tables. He nuzzled her nose a moment, then with a tweak of his fingers the bra was unfastened. But they were chest to chest, so it remained in place in front, even as the back straps swung open. "That's a nice trick," he said hoarsely.

"Thank you, I just thought of it now." She glanced back over her shoulder at the crowd, returning her attention to Madden a few seconds later. "I think we've given them enough for tonight. Always leave them wanting more, right?"

"Wise words." Madden wasted no time sliding his forearm under Eve's backside, lifting her off the floor, and carrying her off the stage to thunderous applause and straight into her office, kicking the door shut behind him and locking it.

THE SEISMIC SHIFT happening in Eve's chest was almost too much to withstand.

She didn't even really understand what was taking place inside her, only that broken pieces that had existed for a long time were trying to glue themselves back together—and that was scary. She'd gone out onstage to destroy any chance of being a respectable wife or a valued member of the community. To claim her title as pariah once and for all so she could stop hoping for better, even in her dreams.

Maybe she had accomplished that.

A room full of people egging her on didn't mean she'd been accepted.

But this man who was holding her so tightly, carrying her across her office to the couch positioned across from her desk, he'd shown up for her in a way she hadn't expected tonight. And his actions were dissolving the loneliness that had lived inside her for as long as she could remember, even at the best of times.

"Nothing I do is going to get rid of you," she said, sounding stunned. "For better or worse. You really mean it, don't you? You want the good, the bad, and the ugly."

"It's about time you realized it, Eve Donahue."

"You just . . . you came out onstage and performed with me." She tightened her cling around Madden, aching to be closer. "You really did that."

"Uh-huh."

"You didn't try to talk me out of self-destructing. You self-destructed with me. I had no idea how much I . . . I needed that." Some of her glittery eye shadow had rubbed off on Madden's chin and the shiny little spot was so endearing, Eve's breath caught. "There's really nothing I can do to make you sorry for loving me."

"Jesus Christ, the fact that you can sound so surprised by my loyalty when you have that six-inch fucking scar on your stomach . . . it's going to kill me. You've given me life in so many ways, Eve. I would walk through hell if you were waiting on the other side." He shook her gently. "Do you accept that now?"

"Yes," she said unequivocally. She'd never meant anything more. And having him know the extent of her devotion was like . . . soaring. Finally, she'd laid it all at his feet, the way he'd laid his love and consistency and loyalty at hers.

Madden set Eve down on the couch and knelt in front of her, burying his head in her lap. He encircled her waist with his thick arms and pressed his face to the scar on the right side of her abdomen, a gruff, prolonged moan coming from his throat. "Did it hurt, love? Were you in pain and I had no idea?"

She combed her fingers through his hair. "It was a typical surgery. No complications. No more than the average discomfort and pain. I was fine."

"No one knew?"

"My father and sister knew, of course. Once we found out I was a match, there was so much paperwork, so many meetings leading up to the day. If I remember correctly, I went on a hunger strike and threatened to run away to California if my father didn't give permission. He thought I was crazy, but they didn't know you like I did." Eve filled her lungs with Madden's scent. "You were always mine."

"*Always.*" Still looking troubled, he bowed his head a moment. "Were they with you in the hospital?"

"Yes." Trying to lighten his mood, she tugged on one of his ears. "I really had to lean into the high-waisted vintage look to keep the secret."

"I never would have let you do this. Never."

"I know. That's why I didn't tell you."

Madden lifted his head slightly, tracing the pink, slightly puckered line with his fingertips, as though he wanted to absorb any past pain. "Why did you do it?"

That shift taking place when they walked into the room was only beginning to settle, but the more Eve let go of doubt, the easier it was to breathe. To look at Madden and say the words she'd kept locked inside since high school. "I've loved you for a really long time," she whispered, watching his chest expand rapidly and shudder back down, his eyes sliding closed. "I didn't give you my kidney because of some girlhood fascination or crush. I *loved* you. I loved your character and the safety you offered me without me having to ask. I loved your intuitiveness and honesty and the quiet ways you showed gratitude to your aunt for bringing you to Rhode Island. For keeping you. I loved how you offered me friendship and acceptance without expecting anything in return."

For several beats, Madden appeared almost shaken. Like he didn't know how to handle hearing so many good things about himself at once. Appearing at a loss, he bent forward and slowly kissed every inch of her scar, top to bottom. "Since we're sharing secrets, when it came time to go back to Ireland, I . . . thought of you. I couldn't leave you."

She looked down at him sharply. "I don't understand."

"I didn't want to go back to the home I'd left behind, but I could have. I could have, if not for you. I stayed because once I'd been near you, that's where I belonged." His mouth dragged up her stomach, kissing as he went. "Something was always there, even when I wouldn't allow myself to have you. My heart brought me back and brought me back to you until you were old enough to decide on me too."

"I love you," she said, haltingly, her lips and scalp tingling with the shock of his revelation. "I love you and I don't know what's going to happen. The kids are gone."

"I know. Elton told me." He pulled her in close to his chest and she went, lifting her arms and wrapping them around his neck. "I'm sorry, Eve. I'm so sorry."

She nodded, rubbing her cheek on his bare skin, deriving comfort from his heat. "My sister said she wants to come back to Cumberland to be close to me, though. When she's had her time in North Carolina and recovered some more. That's something, at least. Isn't it? I don't know where they'll live, but I can figure it out."

"*We* can figure it out."

After a moment, Eve nodded. "Okay."

"But, Eve . . ." Madden pulled back slightly to scrutinize her face. "Is Cumberland really where you want to be? If it is, good. We'll make anything work, you and me. I just want you to know you have options. You are not shackled to this town."

The thought of living anywhere else—and not in a make-believe scenario—was scary. But it could have been a lot scarier if this man's bare skin wasn't pressed to hers, his blue eyes radiating so much love it could fill the deep end of the ocean. His nearness, his affection, his willingness to join her in her weakest moments and transform them into moments of strength were an armor she'd refused to accept until now.

"I'll think about it," she said finally.

Madden nodded, his attention falling to her mouth and holding. Music and the muffled croon of Veda's voice started to filter into the office, the band obviously starting their second set. The din of the club—voices and laughter—wove together with the music to make a full, beautiful sound around Madden and Eve. And Eve knew her lover's body needed relief. She could sense it while wearing a blindfold. His breath started to get shaky, and his skin seemed to be stretched tighter than usual across his abs. Nipples swollen. The fly of his jeans at a prominent angle, his hips pressing the bulge tightly to the couch, his pupils expanding to hide a significant amount of blue.

It was going to take next to nothing for Eve to be ready.

She was already turned on from being onstage. Now her horny, hulking husband was kneeling in front of her with no shirt, visibly aware that she wore nothing but tight boyshort panties and stilettos, his forehead starting to shine with sweat.

"Eve."

"Yes?"

"If a meteor hit this club right now"—he gripped the sides of her underwear, waited for her subtle hip lift, then ripped them down to her feet, throwing them aside—"it still wouldn't keep me off this pussy."

She blinked at him. "How do you want it?"

"Licked." He pushed her knees open and breathed a curse. "Every sweet inch of it."

Confident beneath the worship in his eyes, Eve settled her ankles on the breadth of his shoulders. Slowly. One at a time. "Can I leave on my shoes?"

"Please leave on the shoes," he said raggedly, tugging her butt to the edge of the couch, squeezing her open knees. "God, it's already wet. *God.*"

Eve beckoned him down for a long, breathless kiss. "You took me so hard last night, I probably taste like you," she said against his ear, her voice almost drowned out by the music. But he heard it. He definitely heard her, because he groaned his way down to her breasts, sucking them eagerly in turn while his thumb traced the seam of her sex, dragging moisture up and back and over and around her clit, teasing her so thoroughly that she was whimpering by the time his tongue parted her flesh and rubbed firmly against her entrance. Rubbed and rubbed until her hips began to writhe, to seek friction.

"Madden."

"Be patient. I've waited a long time for this."

"This isn't the act I fantasized about while I waited for you," she managed, her breath choppy. "But I think it might be from now on."

Madden razed his two-day beard against the insides of her thighs, kissing the sensitive skin, meeting Eve's gaze up the heaving length of her body while he pressed his middle finger inside her and held it deep. "What did you fantasize about?" He tugged out his middle finger and added a second, growling when her walls clenched around the digit, her thighs attempting to jerk closed. "Fucking?"

"Yes."

"You dreamed about getting it rough from me, didn't you?"

Oh wow. Wow. She could feel herself getting soaked around his exploring fingers. Eve nodded vigorously. "I don't think I was ready for soft. Not in bed or out. From anyone."

"And now?"

"I'm ready for anything with you now."

Emotion crowded into his eyes as they drifted briefly to her scar, then back to her face. "You saved up all your vows for a night where I'm barely holding it together."

Her nature caused her to push even more. "Did I mention I'm in love with you?"

Madden buried his mouth against her flesh with a moan, his tongue finding her clit, oh god, oh god, finally, but the firm, wet drag of his tongue was nothing like she expected. It was better. So much better. Because she could feel him communicating to her without words, could feel his need to impress upon her how much he cherished her love, her body, her taste. And she welcomed the fingers moving inside her with ownership, because she was safe in this man's care. Eve trusted him with her body and her soul. She handed over both at the same time—and he took. Greedily. Filthily. Using his tongue on that source of pleasure, batting it with the tip of his tongue, before sinking in and lapping her roughly.

"Madden," she gasped, her knees starting to tremble.

He grunted in response, as if to confirm he already knew. Already knew she was on the verge of an orgasm and he wanted to experience all of it as closely as possible, his catcher's hands scooping under her bottom and lifting her for his hungry mouth, giving her nowhere to go but up into the clouds.

"God, oh my *god*," she screamed through her teeth, her intimate muscles quickening and releasing, followed by rhythmic spasms that forced her to stop breathing, because she couldn't physically accomplish both things at once and one was so much better than the other. Orgasms over breathing any day. "I'm . . . I can't breathe. I can't . . ."

"Breathe, love," Madden was saying into her neck, his teeth raking upward from her shoulder to the skin beneath her ear.

"Catch your breath so I can fuck you." His forehead rolled across hers, leaving sweat behind. "I really need to fuck you."

"Fuck me," she whispered, kissing his jaw, his mouth. "I'm ready."

Madden's hand moved out of sight, the sound of his belt buckle distant in the pounding of music on the other side of the wall. And then with his mouth on top of hers, he entered her in a swift thrust, pinning her to the edge of the couch, her thighs wide open to accept him, along with her heart. "Damn," he bit off, his eyelids at half-mast. "I'm never going to get used to how perfect you feel around my cock, Eve. And those thighs are always so restless. Antsy. Excited for me to ride what's between them. Is that right?"

"Yes," she whimpered, arching her back to show off her breasts, wanting him to look. Wanting to show him everything, every part of her body. *Look. Look at what's yours.*

"Gentle," he said, his teeth clamping lightly to her jaw, a mere angling of his hips causing her to sob his name. "You said you're ready for gentle with me."

"It doesn't have to be now," she gasp-laughed. "Maybe tomorrow."

One corner of his mouth ticked up. "Ah, but you told me you love me tonight," he said, beginning a slow pump inside her. Slow. Slow. Slow. "A man ought to make love to his wife on an occasion like this one." He wrapped his arms around her in a protective embrace and looked her in the eye while he rolled his hips. "Even if we are on the couch in the back of a club with hundreds of people wondering what we're doing in here."

"That's kind of our style, right?"

"Aye, it is. Proud of it." He bent her backward on the couch, her body partially on the cushions, her shoulders curved against the backrest while their mouths met and took hungrily, his hips keeping up their slow, measured assault, her legs shamelessly wide for her husband, wanting to feel every inch of that hot pressure he pushed inside her, every grind of his testicles against her backside when he couldn't go any farther, his growl catching against her lips. That shudder that dashed through his muscles. "You were so fucking sexy out there," he rasped, watching her breasts jiggle between them. "In your little see-through bra."

Oh. Okay.

This man had her number.

He knew what made her hot.

It was possible this man knew every single thing about her. And instead of that truth making her panic, it made her feel like the best judge of character on the planet. She'd found a man who celebrated her flaws and needs and strengths in equal measure.

"Was it see-through?" she teased, breathless. "I didn't notice."

"You noticed." Madden's lower body started to move faster. "Everyone noticed, believe me." He laughed a little darkly when her sex squeezed involuntarily. "It's okay, love. You can't help having tits so hot they deserve an audience."

Eve felt the cells in her blood expand and rush, thrilling to the words targeting her libido so accurately, she almost bit him. Or she would have if he wasn't turning her over face down on the couch, her knees on the cold floor, her butt curved over the edge of the leather furniture, wearing nothing but her heels and open-mouthed shock.

Or excitement.

Both.

But her shocked excitement turned to awe when Madden thrust inside her from behind, his sweaty chest pinning her down, his mouth shoving up against her ear. "I'll learn to live with showing you off once in a while. We both know this cunt belongs to your husband."

Truer words were never spoken. She would never let anyone but Madden see her in the state he kept her in for the next five minutes, whining into a couch cushion, her nails leaving indents on the leather, unintelligible praise coming out of her mouth while he took her aggressively from the back, urged on by her begging, that thick part of him slapping deep into her body and expanding her with pressure, her middle and ring fingers playing with her clit, his groans loud and continuous in her ear, that part of him growing stiffer, larger, Eve lifting her butt higher in response and making him curse gutturally, biting her neck. Sucking on it. Their bodies slick with perspiration, humping and straining while the band boomed in the other room.

"No more maybes between us," he said in her ear. "That's done. No matter what happens, we're rock solid."

"Rock solid," she agreed, her climax beginning to swim around in her belly. Oh god, just a little more. A little more. And her throat was tight from all the emotion packed into his voice, every roll of his body that made them one. "I promise."

"Call me your husband."

"You're my husband." She crested, the muscles of her sex bearing down so intensely she could only gasp for breath, wait out the sweet agony. "For real."

Heat rocketed out of Madden where he'd pushed to the deepest recesses of her body, his thick frame tensing to the point of shaking atop her back, his breath blasting into her neck in the form of an exhale, followed by several rasping inhales, his abs clenching and releasing against the lower back. "Oh fuck. Fuck. This is my wife. *Fuck.*"

His big body sagged on top of Eve's, moisture gathered between their legs, messy and glorious and neither one of them cared to clean up yet as Madden turned Eve back over and cuddled her into his lap, laying kisses on her temple, hairline, and cheeks. When she smiled up at him, unafraid, he looked almost shaken with relief. The beginning stages of trusting that he didn't have to chase her anymore.

She'd been irrevocably caught.

"What do we do now, Mad?" she asked in between shallow breaths.

"We go home and see what tomorrow brings. Face it together." He stroked her hair back out of her face. "You're with me?"

She looked him in the eye and made sure he knew she meant what she said. "One hundred percent."

CHAPTER THIRTY-FOUR

Madden stood in the center of his aunt's living room. Stepped forward and dragged his index finger through the fine layer of dust on top of the fireplace mantel. Around him, the silence was thick in a way that only five o'clock in the morning could bring. He wasn't sure what had compelled him to leave Eve's bed and go for a run until he ended up here, at the house that was once the only safe place he'd ever laid his head, only that he'd woken up with a sense of urgency and it only grew stronger when he looked at the glorious woman asleep beside him.

Last night, she'd finally let her walls come crashing down, surprising herself by revealing an even stronger version of herself inside them. A side that was going to trust Madden's intentions from there on out. Trust his ability to decide what he wanted and what would make his own life complete. Her. It was never going to be anything but her and, god, watching Eve accept that would carry him for the rest of his days.

Nothing I do is going to get rid of you. For better or worse. You really mean it, don't you? You want the good, the bad, and the ugly.

Madden closed his eyes now in the predawn light, letting that moment play out in his memory for the fifth time this morning, but instead of contentment sweeping in, the urgency to *do something* heightened. He could lie in bed with Eve all day and make her promises in between rounds of sex and that was all well and good—frankly, he couldn't fucking wait—but she'd set aside her fear of being a stain on his reputation, even though it clearly terrified her, and Madden meant to reward that bravery.

And pacing slowly in front of the fireplace, he had a good idea how.

This place had always been his aunt's house. Not his. Fine, he'd found sanctuary here and never felt anything less than welcome, but he'd left her things exactly as they were when she died for a reason. He'd never felt entitled to claim this place as his own. His lot in life was back in Ireland, and while he'd left that reality behind, it wasn't easy to stop thinking of oneself as a burden when that's all he'd ever been. He'd been taught to accept the bare minimum of privileges and care.

Perhaps it was Eve's love that had stretched the boundaries of what he could and couldn't accept. If such a discerning and intelligent woman loved him, goddammit, he'd done some things right. He could look around now at this house that had been passed down to him in his aunt's will and claim it as his own.

And as such, he intended to renovate at the earliest opportunity.

No more hiding in silence. Eve's love made him want to take up space, if for no other reason than to give her room to stand beside him.

Eve didn't know if she wanted to remain in Cumberland or go somewhere else. But she would always have strong ties to this place. She'd always have a sense of responsibility to her family name and wish to have it respected. In the interest of showing Eve how much her trust meant to him, Madden would finally accept the gift he'd been given in the form of this house . . . and rebuild it for a new purpose.

If Eve wanted to stay in Cumberland, their home would stand on this property.

If she chose a different adventure outside the confines of this town, the new house wouldn't go to waste. When Ruth, Lark, and Landon were ready to return from North Carolina, a home would be waiting for them.

Madden nodded in the quiet, saying a mental thank-you to his aunt. For giving him a home. A chance. And now, the means and opportunity to thank Eve for loving him.

Already making a list of construction-related tasks in his head, Madden turned for the door, only to have his phone ping in the pocket of his hoodie. He assumed it was a text from Eve wanting to know where he'd gone, despite the note he'd left on the coffeepot, but no. It was three simple letters from Elton—WTF—a link to a *Daily News* article included in the same message bubble.

"Bad Madden & the Girl Who Saved His Life."

With his pulse already beginning to race, Madden clicked and read the first few lines, his footsteps carrying him out the door until eventually he was in a dead run.

Eve woke up to find Madden sitting on the edge of the bed with his head bowed, sweat soaking through the back of his gray T-shirt. His sides puffed in and out as if he'd run a long distance at a very fast pace. But that wasn't unusual for Madden. As far back as she could remember, he'd been the type to wake up early and train.

"Good morning." She yawned, rolling over in the sheets and stretching, not bothering to hide her complete and total nudity. Reveling in the fact that she was no longer hiding the scar on her abdomen from him. From anyone. "I'm going to kindly ask that you take a shower before crawling back in here."

Madden didn't say anything in response.

Instead, he raked a hand through his hair and looked at her over his shoulder—and that's when Eve knew something was wrong. His eyes were dark with worry.

"What happened?" she asked, sitting up, her first instinct to fear for the kids and their safety, perhaps because she hadn't quite shaken off the morning grogginess yet. After all, how would Madden know if something happened to the twins? "Are Lark and Landon okay?"

"Yes." He half turned, squeezing her ankle through the sheet. "Ah, love, it's nothing to do with them. There's just this article . . ."

Relief swam in her middle. Briefly. The kids were all right and that was the most important thing. But another article? Really? When was the public's fascination with them going to die down? It wouldn't occur to Eve until later that she didn't question whether or not she and Madden could handle the situation together. Or if the content of the mystery article would force them apart, Madden better off without her.

Those possibilities never crossed her mind.

She was all in on this man. He was all in on her.

Whatever happened, they would face it together and be stronger on the other side.

"Article?" she asked, gathering the sheet over her body, sensing this conversation wasn't the kind one had with their boobs showing. "Is it . . . about our performance last night?"

"Oh, it's definitely mentioned, yes, but that's not the . . ." Madden stood and paced to the window of her bedroom, hands planted on his hips. "That's not the subject of the article."

"You're being so cryptic—"

Eve's phone dinged, interrupting her. Then it dinged again. And again.

An object slowly formed in her throat.

"What is it, Mad?"

"They know you're my kidney donor. It's out there." He expelled a breath, slowly coming toward Eve, towering over where she sat cross-legged in a huddle of sheets. "You've just gotten the courage to tell me and less than a day later, the whole country knows. I'm sorry, love. I'm sorry they invaded your privacy like that." He shook his head. "I can't even figure out how they got that information. I tried for years and was told your identity was sealed up tight unless you chose otherwise."

Eve stared, scenes from the night coming back to her in flashes. "A reporter asked me last night. With all the media interested, someone must have tipped her off, because she knew enough to ask, right? I was caught off guard and my reaction . . . it might have been enough to confirm. Not to mention, my scar would have been visible when I danced. They just connected the dots." She looked up at Madden, unable to read his expression. "I should have been more careful. I'm sorry—"

"Eve." Madden looked stunned as he sat down on the side of the bed and reached for her face, cradling it in his hand. "If it was up to me, I would have told the whole world a long time ago. Jesus, Eve. A sacrifice like yours should be acknowledged."

Eve sat there for long moments, her face supported in the hand of the man she trusted as much as she trusted herself, a man she loved madly. And she realized there was no way to go back to loving him with reservations or fears. She'd let her love break through the barriers last night and it was too strong to be contained ever again.

"I don't care who knows," she whispered. "It's the best decision I ever made. You're the best decision I ever made. If I've learned anything since marrying you, it's that people can feel how they want to feel about me—their opinions have nothing to do with us. You were never going to stop showing up for me until I believed that."

"Damn right," he rasped. "And by the way, their opinion of you is that you're a bloody hero, love. That's exactly what you are. You're my hero."

His image blurred in front of her eyes. "You're mine too."

Madden leaned down to give her a tender kiss, but when Eve lifted her hands to run her fingers through his hair and the sheet slipped down, the kiss veered toward hot. Hungry. "You know, I wouldn't mind a shower too," she said, smiling against his lips.

"I was hoping you'd say that," Madden growled, scooping her off the bed and carrying her toward the bathroom while her laughter filled the room. Once there, he settled her on the sink while he set about turning on the shower and adjusting the temperature. "The day is ours, Eve. We can do whatever you want."

She closed her eyes as the steam started to build in the small bathroom. "I think . . ." She ignored the little leap of nerves in her fingertips. "I think I want to go to breakfast. In town. Just walk into a restaurant and sit down."

When she opened her eyes, Madden was standing shirtless in the steam, looking at her with so much tenderness, she almost clutched her chest from the pressure. The love.

"After we shower, though," she murmured, sliding off the sink and pushing down the waistband of his sweatpants as she went, biting her lip when he stepped out of them, banded her waist with a forearm, and walked her into the shower, pinning her to the wall and demolishing any hint of nerves with a kiss that spoke of forever.

"Aye, love," he breathed, drawing her thighs up around his hips. "After."

LATER THAT MORNING, Madden held Eve's hand tightly in his own, trying not to show his apprehension over walking with her into the local diner, smack-dab in the middle of Main Street. Not because he wasn't proud to be seen with his wife—there was no one prouder on this earth—but because if anyone said a negative word to her, he'd be throwing them headfirst through one of the plateglass windows.

Protectiveness of the woman to his right hummed in his blood like the chorus of a familiar and beloved song, made more potent now that their future was on solid ground.

"Ready?" he asked, looking down at her.

"Yes," she said, smiling, sunlight spilling across her cheeks. "For anything."

Madden swallowed hard, knowing he would be overcome with love every single time he looked at his wife for the next seventy-odd years. Probably more so with every new day. "Let's go," he said gruffly, opening the door, the little bell ringing overhead to signal the arrival of customers—

Applause broke out.

Both of them looked around the diner, searching for the reason for everyone clapping . . . until they slowly realized the applause was for them.

Rather, for Eve.

Madden recognized more than a few faces in that crowd. People who had attended high school at the same time as them. Women who'd been picketing outside Eve's father's club years earlier. Town familiars. They were looking at his wife with a combination of regret and pride, applauding her, leaving Eve visibly stunned. And he knew her well enough to know something healed itself inside her in that moment. Something even he was incapable of reaching. A misconception about her character she'd disproved long before anyone else in this town had caught on.

Madden's own pride in her nearly took him down.

"This makes a good case for staying in Cumberland, I suppose," he said to his wife out of the corner of his mouth.

She looked up at him in a way that allowed him to see all the glorious years ahead with this woman at his side. "Actually . . ." Her throat worked. "I think it's a good case for leaving. I have nothing left to prove."

"You never did, love." Madden brought Eve's hand to his mouth and kissed her knuckles. "Whatever you want to do, wherever you want to go, I'll be there."

"I know," she said, confidently, squeezing his hand.

"What will you do with the club?"

At first, she appeared thoughtful, then decisive. "I know exactly what to do with it."

EPILOGUE

Eve looked back at Madden where he sat in the driver's seat of his truck and she couldn't remember a time in her life when she'd felt lighter and more confident in the direction she was going. In the last two weeks, she'd broken the lease on her apartment and done countless hours of paperwork to relinquish the Gilded Garden. With his shoulder nearly healed, Madden had been going back and forth to New York for practices and games, helping her pack during every available moment in between.

Truthfully, they probably could have packed up her place in one week, instead of two, but they couldn't stop ending up in bed. Eve's neighbors were being a whole lot nicer to her since the media frenzy had catapulted her from devil incarnate to saint in the eyes of Cumberland's residents, but the constant moaning and squeaking bedsprings coming from her apartment had to be testing the limits of their goodwill.

Today, she would move to Madden's apartment in New York. From there . . . who knew?

The world was suddenly a big place full of possibilities and enough to make even the strongest person doubt themselves a little, but she had faith. And she had love. Her next endeavor, whatever it might be, would be about proving her skill as a businesswoman, not about proving herself as a human being. As someone who deserved respect.

She'd had that earned since the beginning. Just by being herself.

Now she smiled at Madden through the windshield and he sent her one back, the pure happiness on his face making her heart roar with joy. What a life they were going to have, she and this man who would rebuild a new home on his aunt's property so her niece, nephew, and sister would have a place to call their own someday soon. The gesture was so purely Madden and one of the numerous reasons she had no caution to throw to the wind.

Caution didn't exist with a safety net this big and wonderful.

Madden nodded at her from the driver's seat and with the added boost of confidence bolstering her, Eve faced the front door and knocked.

Veda answered after about thirty seconds, wearing one sock and a gigantic T-shirt, her bangs facing fourteen directions. "Yo?"

Eve suppressed a smile. "Hey. Got a minute?"

"Sure," Veda said, visibly confused. Nonetheless, she stepped back, allowing Eve to enter the small Cape Cod–style home. "My parents are out of town, so there's not a lot in the fridge I can offer you," Veda went on, quickly peeling off her other sock and stuffing it behind a couch cushion. "Sorry about that."

"Don't worry, I already had breakfast and way too much coffee."

"Is that Madden out in the truck? Does he want to come in too?"

"He's going to wait for me," Eve said, smiling as she took a seat in a leather wingback chair at the edge of the living room. "This is just between us."

"Wow." Veda sank down onto the couch. "Sounds serious. Did something happen with the construction at the club? Everything looked to be running smoothly when I stopped by last night. We're still on target to have the addition completed in a week."

"I know. Thanks to you. Veda . . ." Eve let out a long breath. "If you hadn't walked into the club that day, I don't know if I'd be where I am right now. You set something in motion I can't really explain. You were my childcare, a sounding board, a crown straightener. You encouraged me. Backed me up. You've been all these things for me . . ." Eve paused to gather herself. "But you're so much more than that. So much more. You're a fucking firework, just about to go off."

It was the first time since meeting Veda that the girl was speechless. She stared at Eve with a mixture of shock and suppressed emotion, her hands clasped tightly in her lap.

"That's why I'm selling you the Gilded Garden, Veda."

The girl jolted into a half-standing position, then plonked back down, dumbstruck. "You're what? But . . . I can't do that!"

"You can. For one dollar down." Eve wet her lips. "My debts might be paid now, but I still can't give you the club for free. It's my father's legacy and that man valued a good deal over just about everything, and nothing worthwhile comes for free, but I'm selling it to you for a song. You'll pay me back in notes over the next ten years." Eve took the envelope stuffed with paperwork and keys out of her windbreaker and tossed it on the coffee table. "And I have a feeling you're going to pay me back a lot sooner than that. Especially since a certain catcher for the Yankees donated five figures to your GoFundMe."

Veda shuddered through a breath, regarding the envelope with a sheen of tears in her eyes. "Eve," she whispered. "I can't. I can't do this. I'm not you. I'm not capable of running a . . . the whole place. Someday, sure. But not yet. I'm not ready—"

"Veda. Look at me." Eve paused for emphasis. "Yes, the fuck you are."

A watery laugh burst out of her young friend, her hands shaking as she reached for the envelope, picking it up and looking down in awe as a set of keys tumbled out into her lap. "Are you sure?"

"Positive. And if you need me, I'm only a phone call away." Eve stood. "I'll consider it my chance to return the favor."

Veda sniffed through a laugh. "I think you already have."

"Come here. We're going to seal this with a hug, whether it makes us uncomfortable or—" Veda launched herself straight into Eve, full force, knocking her backward several steps. "Believe in yourself, okay?" she breathed into Veda's hair. "You got this."

"Is it weird to say I think I love you?"

Eve let out a watery laugh. "No. I think I love you too—"

"Should I run out and get us some breakfast?" came Elton's voice from upstairs, followed by a prolonged, bearlike yawn. "I'm ready and willing to drive us to Krispy Kreme for nostalgia's sake . . ."

Elton—clad in nothing but a pair of blue boxers—trailed off when the living room came into view and he saw Veda standing there, hugging Eve.

Veda stepped back, a very distinct blush painting her cheeks. "Funny story . . ."

Seven Years Later

Madden stood in the driveway of his Wisconsin home, heart in his mouth.

Equipment bag at his feet, he watched Eve frost cookies in her black silk robe at their kitchen counter. Skylar came into view with a baby on her hip, saying something to make Eve laugh and she dropped the piping bag, not bothering to pick it up, letting her arms dangle in her relaxed state. Behind the women, in the living room, Robbie wore the ugliest Christmas sweater Madden had ever seen, stoking the fire in the fireplace and smiling over his shoulder at the giggling women in the kitchen.

Madden tipped his head back, tracing the line of purple lights strung along the eaves until the image started to blur. He'd only gone to the field to do an off-season workout with the Brewers' team trainer. Hadn't even been on the road. But then, the purple lights punched him in the chest every time he pulled into the driveway, didn't they?

They brought back memories of that first night he'd spent with his wife. Eating crackers and marmalade, no inkling of the test that awaited them.

Or how soundly they would pass it.

They'd passed every single one since then too. Together.

Down Bad Madden—yes, the nickname had stuck, much to his eternal irritation—had been traded last year to the Brewers, and by that time he and Eve had been all too ready to move out of Manhattan and find their forever home.

This was it.

That truth was apparent in the happiness he witnessed from the driveway, watching the love of his life and every life to come, looking so beautifully secure. Did he have a lot to do with that security? Madden hoped so. But Eve had achieved it for herself too. After going back to school for business while they still lived in New York, she'd recently started a commercial interior design firm from scratch. She'd named it Gilded, a nod to the burlesque club she'd decorated so lovingly once upon a time.

A club that still thrived under its new ownership back in Cumberland.

Inside the house, Madden watched Eve accept the five-month-old baby from Skylar, cuddling the child close and swaying with her around the kitchen, probably singing one of Veda's most recent hits. And Madden smiled, knowing the frequent visits from Elton, Veda, Skylar, Robbie, and the baby, not to mention Lark and Landon—now twelve years old—were enough for her. Him as well. They didn't plan on having children of their own, but they got a lot of enjoyment spoiling the kids in their lives when given the chance.

Eager to hear his wife's voice, Madden swung his equipment bag onto his shoulder, giving the purple Christmas lights a final, prolonged look before walking into the house to a chorus of greetings, the sweetest of which came from his Eve.

And always would.

ABOUT THE AUTHOR

Number one *New York Times* bestselling author **Tessa Bailey** can solve all problems except for her own, so she focuses those efforts on stubborn, fictional blue-collar men and loyal, lovable heroines. She lives on Long Island avoiding the sun and social interactions, then wonders why no one has called. Dubbed the "Michelangelo of dirty talk" by *Entertainment Weekly*, Tessa writes with spice, spirit, swoon, and a guaranteed happily ever after.

   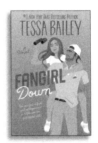
 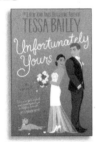  

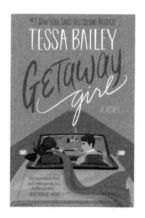 
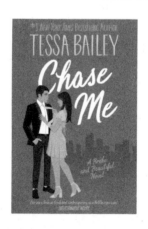  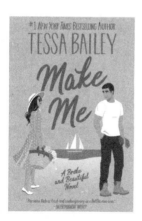